DATE DUE

SEP 2 6			
OCT 1 6			
NOV 1 5			
NOV 29			
DEC 1 4			
FEB 1 1			
GAYLORD			PRINTED IN U.S.A.

GIVE ME LIBERTY

BY NOEL B. GERSON

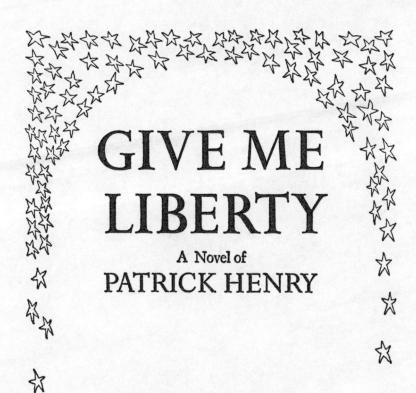

GIVE ME LIBERTY

A Novel of
PATRICK HENRY

By NOEL B. GERSON

DOUBLEDAY & COMPANY, INC.

GARDEN CITY, NEW YORK

1966

f

For
Marilyn

The first thing I have at heart is American liberty; the second is American union.

PATRICK HENRY
June 3, 1788

GIVE ME LIBERTY

ONE

1747–1754

1

The rawhide harness strap cut viciously through the air. The children half-concealed in the pine grove beyond the barn and tobacco storage silos winced when they heard it strike its target, and Anne Henry chewed on the ends of her cotton bonnet ties to keep from crying aloud. John Syme, her half brother, almost a man in his late teens, patted her shoulder and then leaned forward intently with the others as the strap sang out again.

John Henry glanced in the direction of his brood, sighed, and let his hand fall to his side, the strap kicking up a small cloud of dust. "I reckon that's enough of a beating for one morning," he said in a strained voice.

Eleven-year-old Patrick straightened, surreptitiously wiped moisture from his pale blue eyes and, in a gesture that seemed almost casual, ran his hand through his thick brown hair.

"You'll be eating your supper off the mantel tonight," his father said, speaking without rancor.

Patrick made no reply.

The man peered at him. "For the last time, lad," he said, a trace of the Scottish burr of his ancestors in his voice belying his calm, "tell me why you insulted your mother."

Hitching up his homespun breeches and resisting the tempta-

1

tion to rub his sore backside, Patrick considered his reply carefully before he spoke. "Ma knows I'm sorry."

John Henry demonstrated greater patience than he felt. "I understand you apologized as soon as the words were out of your mouth. But that doesn't explain why you were so rude to her."

The boy stiffened, respectful but defiant. "I can't tell you, Pa."

John knew it was useless to pursue his subject. The most obstinate of his stubborn children was capable of withstanding Indian torture rather than reveal his secrets. Turning swiftly, he glared at the group of youngsters in the pine grove. "If you have nothing better to do than stand around all day," he called, "I can give you enough chores to keep you busy."

His five daughters promptly scattered, two hurrying to the house, two others making for the stables and the fifth darting off to the fowl pen to feed the chickens.

But John Syme came forward, his walk relaxed, his smile easy. Man and youth exchanged a quick look, and no further communication was necessary. Perhaps the young man might succeed where his stepfather had failed.

"Hereafter," John Henry declared, "mind your manner, lad." He went off toward the house, where his anxious wife was waiting for him.

Patrick stared out across the fields of glistening, deep green tobacco plants ripening in the Virginia sun, past the stands of corn and wheat that the family raised for its own consumption. Soon the end of October would be at hand, and the season's second crop would be ready for harvesting. Visitors from the Northern colonies were always telling Pa he was lucky to live in Hanover County, where the weather was so mild. But Patrick hated farming, and was determined to follow some other vocation when he grew to manhood, though he didn't yet know what it would be.

"Want to go fishing in the Pamunkey?" his half brother asked.

The boy shrugged.

"How about a swim?"

Patrick remained silent.

"Maybe," John Syme said casually, "the water is too cold for someone of your age."

Patrick snapped at the bait. "It ain't!"

"Isn't."

"I can swim in cold water a blamesight longer than you can, Johnny."

"Want to prove it?"

They started off together toward the pine grove and the Pamunkey River beyond it.

"What was this ruckus all about?" John asked quietly.

The boy's pale eyes blazed scornfully. "You're a spy for Pa."

The accusation was just, and couldn't be denied, but John was overcome by curiosity. "Suppose I promise not to say a word to Pa."

"Will you swear in the King's name that you won't say a blame thing to nobody?"

"I—all right. I swear it."

Patrick looked down at the ground and kicked a pine cone out of his path with a bare foot. "I told Ma to soak her head in a bucket of dishwater."

John blinked in astonishment. "What had she done?"

The boy continued to walk with lowered head. "Nothin'."

"There's a 'g' at the end of that word."

"All right. Nothing."

"But it makes no sense. You've always loved Ma more than any of us. It hasn't been six months that you tried to fight me because you thought I'd shown her too little respect at supper."

Patrick made no reply. Instead he looked up at an oak tree, emitted a sharp whistle between his teeth and called, "You there, Willie! I knowed all along you was there."

John was too startled to correct his grammar when William Henry, an inch shorter than Patrick but already huskier, dropped out of the branches to the ground.

"You saw me get the lickin'. I reckon you're satisfied now."

William wiped his face with the back of a grubby hand and looked apprehensively at John.

"He swore he wouldn't say nothin'." Patrick planted his hands on his hips, thrusting his jaw forward belligerently.

John watched them, knowing it was his duty to prevent a fight, but certain the tension between them would help explain Patrick's unexpected and mystifying conduct.

3

William made an effort to control himself, failed and giggled.

Patrick turned to their half brother. "Willie dared me to say it to Ma."

"I see." John was still confused, but tried to look wise.

Patrick gestured impatiently. "You don't see nothin', Johnny. But Willie does. He knows I always accept a dare!"

William smirked.

"Let me get this straight." John spoke slowly, trying to put the pieces of the puzzle together. "You insulted Ma on a dare—"

"I apologized right off, so's she wouldn't feel hurt!"

"—because Willie dared you to do it. Surely you knew Pa would give you a hiding!"

Patrick's shrug was eloquent, his thin shoulders rising and then falling again gracefully.

Consciously or otherwise, John thought, he was giving a perfect imitation of his uncle and namesake, Hanover County's Anglican vicar. "What have you gained, Patrick?"

"First off, I prove to Willie I ain't scared. There's nothin'— nothing—in the world that scares me." Patrick's eyes gleamed balefully as he turned to stare at the other boy. "And now it's my dare. Willie, I dare you to tell Pa he's an old fool!"

"But he ain't an old fool!" William grew pale beneath his dirt-encrusted tan.

For the first time that morning, Patrick laughed. "I didn't really want Ma to soak her head in dishwater, Willie. You goin' to tell him?"

"He'll hide me raw!" William's protest was an anguished wail.

"I dare you!"

William needed little time to ponder the matter. "I'm the one who'd be a fool if I said it to him!"

"If you won't do it," Patrick told him, "I'll lick the turkey stuffin' out of you right now!"

John started to intervene, but changed his mind. William had taken advantage of Patrick, who seemed incapable of refusing a challenge, and had enjoyed watching the beating from his safe place of vantage in the oak. Now he would have to pay for his pleasure.

Patrick lunged suddenly, doubling over and driving a shoulder

4

into his brother's middle. Both boys fell to the bed of pine needles that littered the ground and, grunting, pummeled each other with more enthusiasm than skill. William was heavier and physically stronger, but he lacked Patrick's ferocity, and within a few moments the smaller boy gained the upper hand.

"Say it out loud," Patrick commanded, sitting on William's chest and drubbing him unmercifully with both fists. "Admit you're as big a coward as a Chickahominy squaw!"

William muttered something unintelligible.

"Say it clear!" Patrick increased the fury of his assault.

"I'm as big a coward as a Chickahominy squaw," the humiliated William sobbed.

Patrick released him at once, jumped to his feet and grinned cheerfully at John. "Now we'll go for that swim," he said, "and I'll bet my gold watch against the musket Pa gived you for your birthday that I'll stay in the water longer than you."

John smiled and shook his head. "It's going to be a friendly swim—and that's all. If I bet against you, I'm sure you'd stay in the water until you froze to death."

"You'd give up long before that. Besides, that's a mighty fine musket, and it'd be worth a mite o' freezin'." Patrick turned to the battered William. "You better come with us."

"I don't want to swim," Willie said under his breath.

"Sometimes," Patrick told him scornfully, "you ain't got the sense you was born with. If Ma or Pa see that blood on your face, you'll get a hidin' sure—for havin' a fight. So do as I say, now, and come along!" Not waiting for a reply, he started off jauntily through the woods. He had won a victory, so his own beating was forgotten and he was at peace with the world.

2

The Reverend Patrick Henry, rector of St. Paul's parish, wrapped his scarf of unbleached wool more closely around his throat and moved his rocking chair of cherry wood closer to the fire crackling in his hearth. "Try the next line."

There was no escape, and his nephew peered miserably at the

5

worn copy of the works of Horace. *"Valet ima summis mutare, et insignem attenuat deis, obscura promens."*

"Your accent is improving, Patrick. Now translate the line, and remember you've used up your quota of mistakes." The clergyman was enjoying the warmth of the fire. "If you make one more error, just one, you'll do without pudding at supper."

Bread pudding filled with raisins and currants and crusted with a thick top of browned coarse sugar was the best dish that Uncle Patrick's housekeeper made, and the boy swallowed painfully.

"Sit straight when you recite!"

"Yes, sir." Patrick cleared his throat and began to translate. "God hath power to change the lowliest with the loftiest, and he maketh the great men weak, bringing to light things hidden in obscurity." He paused for a moment. "I don't think Horace rightly means obscurity here, Uncle. I believe he means—well, now—a oad darkness, or somethin' like that."

The man clapped his hands together. "Excellent!"

"Can I have some puddin' at the end of supper?"

"May, Patrick, not can."

"May I?"

"Of course. But don't you ever learn for the sake of learning, lad?"

Patrick shook his head.

"You should! There's no joy greater than that of mastering knowledge—for its own sake."

The boy braced himself for a sermon.

But his uncle surprised him. "Obviously, you don't agree, even though you have a remarkable capacity for learning—when you apply yourself to your studies. What do you want instead of knowledge?"

Patrick felt confused. "I'm blamed if I know, and that there is God's truth."

"No, lad. God's truth makes man free. If you tried to live according to His truth, you'd let Him guide you. Instead you set your mind against His, and you're unhappy."

Patrick took a deep breath. "You and Ma and Pa all want me to preach God's holy word. But I ain't had no sign from the Almighty that He wants me to do His work."

6

"I'm inclined to doubt that a boy of fourteen would recognize a sign from the Lord," the Reverend Mr. Henry said dryly. "Be that as it may, you're old enough to start planning your future. All we've heard so far are the vocations you don't want. The clergy isn't for you, nor is owning a tobacco farm. There's talk of a hospital being opened in Williamsburg or Richmond, but you won't go to the College of William and Mary, much less think of working for a medical license in England."

"I ain't much of a one for books, Uncle," Patrick said defensively.

"Ah, but you're wrong!" the clergyman thundered. "I doubt if there's another boy in the whole colony who has read the *Republic* of Plato and Aristotle's *Politics* in Greek!"

"That don't—doesn't prove anything, sir."

The man ignored the interruption. "You've even memorized some of Cicero's orations in Latin. Does that prove anything to you?"

Patrick hated being maneuvered into a corner. "I like the sound of old Cicero, so I've read him nights when there's been nothin' better to do. If you'd like to hear what I really want, Uncle, I've got me a hankerin' to explore the new lands west of the Blue Ridge Mountains."

"Romantic, childish nonsense!" Unable to conceal his agitation, the Reverend Mr. Henry rocked rapidly in his chair. "Scum from the prisons of England go out to the frontier, lad. It's no place for a gentleman."

Patrick wiped the palms of his hands on the sides of his faded buckskin trousers. "At home, now, they tell me every day of my life that I'm no gentleman, and I believe 'em. When a fellow has five sisters poundin' away at him day and night, he takes what they tell him to heart."

The clergyman was not deceived. "I've never known you to listen to advice from anyone. You're a gentleman, all right. Don't ever forget that you can trace your Scottish ancestors for at least ten generations, and the French Huguenot side of the family for six or more."

"Havin' great men as ancestors don't win prizes in free-for-all fights at the Hanover Court House fair. It don't improve my aim

7

when I use the long rifle I bought with my chore money." Patrick looked up at the portraits of the dignified, portly Scotsmen that lined the far wall. "Maybe one of them there lads was good at catchin' salmon, but I've got to bait my own hooks when I go trout fishin' in the South Anna or the Pamunkey."

The Reverend Mr. Henry sometimes said that one of the least attractive of the family's traits was a refusal to admit defeat. Nevertheless, he could not tolerate the impertinence of a know-it-all boy. He stood, walked to the sideboard and poured himself a small glass of white rum from a jug a parishioner had brought him from a successful trading venture to the West Indian islands.

Patrick watched him in wary silence.

Ordinarily the clergyman relished the taste of the fifty-year-old rum, but now it tasted flat and burned as it slid down his throat. "Open your book of sums and figures," he ordered, "and we'll see what progress you've made with Euclid's *Elements* in the past two days. Explore beyond the mountains, indeed! I'll double your work load, and you'll have no time for daydreaming."

3

Patrick sunned himself, sprawling on the moss-covered bank of the South Anna River, the base of his fishing pole secured in the ground beside him as the baited hook, supported by two corks, bobbed in the fast-moving stream. He was pleased with himself, and felt he had good reason to be proud of his acumen. Other boys had demanded sixpence in cash return for scrubbing the floor of the Royal Arms Tavern in Hanover, but he had made a shrewd bargain with John Shelton, the proprietor. The man had been delighted to give him six corks from wine bottles for his labors, and Patrick could now take his ease when fishing. It was far more comfortable to loll in the sun than to keep watch on the fishing line.

He heard footsteps in the distance, but made no move other than to yawn. His summer vacation would soon end and he would be forced to return to his studies with his uncle, but for the present he was content. How wonderful it would be to spend his whole life this way, doing only the things he enjoyed.

Two young men in buckskin trousers and rough shirts of home-spun wool emerged from the woods, and Patrick waved lazily. He wasn't fond of the Buehler brothers, Tim and Ed, whose family owned a small farm about two miles from the Henry property, and he had heard his older sisters speak disparagingly of them. But he had no quarrel with them, and assumed they would try their luck elsewhere with their fishing poles.

Tim Buehler, the elder of the pair, glared at the reclining boy. "What the hell do you think you're doing?" he demanded.

"Fishing," Patrick replied, his tone polite but a hint of sarcasm in his eyes.

"This here," Ed Buehler declared, "is where we fish. Take yourself off somewheres else."

Patrick shaded his eyes with a hand. "This land don't belong to you," he replied, still calm. "It's public property, and anyone can use it."

"Everybody in the county knows this is our place," Tim said, his voice becoming ugly. "We staked it out two years ago, maybe three, when we found that the fish bite good in the pools here."

"So go away before we get riled at you," his brother added. Patrick made no move.

The brothers looked at each other. "Henry," the scowling Tim said menacingly, "you had your chance. Now we'll beat you so's you'll be lucky to crawl home on all fours!"

Patrick reached into the tall grass off to his right and, swiftly, raised his long rifle to his shoulder, simultaneously cocking it. "If either of you comes one step closer," he said quietly, "I'll blow off your head."

The Buehlers halted. "What's a little boy like him doing with a rifle like that? Let's take it away from him." Ed spoke in a muf-fled growl.

But his voice carried. "I wouldn't, if I was you," Patrick told him. "In case you've forgotten, I won first prize for marksmanship at the fair last month."

Tim Buehler wiped a film of sweat from his forehead. "He did. And he means what he says." He stared at the boy's icy eyes.

9

"Don't make threats," Patrick said, "unless you're ready to carry them out. As it happens, my right to fish here is as good as yours. I'd have been glad to share the place with you—if you had behaved decent. But your threats have changed the situation. I've took *de facto* possession of this strip of river bank."

"What in hell is he saying?" Ed asked.

"I'll put it to you in words you can understand," Patrick said, making no attempt now to hide his contempt. "From now on, this here is where I fish. Anybody who uses this spot without my word for it will get a bullet in his head."

The brothers began to back toward the safety of the woods.

"If you value your hides," Patrick called, "you won't come back. It's a funny thing, but bullies make my trigger finger itch somethin' awful."

The Buehlers vanished, cursing under their breaths.

Patrick remained alert, and when he could no longer hear the sound of their retreating footsteps, he held his ear to the ground, Indian style, to make certain they weren't trying to sneak back to the clearing and rush him. But he heard them continuing to move off, and smiled. Thucydides had been right when he had written that behind the façade of every tyrant was the soul of a coward. The Buehlers wouldn't return.

Placing the rifle within easy reach, Patrick leaned back on his elbows. The combination of sun and breeze was perfect, and the whole afternoon stretched ahead. He had literally nothing to do until it was time to chop Ma's supper firewood, and with luck he might be able to bring her a mess of fish. Then she might be less likely to berate him for doing nothing all afternoon.

He let his mind drift, the Buehlers all but forgotten. For the next three hours he would haul in fish—and daydream. No prospect could have been more gratifying.

4

John Henry folded his hands on the leather-inlaid top of his study desk and looked sternly at his son, who sat opposite him. "Your mother and I," he said, "are worried about you."

Sarah Henry, a Bible clutched in one hand and a scented hand-kerchief in the other, perched on the edge of the window seat that overlooked the rolling hills of Mount Brilliant, the most prosperous farm in the county. "We're not complaining about your conduct, Patrick. You don't spend your evenings gaming and drinking at the Royal Arms, and I thank the Lord every day of my life that you treat young ladies with the respect that's their due."

"All the same," her husband added, "you're sixteen, and you haven't yet decided on a career. You've given up your studies with your uncle, and you do nothing but wander through the woods every day."

Patrick grinned and wiped his palms on his faded buckskins. "Last night I came home with a wild turkey that weighed twenty pounds if he weighed an ounce. And if my nose smelled rightly when I came past the kitchen just now, we're having him tonight with an oatmeal and sage dressing. Day before yesterday I bagged those quail, but I'll admit I was lucky. It was more than luck, though, that brought down that buck in the woods on the other side of Johnny's farm. He was so heavy I needed help from Johnny and his foreman to load him into the cart so I could bring him home."

"We'd be the last to deny your talents as a hunter, and we enjoy eating well," Mr. Henry said dryly. "But we feel that your classical education is being—wasted, shall we say?"

"Patrick, dear, I've been praying you'd soon become sensible." Mrs. Henry looked as though she might burst into tears, and her eyes, as pale a shade of blue as her son's, looked enormous.

"What your mother is trying to say is that you're living the idle life that only the sons of the wealthy can afford. You forget that we've had seven children of our own, and that I feel as obligated to Johnny as if he were my son as well as your mother's. That means my estate will be split into nine parts when I die. Your mother will get half, and you children will get the other half. Damnation, boy, you just plain can't afford to be idle!"

"And please, Patrick, don't tell us again that you want to go exploring in the Kentucky District."

"Lieutenant Governor Dinwiddie thinks it has possibilities, Ma. He's organizing a land company out there. And it isn't being called the Kentucky District any more." Patrick tried not to sound smug or superior. "The new name for it is Transylvania."

"No matter what it's called, you aren't going." There was a note of grim finality in Mr. Henry's voice. "If you're interested in land, there's plenty of fine property close to home."

"I'm not one for farming, Pa." Patrick watched his father open a tiny silver snuffbox, place two tiny pinches of tobacco on the back of his hand and inhale them. The use of snuff was silly, but this wasn't the time to voice criticisms of parental habits.

"We're rather painfully aware of all the things that don't interest you. Unfortunately, we've yet to hear of things that do. So we're making your decision for you."

Patrick stirred uneasily; this talk wasn't following the pattern of similar conversations in the past.

"Willie is ready to settle down after his year in Richmond," Mr Henry said. "He's decided he wants to become a storekeeper, an honorable vocation and one that will pay high profits to those who are willing to work."

"You find it so easy to talk with people," his wife added, "that we're amazed we didn't think of it ourselves."

"Of what, Ma?"

"It's the perfect business for you, too."

"I own a small piece of property at The Forks, near John Shelton's land," Mr. Henry said. "I'm converting the house into a general store, and I'm setting up you and Willie there as equal partners."

For a moment Patrick was too stunned to think clearly, but he tried to accept his parents' decision philosophically. If he remembered correctly, it was Aeschylus who had written that merchants were men of esteem.

"Willie will do the buying and will be in charge of the stock," Mr. Henry continued. "And you'll do the selling. First, though, the house will have to be cleaned and painted, inside and out. You'll start putting your store in order tomorrow morning, right after breakfast."

Willie was probably responsible for all this, Patrick thought, but it was too late now to give the idiot a piece of his mind. The die was cast, and Patrick was conscious of the grim expression in his father's eyes, the tremulous hope in his mother's. Ordinarily he found it as easy to talk as to breathe, but right now he couldn't think of anything to say.

5

William Henry, so plump at eighteen that he looked as though he would burst out of his black merchant's tailcoat, stood behind the counter and dipped his quill pen into a jar of ink. "Six bags of pure, unadulterated flour," he said.

Patrick remained stretched out on top of a mound of salt bags in the far corner of the store, his favorite resting place. He was still growing at seventeen, and his buckskin trousers looked cut off above the ankles, while his bony wrists jutted out of the sleeves of his soiled leather shirt.

"Patrick, wake up! I've been telling you for the past three months that we've got to take inventory. And if we don't hurry, we won't be home in time for Ma's dinner of venison ribs and baked grits."

Patrick opened one eye. "How do you know that's what we're having for dinner?"

"I looked in at the kitchen before we left home, and asked old Isobel. Now, damn you—"

"Don't curse, Willie."

"My God!"

"And don't take the name of the Lord in vain." Patrick couldn't resist tormenting his brother, but at the same time his admonitions were sincere. After the countless hours he had spent at the parsonage of St. Paul's, studying with his uncle, he had become sensitive—perhaps too sensitive—to blasphemous and abusive language.

"When you've finished delivering your sermon, Vicar," William said with elaborate courtesy, "maybe I can impose on you to help with the inventory."

Patrick, eyes still closed, reached out toward a pile of nearby supplies and ran a hand up and down them. "Six bags of flour."

"Five bolts of prime-combed calico."

"You know as well as I do that there are five bolts," Patrick

13

said with a chuckle. "We counted them yesterday when that sales-man from Massachusetts Bay dropped in to see us."

William remained loftily efficient. "Four barrels of molasses."

"Can't you see them from over there?"

"No."

Patrick groaned and raised himself to one elbow. "All right. Four barrels of molasses, three casks of white sugar and two of brown. We have two cases of coarse gunpowder and I sifted two bags of it last week. You can count the hams and bacons in the storage shed yourself, and if you think I'm going to sort hairpins, shoe buckles, combs and the like, you got another think coming." He lowered himself to his makeshift couch again.

Before William could reply an insistent tap sounded at the door.

"Tell them," Patrick said, "that we aren't serving customers today. We're closed for inventory."

William walked to the door and opened it. "It's a pleasure to see you, ma'm," he said cordially. "Come in."

His tone, more than the invitation, aroused Patrick's curiosity and he peered in the direction of the entrance with half-open eyes. The visitor was John Shelton's daughter, Sarah, a girl of about his own age. She looked exceptionally pretty in an ankle-length dress of yellow silk that matched her windblown hair, and she was swing-ing her bonnet in her hand as she came into the store. But she stopped short when she saw the outstretched figure in the corner.

"Oh, dear, I hope your brother isn't ill, Willie," she said.

Patrick flushed, and tried to compensate for his feelings by laughing loudly.

"Drunk," the girl declared, and dismissed him from her mind. "May I buy a little salt?"

"We just sold the last peck," Patrick told her in a loud voice, shifting his weight on the salt bags.

Sarah Shelton stared at him for a moment, then nodded to Wil-liam and marched out, her head high and her back rigid.

William was unhappy. "You had no right to be so rude."

"She had no right to say I was drunk." Patrick swung his long legs to the floor and ran his fingers through his thick hair, which was falling into his face. "Here I was, feeling peaceful and content, and now that fool girl has spoiled everything." He went to a shelf, took down a battered pewter mug which he dusted with a square of cotton cloth that he took from his back pocket.

His brother looked at him in dismay as he removed the cork from a jug of West Indian rum and splashed liquid into the mug. "That's store stock, Patrick!"

"We paid for it." The claim wasn't accurate, as both brothers knew. The ship's master who had sold them the merchandise had accepted partial payment in cash and had granted them credit for two years to pay the balance of the debt.

"What in tarnation do you think you're doing, Patrick?"

"I've never in my life been drunk, but that stupid Shelton girl thinks I'm like the men who stumble around her father's tavern. If I have the name, I may as well get drunk as a weasel in a lettuce patch." Patrick raised the mug to his lips, swallowed a large quantity of rum and gasped. His insides felt as though he had lighted a hearth fire in his stomach, but he saw William watching him, and continued to drink steadily.

"You can't blame her, you know. You did look sick—or drunk." William became concerned. "That's grade-three rum, Patrick. It's supposed to be used in mulled drinks and cooking. You're throwing it down too fast."

"Mind your own business, and let's finish the inventory." Patrick refilled the mug. "Confound that girl! Who does she think she is?"

6

John Syme helped his visitor into a cushioned chair before an open window in his parlor and turned up two small oil lamps. The odor of rum filled the room, but he remained silent, waiting for his guest to speak.

"Your brother," Patrick told him in a hoarse voice, unfastening the loop that held his shirt closed at the throat, "got sick this morning. On rum. Then I fell asleep out back of the store, and Willie couldn't wake me up. I can't go home for the night when

I feel this way, Johnny. I don't want Ma and Pa to see me like this."

"I'll put you up, naturally."

"Thank you kindly. My head aches, and I feel as though I'd been hit between the eyes with the blunt end of an ax." Patrick blinked and wiped his face on his sleeve. "I'm sober again, but I couldn't hold my own in a free-for-all with your baby son."

"Have you had anything to eat?"

Patrick started to shake his head, but stopped when the ache became worse.

"I'll get you some meat and a pot of strong tea."

"I—I'm not hungry, Johnny."

"You won't feel better until you eat, boy. In the meantime, let me give you a dram of rum to start the biles and humors moving out of your body."

Patrick shuddered, "No rum, thanks. No brandywine or any other strong spirits. Riding over here just now, I took a solemn oath never to touch anything stronger than beer or porter again as long as I live."

John chuckled sympathetically. "I know how you feel. You aren't the first or the last to think you'll never touch spirits again."

"I reckon you didn't hear me, Johnny. I took a vow. I wasn't myself when I'd drunk all that rum. I couldn't make my mind or body do what I wanted, and I don't intend to be that helpless again until the day I die and stand defenseless before my Maker."

He sounded as though he meant it, and John was willing to acknowledge that he might keep his promise to himself. The whole family knew that Patrick was as unpredictable as he was strong-willed.

When John went off to the kitchen outbuilding, Patrick buried his face in his hands and tried to think clearly. The day's experience had frightened him, and for the first time in his seventeen years he began to think in terms beyond the immediate present. That's what happened, he told himself, when a man thought he was about to die.

For one thing, the store was proving an unsatisfactory experiment. He wasn't suited for a life of clerking and waiting on folks, and Willie, for all his perseverance, wasn't much better. The

Henry and Henry General Store would go bankrupt within the next three months unless they got Pa to help them out. And Patrick had no intention of asking his father to throw good gold half sovereigns after bad.

What he'd do after the store closed its doors, Patrick didn't know. He couldn't make a serious decision on a moment's notice, particularly when his head hurt. He'd been wrong to accept Pa's offer in the first place, and he had no intention of leaping too quickly again.

Besides, there were other matters on his mind, too. He held Sarah Shelton responsible for what had happened to him today. Not that she had forced him to drink himself unconscious, of course, but her contempt had goaded him. It was odd, but he'd always been like that, flaring up unexpectedly when people rubbed him the wrong way. He'd settle his score with Sarah, and then he'd be better able to contemplate his future calmly.

7

A belt of deep green gleamed dully as far as the eye could see, off to the west, and the sun looked as though it were suspended above the horizon like a huge, orange ball held by invisible ropes. "I wanted you to see the view from here," Patrick said, breaking the silence. "I don't reckon it's especially pretty. There are higher hills in other counties." His hand found Sarah Shelton's. "But I don't know any better spot around here. I've been riding up to this spot ever since I was a boy."

Sarah made no attempt to free her hand. "I think it's lovely. And thank you, P.H."

He grinned, as he did every time she called him by his initials, which he always signed beneath the poems he wrote to her.

"You feel very strongly about the outdoors."

"Only the wilderness. Beyond that forest are more farmlands. Then you come to the Allegheny Mountains. On the other side is the real wilderness. Millions of acres, millions of square miles, really, where people can be free."

"What can they do out there that we can't do here?"

"The men who settle in Transylvania will make their own rules. They'll draw up their own laws. They won't be chained by the mistakes of the past."

The girl looked up at him, her green-blue eyes uncomprehending.

"Did you ever hear of a philosopher named John Locke? No? Well, I was reading his *Essay Concerning Human Understanding* a day or so ago. Let's see if I can quote him right." He raised his voice, and his baritone, surprisingly deep and mellow, echoed across the rolling hills. " 'All men are liable to error; and most men are, in many points, by passion or interest, under temptation to it.' " He turned to her again, earnestly. "The governor, off in Williamsburg, keeps making all the mistakes that the Crown has made since William the Conqueror joined his Norman system and customs onto that of the Saxons in England nearly seven hundred years ago. The men who sit in the House of Burgesses are supposed to advise the governor, but they're prisoners of the past, too.

"I don't expect the world to be changed overnight, even in Transylvania. I realize that human nature don't—oh—doesn't change. But I keep thinking of that wonderful passage from the *Book of Common Prayer*: 'The fear of the Lord is the beginning of wisdom; a good understanding have all they that do thereafter; the praise of it endureth for ever.' "

He spoke the line from the *Book of Common Prayer* in a tone so hushed that the effect was startling. Sarah was impressed, but had been trying in vain to follow him, and her eyes were troubled. "You don't think very highly of the governor, P.H.?"

Patrick knew he was showing off now, but didn't care. "I have no reason to dislike Dinwiddie or his decrees. All royal governors are the same, you know. They take their orders from London and do what they're told."

Sarah's frown deepened. "You—aren't opposed—to the Crown?"

Patrick laughed. "Certainly not!" He realized she was worried because some of the men who frequented her father's Royal Arms Tavern voiced disloyal thoughts on occasion after they had spent a long afternoon or evening drinking. "King George II has no more faithful subject anywhere in the colonies."

She looked relieved.

He tightened his grip on her hand, looking at her intently. "Thank you for caring what I think."

Color rose in Sarah's face.

"By now," Patrick continued, "I reckon you know what I think of you."

She couldn't help giggling. "Folks are talking about us all the way to Richmond. One of my cousins there wrote a letter to Mama just the other day. She's heard tell that you come calling on me near every night."

"Every night, without fail," he replied, correcting her gently. Suddenly his poise deserted him, and he felt awkward, ill at ease. "Sarah," he said, "I'd like to have a talk with your father. But first I'd like to know whether you'd object."

She sighed. "For a body who's so smart he remembers every word he's ever read, you can be right stupid, P.H. I've been wondering these past weeks if you'd ever get it into your head to stop quoting philosophers and such-like long enough to spare a few words for Papa."

Again they looked at each other, and Patrick took her into his arms. He was uncertain whether he felt the beat of her heart or his own, but he wasted no time in idle contemplation. Bending his head down to kiss her, he marveled that Sarah could love him. She was pretty enough and sweet enough to marry a member of the governor's staff or an officer of the Royal Household Infantry Regiment stationed at Williamsburg.

It was miraculous that she should care for an eighteen-year-old nobody from the Hanover hill country.

8

John Henry inclined his head in the direction of the balding tavern owner who sat in the cushioned seat of honor, then looked across his desk at the young couple who stood before him, shoulders touching. "Mr. Shelton has asked me to speak for both of us, so I shall," he said. "Neither of us is surprised at your desire to be married, of course. But we think the situation is rather delicate. You're both too young to marry, yet you seem to know what you want."

"We do, Pa." Patrick had promised Sarah he wouldn't interrupt either of their fathers, but he couldn't keep silent. "We don't want to wait," he added, ignoring the girl's surreptitious tug at his sleeve. "We're sure we love each other. As Pindar said—"

"Spare me Pindar." Mr. Henry smiled at Sarah, and looked less forbidding. "I admire your taste, lad, even though I question Sarah's judgment. A man should be able to support a wife before he thinks of marriage. But the store is closed, and you've paid off only sixpence per shilling on your debts."

"I'm grateful to you for assuming those debts, Pa, and I intend to make sure you don't suffer a ha'penny's loss. The first two hundred pounds I earn will go to you."

"We'll consider that two hundred pounds a gift to your first child from your mother and me." Mr. Henry chuckled, then sobered. "The question in Mr. Shelton's mind and mine is: How do you plan to earn two pounds, much less two hundred?"

"My girl hasn't known great luxury," Shelton added, "but she's always had a solid roof over her head, warm clothes on her back, and the best of food on her table. What can you give her, Patrick?"

"A promise of hard work, sir."

"Doing what?" Mr. Henry demanded.

Patrick was heartened by the pressure of Sarah's arm against his. "The way I see it, the work I know best is farming. I grew up on this plantation, and I understand tobacco. I can grow enough corn for our cattle, and wheat for our table. If you'll give me my three hundred acres now, Pa, instead of leaving it to me in your will, I'll build us a cabin of pine and locust, and go to work straight off."

The two men exchanged glances. "He makes sense at last," Mr. Henry commented.

The tavern owner nodded. "It's what we've had in mind, lad, but we wanted to hear you say yourself that it's what you wanted. I'll add three hundred acres on my side of the fence to your father's, as Sarah's dowry."

The girl seemed to float across the room, and hugged her father.

"Not so fast," he cautioned. "The dowry isn't as grand as it sounds. You'll find little but scrub pine and pasture land on the property. It runs downhill and the soil is rocky, so it's good for little but grazing. Come to think of it, I'd better give you some cattle and sheep as a wedding present."

"I'll match your gifts, sir," Mr. Henry declared.

Patrick caught his breath and stammered his thanks. Every obstacle to the marriage was being swept aside, and he would be the master of six hundred of his own acres. While it was true that the life of a plantation owner had never appealed to him, and he had spent the better part of his boyhood avoiding chores on his family's farm, life would be different on his own property. For Sarah's sake he'd be willing to work in the fields every day of his life from dawn until sundown.

TWO

1756–1762

1

Two-year-old Martha raced across the front yard of "Pine Slash" when she saw her father dismount. A slave took the horse to the stable at the rear, and Patrick, gaunt and heavily sun-tanned, picked up his daughter and, carrying her in his arms, wandered around to the kitchen, the most substantial building on the property.

There old Isobel, who had insisted on accompanying the newly-weds from the day of their marriage, greeted him with a frown. "Miz Sarah's in the house, Patrick." Having called him by his Christian name from the day of his birth, she hadn't changed her habits just because he had, technically, become her master.

Patrick peered into an iron kettle on top of the wood-burning stove, then reached for a crust of fresh-baked bread.

Isobel promptly slapped his hand, and little Martha shrieked gleefully. "Don't you go teaching that baby bad habits, eating food when your hands are dirty," Isobel said sternly. Looking at him intently, she repeated, "Miz Sarah's in the house."

He left Martha in the kitchen, and not until he was halfway to the main cabin did it occur to him that the old woman had been trying, in a subtle way, to tell him something. He increased his pace, and frowned as the shadows of two locust trees fell

23

across the little house. He'd been promising Sarah for more than a year that he intended to double the size of the building, but other considerations had come first. He'd put an addition on the barn, built new tobacco storage sheds and servants' quarters, but the cabin itself still consisted of its original three rooms and the new bedchamber that his brothers had helped him construct hurriedly in the weeks before Martha had been born.

The partly furnished parlor was empty, and he found Sarah in their own room, stretched out on the four-poster bed that was their most precious and impressive belonging.

She smiled up at him, and he bent down to kiss her, but hesitated. "I've got half the dirt of the county on my face and hands. I've been spending most of the day with my nose to the ground, weeding in those south acres I planted six weeks ago."

"As if I cared." Sarah curled her arms around his neck and held him close.

"Are you feeling well? I mean, there's nothing the matter?" Patrick stripped off his shirt and, crossing the room, poured some water from a pitcher into a basin of tightly seamed oak.

"Of course, dear. Why should something be the matter?" Sarah rearranged her calico dressing gown.

"Blamed if I know." He scooped a handful of soft, yellow soap from a little earthenware bowl and spread a thin film on his face, hands, and neck. "I went looking for you in the kitchen just now, and Isobel—"

"—will never learn to mind her own affairs," Sarah said, and laughed. "I drove into Hanover this afternoon. Dorothea took me in her carriage."

"That was nice of her." He worked up a lather.

"She and Nate want us to drop in this evening, and they'd like you to bring your violin."

"Mmm." Patrick enjoyed the company of their neighbors, Nathaniel and Dorothea Dandridge, but was always conscious of their wealth and his own poverty when he visited their handsome red-brick mansion. Nate, a former Captain in the Royal Navy, had retired to colonial plantation living after inheriting a fortune, and Dorothea was an heiress in her own right, her father having been the late Governor Alexander Spotswood, one of the Duke of Marlborough's more distinguished veterans. What always disturbed Patrick was that Dorothea never wore the same gown twice, it seemed, while Sarah had nothing but the dresses that had been part of her small trousseau. Not that the Dandridges were snobs; on the contrary, Dorothea went out of her way to be friendly, and her own two-year-old daughter, also named Dorothea, had become Martha's inseparable playmate.

"You're too thin," Sarah said, studying Patrick from the bed.

"I eat enough."

"You work too hard, dear. You're out in the fields before sunrise every morning."

"And I still haven't shown a profit." Patrick didn't want to dwell on a distressing subject. Squinting to protect his eyes, he carried the basin to the nearest window, which was covered with heavily oiled paper instead of expensive glass. Then, after hastily dumping the contents and closing the window again, he poured fresh water into the basin and started to rinse thoroughly. "I was planning to start the second volume of Sir Edward Coke's *Institutes* tonight, but he can wait until tomorrow, if you really want to go visiting."

"Who is Sir Edward Coke?" She really wasn't interested, but thought the question polite.

"Lord Chief Justice under James I. I guess you've forgotten how much I enjoyed the first volume of his court decisions, *Coke Upon Littleton*."

Sarah's sigh was patient. "I can't for the life of me see what pleasure you get reading a law book that's a hundred years old."

"A hundred and fifty. I enjoy Coke's logic, the way his mind operates. His application of abstract judicial theories to specific legal situations is fascinating." Patrick realized she wasn't listening, and changed the subject as he reached for the towel Sarah had made herself from their own flax. "What did you do in town?"

"Oh, I stopped in at the Royal Arms for a word with Papa. And I saw Dr. Prescott."

"At his office?"

She nodded casually.

He realized anew the significance of Isobel's hint.

25

"You needn't look as though I'd slapped you, P.H. I merely went to see him about the baby."

Martha was in good health, as he knew, but he took two steps in the direction of the nursery. It hadn't occurred to him until this instant, but one-year-old Johnny was usually awake at this time of day.

Sarah seemed to read his mind, and smiled. "Both the children are fine, dear, and so am I. My health is always good when I'm this way."

Patrick dropped the towel onto a straight-backed pine chair and stared at her.

"Yes," she continued, answering his obvious but unspoken question. "I'm going to have another."

He went to her, and Sarah sat up for his kiss. Patrick hoped, desperately, that she couldn't sense his dismay. Now it was more urgent than ever to build an annex to the house, and he was so busy trying to put the plantation onto a paying basis that he'd have to hire workmen to do the job for him. That would cut into his perilously thin cash reserves, and he had no need to look at his ledgers to know his financial state.

He had only nineteen pounds sterling in his strongbox, and the annex would cost at least half that amount. Now, with still another mouth to feed, he'd never get on his feet. Thanks to game in the woods, fish in the rivers, and vegetables in the kitchen garden, his family wouldn't starve. But there seemed to be little hope of climbing out of an ever-deepening morass.

He felt far sorrier for Sarah than for himself. After less than three years of marriage she was being robbed of her youth. She never complained, but he had often seen the quick flicker of envy in her eyes when she had looked at one of Dorothea's velvet gowns or the handsome furnishings in the elegant drawing room of the Dandridge mansion.

He could only hope that Sarah didn't regret having married him, but he was afraid to ask her true thoughts. He wouldn't blame her if she despised him as much as he loathed himself. No woman wanted to be the wife of a failure, just as no man wanted to fail.

2

It was hot in the blazing sun, and Patrick was stripped to the waist, as were his four slaves. All five were doing identical work, cutting down high weeds with double-edged cutlasses as they prepared a previously uncultivated field for planting, and they slashed in rhythm as Peter, the foreman of the crew, chanted the beat. "Hee-yuh! Hee-yuh!"

Heat waves danced on the horizon and all five were bathed in sweat, but they did not halt until they had cleared the north half of the field. Then, at last, Peter straightened and grinned. "Rest now," he said, and drank from an earthenware water jug as the others stretched out on the ground.

Patrick took the jug and drank next, then passed along the jug. He and his men were on the same level, and he was proud of their ability to work together. Peter was in charge because Peter knew more than anyone else about the soil and tobacco growing, and that was that. Certainly Patrick rejected the criticisms of some plantation owners in Hanover, as well as in Louisa and other nearby counties, that he was lowering his dignity by working in the fields with his slaves.

The institution of slavery was a denial of humanity itself, and as he had told his father-in-law only a few evenings earlier, "I'm opposed to the whole system. I no more condone black slavery here than I'd approve of white slavery in Africa. Maybe I can't change our society, but I can treat my own slaves with as much responsible consideration as I treat my own children."

He had heard that Edmund Pendleton, Speaker of the Burgesses, who had earned a fortune growing tobacco, thought him mad. The criticism didn't bother him in the least. He had to live with his own convictions, not Pendleton's.

A sudden shout from Peter brought him to his feet. "Fire!" the foreman shouted, and pointed in the direction of the "Pine Slash" compound.

A column of thick, unusually black smoke was rising high into the air, and from a distance it looked as though the main house was ablaze. Ugly, orange-yellow flames flickered in the still summer air, and Patrick began to run, the slaves racing beside him.

Peter soon outdistanced him, and was organizing the household staff into a bucket brigade by the time Patrick and the others reached the compound.

Patrick's first concern was his family, and he was relieved when he saw Sarah standing in the front yard, holding the newborn baby, Neddy. Isobel was beside her, firmly clutching the hands of the squirming, excited Martha and wide-eyed John, who was dancing up and down in his excitement. Too breathless to shout a greeting, Patrick raced to the rear, where the clouds of smoke were thickest.

There he saw that the tobacco storage sheds were on fire, but that the conflagration had not yet reached the barns, the main house, or the servants' quarters. He joined Peter at the well, directed one of the servants to release the animals from the barn and immediately assumed charge of the fight.

The oily smoke became thicker, and Patrick found it difficult to breathe as he drew bucket after bucket from the well. His arms ached, his eyes smarted and tears ran down his grimy face, but he didn't dare pause for even a moment's rest. His lungs felt as though they would burst, but he shouted encouragement to his servants, whose efforts seemed useless. "Peter," he called hoarsely, "dig a trench this side of the sheds."

Patrick was too preoccupied to hear a party of horsemen arrive, and blinked in surprise when he saw Nate Dandridge running toward him.

"I saw the smoke from my place," Dandridge said, "and brought my field gang with me. What do you want us to do?"

"Help Peter with the trench. I don't want this thing to spread to the house."

The planter raced off, and began to give rapid instructions to his own men.

Patrick continued to work doggedly, without pause, for another half hour or more. His heart sank when the last of the tobacco sheds vanished, their precious contents—his sole source of revenue—drifting skyward in a blue-gray haze. And he wanted to weep when the roof of the main barn collapsed with a roar,

28

while the skeletal framework of the structure glowed fiercely before crumbling away and spewing on the ground. The tobacco crop was gone, and so were the corn for the livestock and the wheat for the family and servants that had been stored in the barn.

"The kitchen! Dig another trench this side of the kitchen!" Patrick's voice was so rough now that he could scarcely speak. Too impatient to wait for his demand to be obeyed, he turned over the task at the well to Peter and, seizing a spade from Nate Dandridge's young son, who was wielding it ineffectually, he raced toward the kitchen and started to dig frantically.

Others joined him and no one spoke as the trench took shape. The smaller of the barns was burning now, the heat was blistering and there seemed to be little hope of preventing the further spread of the fire. But Patrick continued to dig, his arms trembling and each breath so painful that he was afraid it might be his last. Suddenly a bucket of cold well water cascaded over him, and he stood for an instant, too stunned to move.

"You'll burn to a crisp," Nate shouted. "Move back, P.H.!"

Patrick shook his head and resumed his digging.

The nightmare continued for another quarter of an hour, the flames creeping ever close to the kitchen and, just beyond it, the new annex of the main cabin. Then, when it seemed as though nothing would prevent the flames from completing their destruction, a slight breeze blew up out of the west. The air was warm and dry, but it relieved the immediate threat to the main buildings.

The fire was fanned and flamed higher, but it was moving away from the house, servants' quarters, and kitchen now. The men concentrated their efforts on deepening and extending the trench, and Patrick still worked furiously, half-blinded but determined not to stop until he lost consciousness.

At last he felt a hand on his arm. "The danger is over now," Nate Dandridge said. "The last of it is dying down."

Patrick straightened, wiped his eyes with a soot-blackened arm and stared at the remains of his property. It was true that the fire was no longer a threat. The sheds and barns were nothing but glowing ashes, and men were pouring water on the embers, sending puffs of foul-smelling, hissing steam into the air.

Isobel was standing at the entrance to her kitchen, as though guarding it, and was weeping bitterly.

"Give everybody something to drink," Patrick told her, "and something to eat." Then, unprotesting, he let Nate lead him around to the front yard.

"Dorothea came over in her carriage," Nate told him. "She's taken Sarah and the children off to our place. We'll join them there later." He drew a silver flask of brandywine from his hip pocket and drew out the cork.

"None for me, thanks." Patrick was surprised to discover that his hair had been singed.

Nate didn't try to persuade him to change his mind, but drank from the flask.

Patrick sank onto a pine bench beneath a towering locust tree and tried to assess the damage. "I thank you for your help, Nate," he said at last, and his voice was remarkably calm. For a few moments he sat quietly, sipping a gourd of water that Isobel brought him, then added in a conversational tone, "I'm ruined."

"Is it that bad?" Nate asked.

"It couldn't be worse. I'd have shown a small profit on my tobacco, I reckon. Maybe I'd have just cleared expenses, as I've done every other year. But 'maybes' are a waste of time. The tobacco is gone. The hogs have run off into the woods, and sure as sin they've headed toward the bramble swamps. We'll never recover them. Well, at least the house and servants' buildings haven't been touched."

Nate joined him on the bench. "You could sell some of your slaves. That would give you fresh capital."

"Never. I promised them they'd stay with me, and I keep my word."

His friend knew better than to argue with him.

"They'll help me put up new barns for the cattle and horses. There'll be plenty for them to do after that around here. And I'll take Peter with me. I've taught him to read, write and do sums." Patrick laughed hoarsely. "His addition and subtraction are better than mine."

Nate probed delicately. "Take him with you—where?"

Patrick rubbed his hands together in a futile effort to brush off the clinging soot. "I haven't been happy as a planter, Nate. Some men are cut out for this sort of life—and others aren't. I've been trying for months to face facts honestly, and this fire is the last blow. I'm no farmer."

"I know how discouraged you feel right now, but don't make any hasty decisions." Nate took another swallow from his flask.

"Oh, I'm not. The fire is just the gold piping on the silk waistcoat. Your soil is the same as mine, and we have the same weather. You make a profit of hundreds of pounds every year, and I'd have been happy to earn seventy or eighty in the year."

"You haven't learned the knack yet, that's all."

"I'd be no better in ten years—or twenty."

"I think you may change your mind after you've cleaned yourself up and eaten one of Dorothea's oyster and beef pies."

Patrick shook his head and managed a weak smile. "As Sir Edward Coke wrote when he was Attorney General for the Crown, the application of pure reason points the way toward the solution of even the knottiest of human problems. The line wasn't original with him, of course. He took it from Bacon and changed the wording slightly. But that doesn't make it any less true."

Only Patrick would quote his beloved Sir Edward Coke at a time such as this, but Nate controlled his impatience. "What do you have in mind?"

"I'll sell some of the cattle and one or two of the horses to give me ready capital, and then I'll open another general store, with Peter to work with me as my clerk."

Nate was astonished. "But you've told me many times that you hated storekeeping!"

"So I do, just as much as I dislike farming. But it's the only work I know, and I have a wife and three children to support. And nine slaves."

"Do you think you can earn enough at storekeeping?"

"I'll have to, Nate."

"I wish you'd reconsider. You're still very young—"

31

"I was twenty-two in May, and I've been married for more than four years. So I'm old enough to accept my burdens. I've got to make the change, Nate. I have no choice."

3

"I know how you feel!" Patrick paced up and down the bedroom, the heels of his one pair of silver-buckled shoes clicking on the hardwood floor.

Sarah sat before the dressing table of rubbed mahogany that had been a gift from her parents-in-law, combing her hair, piling it high on her head and holding it in place with gilt-painted pins. "Please, dear, not so loud. The children will hear you."

"They're asleep."

"Martha is still awake. She was playing out in the yard a few minutes ago."

"If she's outdoors," Patrick said with cold logic, "she surely can't hear me."

"Let's not quarrel before a party."

"I'm not quarreling, I'm trying to apologize. I—I wish we weren't going tonight. Dorothea and Nate don't have to include us at every party they give."

"Would you rather wear out your eyes reading Coke—and those French books?"

"The legal codes of Henry the Great of France. They're fascinating, and there's nothing wrong with my eyesight." Patrick halted behind her, and met her gaze in the bronze-framed mirror set into the top of the table. "Sarah, I'm truly sorry. It makes me ashamed of myself when I know you'll be the only woman at the party who isn't wearing a new gown."

"You're very sweet, P.H., but I don't need one."

"That's beside the point. You'll be the most handsome woman there, and I'm sure you'd feel more in a party mood if you had—"

"There's nothing wrong with my red velvet." There was a note of finality in Sarah's voice that silenced him. She turned, put her hand on his arm and thought it best not to mention that his need for new clothes was greater than hers. The fabric of his black broadcloth suit had become shiny, and was perilously thin at the elbows and knees, which she couldn't mend as discreetly as she could his white silk stockings. "Everyone knows," she said loyally, "that we've had a hard struggle since the fire."

"That was more than a year ago, and a man ought to recover his balance in that length of time." Patrick gloomily took her lightweight cloak of unlined silk from a wall peg, draped it over her shoulders and settled his battered tricorn hat on his head. He was beginning to grow bald, but still had enough hair to make it unnecessary to buy a wig, which he couldn't afford.

"You're unhappy because of the remarks that were made at your parents' house on Sunday."

"Not really. Ma and Pa are ambitious for me, and they're sorry I frittered away my time when I was a boy, nearly as sorry as I am."

"You've more than made up for those years with all the reading you do now," she replied as they left the house and walked to the new, small stable where two saddled horses awaited them.

"It isn't the same," Patrick said glumly, and refused to be drawn into further conversation on their ride across the fields.

His mood failed to improve at Dandridge mansion, where more than a dozen guests gathered. Nate's sack, which he poured into silver goblets, came from an expensive cask that English free-booters had captured from a Spanish merchantman off the coast of the Floridas, and couldn't be duplicated in a tavern for less than thruppence a cup. Even though England and France were at war, there were handsome, smokeless French tapers in the crystal chandeliers, a cloth of thick linen was spread on the dining-room table and the chinaware, which bore Governor Spotswood's crest, had been a gift to him from the Duke and Duchess of Marlborough.

The air of opulence was so overwhelming that Patrick was scarcely polite when remarks were addressed to him.

Dorothea exchanged a swift glance with Sarah. "The saddle of venison we're eating tonight was a gift from Mr. Henry," the hostess announced. "When you've tasted it, I'm sure you'll agree he's the best hunter in the colony."

The achievement might mean something in Transylvania and

other parts of the Kentucky District, Patrick told himself, ignoring the smiles of the other guests, but it was meaningless in a part of Virginia so civilized that most people bought rather than shot game. His only reason for hunting was to provide his household with meat.

Nate tried a different tactic. "P.H.," he said, "tell them about the Scotsman who wanted to buy a keg of nails."

Patrick realized that everyone was looking at him, so he reluctantly launched into the anecdote. The story was at best mildly amusing, but his Sassenach accent was perfect, and a roar of laughter rewarded his efforts. He began to brighten in spite of his worries.

"Now," Nate prodded, "the one about the carpenter from Southwark."

Patrick's ear for the dialect of the London borough on the south bank of the River Thames was remarkable, and his talent for mimicry was astonishing. Encouraged by louder and prolonged laughter, he continued to shed his cares, and spun a succession of tales in which he imitated, faultlessly, the dialects of a New England merchant, a Dutch sea captain and a Pamunkey warrior. The dinner was a huge success, Patrick enjoyed the limelight and, as a climax, he carried on an imaginary dialogue between King George II, who spoke English with a thick German accent, and the royal valet, whose only language was Welsh.

The dinner ended on a note of gaiety, and Patrick had paid so little attention to his food that he couldn't recall what he had eaten. The ladies left the table, and the conversation turned to the war. Nate passed a decanter of rare port wine to his left, and only two guests refrained from drinking, Patrick and a youth named Jefferson, from Albemarle County, who was a student at the College of William and Mary and had been invited to spend the night because he was related to the socially prominent Randolph family.

"Cut off French Canada by sea," Nate said, "and we'll starve her into submission."

Richard Henry Lee, a tall, wealthy aristocrat who, although approximately Patrick's age, represented Westmoreland County

34

in the Burgesses, disagreed vigorously. "I say you're wrong, sir. Strike at the enemy through the wilderness."

Patrick laughed, and so did the student, Tom Jefferson, whose home was on the frontier.

Lee flushed. "I'm not thinking in terms of an abortive campaign, like Braddock's, conducted by Redcoat regulars. We need columns of colonials familiar with forest living."

Patrick felt impelled to enter the discussion. "Even the best Indian fighters have only a limited range in the wilderness," he said. "It's too vast." He glanced at Jefferson for corroboration, and the youth nodded. "As for your sea blockade, Nate, that won't be effective, either. There can't be more than about one hundred thousand people in French Canada, and they can live off the land. It seems to me the Royal Army is using a wise strategy. Reduce Quebec City, as General Wolfe is trying to do in his siege, and the French will collapse!"

There was a murmur of agreement around the table, and Lee smiled. "You make sense, sir, and I stand corrected. Are you a militia officer, Mr. Henry?"

"No, sir, merely a student of military affairs." Patrick refrained from adding that the responsibilities of supporting—or trying to support—a family had prevented him from volunteering his services. "My opinions are based on my own logic rather than on specific information. But common sense tells me the French can't hold out for very long. The question is no longer whether we'll win, but when we'll beat them. I think our own problem is far more pressing."

"What problem is that, sir?" Lee asked.

"I thought until recently that our own unfortunate tax situation here in Virginia was unique. But I happened to see a copy of the *Pennsylvania Gazette* a few days ago, and I discover the malady is universal. The governors of all thirteen colonies have imposed special war taxes on no authority but their own."

Lee warmed to him. "I hope to make an address in the Burgesses on that very subject."

"It takes money to prosecute the war," Nate protested, "and we can't expect the Crown to pay the whole cost."

"Let me make myself clear," Patrick declared. "I don't in the least object to taxation itself. But I feel it's unjust to impose a tax on salt, for example, as was done six months ago, without giving the people who are taxed a voice in the matter."

"Yes," Lee added. "Just for the sake of argument, we might have preferred a tax on sugar."

Nate poured himself more port and started the decanter on another round. "Frankly, gentlemen, I don't see what difference it makes. We must pay, regardless."

Patrick hitched forward in his seat. "There's a principle of justice at stake, Nate, one that Coke took from Bacon and enlarged. Even the French recognized it in the Code of Henry IV, when the Estates were granted a voice in ratifying major tax measures. As Coke points out so strongly, ignore the goddess of justice in small matters, and she'll refuse to serve you in large. Suppose a new governor came to Williamsburg, a stupid tyrant who decided to line his own pockets. And suppose he imposed a tax confiscating fifty percent of every man's land holdings. What would you do?"

"I'd tell him he could go to the devil," Nate said.

"Ah, but you couldn't." Patrick slapped the table. "Once you accept his right to impose any tax whatever without your consent, he can then tax you at will. You shrug off the tax on salt because it's only a ha'penny per peck. But unless you take your stand on salt, your fundamental legal right, which has been unwritten and assumed, withers away. Then you have no grounds under law for opposing the confiscation of half your property."

"I'll mount a cannon on my portico before I'll let anyone confiscate my property," Nate said. "And I'll ask you to serve as chief gunner." He stood, everyone laughed, and the men started toward the drawing room.

Patrick found himself beside young Jefferson, and was surprised at the ungainly youth's height. He himself was more than six feet tall, but the freckled, red-haired boy, who probably was still growing, towered over him.

"Do you practice in Hanover, Mr. Henry?" Jefferson asked.

Patrick looked at him blankly for a moment, then shook his head. "Don't be misled because I can cite Coke and Bacon and the Code of Henry IV," he said. "I'm afraid I'm no lawyer."

36

4

"I assure you, lad, I have no intention of laughing at you." The Reverend Patrick Henry sipped his glass of watered rum. "I took you seriously when you were a child, and I shall listen to you now."

Patrick felt cold, but his tea was scalding. "I didn't really think you'd laugh. What I meant was to hope you won't preach to me."

"It's a vocational failing." The old man sat back in his chair and tried not to smile.

"You wanted me to follow in your footsteps, Uncle, but I've always lacked the humility. I don't believe I could start each day by asking, 'Thy will be done.' I need to be kicked and punched into submission. Let me read you some revealing figures." Patrick opened his worn ledger. "In twelve months, from March of '59 until March of this year, I did a gross volume of business amounting to slightly more than four hundred and fifty pounds."

"I know very little of finances, lad," the clergyman interrupted.

"One doesn't need to be Master of the Virginia Exchequer to understand these sums. My profit, on paper, amounted to forty-two pounds, eight shillings, or a little less than ten percent of my gross business. Fair enough. But I've had to buy new stock, and I have only twelve pounds sterling to my name. I propose to sell everything, stock and store. I've found a buyer who'll give me a fair enough price. And I'll stop trying to pretend I'm a storekeeper."

The Reverend Mr. Henry took another swallow of his drink. "Your mother was telling me the other evening that Sarah is expecting a baby in the autumn."

"Yes, Uncle, our fourth—and all the more reason for me to make my right place in the world. Oh, I'm paying for my folly. I was lazy and shiftless as a boy, and I dreamed of living on the frontier. I didn't realize the meaning of hard work, and I expected it would be as easy to support a wife and children as it

37

is to pull a fish from the river or shoot a fat doe in the forest."
Patrick's eyes were bleak as he looked at his uncle. "Well, the
Lord booted me until I disabused myself of the idea. He pushed
me to my knees, and His hand has been holding me there until
I've come to my senses."

"It seems to me," the clergyman said mildly, "you needn't have
worried that I'd preach to you. You deliver a rather powerful
sermon yourself."

"Martha starts school next year, and Johnny goes a year later.
It gave me something of a shock when I realized it a couple of
nights ago. I was reading Justinian's *Digest*—"

"In Latin?"

"Of course, Uncle. Peyton Randolph sent me an English
translation made about fifty years ago, but it's abominable.
Justinian's code is really clear only in the original."

The old man was unable to conceal his pleasure. He had done
his work far better than he had realized when he had been trying
to tutor his intense, restless namesake.

"Anyway, I found I couldn't concentrate. I reckon Sarah
thought I was going mad, and it may be I really was losing my
wits. I went outdoors and walked until dawn. She was awake
when I came in, and I told her right off that I'd get rid of the
store as soon as I could. It's strange, but she actually looked
relieved." Patrick closed the ledger and found his tea palatable.

"What do you intend to do, lad?"

"I took a long look at myself. I'm twenty-four years old, and
I've already had three failures. I can't afford another. I reviewed
my interests, and I finally decided I want to be admitted to the
bar."

The clergyman chuckled.

Patrick stared at him, offended.

"It's been so obvious to me that you were developing strong
interests in the law," his uncle explained. "Knowing how you
carry that perpetual chip on your shoulder, daring the whole world
to knock it off, I thought it best not to say anything to you."

"I'm sorry."

"No need to apologize. You can't change your nature. Only

the Almighty can do it for you, and you're finally putting your-self in His care." The Reverend Mr. Henry drained his drink. "Coke, Henry IV, Justinian. And every law book in Peyton Randolph's library. Couldn't you see it yourself?"

"Not until two nights ago." Patrick grinned sheepishly, then sobered. "I've never before come to anyone for advice, but I don't dare gamble unless I'm reasonably sure that what I'm doing is right."

"Have you told your father this decision?" the clergyman countered.

"I've caused him enough heartache. I want everything settled before I speak to him."

"You'll find he's wanted a professional career for you since you were old enough to walk. The trouble was that you insisted on walking alone from the time you began to toddle. You've always been too independent for your own good, but I'm sure he'll give you what financial help he can afford, in spite of his own reverses in recent months."

"He and Ma have done enough for me," Patrick said flatly. "I can't take charity from anyone."

"How will you support your family?"

"I'm not rightly sure, Uncle. I'll send off a letter to the judiciary committee of the Burgesses today, asking for an examination later this month or next. The money I'm getting for the sale of the store will pay our expenses until September or October. Sarah can stretch a shilling into a half crown. I know I won't be able to set up a law practice overnight, so I'll have to find part-time work until I get enough clients to earn a living at the law. One way or another, we'll have to manage."

The Reverend Mr. Henry kept his thoughts to himself. Patrick was showing courage and daring, but he still seemed incapable of looking beyond the fairly immediate future. Apparently it hadn't occurred to him that he might be as unsuccessful a lawyer as he had been a storekeeper and farmer. His uncle couldn't be sure whether, under the circumstances, this stubborn blind spot was a handicap or a virtue.

5

Williamsburg was so crowded when the Burgesses met that the judiciary committee was forced to conduct its interviews with prospective members of the bar in the back room of the Raleigh Tavern. Some candidates, nervously awaiting their turn, availed themselves of the establishment's facilities, and neither the chairman, Peyton Randolph, nor his four associates were surprised when tense young men stumbled into the hearing room reeking of spirits.

Patrick proved to be the exception. Cold sober and surprisingly calm, he bowed to the members of the board and accepted Randolph's offer to sit opposite them.

White-wigged George Wythe, professor of law at the College of William and Mary, opened the questioning. "Where did you study law, Mr. Henry?"

"At home, sir."

Wythe raised a bushy eyebrow. "You attended no formal courses and took no instruction from members of the bar?"

"No, sir."

Wythe thrust a taper into the glowing coals of the hearth behind him, and took a long time lighting his pipe. "Then I don't suppose you can tell us Coke's definition of common law. Assuming you've heard of Sir Edward."

Several of the others chuckled at his witticism.

Patrick refused to let himself become irritated. "In his *First Institute*, Coke said that reason is the life of the law. Going still further, he insisted that common law itself is nothing but reason. The law, he wrote in summation, is the perfection of reason."

He sounded so sure of himself that he seemed almost glib, and the board members exchanged swift glances. "It would appear you've done considerable reading, Mr. Henry," Peyton Randolph said.

Patrick knew he had at least one supporter on the board. The chairman had allowed him to borrow every law book in the extensive Randolph library over a period of several years.

"Can you tell us Justinian's definition of justice?"

"Justice is the constant and perpetual desire to render to every man his due."

"If you please," Wythe said testily, "the fourth article of the Code of Henry IV."

Patrick hadn't known what to expect, but felt completely at ease. The interrogation concerned only basics that he knew as well as the woods of Hanover County. "No authority other than a Crown bailiff has the right to break into the home of the individual."

Robert Carter Nicholas, who had taken his law degree at Oxford University, rested his elbows on the table, a quizzical expression in his eyes. "The English have adopted that portion of the Code of Henry IV."

"They have not, sir." Patrick thought the attempt to trap him obvious and clumsy. "In his *Third Institute*, Coke defines a man's home as his castle. He amplifies this view somewhat in Semayne's Case, where he says, 'The house of everyone is to him as his castle and fortress, as well as for his defense against injury and violence as for his repose.'" He had made no special effort to memorize the passage, but remembered it without straining.

"Let's assume a hypothetical situation, Mr. Henry," Randolph said. "We'll say that Wolfe's corps hasn't yet taken Quebec City, so the outcome of the war is still in doubt. One of your neighbors, a man of French descent, is believed to be in the pay of the enemy. The officer commanding the military forces in your part of the colony, who is charged with making that portion of Virginia secure against military attack, decides to break into the man's house in order to search for evidence against him. May the officer do this?"

"Not unless he first obtains a search warrant from a magistrate, who will issue the warrant only if he considers that valid grounds for a search exist."

The interrogation continued for almost two hours, and Patrick knew the board members were bearing down because of his lack of a formal law school education. Most candidates were questioned for a half-hour or less. At last he was sent out of the room while the committee made its decision, and he wandered out into

Duke of Gloucester Street, the main thoroughfare of Williamsburg, where he stood watching a steady procession of open and closed carriages, horsemen, and pedestrians moving in two directions.

Never had he seen so much traffic, so many expensively dressed people, and it hadn't occurred to him that there could be so many wealthy people in Virginia. Some of their gaudier carriages, with gold-encrusted crests on their doors and velvet-lined interiors, had cost at least three or four hundred pounds, enough to support his family in style for two years.

He refused to let himself dwell on the possibility that his application might be refused. To the best of his knowledge he had fumbled only a few times in the examination, but no one on the board had indicated whether his answers had been considered satisfactory. If his gamble failed, his future was bleak, and he might be forced to migrate to the western wilderness. The prospect was anything but pleasing, and he smiled at the irony of his situation. As a bachelor there had been nothing he had wanted more than to stake a claim to land west of the mountains. But a married man with three children and a fourth on the way had to think of his family rather than himself. Sarah was too delicate for wilderness living, and educational opportunities for the children were limited in the Kentucky District. A man's dreams died hard—but they died.

A barmaid opened a leaded window and called to Patrick that he was wanted. He hurried through the front room of the Raleigh, where members of the colonial legislature were eating and drinking, and tapped politely on the door of the private chamber at the rear.

"Come in, Mr. Henry." Randolph's voice was devoid of expression.

Two clerks sitting at a table near the windows were writing busily, and for a few moments there was no sound in the room but the harsh scratching of their quill pens. The committee members were solemn, and Wythe actually looked out of sorts.

Patrick bowed, then stood erect and held his breath.

"Are you intending to return to your home today, Mr. Henry?" Randolph asked.

The question was puzzling. "I am, sir."

"Perhaps you'll want to stop here before you leave. Your official copy of your license will be ready in an hour or two." Randolph stood and extended his hand. "Welcome to the ranks, Attorney Henry."

6

A crudely painted shingle reading, PATRICK HENRY, ATTORNEY-AT-LAW AND COUNSELOR, hung from a second-story window above the Royal Arms Tavern in Hanover, opposite the Court House, and creaked dismally in the autumn wind. But the room inside was empty, a coat of dust covered the straight-backed chairs and the pine desk was bare. Worn copies of Coke's *Institutes*, Parkhurst's *Lexicon*, and Hawkins' *Pleas of the Crown* stood on the center shelf of an otherwise empty bookcase, and three new, leather-bound copies of *Laws of Virginia* reposed on the top shelf, looking untouched.

In the taproom directly below, however, there was an air of bustle and gaiety. The county court had reopened after a summer adjournment, and the two magistrates were dining on mutton and ham pie at a table in the corner. Their bailiffs and clerks occupied the long table near the entrance to the kitchen, and a dozen lawyers were eating with their clients at other tables, conferring in low tones.

John Shelton stood inside the front door, making certain that none of his patrons was neglected, and occasionally he signaled unobtrusively to the two barmaids who hurried in and out of the kitchen with heavy trays. A long bar occupied the inner wall of the taproom, and behind it, in racks, were arrayed jugs of sack, whiskey and Dutch gin, West Indian rum, and both French and English brandywine. There was a collection of wines from England, Spain, and France, Portugal and the German states, too, including Madeira and Malaga, Muscadine and Canary and Fayal, as well as a scattering of lesser known products. Three kegs blocked one end of the bar, and each was neatly labeled in thick black paint that resembled tar. The largest was identified as small beer,

43

another as porter and the third as mead, the popular brew made from honey that came in limited quantities from North Carolina.

In charge of the bar was Patrick, wearing a leather apron into which he had tucked a towel. His sleeves were rolled above his elbows, although the day was cool, and he worked without pause, filling tankards and cups, glasses and mugs as the barmaids brought him a steady stream of orders. Even though he was frantically busy, his mind remained unoccupied, and he listened wistfully to snatches of conversation. The other lawyers in the room were real attorneys, counselors who were paid fees in sterling by clients.

He himself hadn't yet earned a farthing as a lawyer, and in the four months that had passed since he had been granted his license, he had done no legal work other than to draw up wills, free of charge, for his father, father-in-law, Uncle Patrick, and John Syme. The worst of his situation was that every man in the taproom was aware of his predicament, and although no one actually treated him with condescension, he could see amusement in the eyes of colleagues who occasionally glanced in his direction. Fortunately or otherwise, the magistrates appeared unaware of his existence.

The two justices were the first to finish their meal, and their departure was the signal for a general exodus. The bailiffs and clerks hurried after the magistrates, and almost at once the attorneys left with their clients, everyone adjourning to the Court House. Only a group of prosperous farmers remained at a corner table, lingering over tankards of hard apple cider, and Patrick joined his father-in-law for a late noon dinner.

Wearily aware that he would have to spend the better part of the afternoon checking the stocks of spirits to determine how much had been consumed, he had little appetite for a meal, and helped himself only to a small platter of scrapple fried with plantain and star apples from Barbados. The odor of spirits still seemed to fill his nostrils, so he preferred a cup of tea to a glass of Shelton's private supply of barley beer.

Patrick toyed with his food in glum silence until his father-in-law inquired after the newest member of the Henry household. "I tell you," Patrick replied, brightening at once, "Anne is going

44

to be a beauty, nearly as pretty as Martha." He was incapable of giving the baby higher praise.

The sound of loud voices and a sudden scuffle erupted at the corner table, and John Shelton was on his feet at once. Patrick jumped up, too, and saw that a slender, middle-aged planter named Wilson was sitting on the floor, a trickle of blood oozing from a cut over one eye. Another farmer of about the same age, called "Greenleaf" Green by his friends, stood over him, both fists clenched.

The other members of the dinner group looked on in dismay, and Shelton intervened with swift efficiency. "I allow no fighting here," he said. "Move apart, pay your reckoning and take yourselves elsewhere."

"There's no more fight," Green assured him. "It lasted for just one punch."

Wilson tugged at Patrick's apron. "I've heard tell you're a lawyer now, Henry. Do something!"

"Are you asking me to represent you?" Patrick found it difficult to take the request seriously.

"Aye! I'll pay you a guinea in sterling, and if this bully gets what he deserves, I'll give you three bags of cured leaf and any ham in my smokehouse that strikes your fancy." Wilson struggled painfully to his feet. "This attack was the lowest—"

"As your attorney," Patrick interrupted, "I order you to say no more at present. Gentlemen," he added to the other farmers, "I'll want all of you to testify as witnesses, and I'll have no subpoenas issued for those who'll appear voluntarily."

"Greenleaf" Green laughed derisively, the thumbs of his huge hands hooked into his rawhide belt. "Henry is no lawyer! We've been drinking the kind of justice he knows. That punch made you weak in the head, Wilson. Henry was admitted to a different kind of bar than you mean!"

Patrick could feel color rising in his face. He had acquired his first client under circumstances so questionable that other attorneys might be justified in accusing him of unethical opportunism, but he had no intention of letting the chance slip from his fingers. "We'll go straight to the Court House," he said to Wilson, ignoring Green. "We'll swear out a warrant on charges of assault and

45

battery, and we'll see that the case is put on the calendar right off."
He went behind the bar, removed his apron and slipped into his
shabby coat of black broadcloth.

7

The unpainted plaster walls and ceiling were peeling, the win-
dowpanes on both sides of the magistrates' bench were cracked
and the chairs of plain pine in the jury box were held together
with thongs to prevent them from collapsing. The principal bailiff
kept his fishing gear and hunting musket under oiled paper in one
corner of the chamber, the justices having appropriated the only
suite of private rooms in the building, and no one had tried to remove the nests of the purple, green, and blue starlings from the
eaves of the building, even though the noisy chatter of the birds
sometimes made it difficult for the magistrates, counselors, and
jurymen to hear what was being said in the courtroom.

In spite of the acoustical problems and shabby décor, however,
the King's justice was dispensed without fear or favor in the Hanover County Court House. The magistrates wore the stiff curled
wigs and voluminous robes of their office, a mace symbolic of
their authority rested on a varnished table in front of the bench
when court was in session and attorneys were required to wear
wigs and gowns only a shade less formal than those of the justices.

Patrick felt uncomfortable in his borrowed finery, but tried to
put his unaccustomed costume out of his mind as he addressed the
jury of Hanover County farmers and storekeepers. "Picture the
scene, gentlemen," he said in a resonant voice that rose above
the incessant chirping of the starlings. "A few friends relaxed in
convivial surroundings. Prices had been good in the tobacco market that morning, and after their many months of hard labor, they
had earned a brief respite from their cares.

"They ate with good appetites, and they joked with the familiar,
rough humor of men who have known and respected each other
for years. You will have no difficulty envisaging such a scene, gentlemen, for you yourselves have participated in many like it.

"You heard my honorable opponent, the respected counsel for

the defense, suggest that several members of the party, including the plaintiff, had been drinking intemperately." Patrick's tone, which had been solemn, suddenly became light and scoffing. "You heard the plaintiff and witnesses deny that allegation. They drank only two or three tankards of mead each, and I ask you, what Hanover County man loses his head after a few gentle drops of mead?"

The members of the jury grinned, and several laughed aloud.

Patrick pursued his advantage. "I know, better than any other person in this chamber, that no one was intoxicated, and had Their Honors permitted me to give sworn testimony, I could have verified what the plaintiff and witnesses told you under oath, for these two hands poured the mead." He was taking a calculated risk, knowing he could be held in contempt, but he was making his point in spite of the refusal of the court to let him testify earlier in the trial. Fortunately, his estimate of the reactions from the bench had been right. Both magistrates were smiling, obviously surprised by the candor of an attorney willing to admit openly in court that he had served as a barman.

"My client," Patrick continued, unexpectedly dropping his voice an octave, scowling and stabbing the air with a forefinger, "suffered sudden, grievous injury. The defendant admits he struck a man half his size who was unprepared for a vicious assault. The defendant claims he had been insulted, but neither he nor anyone else can remember what caused him to take leave of his senses.

"But you and I know why he struck that cruel blow, gentlemen!" Patrick's voice soared theatrically now, and he snatched his wig from his head. "You heard the defendant admit that he was jealous of the plaintiff's higher yield of tobacco per acre this year. Jealousy, gentlemen, was the monster locked in his breast, the monster that burst into the open and caused my client to suffer.

"The plaintiff seeks no revenge, gentlemen." Again Patrick's manner changed, and now he sounded calm and reasonable. "He wants only his due. He does not ask that the defendant be sent to jail for this attack. He has no wish to stain forever the good name of one who, until this black day, was a law-abiding subject of His Majesty, an honorable father and a loving husband. The plaintiff asks justice, no more and no less, and offers his hand

47

once again in friendship to one who basely attacked him. For the sake of justice, gentlemen, I ask that the plaintiff be awarded ten guineas in sterling as recompense for his suffering, and that the defendant be required to pay court costs. By your leave, Your Honors, the case for the plaintiff rests."

Patrick bowed to the magistrates and walked stiff-legged to the table where Wilson was sitting. He felt something limp in his left hand, saw it was his borrowed wig and was bewildered for a moment, unable to recall how it had left his head. But he clapped it on again with a feigned air of nonchalance, and took his seat beside his client.

A few minutes later the jury retired, and the magistrates left the bench temporarily, but did not adjourn the court.

"How do you suppose I'll make out?" Wilson asked anxiously.

"With luck, you'll get half of what we've asked," Patrick told him, speaking softly, so that Green and his attorney, sitting at an adjoining table, could not hear him.

"That's all?"

"Friend, I suspect that you may have been responsible for that punch. I was careful not to dwell in my presentation on your table talk at dinner that day. But I have an idea you were taunting Green about your bigger tobacco yield until you drove him into a fury. If the jury shares my suspicion, you'll get nothing."

Wilson blanched and averted his eyes.

Conversation was desultory until the jury returned, and everyone stood as the magistrates came back into the chamber. Then the foreman was directed to deliver the verdict.

"We find the defendant guilty as charged, Your Honors. We suggest he be fined damages as requested by counsel for the plaintiff, and recommend that he be shown personal clemency."

The magistrates conferred in whispers, and passed judgment accordingly.

Court was adjourned, and Wilson was ecstatic, but Patrick accepted his thanks with the air of a man accustomed to winning cases by the score.

Several men came forward to shake his hand as he made his way from the Court House, and he accepted their congratulations with the same faintly pleased but detached air. Not until he reached home, he thought, would he be able to celebrate in private with Sarah.

"Mr. Henry!"

Patrick turned to see Ewell Dabney, the wealthiest planter in the area, beckoning to him. "Your servant, sir."

"Yours, Mr. Henry. That was one of the most impressive performances I've ever had the pleasure of watching, and I offer you my felicitations on fashioning a victory out of the flimsiest of evidence."

Unable to admit aloud that his case had been weak, Patrick merely bowed.

"I've been looking for someone of your caliber to represent me in some unpleasant litigation in Louisa County. I won't bore you with the details now, Mr. Henry, but I'm trying to recover some valuable property from a cousin. If you can spare the time, I can offer you a retainer fee of twenty-five guineas, with a promise of another twenty-five if you win the case."

Patrick caught his breath. Not only was he being offered as much for one case as he had previously earned in a year of farming or storekeeping, but the prestige of representing Dabney would bring him other clients. And never again would he be forced to suffer the humiliation of serving as his father-in-law's barman in order to support Sarah and the children. "I'm sure, sir," he said, "that I can spare the time."

8

"I wasn't expecting you until tomorrow, P.H." Sarah hurriedly lighted two oil lamps shaped, in the newly fashionable design, like sailing boats.

Patrick sank into the cushioned chair they had bought in Richmond the previous year, but demurred when his wife offered to help him remove his boots. "I'm not that tired, my dear."

"But you must have spent a long day on the road."

"I changed horses twice after staying the night in Baltimore." He caught hold of her hand and drew her to a chair beside his. "Don't fuss over me, Sarah. I had a good supper at an inn on the

49

road, and I want nothing to eat or drink. I'm only sorry I didn't arrive before the children went to bed. Now tell me the news."

"Nothing is changed here, P.H. Martha is spending the night with Dorothea because they're going together to a schoolmate's birthday party tomorrow. Nate will bring her home in the afternoon."

"There's no need for that. Peter can drive to the Dandridge house for her, unless you have other plans and intend to use the carriage."

"No, dear, I don't." She hesitated for an instant. "I know that Nate hopes you'll represent him in a law case in Williamsburg. But he hesitates to ask you."

"I'll never be too busy to do work for Nate Dandridge. Now, then. Has John's new tooth come in, and has Anne's rash disappeared?"

"Yes, to both questions." Sarah giggled. "Gracious, sir, all Virginia is talking about you, and you're only interested in children's rashes and teeth!"

"I thank the Almighty because I can afford the luxury. Why are tongues clacking over me?"

"Because of the verdict you won in the case against the clergymen, of course! Your office received more than two hundred letters today—from all over the colony—thanking you for saving them from having to pay their ministers more money everytime the price of tobacco goes higher."

"Or less when it drops." Patrick sat back contentedly in his chair, and spoke candidly, without false modesty. "I did well in that case, and I was relieved when Uncle Patrick took no offense. I should have known he'd realize there was nothing personal in my stand, that I must do my best for my clients."

"You can be maddening, P.H."

"What have I done?"

"I'm so anxious to hear about Philadelphia! And you just sit there, as though you hadn't even made the journey!"

"It's a gracious city, although I don't care for Pennsylvania food. What I found of the greatest interest is that people there feel as we do about the young King. They're afraid George III is determined to show us he's our master, and they don't like the new tax laws that Parliament is passing. In fact, people everywhere share the same feelings. It's astonishing—and heartening. I saw a copy of a Boston newspaper called the *Gazette*—"

"Politics and taxes again. I might have known."

"You asked my impressions." He looked at her with affectionate amusement.

"You haven't told me yet whether you won your case."

He was surprised that there might have been any doubts in her mind. "Yes, the Richmond interests were awarded damages. The High Court was very courteous, and allowed me to present our case myself, with local counsel stepping in whenever major differences between the laws of Virginia and Pennsylvania might have caused confusion." He became more animated. "I certainly liked the bookshops. I packed seven or eight volumes on the law in my saddlebags, and a crate with about thirty more is being sent down to me by wagon cart. There's the real advantage of city living. They have the newest books six weeks after they're published in London."

Sarah listened politely, but had no intention of listening to a detailed description of the legal studies he had acquired for his constantly expanding library. "Tell me about the ladies of Philadelphia."

"Each of them has two feet, two hands, and two eyes. English is the common language, but people from the hill country speak German, a barbarous tongue."

"Don't tease me, P.H. I want to know how they dress."

Her request made no sense. "Much as they do here, I believe."

"I very much doubt it. And you're hopeless."

"Not too hopeless, perhaps." Patrick reached into the inner pocket of his coat and drew out a small box of varnished elmwood, which he handed to her.

She opened it, and gasped when she saw a heavy bracelet of gold, with her name engraved on the inner rim. "This must have cost the whole fee you earned there!"

"Hang the fee. I think that, after eight years of marriage, it's time you own some jewelry." He stood when she rose to her feet and kissed him. "I brought Ma a bracelet of sterling," he said, "and smaller bangles for Martha and Anne." He paused, and his tone became slightly defensive. "You won't approve, but I bought smallswords for the boys. Dress swords, with dull blades, so they can't cut themselves."

"Did you have a new suit of clothes made for yourself, as you promised?"

"I didn't have time," he protested.

Sarah's exasperation rendered her inarticulate.

"I wouldn't feel at home in the English watering places, my dear. The life of a beau and dandy wouldn't appeal to me."

"But you have no pride, P.H. How can you appear in court year after year in that shabby old suit?"

"The magistrates are impressed by arguments, not appearances. Besides," he added with a chuckle, "my robes cover my suit."

"If you won't do something about it, I will. I'll send an order to Nate's tailor in Williamsburg!"

"We don't have money to waste, Sarah."

She fingered the bracelet, thrusting her wrist under his nose. "You could have bought a whole new wardrobe with the money you spent for this."

"By next year," he said, "our financial situation should be much improved, provided clients keep coming to me and the Crown doesn't impose too many new taxes. In fact, we'll be able to afford a new house before too long, so you might keep watch for a place in the area that strikes your fancy." Patrick yawned, stood, and began to unwind his neckcloth of inexpensive cotton. It was time he moved his family to a house in keeping with his increased prosperity, but he realized he would hate to leave the unpretentious dwelling that had been his home for eight years.

In fact, he was surprised to discover that his character was developing in unexpected ways. Now that he was establishing himself in a career and, for the first time in his life, was earning an aristocrat's income, he found that he had no craving for the things money bought. It was one thing to give gifts to Sarah and the children, but the very idea of lavishing luxuries on himself was abhorrent to him. Only now, with his financial worries eased, was he learning that the prospect of becoming wealthy didn't particularly appeal to him.

He thought it wise not to mention his feelings to Sarah, however. Not that she was avaricious, but she would be sure to ask what he really wanted, and the truth of the matter was that he didn't know.

9

John Syme added a hickory log to the fire in his parlor hearth, stood erect and dusted his hands. "I enjoyed my stay in Williamsburg," he said, "and I don't believe I did discredit to the people of Hanover County in the Burgesses. But I certainly didn't find the experience as exciting as you seem to think it should have been."

Patrick warmed himself before the fire, occasionally running a hand through his thinning hair. "I don't see how the session could have failed to be dramatic. The spirit that's being shown everywhere in the colonies is extraordinary."

His half brother looked at him blankly. "What spirit?"

"The growing resistance to the belief of the King and his ministers, of course! The laws aimed at Massachusetts Bay that permit agents of the Boston Port Collector to search where they please for alleged smuggled goods is an outrage! It denies the basic principle of English liberties!"

John was accustomed to the younger man's outbursts, and smiled. "You exaggerate, of course. No one has broken into your house seeking untaxed imports."

"Not yet, but what the Collector at Boston is allowed to do, the Collector at Williamsburg may do, too." Patrick grew increasingly incensed, and began to pace up and down the confines of the little parlor.

His half brother looked at him with ill-concealed amusement. "Suppose an official party did break in? Would they find any contraband?"

Patrick's ferocious air melted, and he laughed. "As a matter of fact, they would. I ordered three kegs of that mild barley beer from Edinburgh, the strongest alcoholic spirits that I enjoy. And a sea captain for whom I handled some litigation last year smuggled it in at Baltimore for me. Your hands aren't too clean, either, you know. That Dutch plate you bought last month was smuggled. And that's my whole point. I don't think there's an American anywhere in all thirteen colonies who doesn't own merchandise that's untaxed."

"Then the people of all thirteen colonies are guilty under the law, aren't they, Attorney Henry?"

"We're all guilty of non-compliance with unjust, unfair laws, yes. But the principle of justice is being subverted by the Crown and the Commons, not the people of America. Our only form of protest is to defy laws that deny our basic rights as free English citizens. Blame short-sighted Parliamentarians like George Grenville and that rabid anti-colonial, Charles Townshend. We served the Crown well, and won the war in the New World long before the fighting stopped in Europe. When a peace treaty is signed, there's no question that France will be forced to cede Canada to the Crown. But the new King is so puffed with his own self-importance, and the members of the Commons are so afraid of incurring his displeasure, that we're being made to pay a penalty for our patriotism!"

John refused to take the situation seriously. "As nearly as I can learn, the rights of search for contraband are being applied sparingly in Boston, Patrick."

"As of the moment, perhaps, but that's no guarantee of what will be done tomorrow. I don't suppose you're familiar with the plea that a Boston lawyer named Otis made before the Massachusetts Supreme Court on the subject. It was brilliant."

"There was some talk of it in the Burgesses. But assembly leaders like Edmund Pendleton and George Wythe are conservative gentlemen, you know. They may practice a bit of smuggling now and then, but they don't actually preach doctrines advocating disobedience to the Crown."

"Pendleton and Wythe are timid old women, and you're shortsighted, Johnny. I'd like you to read a copy of a pamphlet that James Otis has written. Some friends in Philadelphia have sent it on to me."

John became concerned. "I hope you aren't letting yourself become involved with those radicals in Massachusetts Bay. You're finally proving yourself as a professional man, and for the first time in your life you're earning a respectable income. Don't jeopardize your security, P.H. You'll lose your clients if you become friendly with the wrong elements."

Patrick was offended. "Anyone who objects to my way of thinking needn't be burdened with my company. And that applies to you, Johnny!"

His half brother smiled wryly. "I'm merely trying to help you, P.H. I know better than to waste my breath trying to influence your thinking. You'll either be knighted by the Crown—or hanged as an insurrectionist. Speaking for myself, I'd enjoy telling people, 'I'm related to Sir Patrick.' It would give me far more satisfaction than helping your widow look after your orphaned children, who wouldn't find it easy to understand that their father died for the sake of a principle he had evolved because he read too many books."

Patrick grinned sheepishly. "I'm inclined to become a trifle hotheaded on occasion. Forgive me, Johnny. I'm disturbed because London seems to be ignoring our rights. We need a spokesman who'll present the colonies' grievances to the Commons and the government ministries."

"You, perhaps?"

"Hardly! I'm no statesman."

"Why not trust Dr. Franklin of Philadelphia, then? He's been in England for some time."

"He's been there too long, if you ask me," Patrick retorted. "His views are too moderate."

"I'm sure he's making a beginning, and that he's being careful not to antagonize powerful men who'll tell the First Minister and the Minister for Colonies that we're worried about the present trend of events. Gentle persuasion is better than antagonizing the Crown, isn't it?"

"Well, I'll admit we aren't strong enough to take up arms."

John was stunned. "You aren't seriously suggesting open revolt because the new King is inexperienced in dealing with his empire!"

"No, I believe we'll arrive at an accommodation that will satisfy everyone, and that there will be no bloodshed. But I'm convinced it's necessary for London to be told how we feel, and why. That's why the position that Otis up in Massachusetts Bay has taken is so important. The government won't listen and the Commons will take no action until New York and Connecticut and Pennsylvania make their own protests. Virginia and Maryland and the Carolinas must speak up, too. We can't let others do our work for us."

"If you think it's so essential to present your philosophy, why don't you run for a seat in the Burgesses?"

"In the first place," Patrick replied unhappily, "I'm too busy earning a living, making up for the years I lost. And in the second place, no one has thought of nominating me for a place in the assembly."

THREE

1764–1769

1

Relations between England and her North American colonies continued to deteriorate, and by 1764 opinions on both sides of the Atlantic were hardening. "The well-being of His Majesty's Empire," said First Minister George Grenville, "is more important by far than that of her separate parts. England is the hub of a great wheel, and silver must flow to London from each distant part of the realm, here to be collected and disbursed again according to the needs of our many peoples throughout the world, as we deem necessary and fitting."

Some colonials agreed that London should be regarded as the fountainhead of political and economic wisdom, but others were vehemently and vocally opposed to the idea. "The Crown," Sam Adams of Boston wrote dramatically in a weekly newspaper, the *Gazette*, "wants to enslave us. We must resist!"

Grenville was aware of colonial opposition to his policies and struck out in a new, seemingly conciliatory direction. A thirty-year-old law, the Molasses Act, which imposed a tax of sixpence per gallon on molasses imported into the colonies, was repealed. As the First Minister told Parliament, the tax was so high that colonials preferred to smuggle in their sugar, and no one bothered to pay the tax.

57

So the Commons passed a new bill, the Sugar Act, which imposed a duty of only thruppence per gallon on molasses, and Grenville expressed the hope that His Majesty's overseas subjects would accept this lower, more equitable levy. He and his colleagues completely failed to understand the American mind, however, and ruined the good effect by including taxes on a number of other imported goods in the Sugar Act.

Patrick Henry read a copy of the new law in the Louisa County Court House, where he was appearing in behalf of several clients, and was so incensed that he made a brief, impromptu speech on the front steps of the building at noon. "We must now pay taxes on wines and silks, coffee and ironware and linen. The Commons has even dared to tax our imports of gunpowder! It's bad enough that we're not allowed to manufacture our own powder.

"Now we must pay for the privilege of defending our frontier settlements against savages! Does the Crown send troops to protect our brave wilderness dwellers against Indian warriors who loot and scalp and burn and pillage? Oh, no. Every family must look after its own safety. But now the brave householder must pay a tax to fatten the King's purse for powder that will save the lives of his wife and children, make his cabin secure and prevent marauders from stealing his corn and cattle.

"These taxes are too much for honest Virginians to swallow. The Sugar Act must be repealed, my friends, and Virginians must speak with one voice. Let our cry of protest be heard in Williamsburg. Then His Excellency will write to London, saying, 'Virginians demand justice, and will be satisfied with nothing less.'"

A crowd of about one hundred and fifty men, including lawyers and their clients, applauded heartily. Patrick was gratified by their cheers, but his pleasure was fleeting, and he had little appetite for the mutton chops and peaches fried in batter that were a specialty of the Louisa Inn.

His unhappy mood persisted, and was so glum that he scarcely noticed a driving summer rain that soaked him when he rode away from the Court House late in the afternoon. Ordinarily he paused at a hilltop for a view of his new home, "Roundabout," an estate in Louisa County about thirty miles from his former property, but this was a day when he took no satisfaction in his own accomplishments. Brooding, he paid no attention to the handsome one and one-half story building of red brick, with its handsome white-columned portico, solid outbuildings and snug barns. Although the place was far from palatial, it was symbolic of his rise in the world, and he frequently encircled the property before joining his family for supper.

Now, however, he rode with lowered head through the mud toward the whitewashed gate at the bottom of the winding path that led from the hilltop house to the road. And he was so lost in thought that he failed to see Martha running down the hill toward him until the child called a greeting.

Patrick brightened immediately, leaned down and lifted her up into the saddle. "Don't you know it's raining, child? You'll ruin the new shoes we had made in London for you." They were the last English shoes he would buy, he thought, as he certainly wouldn't pay the new tax on footwear.

The girl laughed and brushed her damp hair away from her face. "No I won't, Papa, because I'm not wearing shoes," she said, exhibiting a muddy foot. "Mama sent me to tell you that some gentlemen are in the parlor, waiting to see you."

He spurred his gelding up the hill. "Who are they?"

"Uncle William is one, and Justice Perkins is another, but I don't know the rest."

William Christian, who had married Patrick's sister, Anne, was a partner in the newly formed law firm of Henry and Christian, and was a frequent visitor. But Meredith Perkins, the presiding magistrate of Louisa County, rarely accepted the hospitality of lawyers who appeared before him in court, so it was apparent that something out of the ordinary was happening.

"Dorothea is coming tomorrow," Martha said, "and she'll stay here with me for a whole week."

"Well, you'll have to wash off your dirty feet before you entertain a guest, won't you?"

Martha's peal of laughter raised the gelding's ears to sharp points. "Dorothea isn't a guest, Papa!"

Sarah was waiting at the front door for her husband, and addressed him in a low murmur as he cleaned his boots on a mat made of plaited vine fibers. "I don't know why they're here. I tried to get Will Christian aside, but he wouldn't meet my eye."

"We'll soon find out." Patrick squeezed her upper arms reassuringly, then walked into the parlor. He bowed to Magistrate Perkins, Harold Walker, a wealthy plantation owner, and his brother-in-law. "I'm honored by this call, gentlemen, and I'm delighted that Mrs. Henry found the sack for you."

"I already knew where it was," Christian replied with a broad smile. "I needed no help from Sarah."

Patrick was pleased that the men had made themselves at home; they could have paid him no higher compliment as a host.

The trio exchanged glances, and the magistrate acted as their spokesman. "P.H.," he said, wasting no time, "I heard your speech this noon from the open window of my chambers. That's why I left the bench early this afternoon. You expressed the sentiments of every man in Louisa County. The new taxes are outrageous. Members of the bench aren't permitted to express opinions on controversial matters, of course, but please accept my private congratulations."

"If men in the seaboard counties felt as we do," Walker declared, "Virginia could stand united in its opposition to the Crown policy."

Patrick was a realist. "They and their fathers—and their grandfathers—have supported the Crown in so many things for so many years that it isn't easy for them to change their habits. They'll need to be jolted out of their complacency before they'll see Grenville's policies our way."

"They won't change of their own accord, we know," Magistrate Perkins said. "They need someone like you to jolt them. For that reason, among others, we want your permission to submit your name to the citizens of Louisa as a candidate for one of the county's representatives in the lower House."

"You're very kind, Your Honor, but you forget I've just lived here for a few months." Patrick knew his brother-in-law had said something about his desire to serve in the Burgesses at an appropriate time.

Christian grinned, then hastily looked away. Sarah, he knew, would not thank him if her husband went into politics. She had often expressed the opinion, at family gatherings, that he was already far too busy, and frequent journeys to Williamsburg would consume still more of his time.

"I've spoken to some of my neighbors," Walker said, "and they'll give you their full support."

"So will the townsmen in Louisa and Mercerville," Christian added. "You've appeared in court here for years, and people think of you as one of their own."

Patrick was more impressed by his brother-in-law's support than by anything the others said. Christian's own income would decline if the senior partner in the firm started spending two or three months of the year in Williamsburg, so it was evident that he was willing to accept a sacrifice for what he considered the public good.

"I'm flattered by your confidence and friendship, gentlemen," Patrick said carefully. "But I'd like to make my position clear before I accept. I hope you realize I have no desire to make a career for myself in the Burgesses. I gladly leave that sort of life to men like Edmund Pendleton and George Wythe. I'd like to do what I can to help this colony clarify its opposition to present Crown policies, and then I want to retire again to my private practice. I don't believe I have the temperament for political compromise, and it's been my observation that only the men who are willing to trade are successful in Williamsburg."

Magistrate Perkins remained amiable. "I think you're a new type of politician, P.H., a type this colony needs. If we aren't represented by honest, frank men, the Burgesses will lose whatever influence they have with the governor. But I'm willing to let the future take care of itself. We ask no more than that you see us through this new crisis."

"Under those conditions, I gladly accept." Patrick hoped Sarah wouldn't protest too vehemently, but her opposition was less important than the principle at stake. Unless he and men of similar persuasion spoke their minds, their children would grow to adulthood in a land the Crown would be free to exploit at will for its own selfish purposes.

2

Patrick felt distinctly out of place, and wished he hadn't accepted Richard Henry Lee's invitation to join a small group of his fellow Burgesses for an informal social hour. The surroundings were pleasant enough, and he was familiar with the back room of the Raleigh Tavern, the same chamber in which he had been examined for admission to the bar. Perhaps he should have worn black broadcloth, like the others, instead of donning the buckskins that were the uniform of delegates from the other western counties.

What really bothered him was that his companions were men who had inherited fortunes and married heiresses. He was the only one at the table who lived solely on what he earned, and he felt they spoke another language. Their families were intimate, they visited each other's estates and they exchanged cheerful insults with the bland familiarity of old friends. Only Colonel George Washington, a militia hero of the recent war against the French and Indians, a patrician with a big jaw and bigger nose, maintained a measure of reserve.

John Tyler, a slender, dark-haired planter with wrists and hands almost as small as a girl's, was as voluble as Lee, and as quick-witted. Between them they dominated the conversation, with occasional interruptions from Washington's close friend and neighbor, George Mason, who was reputedly the wealthiest member of the Burgesses, and heavy-set Benjamin Harrison, whose shoulders and humor were as broad as a blacksmith's.

After commenting at length on the quality of each other's racing horses and wine cellars, the young assemblymen began to speak of political matters, and soon the atmosphere became so charged that even Washington twirled the stem of his glass and spilled Madeira on the table. "I tell you, lads, we must accept reality," Lee said. "Don't for a moment forget that Parliament passed this new Stamp Act without a dissenting vote being recorded against it."

"Does that mean you'll willingly pay a tax on every document you use, your bills for your wife's gowns and your own wine, your sales of tobacco and your nephew's marriage license?" Tyler was scornful.

"If I must, I'll accept the law, no matter how much I dislike it." Lee spread his fingers in a helpless gesture. "No one can accuse the colonel of being a coward, but you don't see him defying Governor Fauquier."

"I'd gladly stand up to him if I thought it would do any good," Washington said. "But opposition for its own sake will make London all the more determined to enforce the law."

"The Act goes into effect in November," Mason added. "So we'd have only five months in which to do something. And I can't imagine what it'd be. Boston has been complaining bitterly, but all the wails and cries haven't accomplished anything."

Harrison drained his mug and placed it on the table with a resounding thump. "At least they're shouting up in Massachusetts Bay. They aren't tugging their forelocks and opening their purse strings to pay the most unfair tax ever imposed on a free people."

Tyler looked at Patrick. "What are your views, Mr. Henry?"

Everyone turned to the outsider.

"Listen," Patrick said, inclining his head toward the main room of the establishment, where a score of patrons were bellowing a simple tune, commonly called "The Stamp Act Song," that was popular everywhere:

> *"With the beasts of the wood, we will ramble for food,*
> *And lodge in wild deserts and caves;*
> *And live poor as Job on the 'skirts of the globe,*
> *Before we'll submit to be slaves."*

Patrick's diffidence vanished. "There, gentlemen," he said, "you hear the people of America crying in the wilderness. Someone must lead them to the Promised Land."

Lee was friendly but skeptical. "Do you propose to be their Moses?"

"I think every assemblyman has two duties," Patrick replied gravely. "We must reflect the views of our constituents. And when they search for a road, we must guide them to it."

"Forgive me if I accuse you of ambiguity, Mr. Henry."

Patrick's expression remained unchanged. "I supported Mr. Lee's motion today to convene the House as a committee of the whole tomorrow for the purpose of considering the Stamp Act."

"All of us supported Richie," Harrison muttered, "for all the good it will accomplish. A half-dozen speakers will deplore the passage of the Stamp Act by Parliament. The conservatives—who always support the Crown—will then vote that the remarks be expunged from the record. And we'll adjourn for the summer. I'm tempted to leave for home tonight instead of being a party to a sorry spectacle."

"Unless you have special reason for leaving early, Mr. Harrison," Patrick said quietly, "I think you may find it worth your while to stay for another day. Now, I hope you'll excuse me, gentlemen. I promised my half brother I'd meet him at the Raleigh for a bite of supper. It's the penalty a new legislator pays for having a relative with seniority in the Burgesses."

Washington put a tanned hand on his arm. "Before you go, Mr. Henry, I think it only fair to tell you that Speaker Robinson and Edmund Pendleton were taking pains today to repeat a conversation that took place last night at the Governor's Palace. The governor is threatening to strike boldly if there's open opposition to the Stamp Act. He went out of his way to remind Pendleton that direct defiance of royal law is a hanging offense."

"Are you warning me, Colonel?"

"Certainly not, sir! I'm merely making you privy to information you may not have heard." A broad smile creased Washington's face, and his air of reserve vanished.

Patrick returned his grin. "In that case, Colonel, I'm grateful to you. You didn't run from the field when General Braddock's corps marched into an ambush, so I'm sure you'll understand that I find retreat distasteful, too. I'd rather die in battle with a clear conscience than expire of fright in my bed."

3

The sun appeared after an early morning rainstorm on May 29, 1765, and most members of the assembly were anxious to return to their homes after spending five uneventful weeks in Williamsburg. But there were rumors that something spectacular would enliven what had been a dull session to date, so the representatives postponed their departure for another day or two. By mid-morning they began to make their way to the Burgesses after a leisurely breakfast, and soon every seat in the auditorium was taken. The word that something out of the ordinary would happen had spread through the town, and the visitors' galleries, which were located above the Speaker's rostrum, were crowded, too. The governor's secretary sat in one front row seat, the Treasurer of Virginia in another, and although women rarely considered the activities of the House lively enough for their taste, several handsomely gowned ladies sat in the section reserved for colonial officials and their families.

A church bell down Duke of Gloucester Street chimed the hour of eleven, and as the last note faded away, Speaker John Robinson came down the center aisle, a powdered wig on his head, his robe of scarlet and gold trailing behind him. He was preceded by the Burgesses King of Arms, bearing a mace, and the members stood until the Speaker took his seat and ceremonially rapped his gavel for order.

"A quorum of members being duly present," Robinson said, hurrying through the ritual, "I hereby declare the House in session, God save the King, preserve him and protect him from his enemies." He leaned back in his leather-padded chair. "In accordance with the motion passed at the close of business yesterday, this House is now convened as a committee of the whole, with the Speaker acting as chairman. The clerk will note that the motion was made by the right honorable member from Westmoreland County."

The clerk's pen scratched, and for a moment or two no one spoke.

"Mr. Chairman!"

Robinson peered toward the rear of the chamber, where the new members sat. "Who seeks the floor?"

"The member from Louisa County," Patrick replied, "for the purpose of moving a series of resolutions."

"The chair recognizes the right honorable member from Louisa."

Patrick walked slowly down the aisle to the well, relieved that

Sarah had forced him to buy a new suit of black broadcloth, silver-buckled shoes and a silk stock. Delegates from Albemarle, Amherst, and several other western counties delighted in wearing buckskins to sessions of the Burgesses, but he had refused to follow their example today. His intent was too solemn, and he wanted to create a solid, conservative impression.

Taking some scribbled notes from an inner pocket, he launched on his maiden speech. "Whereas, the honorable House of Commons in England have of late drawn into question how far the General Assembly of this colony has power to enact laws for laying of taxes and imposing duties, payable by the people of this, His Majesty's most ancient colony; for settling and ascertaining the same to all future times, the House of Burgesses of this present General Assembly have come to the following resolves:

"One. Resolved, that the first adventurers and settlers of this, His Majesty's colony and dominion, brought with them and transmitted to their posterity, and all other of His Majesty's subjects, since inhabiting in this, His Majesty's said colony, all the privileges, franchises, and immunities that have at any time been held, enjoyed, and possessed, by the people of Great Britain."

It was obvious that he was issuing a challenge to the validity of the Stamp Act, and a stir went through the House. Pendleton, Wythe, and others in the front row who had long been leaders of the Burgesses glared at the young speaker, but Patrick ignored them. Richard Henry Lee, who was sitting in the third row, grinned at him, and John Tyler, directly behind Lee, nodded his encouragement.

"Two. Resolved, that by two royal charters, granted by King James the First, the colonists aforesaid are declared entitled to all the privileges, liberties, and immunities of denizens and natural-born subjects, to all intents and purposes as if they had been abiding and born within the realm of England."

Patrick knew that no matter how much the colonists might think of themselves as Englishmen, Parliament had denied them fundamental rights, and his voice rose dramatically as he reached the heart of the dispute. "Three. Resolved, that the taxation of the people by themselves or by persons chosen by themselves to represent them, who can only know what taxes the people are able to bear, and the easiest mode of raising them, and are equally affected by such taxes themselves, is the distinguishing characteristic of British freedom, and without which the ancient constitution cannot subsist."

Speaker Robinson's face was red, and he conferred hastily with his law clerk in an undertone, apparently trying to determine whether he had the right to silence the speaker.

George Mason chuckled, then whispered something to Washington, whose eyes, almost as intense a blue as Patrick's, belied his seeming calm.

"Four." Patrick lowered his voice so the guests in the visitors' galleries had to strain to hear him. "Resolved, that His Majesty's liege people of this most ancient colony have uninterruptedly enjoyed the right of being thus governed by their own Assembly in the article of their taxes and internal police, and that the same has never been forfeited, or any other way given up, but has been constantly recognized by the kings and people of Great Britain."

The chief clerk and his assistants were writing rapidly, taking down every word of the first coherent reply to the Stamp Act.

"Five." Patrick raised his voice now, and every phrase, every word soared toward the high dome of the chamber. "Resolved, therefore, that the General Assembly of this colony have the only and sole exclusive right and power to lay taxes and impositions upon the inhabitants of this colony; and that every attempt to vest such power in any person or persons whatsoever, other than the General Assembly aforesaid, has a manifest tendency to destroy British as well as American freedom."

Benjamin Harrison leaped to his feet and led the younger members in applause.

Elderly John Randolph, who served as Attorney General of the colony and was fanatical in his loyalty to the Crown, shook his fist at the speaker.

Patrick raised a hand for silence, and continued in the same clear, resonant voice. "Six. Resolved, that His Majesty's liege people, the inhabitants of this colony, are not bound to yield obedience to any law or ordinance whatever, designed to impose any taxation whatsoever upon them, other than the laws or ordinances of the General Assembly aforesaid."

No man could have issued a more sharply defined call to combat. The authority of the Commons was being denied, and so was that of the Crown itself. John Randolph was apoplectic, and the governor's secretary stalked out of the visitors' gallery, the treasurer behind him.

Patrick was conscious of the furor he was creating, and a deceptively mild smile lighted his face. "There is one more resolution," he said calmly, then raised his voice to a defiant shout. "Seven. Resolved, that any person who shall, by speaking or writing, assert or maintain that any person or persons, other than the General Assembly of this colony, have any right or power to impose or lay any taxation on the people here, shall be deemed an enemy to His Majesty's colony."

John Syme twisted in his seat and looked apprehensively at the sergeants-at-arms in their scarlet tunics who stood at the rear doors. It was evident that he was afraid his half brother would be placed under arrest, and the more conservative members were calling, "Shame! Expel him!"

"I haven't yet yielded the floor, Mr. Chairman," Patrick said. "Fellow members of the Burgesses, these resolutions express the sentiments near to the hearts of us all, and to the people whom we here represent. Let London heed our words and rescind a law we find odious. I urge the passage of these resolutions so that none in His Majesty's service will doubt our resolve.

"Tyrants have throughout all history been deaf to the demands of free men for their liberties. Caesar had his Brutus, Charles the First his Cromwell, and George the Third—"

"Treason!" Speaker Robinson called, striking his gavel repeatedly.

"Treason!" The shout arose from every part of the chamber.

Patrick stood still, his chin thrust forward, his fists clenched, waiting for the furor to subside. "And George the Third," he resumed, "may profit by their example." He glanced around at Speaker Robinson, then faced the members again, both arms raised. "If this be treason, make the most of it!"

In the pandemonium that followed, Lee and Tyler were the first to shake Patrick's hand as he made his way back to his seat. Then others crowded into the aisle, among them Washington and an exuberant Mason, who pounded him on the back.

Representatives loyal to the Crown opened a spirited rebuttal, but Patrick sat quietly in his seat through arguments that raged for hours. The usual three o'clock dinner recess was forgotten, and supporters of the resolutions, led by Lee and Tyler, combed the chamber for votes. Their foes, who had always deplored such blatant tactics, were forced to forget their dignity and do the same. Both sides realized the count would be close, and the leaders allowed the debate to continue while they harangued, pleaded, and argued with the few representatives still on the fence.

Tempers frayed as men became hungry, and finally Speaker Robinson took matters into his own hands. "The members," he said, "will take their seats, and the clerk will call the roll on the resolutions."

Several members protested angrily, claiming the right of unlimited debate, but the chair ruled against them on the grounds that it was his prerogative to terminate the discussion when the House sat as a committee of the whole.

Patrick had taken no part in the talks that had followed his own initial presentation, but he hunched forward in his seat, keeping his own tally as the chief clerk began to call the roll alphabetically, by counties.

At the halfway mark, the vote of Norfolk County, ten members were opposed to the resolutions, and nine favored them. The tension increased, and the visitors' galleries, which had emptied during the long hours of heated debate, were filled again.

York County was the last on the list, and after both of its representatives declared themselves in favor of the resolutions, Benjamin Harrison's ear-splitting Chickasaw war whoop rattled the crystal ornaments dangling from the overhead chandeliers. The resolutions were adopted by a vote of twenty-two to twenty.

The younger members surrounded Patrick, pumping his hand, slapping him on the back and shouting his praises. The power of the long-entrenched conservatives had been curtailed for the first time within the memory of living men. Someone in the crowd of Patrick's admirers said, "This will encourage the Whigs in Parliament. The King and his Tories won't have such an easy time of it now."

"Come along, you Whigs," Harrison called in his deep voice. "To the Raleigh for supper."

The victors moved together up the aisle, only a few of them dimly aware that a Whig party in Virginia had just been born.

Patrick approached the door just as Edmund Pendleton, elegant in a suit of dark green velvet, reached it simultaneously. They exchanged stiff bows, each waving the other through the exit first, and Pendleton could not remain silent after his defeat.

"I trust you're pleased with yourself, Mr. Henry," he said stiffly. "The governor has been our friend, and so have the officials of the Colonial Ministry in London. Now, thanks to you, they'll be our enemies."

"I bear them no malice, sir," Patrick replied carefully, "and I hope that within a short time this expression of the people's sentiments will make their task easier. The willingly governed are the best governed, and I feel certain that, when the Stamp Act is repealed, the whole colony will give His Excellency full cooperation in all things."

"By what right do you presume to speak for the plain people of Virginia, Mr. Henry?" Pendleton demanded.

Others had grown quiet, and were straining to hear.

"I make no presumption, sir." Patrick's voice was soft, but carried to the far reaches of the crowd. "If I know the plain people, it's because I'm one of them. And I tell you they won't be satisfied until the rights of taxation are returned to their own representatives and the Stamp Act is rescinded."

4

Drops of early morning dew still clung to blades of grass on the neat lawns of Williamsburg's homes as Patrick Henry and John Syme rode up Duke of Gloucester Street on their homeward journey. As always, John looked like a member of the Burgesses in his dark suit and bicorn hat, but a casual observer who had not been present in the Assembly chamber the preceding day would have found it difficult to believe that Patrick had been the author of a history-making document.

His new clothes were crammed into his worn saddlebags, along with several new law books and volumes of history he had bought during his stay in the capital. His buckskin trousers and shirt were limp and shabby, his moccasins were worn thin, and his stained, battered headgear was shapeless. It was wasteful, he contended, for a man to risk ruining expensive clothing on dusty country lanes, and it didn't bother him if other travelers mistakenly assumed he was a wilderness farmer. It was not customary for gentlemen to carry muskets, but tradition meant little to him; it was far more important that he try to bag a deer or a wild boar on the homeward journey, so his long rifle, loaded and ready for use, was laid across his pommel.

John was still excited, and could think only of the scene in the Burgesses. "No one at home will be surprised to hear you made a great speech," he said, "but I'll never forget the expressions on the faces of the men who listened to you. Robinson and Wythe and Pendleton were ready to hang you from the nearest tree. And your friends would have followed you into battle if you'd asked them to make war on the Crown."

"I pray to the Almighty that neither we nor the English will ever be stupid enough to use force against each other. Parliament may think seriously of changing its policies when the action of the Burgesses yesterday is officially received by the Commons. If not, we have other weapons in our arsenal." Patrick made himself more comfortable in his saddle. "You heard Colonel Washington's suggestion last night at supper."

"I think it's unrealistic to hope that the people of every colony will agree to buy no goods made in England. We can't even work out common defense plans to protect the wilderness settlements from Indian attacks."

Patrick smiled. "Now you know why I was so willing to be the Burgesses' representative at the conference in New York Town in September. We'll talk about Indians, right enough. We'll also arrange ways to make non-importation agreements effective."

John stared at him as they rode their horses at a rapid walk on the road that would take them along the banks of the Chickahominy River toward Richmond. "P.H., you're letting yourself in for trouble."

"Am I?"

"You were so busy celebrating with the young Whigs last night that you didn't hear what was being said around town. You've challenged the authority of the King, you know, and George III is a headstrong man."

"It's high time he learns we're his free subjects, not his slaves." Patrick's good humor dissipated.

"I'm thinking of you, a man of twenty-nine with a wife, children, and an expanding law practice!" John wondered if his half brother would ever settle down and become practical. "Some of the Tories were wondering—aloud—whether the King or Grenville will order you arrested."

"It would be an interesting trial. Not only would the Crown's legal position be weak, but I don't believe there's a magistrate in Virginia, not even one of the justices of the General Court in Williamsburg, who'd send me to prison."

"Has it occurred to you," the irritated John asked, "that you might be sent to England for trial?"

"There's no legal precedent for that."

"Legal precedent be damned. London newspapers have been demanding English trials for Otis and Sam Adams of Massachusetts Bay, and now they'll certainly add your name to the list. They won't be satisfied until you've been hanged."

Patrick was unable to consider the possibility seriously, and shrugged. "The experience would be unique." He laughed, but stopped short when he saw that John was exasperated. "I hope there will be so many of us open to the same charge by the time the Crown decides to take such action," he added, "that there won't be enough ships in the Royal Navy to carry all of us off to jail in England."

"Then you're really planning to devote time and effort to arousing opposition to the Stamp Act?"

"I must."

"You'll lose clients who hold different political views, P.H."

"Others will replace them."

72

"You can't compensate for the time you'll spend in New York Town. And if you and Lee meant what you said last night when you offered to speak anywhere in Virginia to rally opposition to the Stamp Act—"

"The people will learn what's at stake only if we tell them." There was a note of grim finality in Patrick's voice that ended the conversation.

A half-hour later the pair approached the sleepy little town of Toano, which had only one road wide enough for carriages, several small churches and a general store distinguishing its main thoroughfare. Two small children were playing on the lawn of a white-washed clapboard house, and on one of the small side lanes a man in a faded shirt and breeches was trimming a hedge with a cutlass. No one else was in sight.

"There he is!" A shout broke the calm.

Mounted men rode into the open, seemingly from nowhere, and headed toward Patrick.

Reacting instinctively, he started to raise his long rifle to his shoulder, but hesitated when he saw that the riders were wearing the distinctive green uniforms that identified them as militiamen who had served on the frontier in the war against the French and Indians.

"Be you Patrick Henry?" the leader, who wore a sergeant's red epaulet on his left shoulder, called loudly.

"I am." It would be virtually impossible to defend himself against so many, Patrick thought, and prudently lowered his rifle.

A drum sounded a long, low roll, then the shrill piping of a fife cut through the air. Twenty or twenty-five men on foot appeared from behind a barn, one of them carrying the Old Dominion ensign, a white banner on which had been sewn a crude representation of the century and a half old seal of the London Company, which had established the first permanent Virginia colony at Jamestown in 1607. The whole company began to sing "The Stamp Act Song," enthusiasm making up, in part, for an inability to carry a tune.

Patrick and John, bewildered by the unexpected display, were escorted to the side yard of the Anglican church, where a feast was spread on bare oak tables. There were platters of baked ham and roasted fowl, heaping bowls of raw oysters and baked crabs, and busy housewives, their smaller children underfoot, were carrying still more food to the tables from a kitchen located behind the church.

Two huge kegs of ale stood at either ends of the rows of tables, and foaming mugs were thrust into the hands of the half brothers before they were allowed to dismount.

"To Patrick Henry!" the former sergeant shouted.

The others repeated the toast.

"To Virginia! And to hell with King George!"

For a moment Patrick and John stood side by side as they were lifted bodily from their saddles and deposited on the ground by the cheering citizens. "I hope," John said in a low tone, "that you're prepared to cope with this, P.H. When men curse the King, it's treason—no matter what anyone may call it."

There were tears in Patrick's eyes. "They don't mean it literally, Johnny, and they won't. Unless the Crown proves to be even more stupid and shortsighted than I believe possible. What this demonstration proves is that our people won't submit to tyranny. And when folks show this kind of courage, I've got to help them, no matter what happens to my reputation or law practice."

He was surrounded by the eager farmers and artisans of Toano, each of them anxious to shake his hand and thank him for his defiance of the Crown. No matter what the King and his ministers might think, no matter how much the Tories in the Burgesses might fume, the common people of Virginia were already making clear their own sentiments in the dispute.

5

Burgess Richard Bland had made a lifelong study of warring Indian tribes, as had many other delegates to the meeting in New York Town, which was attended by representatives from nine of the thirteen colonies. Bland and the other experts settled down to discussions of how to pacify the savage nations, and while they debated fine points of strategy, the deputies who were less familiar with the Iroquois, Cherokee, and Chickasaw acquainted themselves with the delights of the town.

New York was the third largest city in the colonies, smaller and less conscious of its cultural heritage than Philadelphia, smaller and less commercially aggressive than Boston. But it had an air, and even a certain charm, of its own. The students at King's College were louder and more boisterous than those who attended Harvard or the College of William and Mary. Ships flying the flags of a dozen nations docked at the wharves and slips of the Sound River, sometimes called the East River. The John Street Theatre presented plays less than a year after their first performance in London, and the young women who strolled in Renelagh and Vauxhall Gardens were as unabashedly bold as the most audacious wenches of the Old World. The flavor of New York made up for its unimpressive size.

"What I like best about the place is its Dutch gin," Sam Adams of Boston said as he added a little finely powdered birch bark and spring water to the liquor in his glass. "I'm told that two thousand gallons are sent here from Amsterdam every year, but not a single drop goes to any other town. What a pity." He sighed and sat back against his hard wooden seat in the Pearl Street tavern recently renamed the Three Georges.

Patrick thought his companion was one of the homeliest, yet one of the most personable men he had ever met. Short, plump, and balding, with ineradicably ink-stained fingers, Adams cared as little about his appearance as Patrick himself. His linen stock was soiled, his cuffs were frayed and he hadn't bothered to have the pewter buckles on his shoes polished for months. The pockets of his old brown suit bulged with papers, and a button was missing from his waistcoat, but his manner was so commanding that two barmaids hurried to the booth the moment he drained his drink and raised his head.

"Are you sure you won't join me, Mr. Henry?" he asked. "I assure you, sir, Dutch gin is superior to the most mellow and fragrant of spiced Madeiras."

"To be truthful with you, Mr. Adams, I'm not fond of Madeira." Patrick dropped a measuring spoon of coarse brown sugar into his tea, and suddenly laughed. "What superb irony, Mr.

75

Adams. You and I, for whose scalps the press of London cries so incessantly, sit together in a tavern named in the King's honor."

Adams did not reply until the barmaid deposited a fresh drink before him and moved out of earshot. "Inns," he said succinctly, "find it easy to change their names."

"Easier by far than men may change their allegiance," Patrick replied.

"My views disturb you."

"No, it's our future that worries me. When we last met to discuss the border wars with the Indians, the Stamp Act Congress that you and Otis summoned was about to go into session, and we had good reason to hope our efforts would succeed. The people in every colony put up great resistance to the Stamp Act—"

"Yes, thanks to our work in organizing their opposition. And we did well, sir! I doubt if more than a thousand guineas went to the Crown from the sale of stamps. Men from New Hampshire to Georgia ignored the law."

"So they did, Mr. Adams, but you simplify a complex situation." Patrick drummed on the table with lean fingers, then ran his hand through his still thinning hair. "Look at our present situation. We've had to use our wilderness disputes with the Indians as a pretext for still another intercolonial meeting."

"It's wise to use discretion when dealing with Satan, Mr. Henry."

"Are we so certain that England is the Devil incarnate, sir? Pitt is our friend, and so are dozens of others in the Commons. I've read the speech in which Colonel Isaac Barré called us Sons of Liberty, and he defended us as ably as you or I could have pleaded our cause. Lord Camden's speech on taxation was a paraphrase of my resolutions before the Virginia Burgesses. I don't see how we can justly condemn all Englishmen."

Adams seasoned his drink with powdered birch bark from a clam shell, and added water to the mixture. "Even you fail to understand our true situation, Mr. Henry, and you surprise me. Privately, I welcome the support of men like William Pitt and Camden. Publicly, I condemn all England, because I must."

The barmaid appeared with a kettle of steaming tea, but Patrick waved her away. "That's where you and I part company, Mr. Adams."

"Hear me out, Mr. Henry." Sam Adams rummaged in his pockets, and finally produced a crumpled newspaper clipping. "Here we are. A cutting dated March 26, 1766, announcing the repeal of the Stamp Act. We lighted bonfires and paraded in all our towns, but we were merely using the occasion to keep public feeling at a boil. Listen to the wording of the Declaratory Act, passed by the Commons on the very same day. 'Parliament possesses the authority to bind the colonies and people of America, subjects of the Crown of Great Britain, in all cases whatsoever.'"

Patrick needed no press clippings to remember the precise wording of what had transpired in the Commons. "Don't forget Pitt wanted to add the phrase, 'With the exception of taking money out of their pockets without their consent.'"

"Pitt's addition was stricken by the Tories! There's the answer to your hopes for a peaceful accommodation, Mr. Henry."

"I find it difficult to abandon hope. The alternative is frightening."

"But it must be faced." Sam Adams lighted his pipe, and his face was hidden for a moment in a cloud of smoke.

Patrick didn't know him well enough to ask that he refrain from smoking. It was embarrassing to admit to acquaintances that tobacco gave him a headache.

"I don't believe in political miracles, and I think it inevitable that America and England must part."

"I've given the matter great thought as I've gone from town to town in Virginia, making speeches, and I'm convinced the Crown won't willingly grant us independence."

"So am I," Adams said calmly.

"Then we'll have to go to war." Patrick stared at him.

"Eventually, yes."

"We lack military strength, Mr. Adams. We'll need aid from a major European power, preferably France. It would do no harm to be assured of help from the Spaniards and Dutch, too, but I'm afraid Holland is too closely allied with England."

Adams' laugh was harsh. "You've been studying the problem with great care, Mr. Henry."

77

"The more closely I examine it, the more convinced I become that the King and the Commons must be made to compromise with us. On our terms."

"We must work for peace, but prepare for war. Let's be realists, Mr. Henry. You control the Virginia Assembly, just as the Massachusetts General Court will do what I want."

Patrick demurred. "Richie Lee and I have been elected leaders of the Whig party, and we've been fortunate enough to win a majority of the seats in the new Burgesses. But no one man can claim that he controls the Virginia Assembly."

"You're too modest. Now, then, your secret Committee of Correspondence wrote mine that you intend to keep stirring the hornet's nest."

"I wrote that particular letter myself."

"I thought I detected the ring of your rhetoric." Adams was pleased with himself. "We've been marching and holding meetings five nights out of seven in Boston, too. Your purpose and mine are the same, Mr. Henry. The King meddles in Parliament's business, and the Tories control the Commons. We hope to create sympathy for our cause in England. But I think it unlikely that patriotism is dead there, and our demonstrations may harden public opinion against us."

"I'm aware of the risk."

"Then you and I are saying the same thing, sir, but in different words."

Patrick shook his head. "No, Mr. Adams. I dread a war in which the odds will be against us, but you apparently look forward to it."

"I look forward to the day when the colonies will unite as a new nation."

"Would you be content to remain a part of the Empire if we're granted our own rights of taxation?"

Adams impatiently emptied his glass. "You dream in vain, Mr. Henry! Neither King George nor the House of Commons will grant us that right! A matter of national pride is at stake now."

"It's true," Patrick replied slowly, "that a nation's pride becomes its principle." He extended his hand across the table. "If the worst comes, Mr. Adams, you may rely on me, and on Virginia."

6

Richard Henry Lee stood at the curtained windows of the Henry parlor and looked gloomily at the children playing in the yard. "We waste our breath wishing that Pitt hadn't been taken ill. We've met our equal, perhaps our master, in Chancellor of the Exchequer Townshend."

"His techniques are effective, I must admit." John Tyler sat on a cushioned cedar bench before the hearth. "His bill forbidding the New York Assembly to meet until it appropriated funds for the billeting of British troops was brilliant—and diabolical, confound him."

"It was also legal." Patrick stood at one side of the hearth, his hands clasped behind his back. "The charter of New York grants rights to the legislature in the King's name. The New York Assembly was forced to accept royal authority, but that was a situation beyond any American's control. However, the new taxes are an even greater test of our ability and will to resist."

Tyler read from a list in his hand. "Sugar, tea, coffee, paint, glass, paper, ironware, all objects made of lead. Alcoholic spirits, pewter, buttons, silk. Townshend is even planning to tax hairbrushes!"

Lee still gazed out of the window. "He intends to try us, it's plain. If we pay import duties on these things, the list will be enlarged. He's rubbing our noses in dung until we reek of the filthy stuff."

For a few moments no one spoke. "Is there any reason to change our plan of rebuttal, gentlemen?" Patrick asked at last. After a day and night of unending talks, he and his colleagues were bone weary, and he was anxious to settle matters.

"Let me go over the details once more." Tyler began to enumerate on his fingers. "You'll make a speech in the Burgesses, P.H., denying the Crown's right to lay any taxes on us."

"My legal position will be shaky," Patrick said, "but Townshend must be challenged if we're to stand firm."

"In the meantime, the Committee of Correspondence will start

79

collecting written pledges from every planter, merchant, and storekeeper in Virginia. Each will be required to swear an oath, in the presence of witnesses, that he'll buy no goods imported from England until the Townshend Act is repealed." Tyler glanced in the direction of the tall man at the window. "Will you prepare the form for the oath, Richie?"

"If you wish, but I'll need someone to go over it for legal knotholes. I'm not an expert lawyer."

"I'll write it," Patrick said.

Lee turned toward him in protest. "You're taking on too many burdens, P.H."

"How much is too much, Richie?"

Richard Henry Lee shrugged eloquently.

"We'll meet again at Colonel Washington's house on Monday —with the full Committee—to divide the colony into districts," Tyler said. "And we'll give each member responsibility for a district. That leaves only the letters to the other colonies to be assigned."

"I intend to write them over the weekend." Patrick began to pace the parlor, slowly. "I have no doubt they're taking steps, too, to make the non-importation boycott effective. There's little doubt in my mind that Sam Adams will seal the port of Boston effectively, and John Dickinson seems to be an effective leader in Pennsylvania."

"What do you know of Livingston in New York, P.H.?" Lee wanted to know.

"I met him on my last trip there. He's efficient, I think, and he needs to be. The Tories in New York Town are bold, and may have to be frightened into compliance. Several of them are shipowners, and may be inclined to pay the new taxes on their cargoes to the port collector unless steps are taken to persuade them they'd be making a grave mistake. However, let's worry about Virginia, and let the Committees in other colonies discipline their own merchants."

His companions nodded agreement, and Tyler voiced the thoughts of all three. "Each crisis is succeeded by another that's worse. When I see squads of Sons of Liberty volunteers marching and countermarching on village greens, my heart sinks to my boots."

"So does mine," Patrick said, "because so few of them own muskets or rifles. But we can't solve all our problems in a day."

"No, not in a day and night." Lee stretched and yawned. "It's time we become acquainted with our own families again."

"You'll have some deer meat sausages and mush boiled in milk before you go, I hope." Patrick started toward the door. "And I'll tap a new keg of mead."

"We've imposed on Mrs. Henry's hospitality long enough," Tyler replied, halting him. "We don't want to wear out our welcome, because if one thing is sure in this uncertain world, we'll be back. Our problems multiply like wild raspberries on low ground."

A half-hour later Patrick saw his guests off, then went in search of Sarah. He found her in her vegetable garden at the rear of the house, and she stood, a basket of green beans on her arm.

"I'm riding over to Hanover," he told her. "We have a case on trial there, and Will Christian wants me to present the summation to the jury."

She brushed a strand of hair from her face with the back of her hand. "How can you make an address on a case you know nothing about?"

"Oh, I'll look through Will's brief on the road."

His capacity for work was limitless, and she sighed. "I don't suppose you'll be home for dinner this noon."

"I'm afraid not, my dear. I'll need to spend the afternoon discussing the handling of some new cases with the junior partners. I have only today—what's left of it—and tomorrow for my private practice. I'll have to spend the rest of the week on Committee of Correspondence business."

Sarah looked up at him, shielding her eyes from the sun. "There's something I want to discuss with you, but it will have to wait."

"Is it important?"

"It will keep until this evening."

Patrick had planned to spend the evening writing letters to the Committees of Correspondence in other colonies, but he kept his schedule to himself for fear she would think he was avoiding her.

"We seem to have so little time to spend with each other these days."

"It's been like this for almost three years, ever since you presented your resolutions in the Burgesses." If Sarah felt bitter, she concealed her feelings expertly. "I can scarcely remember those first years we were married."

"Let's go into the house and talk right now," Patrick said abruptly. "The jury in Hanover can wait a little longer."

Sarah gave the wicker basket of beans to Isobel at the kitchen door, then preceded her husband into the house and sat down in the parlor. "You're so busy I sometimes feel I should ask you in advance for an appointment."

"I wish I could promise you a lull, but I honestly don't see one ahead. I'm sorry."

"I'm afraid you'll have to squeeze in a few hours on Sundays for family business, P.H." She tried to smile, but the effort was too great. "We're going to need a bigger house, and I'd like you to come with me when I tour the neighborhood."

"A library would be convenient for my meetings, but I can make do with the parlor for a few more years. After that, maybe, we'll have come to an understanding with England and I won't need to hold so many conferences here. I'll grant you that Martha and John are growing old enough to want space for entertaining their friends, but they'll have to be patient. The ground drops away so sharply on all sides of this place that it isn't practical to think of building an addition."

"We need a new house now," Sarah said, "because I'm going to have another baby."

He sat down. "Are you sure?"

She laughed humorlessly. "I should know the signs by now, don't you think? Besides, I went to the doctor last week when you were meeting with the Whig leaders in Williamsburg, and he said there's no doubt of it. So we'll need quite a bit more space. I intend to change all of the children's present sleeping arrangements. Martha and Anne squabble so much they should have separate rooms. John simply won't go to sleep at bedtime, and the lamp he uses for reading disturbs Neddy, so it will be best to give them rooms of their own. I want a big nursery. The one

82

we have here is too cramped. And you really should have a library, P.H. Your books are all over the house, and so are your political visitors."

Patrick's mind reeled. "Buy any house that suits your taste. I can give you fifteen hundred guineas in silver, and you can add that to the price we get for this place."

An unaccustomed, stubborn expression appeared on Sarah's face. "I made the mistake of selecting this place alone. And now we'll have to move again before we've settled into it. I don't intend to stumble again. P.H., I need your help."

Patrick quickly rearranged his mental schedule, and knew he'd have to send a note to Colonel Washington saying he'd be late for the forthcoming Committee meeting. "I reckon we ought to look for a house with two or three guest rooms. And a kitchen where Isobel won't be so cramped when half the Whig party stops in for a meal."

"I—I'd like to go back to Hanover County. People here are good to us, but I miss my friends and family. You're away from home so much that I'm sometimes lonely." She hated confessing what she regarded as a weakness, and began to tug at a lace-edged handkerchief that he had brought her as a gift from Philadelphia on his last trip out of the colony.

He went to her, sat on the arm of her hickory-wood chair and the pegged joint creaked. "The cost of a fight for liberty is high," he said, awkwardly stroking her hair, "and you're paying a higher price than I am. We'll blamed well find a suitable place in Hanover County!"

"I didn't mean to complain." Sarah continued to pull at the handkerchief.

"You have every right to say what's on your mind. If it's any comfort to you, Colonel Washington says his wife is unhappy over the time he spends on Whig and Committee affairs these days. But they have no children, so it makes a difference."

Her smile was wan.

"If my conscience would let me live in peace with myself, I'd find someone else to do my work."

"I wouldn't let you do it, P.H. Just last night Mr. Lee was telling me that the people of Virginia look up to you—and depend

83

on you. I'm sure you don't like this frenzied kind of living any more than I do, but I'm proud of you. I wouldn't have you change for anything on earth." Sarah managed to sound convincing.

Patrick was relieved, which was her purpose. "Do you want the new baby?" he asked.

"Of course!" Her eyes asked him the same question.

He nodded, unable to admit that he was reluctant to see any child born into such a troubled, uncertain world.

7

"The tea we drank at breakfast this morning," said Thomas Jefferson, the Whig party's newest recruit, "was made of mullein, catnip, balm, sage, and raspberry leaves."

Patrick shuddered as he deposited his hat on a wooden wall peg in the Burgesses' cloakroom. "How do you know?"

"I made it my business to ask the barmaid in the Raleigh's Apollo room." Jefferson's grin was still boyish.

"Your curiosity will get you into trouble, lad. For the past six months, ever since the non-importation agreements became effective, I've been trying hard to delude myself. Some mornings, when I'm particularly sleepy, I'm almost convinced I'm drinking green East India tea imported from Holland. Catnip and raspberry leaves, indeed. Hereafter I shall feel like a goat wandering through a pasture."

They strolled together toward the floor of the House, but were halted by two musket-bearing soldiers of the King's Own Infantry, Third Battalion, who were normally used for ceremonial duties at the Governor's Palace.

Patrick took offense immediately. "What's the meaning of this?"

A young captain, elegant in a scarlet tunic and plumed brass helmet, appeared from the floor and raised a hand to his visor in a half-salute. "Mr. Henry?"

"Correct, and Mr. Jefferson, who'll take the oath this morning as a new member of the Assembly. Why are we being prevented from going onto the floor?"

The officer was embarrassed. "This section of the Burgesses has been prorogued, sir." He acted as though he had been directed to handle Patrick with particular care.

"On whose authority?"

"The King's, Mr. Henry."

Patrick was outraged. "I demand an explanation."

Jefferson touched his arm. "I'm sure the captain is merely following orders."

The officer, who was about Jefferson's age, was grateful. "That's right. I'm not invited to read letters from the ministers in London."

Patrick was in no mood to enjoy the pleasantry. "Have you turned away others?"

"Yes, Mr. Henry. I've been directed to let no one into the House chamber."

"I'll demand an explanation from the governor!"

"His Excellency has gone for a cruise in a Royal Navy frigate on Chesapeake Bay, sir. I believe he's planning to pay a state visit to Baltimore, so he won't return to Williamsburg for several weeks."

Patrick's feeling of impotent rage mounted, but before his anger could explode, Richard Henry Lee hurried into the cloakroom. "You've heard?" he called, not bothering with a greeting.

"Only that we're being prevented from meeting by force of arms, and that the governor has conveniently absented himself from the colony."

Lee guided him onto the portico, with Jefferson flanking him on the other side. "There's been trouble in Boston, P.H., and the legislatures of other colonies have been prorogued for three months as a precautionary measure."

"The Crown has no legal authority to close the Virginia Burgesses!" Patrick made a great effort to calm himself. "What's happened in Massachusetts Bay?"

"You'll recall that a merchantman, the *Liberty*, landed her cargo in Boston last summer, refusing to pay the port collector a farthing in import duties."

"I wrote her owner—a man named Hancock—a letter of congratulations," Patrick said impatiently.

"On orders from London, the *Liberty* has been seized by two ships of the Royal Navy," Lee said soberly.

"The legal grounds validating the impounding of a British subject's property must have been very flimsy," Jefferson declared. "I know of no precedent for such an act."

For the moment, at least, Patrick had no interest in legalities. "What's been done up there, Richie?"

"Sam Adams sent us a letter by courier. Had it come yesterday, we'd have been prepared, and might have circumvented the closing of the Burgesses."

"What action has been taken in Boston that impels the Crown to put troops at our doors?"

"The Massachusetts Bay legislature protested with great violence, apparently. They were so defiant that two regiments of troops brought down from Halifax were landed there to keep order."

Patrick's face was white beneath his tan. "It's obvious that the whole move was planned with great care. Two regiments aren't transferred from Halifax to Boston on a moment's notice."

Jefferson, although lacking experience, demonstrated an ability to remain cool in a moment of crisis. "Do you know whether martial law has been declared?"

"No, Adams' letter was written hurriedly," Lee said. "He mentioned few details."

Jefferson fingered the gold watch fob that had been his prize as valedictorian of his class at the College of William and Mary. "It's de facto martial law if not de jure. Boston is an occupied city."

Patrick wasn't listening. He walked to one side of the little portico, leaned against it and stared with unseeing eyes at the traffic passing through the busy streets of Williamsburg. "Tom," he asked suddenly, "is the college holding classes?"

"No, the students went home for their Christmas holidays last Tuesday."

"Then the House will assemble this morning in Brafferton Hall. We'll be a little crowded, but no one will mind standing."

Jefferson was concerned. "We'll be compromising the college authorities."

"I have no intention of causing difficulties for them. We'll appropriate the building for an hour or two without asking their permission." Patrick's voice began to soar, as it did when he was delivering an address. "Bullets and bayonets may seal the Burgesses' chamber, but neither the King nor his armies can prevent free men from expressing their freely held views. We'll meet for a single session, just long enough to vote an expression of sympathy with the Massachusetts legislature—and to make certain that copies are sent to King George, the Ministry for Colonies, and the House of Commons. We'll maintain our rights, even if they send troops to occupy every city, town, and village in America!"

8

"Scotchtown," in Hanover County, was by far the largest and most handsome home in which the Henry family had ever lived. Patrick had emptied his strongbox to purchase and furnish the place, but neither he nor Sarah regretted the expense. They owned one thousand acres, and Peter, who had been freed from bondage, adopted his former master's name and managed the plantation. Within a few years, he estimated, tobacco growing and cattle raising would make the farm self-sufficient, and by 1775 Patrick would be independently wealthy.

The house itself was made of clapboard, painted white, with a shingled roof, a portico supported by Doric columns and eight fireplaces. The largest of them, in the drawing room, was twelve feet long. Bookshelves lined every wall of the library from floor to ceiling, and the house boasted nine bedchambers, more than enough for the family's needs and the demands of Patrick's expanding political career. Sarah was satisfied, and confided to Nate and Dorothea Dandridge that for the first time since her marriage she didn't feel crowded.

Her sewing room soon became the family gathering place, however. Martha and her friend, Dorothea, paraded experimentally there in their first adult clothes. John insisted that he found the rug before the hearth the most comfortable place in the house to study Latin and mathematics, the younger children scattered their toys about the chamber and the crib of the new baby, a boy, was carried to a corner niche daily from the nursery.

Patrick liked to relax there, too, on the rare occasions when he was able to spend an evening at home. The Assembly adjourned for the summer of 1769 in June, and for the next month the Whig leaders traveled in pairs from one end of the colony to the other, making speeches, attending rallies and encouraging the people of every community to maintain their boycott of all English-made goods. In August and September the thriving practice of Henry and Christian, counselors-at-law, kept Patrick at his Hanover office until long after dark, and when he returned home he usually closeted himself in the library until midnight or later, often eating a light, solitary supper there while he worked. Clients had such great faith in him that they insisted he appear personally to represent them in court, and he often rode sixty or seventy miles in a day to distant county seats in order to oblige them.

In October, however, he began to enjoy a period of relative quiet. The Assembly was not scheduled to meet again until late in the year, and the non-importation agreements were so effective that the House of Commons gave up its efforts to put new teeth into the Townshend Act. Port collectors in the colonies abandoned their attempts to tax goods manufactured in England. Only the tax on tea was retained as a symbol of the Crown's right to levy duties where it saw fit.

Three new junior partners were taken into the busy law firm in Hanover, and Will Christian hired four new clerks to prepare briefs. Patrick's work load was relieved, and although he still had to make court appearances in towns as widely separated as Fredericksburg, Hopewell, and Charlottesville, his evenings were free.

One night in mid-November he reached home a short time after the family had finished supper and, tired after a grueling day in court and a long ride, contented himself with a light meal of oxtail soup and iron-hard water biscuits. Sarah sat with him, and then they walked together to her sewing room, Patrick still munching a biscuit.

"I can't imagine why sailors don't like these," he said, scattering crumbs on the new hall rug.

"They'd break my teeth," Sarah replied, and laughed.

"I suppose I'm pleased because I still have my own teeth. That's more than I can say for my hair." He ran his free hand over the light fuzz on the crown of his head.

88

The usual bedlam prevailed in the sewing room. John was reading aloud to himself in Latin, translating sentence by sentence, Martha and Dorothea were practicing walking in front of the windows in their first high-heeled slippers, and the smaller children were playing a military game of some sort with an ivory chess set. Only the baby was quiet.

Patrick brushed several toys from his favorite chair, scooped up Anne and deposited her on his lap as he sat down.

Sarah glanced at the porcelain clock on the mantel, and announced that it was time for bed. Martha and her friend were not included in the edict, nor was John, but Anne and Neddy protested bitterly. Patrick made it a rule not to interfere with his wife's management of the household, but he looked at her in mute appeal.

She relented, knowing his opportunities to spend time with the children were limited, and everyone relaxed. Patrick immediately took charge. "Speak up, John. I can't hear what you're reading."

His son obediently raised his voice. *"De duobus malis, minus est semper eligendum."*

"And the translation?"

"Of two evils, always choose the lesser."

"Good boy. And a motto worth remembering. Who wrote it?"

John made a wry face. "Thomas a Kempis, a papist," he said scornfully.

His father glared at him. "I'll tolerate no such talk here!"

Martha and Dorothea giggled.

"Hold your heads higher and stop peering down at your toes when you walk, girls, and you won't look so awkward." Patrick turned back to his son. "What's your complaint against papists, lad?"

"Well, I—I don't know, exactly."

"Then why do you speak of them disparagingly?"

"Because—everybody else does." John knew he was in trouble, but there was no escape.

"By everybody, you mean the young bigots—sons and grandsons of bigots—who go to school with you, no doubt. Has it ever occurred to you that you and they worship the same God?"

"No, Papa, I hadn't thought about it."

"Then think! Now! Have you ever known any papists?"

Sarah wished he would treat the boy more gently, but concentrated on the scarf she was knitting.

John was near tears. "I—I don't—think so, Papa."

"Well, you do. Mr. Carroll, of the Maryland Committee of Correspondence, who visited us this summer—and brought you that hunting knife you like so much—is of the Roman faith." Patrick's manner became softer. "They have no horns on their heads. They came by the thousands to Maryland because they sought the right to worship as they believed right. Their motives were the same as those of the Dissenters who founded Massachusetts Bay. I suppose you've heard that the Baptists are a miserable lot, too."

John was cautious now. "I haven't really heard much about them."

Patrick turned suddenly to the two teen-aged girls. "But you have. I can see it in your faces. You don't hold very high opinions of them, eh?"

Martha and Dorothea looked uncertainly at each other.

"Perhaps you'd like to hear where I've been today. I rode up to Fredericksburg to defend three Baptists who were thrown into prison there. The poor wretches were guilty of no offense except that of preaching the Gospel as they interpret it. The prosecutor actually based his whole case on the grounds that they ram a text of Scripture down a man's throat when they meet him. Those were the prosecutor's words."

Dorothea Dandridge was more courageous than Martha. "What happened in the trial, Mr. Henry?"

"The charges against them were dismissed, of course! And I refused to accept a fee for my services." Patrick glanced in his wife's direction for an instant.

Sarah smiled and nodded, obviously pleased.

"I'm spending my time and effort fighting for liberty so that all of you children will live in a free colony," Patrick declared solemnly, his voice becoming resonant. "The Crown isn't the only culprit who would steal our liberties from us. Freedom is indivisible!"

Anne and Neddy were too young to understand him, and the older children looked puzzled.

"That means it can't be divided. If you take away part of a man's freedom, you rob him of all freedom. And in this land all men must be free. That includes the right to worship as they wish, and to be respected for it! Americans must dedicate themselves to the cause of religious liberty, or we'll perish." Patrick jabbed a finger at Martha, then at John. "One of your ancestors fled to this country from France because he'd have been thrown into prison for his beliefs. Just as the three Baptists were locked behind the Fredericksburg jail."

Martha's eyes were proud. "But you saved them, Papa."

"I helped. And all of you must do your part. You don't need to wait until you're grown men and women. When you hear bigotry, challenge it! If you lose a friend, it's been a worthless friendship."

Patrick was still warming to his theme, but a servant appeared in the entrance, interrupting him. "Mr. Henry, sir, there's a visitor here to see you."

Benjamin Harrison's bulky figure filled the frame. "Mrs. Henry, your pardon for this intrusion. You'll have to forgive my informality, P.H., but it's urgent that I see you."

"It's good to see you, Ben. We'll go into the library, where it will be a little more quiet." Patrick deposited Anne on his chair. "You'll let me fix you a rum and canary toddy?"

"And I insist you have some supper," Sarah added calmly, unperturbed by the sudden appearance of the visitor.

"Later, ma'am, if you don't mind," Harrison replied, bowing. "I'd like to talk first, and I think you may be interested in what I have to say."

Sarah so rarely was present at her husband's political discussions that she was as surprised as Patrick. Recovering quickly, she gathered her skirts and, absently telling the children to go off to bed, preceded the men into the library.

Patrick poured rum, wine, and spices into a tankard, then plunged a glowing metal poker from the hearth into the brew.

Harrison sipped appreciatively. "This is good. I've ridden here from Richmond without a stop on the road."

Patrick braced himself for bad news, and looked apprehensively at Sarah.

"I don't want to alarm you, Mrs. Henry, but you have a right to hear of your husband's situation," Harrison said.

Sarah's hand crept to her throat.

The visitor stood before the hearth, feet planted wide apart. "I own a part interest in a brigantine that was due to arrive from London yesterday. Well, she was a day late, and her captain came straight to Will Byrd's house as soon as he cast anchor. We sat down to supper right off, and asked him the latest from London." Harrison drew a copy of the London *Post* from the inner pocket of his cloak, and unfolded the newspaper. "I never did eat my supper," he added with a wry smile.

Patrick took the newspaper from him.

"Look at the columns on the second page relating the news of Parliament."

Patrick scanned the paper in silence, nodded and spoke gently to Sarah. "This is dated three and a half weeks ago. A bill was being prepared for submission to the Commons, naming six colonial leaders as traitors to the Crown."

"You're one of them, dear?" Her voice was high-pitched, but did not falter.

"I have the honor," Patrick replied dryly. "And I'm in good company, with Otis, Adams, and Hancock of Massachusetts—"

"What will they do to you?"

"According to this rather bloodthirsty account, we'll be sent in irons to England and tried by the House of Lords, acting in its capacity as a Star Chamber."

"The Tories rammed the bill through the Commons that very day, P.H.," Harrison said. "The captain delayed his sailing until he received word."

Patrick astonished both his wife and his friend by laughing heartily. "This is magnificent! They united us with unjust revenue taxes, and now they'd cement the bonds by creating some genuine colonial martyrs." He sobered and stroked Sarah's shoulder. "Never fear, my dear. This is a little political game the Tories are playing."

She looked at him, fearful and confused.

"They couldn't collect taxes from us, and of course they don't want to admit failure. So they've tried to make a case against some of us over here—on the flimsiest of charges—in order to keep their hold on the English electorate."

Harrison frowned over the rim of his tankard. "What makes you say the charges are flimsy, P.H.?"

"I'm innocent of treason, and so are the others. That stupid ninny who has been gaining favor lately with King George, Lord North, is behind this, I'm sure. He's no lawyer, or he'd know better. The case would collapse in court. If the Crown actually put us on trial."

Sarah drew a deep breath. "If?"

"Of course. We'd have to be tried here first. Not even the Crown dares to upset basic common law. That means I'd be tried by the high court of the colony, the General Court in Williamsburg."

Harrison relaxed and grinned. "I see."

"I'm afraid I don't," Sarah said.

"Three of the five justices are Whigs," Patrick told her, "and even the two Tories wouldn't agree to anything as outrageous as exporting a citizen of Virginia for trial in England. This is another of the government's blunders, and you can take my word for it, nothing more will come of the matter."

His wife sighed, relaxed for a moment and then remembered her duties as a hostess. "I must get you something to eat, Mr. Harrison. And I insist you spend the night with us."

"You're very kind, ma'am." Harrison said no more until she closed the library door behind her. "Is it really going to be that simple, P.H.?"

"I think so," Patrick said.

"The whole colony would revolt if you were hauled off in chains. Just thinking about it makes my blood boil."

"Exactly, Ben, and there are men in London wise enough to know that Americans would be unable to refuse such a challenge. The Tories don't want to deal with a revolution over here, you know, any more than we want it."

"I hope you're right."

"So do I. When I was a boy I wanted to go west across the mountains, but the prospect doesn't appeal to me now that I'm a middle-aged man of thirty-three. I'll be on the safe side in all this, of course. The General Court in Williamsburg would have to issue a warrant for my arrest before the Crown could lay hands on me, so I'll ask our friends there to keep us informed. If need be, I could disappear for a time."

"I believe," Harrison said thoughtfully, "that we'll give you an escort of French and Indian War veterans hereafter."

"That would be a nuisance."

"I'm sure it's what the Committee will want to do."

"Whatever happens, I'm grateful, and I'm sure the New Englanders will be, too, when I write them the news."

Harrison was startled.

"This development is a guarantee of my political integrity and reputation, Ben. We've always thought of ourselves as Englishmen, but I'm beginning to wonder if we've been wrong. The separation of the Atlantic does something to men's minds, and we don't think alike. If the King paid a visit to his loyal colonies, I can't help wondering whether we'd put him on trial."

9

Meetings of the Burgesses had been lively for so many years that the younger members could scarcely remember a time when sessions had been boring and dull. But the Assembly had dealt only with routine matters since reconvening early in December, and even the appropriations bills, which usually sparked a tug-of-war between the conservative tidewater counties and the more radical hinterlands, were handled with dispatch. Patrick Henry and Richard Henry Lee were in firm command of the legislature, and their Whigs, with a majority of more than two to one over the Tories, were proud of their ability to handle the public business efficiently.

Patrick had discouraged his colleagues from taking any notice of the Act of Parliament branding him as a traitor. No attempt had as yet been made by the Crown to bring him to trial, and he didn't want to be the cause of making bad feelings worse. Most of the Whigs disagreed with his strategy, but as it was his personal

94

future at stake, they reluctantly agreed not to make an issue of the matter.

A few days before the Burgesses were scheduled to adjourn for Christmas the atmosphere became tense again. A Royal Navy sloop-of-war dropped anchor at Newport News, and a courier, escorted by a detachment of heavily armed Marines, rode to Williamsburg with a sealed bag of striped red and white canvas, the colors of the Colonial Ministry. Patrick's bodyguard of war veterans was doubled, but he rejected suggestions that he make a "journey of inspection" into the Kentucky District beyond the mountains.

The next day elderly John Randolph, who had threatened to migrate to London if relations between England and the colony failed to improve, was invited to the Governor's Palace for dinner. Apparently he was being told at least some of the secrets contained in the bag from the Colonial Ministry, and his fellow Tories were jealous of the treatment he was being accorded. The Whigs were curious, too, but tried to pretend they didn't care what he learned.

In late afternoon, about an hour after the Assembly had reconvened, Randolph reappeared in the chamber, looking smug and well fed. There was a rustle in the hall as he made his way to his seat in the front row on the right side of the hall, leaning heavily on his walking stick, and his smile indicated his appreciation of the stir he was creating.

He sat for a few minutes, listening to the desultory debate on road improvements in Nelson and Albemarle Counties, which were so remote from civilization that tidewater men considered any roads there a luxury. Then he rose to his feet, asking for the floor and requesting permission to interrupt the discussion of the measure under consideration for the purpose of making a special announcement.

The Speaker promptly granted the privilege, and Randolph walked slowly to the well of the chamber as a hush settled over the Assembly. Benjamin Harrison, sitting near a window, signaled three times, alerting Patrick's bodyguards on the lawn outside, and everyone braced for a revelation that might mean trouble.

"Gentlemen, I have long pleaded for greater friendship between the mother country and this colony. It has long been my unalterable belief that there exists in London a special love for Virginia, a love as stanch as that of a mother for a wayward daughter."

Lee, sitting directly before him on the left side, began to tap on the top of his desk with a quill pen. But Patrick, in the next seat, looked far more at ease than he felt, and smiled blandly.

"I have reason to believe that love remains undiminished," the old Tory cried eloquently. "And while I am not privileged to reveal my sources of information, I assure you they have not misled me." He looked surprised when everyone in the chamber laughed; his own wit was so feeble that the humor of his remark did not occur to him.

"Nearly two months ago," he continued, "the Commons passed a law for the purpose of warning the sons of Britain in the New World that they could try the patience of His Majesty's Government too severely. To the surprise of the wise and humane men who comprise that Government, many colonials have chosen to interpret that Act literally. Nothing was farther from the intention of those who drew the bill and those who passed it.

"It is their purpose to raise a stern and admonishing finger to the impertinent. If they are prudent, they will heed this sign of displeasure, and act discreetly hereafter." He bowed to the Speaker and hobbled back to his seat.

Whigs immediately surrounded Patrick to congratulate him, and Speaker Robinson pounded his gavel in vain for order. Randolph's words had been deliberately vague, but his meaning was clear. The Commons had reconsidered its rash decision to prosecute the colonial Whig leaders for treason, realizing that such trials would stiffen rather than dispel resistance.

But the Act could not be rescinded without a loss of dignity, so it was being allowed to stand, although no attempt would be made to enforce it. Even the announcement, made through a colonial sympathetic to England, was not a formal withdrawal, so Parliament, in its own eyes, at least, had not lost stature.

Patrick shook the hands his friends held out to him, but could not rejoice with them. His own forecast of what would happen had been right, but gave him small comfort. "I'm still a traitor in the eyes of the Crown," he murmured to Lee after the others had gone back to their seats. "It's a shrewd move, you know. They're suspending a sword over my head, hoping to frighten me into silence. Sam Adams and I have become England's hostages."

Lee was unhappy, too. "In the future," he said, "you'll have to let others—who are less vulnerable—speak out against injustices."

"Never! No threat can destroy my hatred for tyranny and my love of liberty."

FOUR

1773–1774

1

There were six children in the Henry family at Scotchtown,
Patrick's private law practice flourished, and even his political
opponents recognized him as the most able and successful trial
lawyer in Virginia. The offices in Hanover now occupied John
Shelton's entire building, and Patrick's father-in-law closed his
Royal Arms Tavern and lived on the rents paid to him by the firm
of Henry and Christian.

Men argued about the reasons for Patrick's ability to influence
magistrates and sway juries. "He's like a play-actor on a stage,"
Edmund Pendleton said. "He fascinates them."

"He doesn't fascinate me," George Wythe replied bluntly.

Thomas Jefferson, himself a lawyer of great talent and now one
of Patrick's first assistants in the Burgesses, disagreed with the views
of the prejudiced Tories. "Some men," he said, "don't realize that
P.H. knows the law so well he qualifies for the post of Chief
Justice of the General Court. He uses so many tricks of rhetoric
when he speaks—and his oratory comes as natural to him as does
breathing—that they forget he's read every law book published in
the English language, and remembers every word he has read."

Relations between England and her North American colonies
were much improved, and many leading citizens of the major

99

colonies believed that Lord North, the Crown's new First Minister, wanted to live in peace with them. Attempts to enforce the tax laws were half-hearted, the non-importation agreements were ignored and trading was resumed on a large scale. Troops were still quartered in Boston, where an unfortunate incident was blown up out of all proportion to reality by Sam Adams, who called it a "massacre." But Boston merchants continued to prosper, and no one made more money than John Hancock, who quietly gloried in his smuggling operations. A half-regiment of troops was stationed for a time in New York Town, but the citizens there were so peaceful that the soldiers were withdrawn. Philadelphia was left to its own devices, and so were Baltimore and Williamsburg, where only one company of Royal Infantry upheld the honor of the Crown by participating in official ceremonies and acting as escorts for the unmarried young ladies of the Virginia capital.

Patrick felt that the aura of serenity was deceptive, however, and maintained a heavy correspondence with the Whig leaders of other colonies. Eventually, he said, a man as shortsighted as King George would make another attempt to force his will on the colonies.

He was proved right in 1773, when Parliament unexpectedly placed a new tax on tea imported by the Americans. Flagging American interest in resistance to the Crown was revived, and in Virginia an emergency meeting of Whig leaders was held at Scotchtown.

"I've had several letters from London," Jefferson said, "and they all say that the purpose of the Commons isn't one of rubbing our fur the wrong way. The East India Company has a monopoly on tea—"

"—and the English market is saturated with the stuff," Lee declared, interrupting. "They want to reopen the American market, and they couldn't have chosen a worse way to go about it."

George Mason was leafing through letters from the Committees of Correspondence in other colonies. "I agree with Massachusetts Bay," he said. "When the British try to land the damned tea, we ought to throw it into the sea."

Patrick had been letting the others talk, and entered the conversation for the first time. "No, I disagree. If the King and North were trying to test our will to resist, I believe we'd be right to smash the boxes of tea sent here. Under the circumstances, I think violence on our part will merely breed counterviolence in England."

Lee stared at him. "You carry the spirit of Christian charity and meekness to far, P.H."

"Hear me out." Patrick beckoned as Martha and Dorothea Dandridge, both looking completely adult, appeared at the door with trays of cold ox-tongue and mutton cutlets. "Leave the food on the table, girls, and thank you. We'll help ourselves when we're hungry." He waited until they withdrew and closed the door. "I'm not for a minute suggesting we accept the tea, Richie."

"I should hope not. The tax of twelvepence per pound is prohibitive and outrageous."

Jefferson smiled. "It's clever. The East India Company pays for the entire cost of transporting tea across the Atlantic out of its share of the tax. Everything else it makes is solid profit."

"We're agreed," Patrick said, "that the tea must not be landed on American soil. Right?"

The others nodded.

"There's more than one way to skin a skunk, provided you don't let your knife slip." Patrick rose from his desk. "I represented the East India Company in a case before the General Court a few months ago, so I know something of their operations. Their representatives in the colonies will pay the tax, presumably, and then pass along the fee to the wholesale buyers here. Eventually, the consumer will be paying the tax—indirectly."

"Anyone who buys tea—or even drinks it—ought to be treated by his whole community like a pox victim," Mason said angrily. "Decent people should stop speaking to him, and doors should be closed in his face."

Patrick held up a hand. "Calm yourself, George. As Colonel Washington says, you can't fight a battle until the enemy sends his troops into the field to meet yours. If there's no tea on sale, anywhere, folks won't be able to buy it."

"The only way to make certain that some greedy merchant

doesn't take part of the cargo," Mason retorted, "is to break up the cases, the way they plan to do in Boston."

"I disapprove of violence as a matter of principle," Jefferson said, helping himself to some mutton. "But Sam Adams may have the only sensible solution."

"Why don't we listen to whatever P.H. has to say before we leap to conclusions?" Lee spoke quietly.

Patrick thanked him with a smile. "The East India Company," he said, "keeps two agents at Norfolk and one at Newport News. All three of them are honorable, law-abiding Englishmen. I've made it my business to find out that they sympathize with us. They're even willing to admit, in private conversation, that the Crown has been wrong in the past ten years."

Lee chuckled. "Might it be that they've been listening to some lectures from someone who strongly favors the colonial position?"

Out of force of habit, Patrick passed a hand over the top of his head, now almost completely bald. "Let's say they were open to persuasion. They're ambitious young fellows—two of them are married and have children—and I believe they'd welcome the chance to make new careers for themselves. The East India Company doesn't pay very high wages, you know." He paused to let the others absorb the significance of his strategy. "I think I've already found a place for one of them up in Fredericksburg."

Lee became enthusiastic. "My cousin needs someone who'll supervise the operations of his plantations. And I know he'll be willing to give the right man several hundred acres of his own."

"That will leave only one more opening to develop, which shouldn't be too difficult. Keep in mind that those cargoes of tea are on the high seas right now. If there are no East India Company agents on hand to receive the goods and pay the taxes, the ships' masters can't leave cases of tea on the docks and sail off, can they?"

Jefferson looked at him admiringly. "You should have kept your store, P.H. You have a real knack for dealing with merchandise."

Patrick laughed. "Only when it doesn't belong to me."

Mason placed a bowl of oysters in the shell on the table beside him and took a sharp poniard from his boot-top. "The beauty of this scheme is that Parliament won't be able to blame us for refusing to pay the tax. They can't hold us responsible if employees of the East India Company improve their lot!"

"For more than one hundred and fifty years," Patrick said, "the poor of the Old World have been drawn to the New. The magnets have been prosperity and freedom. Those are our real weapons, and no laws that Parliament passes will lessen their appeal. That's why, if we keep our heads, we can't lose this struggle."

2

Pennsylvania, New York, and South Carolina quickly adopted the Virginia scheme for dealing with the East India Company's ships, and everywhere the results were the same. The bewildered masters found no one to accept their cargo, and the vessels returned to England from Philadelphia and New York Town, as well as Norfolk and Newport News, without landing their wares. A slightly different situation developed in Charleston, although the results were substantially the same. Crown officials ordered the tea landed and stored in warehouses, but no one came forward to pay the duty, and the cargo slowly rotted.

Only in Boston was there violence. Supporters of Sam Adams and John Hancock dressed as Indians and destroyed vast quantities of tea. That raid prompted Lord North and Parliament to retaliate so swiftly and with such vengeance that Patrick, in a letter to Colonel Washington, declared, "I harbor the terrible suspicion that the First Minister and the Commons were seeking an excuse to destroy the liberties more precious to us than life itself."

The Royal Navy sealed the harbor of Boston, and all trade with the city was cut off until her citizens paid the East India Company for the tea that had been destroyed. Boston refused.

The most alarming of all the new acts passed early in 1774 by the Commons arbitrarily withdrew the charter of Massachusetts Bay, converted it into a royal province and decreed that henceforth public officials in the colony would be appointed by the Crown rather than elected by the people.

Americans were shocked. "Parliament has made its worst blunder," Jefferson said.

"Our Magna Charta has been destroyed," Patrick told the Burgesses. "No man will fight for a dish of tea, but we will make any sacrifice to protect the rights we hold dear."

Lord North added insult to injury, and the Commons passed still more acts that aroused the men of every colony. A new billeting bill compelled the Americans to make their homes available, at least in theory, for the housing of troops. Royal officials accused of committing crimes in the New World were granted the privilege of returning to England for trial. And, as a final blow, the entire territory between the Appalachian Mountains and the Mississippi River was summarily transferred to the Province of Quebec, nullifying the claims of Virginia, Connecticut, and Massachusetts to lands those colonies regarded as their own.

"We can't submit to this injustice," Patrick told Sarah as he prepared to leave for a special session of the Burgesses in Williamsburg. "Spend the money in my stronghox with care. I'm accepting no more private cases, and I don't know when I'll return to my practice. I must see this situation through to the end, no matter what may happen."

Sarah withheld her tears until he rode away.

3

The stage had been set with great care. Whig leaders debated endless schemes, but finally, at the urging of Lee, Colonel Washington, and Patrick, they agreed that a resolution condemning the royal usurpation of the Kentucky District would be futile. It would be far more fitting, the trio argued, to make a simple gesture that every man on both sides of the Atlantic would understand. The nature of that gesture was worked out with great care.

A subcommittee composed of Jefferson and Mason was appointed to approach the leaders of the Tory minority and seek its cooperation. Edmund Pendleton and George Wythe proved to be as indignant as the Whigs over London's attitude, and only a few diehards insisted that the Crown was acting within its rights. Care was taken to prevent those loyal to the King to learn of the legislative leaders' plan, but old John Randolph got wind of it, and left

Williamsburg for his home, swearing that Virginians were traitors and that he would leave the colony permanently unless his fellow citizens came to their senses.

The Assembly convened on May 5, 1774, and as its first order of business elected Benjamin Harrison as the new Speaker. Lee and Patrick were in control of the legislature, but had to spend several weeks dealing with problems created by the governor, Lord Dunmore.

The colony was engaged in a senseless border dispute with Pennsylvania, created by Dunmore, and the Indian tribes living in the western part of the colony sent representatives to Williamsburg, claiming that the governor was breaking Virginia's long-standing treaty agreements with them. Patrick suspected that Dunmore was deliberately trying to create diversions, and dealt swiftly with both problems. He himself headed a committee that reached a new agreement with the Indians, and Lee was chairman of another that drafted a long, friendly letter to Pennsylvania, promising that an amicable understanding could be reached.

By late May, everything was ready for the enactment of a dramatic scene, and tension was heightened by the surface cordiality of the relations between the governor and the Burgesses.

On the last night of the month a reception was given by the Burgesses in their chamber, honoring Lady Dunmore and her daughters. A spiced punch of Madeira and sack was served, long tables were laden with such delicacies as quail stuffed with peppered sausage, ham baked in mead, and gooseberry tarts made of liver dumpling dough. The delegates made a point of treating the ladies of the governor's family with great respect, and the atmosphere was spirited, if somewhat artificially gay.

Dunmore, a florid-faced man who favored suits of cream-colored satin and towering, powdered wigs, played the game blandly. He exchanged amenities with Lee and Colonel Washington, then sought Patrick and Harrison for a seemingly innocuous chat.

"I sometimes wonder," he said, "whether you gentlemen find the climate of Williamsburg oppressive."

"No, milord," Patrick replied in his blandest voice, "Virginia is our home, so we've been accustomed to the climate here from birth. I believe that only you who come here from England for a stay of a few years suffer."

The governor's dark eyes were cold, but he smiled broadly. "You may be right, Mr. Henry. I do feel it's warmer than usual this spring."

Harrison coughed behind his hand and reddened.

"I believe it's going to become far warmer, milord," Patrick said cheerfully.

"I wouldn't doubt it, Mr. Henry. I trust you aren't particularly susceptible to heat?"

"I enjoy it." Patrick made a courageous stab. "And you, milord?"

"I'm as impervious to heat as I am to cold, Mr. Henry." Dunmore nodded pleasantly and wandered off to speak to someone else.

"He knows," Harrison muttered.

"Maybe so. Or else he guesses."

"The law branding you as a traitor has never been rescinded, P.H. Perhaps you'd better let someone else take over your part tomorrow."

"No, not if I hang for it."

"You may."

"If I do, the rest of you can join me on the gallows. No man can afford to hide in shadows any more, Ben. The Crown is demanding that we stand free and clear, so the whole world will know us."

4

The House convened at the unusually early hour of nine o'clock on the morning of June 1, and the Reverend Angus Moran, the chaplain, opened the session with a prayer, which consisted of selections from the fifth chapter of the Book of Nehemiah.

"Ought ye not to walk in the fear of our God because of the reproach of the heathen our enemies?" he intoned. "I, likewise, and my brethren, and my servants, might exact of them money and corn: I pray you, leave off this usury.

"Restore, I pray you, to them, even this day, their lands, their vineyards, their oliveyards, and their houses, also the hundredth part of the money, and of the corn, the wine, and the oil, that ye exact of them.

"Then said they, We will restore them, and will require nothing of them; so will we do as thou sayest.

"And the people did according to this promise.

"Think upon me, my God, for good, according to all that I have done for this people. Amen."

The invocation was unusual, but made complete sense to the members. Sir Thomas Philby, Lord Dunmore's secretary, who was sitting in the visitors' gallery, seemed to understand it, too.

"Mr. Speaker," Patrick called as soon as everyone sat down, "I request recognition for the purpose of making a motion."

Harrison struck his table with the Speaker's silver-handled gavel. "The chair recognizes the right honorable member from Hanover for the purpose of making a motion."

Patrick stood, and slowly inspected the assemblage. "Mr. Speaker," he said, "this is the first day of June, a day of infamy. It is this day that the town of Boston is cast into purdah. It is this day that the Boston Port Bill becomes effective.

"Great ships of war stand in her harbor, their gleaming guns refusing entry to merchant ships. Armed troops stand guard at the roads and quiet country lanes that lead into her thoroughfares, refusing entry to the good farmers and merchants from other colonies who would take their wares to sell in that proud city.

"It is the intent of the House of Commons to humble Boston's pride. It is not our place to call the Commons wrong, nor should we tell her right honorable members that they err. Time will prove to them that they have misjudged the temper of the good people of Boston, and of all these colonies.

"The blow that strikes Boston strikes you and me, here, with as stunning a blow as it strikes Massachusetts Bay.

"I call upon Virginia to stand beside Massachusetts Bay, so that degradation may be turned into triumph, so the whole world will know we Americans share our sorrows as well as our joys. Mr. Speaker, I submit the following resolution for the consideration and approbation of this House. 'Resolved, That the first day of June be set aside by the people of the colony of Virginia as a day of fasting and prayer, that we fast as a sign of humility in sharing the cruel and unjust punishment being inflicted upon the town of

Boston, that we pray to the Almighty for the relief of her burdens."

Everyone present knew that the audacious motion was a direct challenge to the Crown, and there was an unnatural silence as Patrick sat down.

Richard Henry Lee rose to his feet without undue haste. "Mr. Speaker!"

"The chair recognizes the right honorable member from Westmoreland."

"Mr. Speaker, I second the resolution. I further ask all members of the Burgesses to take their stand without equivocation, and make the expression of our sentiments unanimous. This, Mr. Speaker," Lee thundered, "is an occasion when all who love freedom must be willing to stand erect and be counted!"

"It has been moved and seconded that the first day of June be set aside as a day of fasting and prayer, as a gesture of sympathy and unity with our fellow citizens of Boston." Harrison cracked his gavel on the table. "All in favor will so indicate by rising."

Every member of the Burgesses stood.

"The resolution is adopted by unanimous vote."

As the legislators sat down again, Sir Thomas Philby quickly made his way from the visitors' gallery to the floor. A lean cavalryman who walked with a slight limp, his bearing was military, and the star of the Order of the Bath, England's highest order of knighthood for her heroes who had distinguished themselves in war, gleamed on the left breast of his black silk suit. His expression reflected his distaste for the task he was being called upon to perform, since Colonel Washington and other veterans of Braddock's army were his former comrades in arms.

The situation required Harrison to simulate surprise. "The privileges of appearing on the floor of the Burgesses are reserved to members of the Burgesses," he said. "What will you here, Sir Thomas?"

The knight's reply was equally formal and stilted. "I bear tidings to the Burgesses from John Murray, Earl of Dunmore," he called, still moving down the center aisle.

Speaker Harrison politely stood aside to make room for him on the dais.

Sir Thomas took a folded sheet of parchment from his pocket,

GIVE ME LIBERTY: 1773–1774

and when he shook it open, the members could see an official seal in red wax, the royal color, in the lower right-hand corner. "Under the authority vested in my person as deputy of His Majesty, George, King of Great Britain, Ireland and the Dominions-over-the-Seas, and viceroy for the colony of Virginia, acting in His Majesty's name, I do hereby declare that the act perpetrated this day by the Assembly of the said colony is lacking in respect for our liege lord and master. Therefore, in accordance with the powers deputized to me, I do hereby declare this Assembly dissolved. Dunmore."

Sir Thomas and Harrison exchanged bows, and the governor's secretary made his way from the chamber. No one was surprised by Lord Dunmore's action, but the swiftness of his retaliation was startling. Nevertheless, the Speaker remained urbane. "The House," he said dryly, "appears to have been adjourned. Since this adjournment is involuntary and lacks the consent of the House, we will dispense with the usual formalities, so that our own attitude in this matter will appear on our records."

He descended from the dais and began to walk slowly up the center aisle. Patrick and Lee, the Whig majority leaders, fell in behind him, and as a show of solidarity waited for Edmund Pendleton and Peyton Randolph, the heads of the Tory party. They linked arms and walked four abreast, scarcely able to squeeze into the space between the desks on both sides of the aisle. The other members followed, and their silence was eloquent.

As they emerged onto the portico and the shrub-lined gravel path beyond it, a waiting observer saw them from the belfry of the nearby Anglican church. The bell began to toll, slowly and mournfully, and other church bells started to peal, too. Virginia was mourning more than the punishment inflicted by Parliament on Boston now; her own liberties had been curtailed.

5

The Apollo room of the Raleigh Tavern was so crowded that members of the Burgesses who had been eating their breakfast there finished their meals quickly in order to make room for colleagues to sit beside them. Word had been sent to every member of the dissolved House that an informal meeting would be held promptly at eight o'clock, and when Benjamin Harrison rapped for order, using an empty porter tankard as a gavel, men were standing three deep along the walls.

"It would be inconvenient, gentlemen, to spend the coming months in prison for disobeying a royal command," he said. "So I distinctly want it understood that this is a gathering of friends, not a rump meeting of the House." He paused, waiting for a roar of laughter to rise to a peak and subside. "Not that we're afraid of jail, but there's too much to be done in the weeks ahead. Some of our neighbors want to tell you their ideas."

Patrick, who was squeezed into a corner, pushed back his chair. "If any man fears for his personal safety," he declared, "let him leave now. Some of us spent the evening together, thinking about our future as Virginians and as Americans. We intend to strike out through an uncharted wilderness, and we don't know what evils may be lurking on the trail we hope to cut. Your vote yesterday was a confirmation of your love for Virginia, but individual circumstances may make it prudent for some of you to take yourselves elsewhere. For example, those who have large families may want to think first of the security of their children."

Everyone present knew he had six children, and another wave of laughter swept through the Apollo room. No one left.

Patrick sat, and Richard Henry Lee stood. "Through extraordinary coincidence," he said informally, "some friends who happened to dine together last night, after our day of fasting, included the leaders and assistant leaders of both the distinguished Tory party and my own Whig party. Naturally, we talked about the dissolution of the House, the unhappy day in Boston and other matters near and dear to us all.

"It was clear to us, as it must be to you, that our freedoms will be destroyed if they are further curtailed. We stand in jeopardy, and so does every other colony."

Patrick looked at some notes he had taken from his pocket, and made minor corrections on them with a scratchy goose quill. Then he passed the paper to Edmund Pendleton, who put on gold-framed spectacles to read what he had written. The Tory leader looked displeased, but his austerity made no impression on Patrick as they argued in whispers while Lee continued to speak.

"The events of the past twenty-four hours have proved, if further proof were needed, that Massachusetts Bay's problems are Virginia's. New York and South Carolina will share our sense of futility and outrage when the couriers carrying word of yesterday's events reach Charleston and New York Town. Our Committee of Correspondence spent a busy evening."

There was a stir in the room, and members of the House looked at each other in surprise. Never before had the existence of the Committee been mentioned aloud at a large gathering, and the mere fact that Lee had spoken its name was an obvious sign that the leaders of the Burgesses were embarking on a bolder policy.

Lee was well aware of the heightened interest he had created, and smiled grimly. "The English colonies of this continent are sisters whose lives have been threatened by a jealous and powerful mother unwilling to see them grow to womanhood. But England's daughters need not cower in their separate chambers, awaiting punishment. Indeed, if they remain separate, they surely will be chastised. But if they join hands, their combined, determined strength will bring a deluded parent to her senses. Colonel, is there anything you'd like to add before we tell them the Committee's decisions?"

Colonel Washington was no taller than the other leaders who stood over six feet, but his unusually erect bearing and the simple cut of his long-tailed, London-made suits created an illusion of height. Unsmiling but courtly, the most moderate of the Whig chieftains made no secret of his aversion to public speaking, and ran a long forefinger inside the rim of his silk neckcloth as he gazed diffidently around the room. "The House," he said, "is proud of its democratic tradition. On this occasion it would appear that those traditions have been ignored. It is true that the few have made a decision for the many, even though those few include Mr. Pendleton and Mr. Randolph of the Tories as well as my Whig associates. Circumstances have made it impossible for us to deal otherwise with a crucial matter. The Assembly having been dissolved, no formal vote on our plan can be tallied without risking

111

the charge that we have deliberately chosen to ignore the governor's order.

"But if any man present thinks our scheme unwise, we will welcome such remarks as he cares to make. And if a majority should oppose the plan, we will withdraw it."

Patrick and Lee grinned at each other. Washington's point was well taken, and by soothing the rank and file now, he was preventing an outburst of opposition later. For a soldier, he demonstrated remarkable political acumen.

Again Patrick stood. "The Committee of Correspondence, which was enlarged last night to include Tory party representation, is sending a special message to the Committees of the other twelve colonies. In it, we will urge that a Congress of delegates representing all the colonies be held as soon as special conventions can elect these delegates. We're suggesting that the Congress be held in Philadelphia, which is not only the largest of our cities but is centrally located.

"Our letter," he continued, glancing at his notes, "will state that a joint meeting is necessary to consider the united interests of America. We must live and work together, and only through union can we convince the Commons and the Crown that a blow at Massachusetts Bay is an insult to Virginia, that a blow at Virginia is an insult to Connecticut. Neither the British troops and warships that would intimidate Boston nor the attempt to silence the Burgesses of Virginia will prevent free Americans from freely expressing the truths we cherish.

"Let us preserve those freedoms. Let each county elect representatives to a convention which will select the delegates this colony will send to the Congress in Philadelphia. The King cannot gag us, nor his Parliament shackle us. We have placed ourselves under the protection of Almighty God, and His justice will prevail."

6

Gold sovereigns and half sovereigns were piled in neat stacks on the library desk, gleaming in the light of an oil lamp. Patrick took still more coins from his strongbox, and Sarah carefully filled another lamp with Arctic whale oil, refined in Amsterdam and so precious that she always performed the task herself. Voluminous curtains of porous muslin, made of Georgia cotton and home-loomed, covered the open windows to keep out mosquitoes, and in a tree near the carriage house a snow owl called mournfully to its mate. Inside the room there was no sound but the clinking of metal as the piles of coins continued to grow.

Sarah inserted a cork stopper into the glazed jar of whale oil and, to prevent evaporation, covered the top with a dimity bag filled with moss from the banks of the James River. Then she poured her husband a small tankard of beer from a thick earthenware jug; trying to conceal her nervousness, she took some clothes from a mending basket as she sat down opposite him.

At last the strongbox was empty, and Patrick made some calculations on paper, squinting as he peered at the rows of figures.

"You need spectacles," Sarah said.

He nodded absently, still preoccupied. "I'll get them in Philadelphia. I've heard Dr. Franklin has invented a new process for making them that's superior to any glass ground in England."

She smiled but made no comment. He was partial to colonial products these days, so she didn't have the heart to remind him that the spectacle makers of London were craftsmen far more experienced than a Philadelphia editor and politician who, apparently, enjoyed tinkering and insisted that everyone he knew experiment with his bizarre inventions.

When Patrick was done, he placed the gold-coated quill that had been a gift from the Whigs in a small container of pebbles, rolled down his shirtsleeves and leaned back in his chair. "Our situation," he said cheerfully, "could be much worse."

Sarah waited patiently.

"Peter is putting enough vegetables, fowl, butter, and milk on our table for us to be almost self-sufficient in food. We're growing enough of our own wheat to barter for beef, and the Dandridge potato crop is more than enough for their needs and ours. We can give them all the oats and barley they want. Peter says the new strain of barley from Scotland that I smuggled past the port collectors last year is the best we've ever tried. We get all the West Indian coffee we need from Ben Arnold and the other New Haven merchants who are glad to take a little of our tobacco, and I don't believe we'll be buying tea for a long time to come. I have enough spirits on hand for friends and beer for myself to last for a long time. So I don't think we'll have to spend more than twenty to thirty pounds per year for food."

"You make it sound as though we're in for a long siege." Sarah tried to speak lightly, but failed.

"I think it may be longer than most people realize, and now that I've been elected a delegate to the Continental Congress, I'll have no chance at all to earn any money in my private practice. What we plan to do is prepare a proposal of some sort to England. The Commons will answer, then we'll formulate another reply, and eventually we'll work out some sort of accommodation. But each step will be long and painful. Men who are elected to public office—and this is as true of colonials as it is of the English—must have the opportunities to express their opinions, reconcile their differences and find common ground to occupy."

"I know nothing of governments, and the more you become involved, the less I understand. Parliament passes acts you don't like, and the Burgesses issue statements condemning them. I keep thinking of little boys daring each other to fight in a free-for-all."

"There are times," Patrick replied with gentle self-irony, "when I'm inclined to agree with you. Unfortunately, there's more at stake than the pride of boys trying to prove they're growing into men."

Only one aspect of the situation concerned her. "How much money do we have, P.H.?"

"Twelve hundred pounds in paper, and four hundred in gold and silver. Enough to last two to three years, if we're prudent."

Sarah laughed.

He detected a note of hysteria in her voice. "I'm not saying our dispute with the Commons will go on that long, but we must be prepared for negotiations over a long period." He decided not to mention the possibility that the disagreement might become worse, and that open warfare might erupt. If that should happen, in part because of his own convictions, he would be obligated to serve the colonial cause until peace was restored.

She shook her head, dabbing at her eyes with a linen handkerchief. "I'm amused, dear, because we've changed. There was a time, not so long ago, when we would have been happy with an income of one hundred pounds a year. It would have looked like a fortune to us. Now we blithely talk in terms of thousands."

He felt guilty, and flushed. His new ceremonial wig, which he loathed, had been made for him in Baltimore at exorbitant cost, but he had paid the price cheerfully, spending more than he had earned in a year when the older children had been small. "At least," he said with feigned brightness, "there will be one less mouth to feed when Martha marries John Fontaine next year."

Sarah's expression softened at the mention of her daughter's forthcoming marriage to an eligible young planter.

"I've already discussed her dowry with John. I'm going to give them the house and land I bought across the river last year."

"Then we'll lose the income our tenants are paying."

"That can't be helped, Sarah. Nate Dandridge may be able to present Dorothea's husband with a bag of gold when she finds the right lad, but I don't have Nate's fortune. I can't afford to hand out either specie or gold when there's no more coming in." He started putting away the money, counting each stack again as he placed it in the strongbox.

She stuffed the shirt she had mended into her wicker basket. "You know I'll be careful, dear."

He went to her, slid an arm around her waist and kissed her. "I've never doubted your ability to manage our household." Her back felt rigid beneath his touch, and he searched her face. "What's wrong?"

"I wish I knew. But I dread your meeting in Philadelphia. When I was in Richmond last week, buying material for the girls' new autumn clothes, people in the shops were actually boasting that we'll be independent of England by this time next year."

If England remained stubborn, the colonies might be forced to cut their ties with her, but he saw no reason to upset Sarah prematurely, and patted her shoulder. "Let me worry about that."

"Now you sound like the men in the drygoods shops. Two of them didn't know me, and they kept telling each other, 'Leave everything to Patrick Henry and Richie Lee. They'll tweak the King's nose.' I—I'm frightened, P.H. I don't want to lose my husband to a royal hangman or my sons in a battle with professional soldiers—who shoot to kill. I've never interfered in your work, but I beg you, find some way at your Philadelphia meeting to compromise with the King and Parliament."

"I'd do it if I could, Sarah. But freedom is like faith in the Almighty. It can't be compromised."

7

City Tavern, where the servings of roasts and meat pies were ample and the spirits generous, was located conveniently near Carpenters' Hall, where the First Continental Congress held its meetings. At four o'clock every afternoon the delegates went there for dinner, their day's work done, and throngs of Philadelphians congregated in Chestnut Street outside to watch and cheer them. The citizens lived on rumors, whispers and snippets of information, and occasionally one of the delegates paused long enough to fill them in on the session's events.

Caesar Rodney of Delaware, tall and painfully thin, was particularly obliging, and so was the wealthy Philip Livingston of New York. The crowds respected their own Dr. Franklin too much to pester him, and the few who approached Sam Adams of Massachusetts found him so shy in public that he became inarticulate. Joseph Galloway of Pennsylvania was well known locally, but his views were too conservative for the taste of the crowds, and Silas Deane of Connecticut, although friendly, developed the art of saying a great deal while actually revealing nothing.

The Virginians who dominated the Congress in its earlier stages were regarded with such awe that not even the brash apprentices who made life miserable for some delegates had the courage to annoy them. Peyton Randolph, who had been elected president of the Congress and, consequently, had thrown in his lot with the Whigs, was a man of great dignity whose manner did not encourage familiarity. Colonel Washington, who usually rode his horse from the meetings to the City Tavern, maintained a patrician reserve, as did Edmund Pendleton and elderly, wealthy Richard Bland.

The two popular heroes of the Congress, Patrick Henry and

Richard Henry Lee, who sometimes made as many as a dozen speeches between them in a single day, were cheered regularly with such lusty fervor that embarrassment forced them to dine elsewhere. Lee became friendly with Thomas Lynch of South Carolina, and they often rode together to one of the old inns on Market Street which specialized in the seafood they preferred. Patrick found the little New Tavern more to his liking, and so did John Adams of Massachusetts, Sam's distant cousin.

A grave, self-effacing man who, like Washington, rarely made a formal address to his colleagues, John Adams nevertheless had become one of the moving forces of the Congress. Patrick soon discovered that Adams' knowledge of law was as vast as his own, and they struck up a close friendship when they found themselves standing together on every issue, prodding the cautious to take a bolder position and tamping down the recklessness of the radicals who were urging that the colonies establish a united, independent government immediately.

Others joined the pair at the New Tavern occasionally, but most found cause for complaint. Colonel Washington said the roast turkey was so tough he couldn't chew it, and Sam Adams insisted the landlord was niggardly with his measures of rum and brandywine. Livingston, who paid a great deal of attention to his food, said that the beef was abominable and the tarts even worse.

But John Adams and Patrick liked the quiet, refined atmosphere, and relaxed before a coal fire. The service was slow, it was true, but they were in no hurry. Patrick drank nothing stronger than an occasional tankard of beer and Adams added so much water to his wine that neither cared if the portions of spirits were small. It didn't matter, either, if the quality of the food left something to be desired; conversation was far more important to them, and they usually became so engrossed in talk they didn't notice what they ate.

Their preoccupation with the multiple problems that Congress was facing became increasingly intense as the weeks passed. The first weeks had been the most harmonious, and no real difficulties had been encountered in gaining support for Massachusetts from the other colonies. Patrick had made an impassioned speech, in which he had said, "The distinctions between Virginians, Pennsylvanians, New Yorkers, and New Englanders are no more. I am not a Virginian, but an American." Lee had taken advantage of the emotional response to the address by proposing a resolution favoring the cause of Massachusetts, and it had been adopted by unanimous vote.

But now, after six weeks of incessant debate, it was proving difficult to obtain agreement of the members on any of the other basic issues. John Adams enumerated them on his slender fingers as he and Patrick sat together over steaming bowls of veal and tripe stew. "The radicals," he said, "want to set too early a date for the start of a non-importation, non-exportation agreement if our demands are rejected by Parliament. Cousin Sam keeps insisting we appoint generals to command a united colonial militia—"

"—which would be certain to alarm the War Office," Patrick declared, interrupting. "What's more, as I pointed out in my speech on the subject yesterday, we have no authority from our citizens to establish an army. I'm not denying we may need a unified military command in the next year or two, John, but we haven't come to it yet. And the citizens should be given a voice in something that significant."

Adams nodded energetically, added large quantities of water to some Burgundy in his glass and continued his recital. "The delegates quibble over the wording of an appeal to the people of Canada, who'll never join us if Jay of New York and the other legal purists keep modifying the language of the resolution. There's even the quarrel over the propriety of issuing a memorial to the people of our own colonies, which is absurd. And the suggestion that we rebuke Georgia for not sending delegates to the Congress is positively dangerous. The letter from Lyman Hall saying they couldn't elect representatives in time, but will send a delegation to our next session, is honorable and reasonable. I don't know why the hotheads refuse to understand that we'll antagonize Georgia if we criticize her."

"You've lined up more than enough votes to defeat a motion of rebuke, so dismiss it from your mind, John." Patrick wiped his knife on a slab of barley bread, then neatly cut a bacon and apple dumpling into quarters. "My worry is whether our Declaration of

Rights will be passed. Aside from the loss of all the work we've put into it, we render ourselves legally defenseless if we adopt Joe Galloway's plan to establish a third House of Parliament in the colonies."

Adams stared gloomily at his stew, and ate without appetite. "I thought your explanation of the weakness of Galloway's plan was brilliant, and I don't see how the men who aren't lawyers can fail to understand it. We'd be admitting the right of the Commons to govern us if we granted it a veto power over our own House, and that's the essence of Galloway's scheme. I'm astonished by the shortsightedness of the Tories."

"So was I, but I've been thinking about them these past few days, and I believe I understand them better now. I don't think they love America any less than we do."

John Adams laughed scornfully. "You give them more credit than they deserve, Patrick."

"Hear me out. Young Jay's attitude is typical of the whole breed. He has great respect for centralized authority, which is vested right now in the Commons. I honestly believe that if we were to establish a central government of our own with the power to approve or veto the acts of the provincial assemblies, most of the conservatives would favor the idea and stop supporting Galloway."

"But that's absurd!" Adams rarely became excited, but he pounded the handle of his knife on the oak table so hard that the pewter plates rattled. "The core of our argument is that the assembly of each colony is as much the representative of its citizens as the Commons is the voice of the English people. Each assembly must have sovereign rights under the Crown, precisely as the Commons has them."

"You don't have to convince me, John," Patrick said dryly. "It took us long enough to hammer out the wording of our Declaration: 'Our rights stem from the immutable laws of nature, the principles of the English constitution and the several charters or compacts.' You've heard me argue that no laws passed by Parliament are binding on us until our own legislatures approve them."

Adams chuckled, but his eyes remained sober. "I can only hope," he said, sipping his watered wine, "that we won't have as much trouble in London as we're encountering from our own conservatives here. They're forgetting that our rights as free Englishmen are at stake."

8

Delegates to the Congress knew that a failure to reach agreement among themselves would be interpreted in London as a sign of weakness, so they closed ranks. A fourteen-hour session was held on the day that a vote was to be taken on the plan of Joseph Galloway, and Patrick, spearheading the opposition, made eleven addresses. Each time one of the proponents of the measure stopped speaking, he leaped to his feet with a rebuttal, finally losing his voice. The Galloway plan was defeated.

Then the self-styled "moderate Whigs" from Virginia and Massachusetts took command. Their Declaration of Rights and Grievances, addressed to King George, was passed by an almost unanimous vote. They won a majority for their memorial asking the people of Quebec to join them, and they won a significant delay for the start of their commercial embargo which would forbid all trade with England.

John Adams and Patrick won their biggest victory when they beat off an attempt to address a petition to Parliament. Inasmuch as Americans refused to recognize the authority of the Commons over them, they argued, it would be better policy to send an open Address to the People of England, explaining their position and asking for support. Lee was chairman of a committee that worked furiously on the Address, which was almost painfully candid. If the rights of American colonials were recognized, it stated baldly, the embargo on trade would be set aside, and men on both sides of the Atlantic would prosper.

The exhausted delegates adopted the Address, voted to meet again the following May if their appeal to the Crown remained unheeded and, at the end of October, Congress finally adjourned.

Most members left at once for their homes, but Sam Adams asked the Virginians to stay in Philadelphia an extra night for a joint supper with the Massachusetts delegation. Pendleton and

Bland protested, but were outvoted, the others agreeing that it was fitting for the representatives of the two wealthiest, most heavily populated and most influential colonies to celebrate together.

The two groups met in a private room on the second floor of the City Tavern, and exchanged toasts in sack, Madeira and Claret. Patrick raised his own glass to each member in turn, but took only token sips from his glass. It occurred to him as he ate raw oysters that he considered inferior to those found in Chesapeake Bay that the party was a mistake, just as Bland and Pendleton had insisted it would be. He was too tired to enjoy himself, and everyone else was suffering from fatigue, too. Colonel Washington was yawning, and Elbridge Gerry of Massachusetts dozed quietly.

Sam Adams soon made it clear that social conviviality had not been his real aim in suggesting the supper. After everyone present had been toasted, a huge tureen of a peppered tripe and fish chowder was placed on the table, and the barmaids who carried it into the room withdrew. Sam promptly refilled his glass and leaped to his feet again. "Gentlemen," he said, "I propose a toast to a new nation, a free and independent America!"

Lee blinked at him, Colonel Washington's jaw dropped and even John Adams, who thought he knew his cousin well, was astonished.

Patrick was the first to recover. "Isn't this a little premature?" he asked.

"No, sir!" Sam's voice was loud and rasping. "I can say in the company of friends what I couldn't on the floor of Congress. We've been dueling with phantoms these past seven weeks, lads, and that's the truth. Mark you, the King will reject our Declaration —because he must. We've put him in an impossible position. If he even receives a document addressed to him over the heads of the Commons, he'll be admitting that Parliament has no jurisdiction over us. You lawyers," he added, grinning at his cousin and Patrick, "ought to realize that every thinking member of the bar in England will be horrified."

Lee cut in swiftly. "Maybe so, but I believe the Crown will be under great pressure to ignore the subtle legalities. Every merchant in England will cry for an accommodation with us, and I predict that the same ship that carries the threat of our embargo to London will return with an agreement. Money talks."

Sam, still on his feet, drained his glass. "Guns talk louder. The first thing I'm going to do when I get home is to have the Sons of Liberty enlarge a foundry in Worcester so we'll be ready to forge cannon when the time comes. I advise you to prepare yourselves, too."

Everyone looked at Colonel Washington, by far the most experienced military man present. He was silent for a time, pondering and rubbing the side of his prominent nose. "Even if I were to grant your assumption that we'll be reduced to armed combat, and I don't, Mr. Adams, I think it would be a mistake to make any openly hostile move. I intend to encourage the formation of new militia companies in Virginia, and I'm sure other colonies will be doing the same. Recruits should be drilled, of course, and I don't believe the Crown will be unduly alarmed. But the building of foundries for cannon would insure the occupation of all our major towns by troops from Halifax, where the British garrison has been reinforced, and from England itself." He was courteous but firm. "In my opinion, Mr. Adams, you're playing with fire."

"It's my view, Colonel, that the fire is already blazing!" Sam reached for a decanter.

His cousin gently nudged it beyond his grasp.

Washington glanced around the table. "Gentlemen, I have a great respect for British regulars. Their generals are experienced and their staff corps is efficient, the officers they send into the field are spirited veterans and their troops are disciplined."

Sam took his seat and accepted a bowl of soup from Patrick, who sat opposite him and ladled it for him. "I'm no soldier, Colonel," he said contemptuously, "but it's been my misfortune to see General Gage and his corps of occupation at close quarters in Boston. I say our Minutemen, who've had no formal training, can beat the tar out of the Redcoats."

Washington remained polite and unruffled. "In a limited engagement, perhaps, but American militiamen couldn't win a prolonged campaign without outside help."

The pepper-seasoned soup burned Patrick's mouth, but he was so engrossed in the conversation that he paid no attention to his discomfort. "It's been my belief that we'd need help from the French, Spanish, or Dutch if we hoped to win a war against England. Is that what you're trying to tell us, Colonel?"

"The Dutch don't have the manpower reserves to send a force across the Atlantic, and they're so closely allied with England these days that it isn't realistic to hope they'd give us help. Without the French or Spaniards—preferably both—I think our chances of winning a real victory would be slim."

Sam was still belligerent. "You military men are all alike," he declared as Washington glared at him. "You don't weigh the spirit of the people in your calculations. Soldiers from Cornwall and Kent and Lincolnshire don't give a tinker-mackerels' dam whether we keep our ties with England or set out in the world on our own. But boys from New Hampshire and North Carolina care! It's their freedom that's at stake. I say that a company of American militia can whip a battalion of Redcoat puppets any day, rain or shine, snow or hail."

Washington was dangerously close to losing his temper, Sam's fury was mounting and Patrick intervened swiftly. "We can only hoped the question will remain theoretical," he said, "and at present it does us little good to speculate. The matter is out of our hands. The Declaration of Rights and Grievances will be presented to the King at Whitehall by early December, and he'll decide whether there will be negotiations—or war."

FIVE

1775

1

It was good to have Martha home again, even for a few days. Patrick stood at the library window, his new spectacles pushed up onto his forehead, and watched his eldest daughter standing in the driveway with her good friend, Dorothea, as they waited for the Dandridge carriage to be driven around from the rear of the house. It was strange to think of Martha as a matron, and Patrick still regarded her as a child, but he realized he was seeing her through a father's eyes, and laughed aloud at his shortsightedness. It required no effort to see that Dorothea, who still scorned marriage and was busily rejecting suitors, had ripened into a mature beauty. So it stood to reason that Martha, after eight weeks of marriage, was a woman, too, rather than a girl.

Reluctantly turning away from the window, Patrick threw another hickory log on the fire and went back to the pile of unanswered correspondence on his desk. It was sheer luck that John Tyler had stopped off at Scotchtown earlier in the day, and had immediately volunteered to pass along the latest news from London to some of the other colonial Committees. He hadn't known that a packet ship had put into Newport News at dawn that morning with the latest London newspapers and dispatches from the three observers sent to England by the Continental

Congress. Without his help, Patrick would have been compelled to spend the entire night passing along word of the complicated and fast-moving developments on the other side of the Atlantic.

The library door opened, and Patrick knew without looking up that Martha had come in; she was still the only one of his children privileged to enter the library without announcing her presence by knocking. "Tell me, Mrs. Fontaine, does your husband have a sensitive nose?" he asked, grinning as he continued to write. "You'll find a jar of musk-and-flower balm on the mantel. I ordered it some time ago from France as a little wedding present for you, but I just received it today, with the documents from London."

"You still spoil me." Martha leaned over him and kissed him on his high forehead.

The news was foremost in his mind. "Our supporters in England are stirring up a great tempest on our behalf. Listen to what Pitt—he's the Earl of Chatham now, you know—said in the House of Lords. He called our Declaration a splendid paper and congratulated us 'for solidity of reason, force of sagacity, and wisdom of conclusion.' I'm sure Dr. Franklin will want to thank him, so I'm sending the *Post* cutting to Philadelphia."

"I want to talk to you, Papa." Martha sat down and smoothed her skirt of rustling, honey-colored silk that matched her hair.

"Edmund Burke has given us even stronger support in the Commons. He's asked for a return to the spirit that united England and the colonies before '63. In effect, he's demanding that the King change his entire policy."

"Please, Papa." The young woman's eyes were troubled.

"We may still be scalped, of course. Pitt mustered only eighteen votes in the Lords on a bill to withdraw troops from Boston. And the King hasn't indicated yet whether he'll receive our Declaration—or what he'll do about it. Everything hangs on his decision, and neither Lord North nor his ministers will tell anyone what recommendations they're making to the Crown."

"Mama is ill," Martha said in a low voice.

The papers on the desk forgotten, her father pushed back his chair and stood.

"No, please don't go to her. I—she swore me to secrecy. She doesn't want you to know."

As hurt as he was bewildered, Patrick sank back into his chair.

"Mama doesn't want to worry you. She knows you've been working day and night, and she keeps thinking about something Mr. Lee said to her after you came home from Philadelphia last autumn. He told her all America is depending on you, and she doesn't want to add to your burden."

"This is nonsense!" he declared angrily. "If your mother isn't feeling well, I have a right to know it!"

Martha extended both hands toward him in a gesture that always had melted him since she had been a small child. "Mama swore me to secrecy. None of the others know, although I think Neddy suspects something."

"I can't pretend ignorance when my wife is ill!" Patrick's voice soared, as it did when he was making a speech, and an ornamental candlestick holder, decorated with a cascade of crystal droplets, tinkled musically.

"Don't say anything to her, Papa, I beg you. It will only upset her and make her feel worse. I've come to you because you have a right to know, but Mama is always more concerned about you than she is about herself, and she'll worry herself into her grave if you say as much as a single word to her."

Patrick's hands were trembling, and he made a great effort to compose himself.

Martha wanted to comfort him, but didn't know what to do. "Just what is her illness, and how bad is it?"

She hesitated. "Well, Mama had cynanche of the lungs while you were attending the Congress meetings—"

"She was given the usual beef tea with herbs and was bled three times," Patrick said impatiently. "Two physicians assured me that cynanche is a mild disease."

"They've changed their minds, since Mama has been running a fever and is losing so much weight."

His fear mounted. "She told me she was taking off weight purposely. That was a deliberate attempt to hoax me." He took a deep breath. "Is she suffering from the tubercle?"

"They aren't sure, Papa. They're watching her very closely, and they'll bleed her more heavily to get rid of the black humors if they diagnose her case as the tubercle."

Patrick's throat felt painfully dry, and his jaws were wooden when he spoke. "If she should prove to be that ill, I hope I'd be officially informed!"

"Of course," Martha replied soothingly. "If Mama's condition proves to be that unfortunate, she wouldn't want to hide it from you. In the meantime, Anne is going to take charge of the house, so Mama can spend more time in bed, resting. And I'll ride over every day to make sure that things run smoothly here. I wouldn't dare interfere in Isobel's kitchen, and neither would Anne, of course. Mama has planned her convalescence very carefully to prevent you from suspecting there might be anything wrong. So, for her sake, pretend to be deaf and blind for the next few weeks—until the doctors have a better notion of what may be ailing her."

"The tubercle frightens me. I've never yet heard of a case cured by bleeding. Nate Dandridge's cousin died of tubercle humors last year after the doctors had tried everything—bleeding, mustard poultices, and even wine-vapor baths."

"Don't be so gloomy, Papa. The trouble with England has been upsetting you, and you're tired."

"Maybe so, but who wouldn't be upset? Wherever I go, I see militiamen drilling on village greens. And I know I bear as much responsibility for the tension as any man in America."

"It's hardly your fault!"

"No," Patrick said slowly, "I'm not to blame, nor are Richie Lee and Sam Adams and the others. For that matter, neither are the King and Lord North. They're doing what they honestly believe right, and their convictions are as courageous as ours. I suppose I keep hoping for miracles. I'm already burdening the Lord, and now I'll have to ask Him for still more." His voice became husky. "I reckon your father is a weak man, Martha."

"You're stronger than anyone I've ever known."

He shook his head. "I have my Achilles' heel. Without your mother—I'd be nothing."

2

Benjamin Franklin's letter to Patrick and Richard Henry Lee was so brief, so lacking in the usual courtesy that at first reading it seemed ungracious. "Sirs," he wrote, "the Virginia Committee of

Correspondence will share my sorrow at the news just received by packet ship. His Majesty has declined to accept the Declaration of Rights and Grievances, and has rejected it *in toto*, refusing to consider its merits or validity."

The Assembly was called into session on only ten days' notice, and even men who had been hoping that a reasonable compromise could be worked out with the Crown lost heart. The pace of military preparations quickened in Virginia and elsewhere, and Patrick received a letter from John Adams saying that the tensions in Boston were rapidly becoming unbearable.

"Dry kindling is piled high," the sober Massachusetts attorney wrote, "and a spark, even a cinder blown across the brushwood by a capricious wind could soon engulf all America in flames."

Sam Adams' followers went to work with a vengeance now, and started enlarging the foundry in Worcester for the forging of big guns. Two cannon in General Gage's Boston arsenal disappeared under mysterious circumstances, and all troops in the area were put on an alert.

Preparations for war were speeded in other colonies, too. Colonel Washington urged all local militia commanders in Virginia to procure muskets or rifles for their men by any means available, and several of his colleagues on the Committee of Correspondence helped him organize the "Old Dominion's" volunteers into two regiments ready to march quickly in the event that hostilities broke out. In Philadelphia feelings ran so high that the homes of citizens known to be unswervingly loyal to the Crown were daubed with yellow paint, and the Loyalists, as such men were now called in most places, were warned by the Charleston Sons of Liberty to leave South Carolina or suffer unnamed consequences.

On March 22, 1775, the day Patrick was scheduled to go to Williamsburg for the meeting of the Burgesses, he received word that several companies of Massachusetts militia had been mobilized, and that all Redcoat leaves of absence in the Boston garrison had been canceled. "The fighting is certain to start any day," he told his somber family at dinner. "But most people don't realize we're close to war. We've pulled back so many times after going to the edge of the chasm—and so have the British—that people are still hoping some way will be found to preserve peace. It's too late now for peace, and Americans must be made to know the truth."

He delayed his departure in order to write notes for a speech that, he said, he would make the following day. His children were impressed, as he ordinarily made no preparations for an address, but he told them the situation had become so critical that he wanted to awaken the men of every colony with a carefully prepared statement.

He spent two hours alone in his library, then ordered his horse saddled and went to the bedchamber he shared with Sarah. She had retired after dinner to rest, as had become her habit, and Patrick peered at her anxiously. However, the color in her cheeks reassured him, as did the knowledge that she had lost no more weight in recent weeks. She put aside the copy of the *Royal American Magazine* she had been reading, and smiled up at him.

"How long will you be gone this time, P.H.?"

"We're planning to hold a short session." Patrick saw no reason to add to her worries by telling her the speech he planned to make was so inflammatory that Lord Dunmore might well dissolve the Burgesses within twenty-four hours.

"You'll take good care of yourself?"

"Of course. My hide is as tough as a bull buffalo's."

Sarah didn't find his assurances amusing. "Everyone knows how you feel, and if things are really so bad now, Lord Dunmore may have you arrested."

"Impossible," he lied.

"It wasn't so long ago that the Crown thought of bringing you to trial," she persisted. "There must be more reason now."

"When only a few of us understood the issues, there might have been a risk," Patrick reassured her. "By now there are two million Americans standing together—maybe as many as three million. The King doesn't have enough jails to imprison all of us." He laughed, feigning joviality.

Sarah's smile was forced.

He was tempted to mention her own illness, but had kept silent for so long that it would achieve nothing to bring the truth into the open now. The physicians had assured him she wasn't suffer-

ing from the tubercle, and although he had been disinclined to
believe their optimistic report, he had to admit that in recent weeks
she had looked better and seemed livelier. "Be sure you take your
blood tonic while I'm in Williamsburg," he said, referring to the
medication she had been given for the polite ailment, ladies'
fatigue, that was her alleged reason for spending so much time in
bed.

"You're as bad as Martha. The very first thing she does when
she drives over here every day is stand over me until I drink a glass
of the wretched brew. I've lost all taste for herbs, and I'm sure I
shall never be able to eat them again in an Italian greens-salad."

Patrick bent down to kiss her.

Sarah's arms slid around his neck, and for a moment she
clutched him hard, her nails digging through the fabric of his coat,
before she gently released him. "May God bless and keep you,
always," she murmured.

By the time he stood erect again, her eyes were calm and her
face was composed.

3

Word had been passed that Patrick Henry intended to make a
major address at the end of the first day's meeting, so the floor of
the House was crowded and guests were standing three deep at
the rear of the visitors' gallery. But Patrick spoke in a reasonable,
almost unemotional voice for more than an hour as he traced the
history of the dispute between the colonies and England. Anyone
who had expected to hear dazzling bursts of oratory from a
celebrated public speaker was sorely disappointed.

Peyton Randolph, who had been elected Speaker as a Whig
gesture of solidarity to the Tories, frequently averted his head and
hid his yawns behind his hand. Williamsburg merchants, some of
them Loyalists, who crowded into the gallery, conversed with each
other in low tones and paid little attention to the speech. Lord
Dunmore had deliberately refrained from sending any representative to the House, and two Redcoat officers whose curiosity had

brought them to the chamber waited for an opportune moment to leave unobtrusively.

Only three people in the hall realized that Patrick was slowly, almost imperceptibly increasing the intensity of his delivery. Richard Henry Lee, sitting beside him in the front row on the Whig side, expressed his admiration for a brother orator by listening intently, his head cocked to one side. Thomas Jefferson, two rows to the rear, made occasional notes as he studied Patrick's technique. And Martha Henry Fontaine, whose husband John sat beside her in the visitors' gallery, listened to her father with rapt attention, her eyes shining.

Gradually the merchants fell silent, Peyton Randolph sat bolt upright and the members leaned forward in their seats as the tension grew. Patrick was playing with his audience "in the manner of a master fiddler drawing tunes from his fiddle," as Lee later said. Pauses became longer, the speaker's voice rose to a booming crescendo, then dropped to a mere whisper that, nevertheless, carried to the far corners of the chamber. Patrick became increasingly eloquent, his air of serene calm gave way to an ever-increasing passion in both the content and delivery of his address, and as he approached his climax, his audience was listening breathlessly to every word.

"They tell us," he declared, "that we are weak, unable to cope with so formidable an adversary. But when shall we be stronger? Will it be when we are totally disarmed, and when a British guard shall be stationed in every house? Shall we gather strength by irresolution and inaction? Shall we acquire the means of effectual resistance by lying supinely on our backs, and hugging the delusive phantom of hope, until our enemies shall have bound us hand and foot?"

His listeners were so thoroughly under his spell now that the cry, "No, no!" rose from every part of the hall.

He waited until the hubbub subsided, then continued, his voice becoming still more powerful. "We are not weak, if we make a proper use of those means which the God of nature has placed in our power. Three millions of people armed in the holy cause of liberty, and in such a country as that which we possess, are invincible by any force which our enemy can send against us.

"Besides, Mr. Speaker, we shall not fight our battles alone. There is a just God who presides over the destinies of nations, and who will raise up friends to fight our battles with us. The battle is not to the strong alone. It is to the vigilant, the active, the brave.

"Besides, we no longer have a choice, an election. Even were we base enough to desire it, it is now too late to retire from the contest, a contest in which right must prevail over right, and justice over tyranny.

"There is no retreat but in submission and slavery. Our chains are forged. Their clanking may be heard on the plains of Boston. The war is inevitable." Patrick paused and waited for a painfully long time. "Let it come!" he roared in his deepest voice. "I repeat, let it come!"

The members started to applaud, but he silenced them by raising both hands over his head.

"It is in vain, Mr. Speaker, to extenuate the matter," he went on, his baritone pulsating. "Gentlemen may cry peace, peace, but there is no peace.

"The war is actually begun.

"The next gale that sweeps from the north will bring to our ears the clash of resounding arms. Our brethren are already in the field.

"Why stand we here idle? What is it that gentlemen wish? What would they have? Is life so dear, or peace so sweet, as to be purchased at the price of chains and slavery?"

Again he paused, and stood with his wrists held together, his head bowed and back bent, as though burdened by links of heavy metal. Then his instinct for the theatrical prompted him to simulate a great effort; slowly he wrenched his wrists apart and even more slowly his back straightened.

"Forbid it, Almighty God!" he cried, and the purity of his sudden exaltation sent a sudden shiver through his audience. "I know not what course others may take, but as for me—give me liberty, or give me death!"

He sat down, and no one moved or spoke. Emotion overcame everyone present, and the spell was not broken until the two British officers in the gallery finally jumped to their feet and hastily departed. Then men on the floor of the chamber began to applaud, gently at first, apparently unwilling to dispel the aura Patrick had

133

created. Little by little other members joined in, as did the visitors, and the hall resounded to their unrestrained cheers. Colonel Washington, who so rarely displayed emotion, made no attempt to brush away the tears that streamed down his face. Lee and Jefferson wept, too, as did a score of others.

Martha buried her face in her husband's coat as he held her in his arms, and her sobs added to the bedlam. Mrs. Harrison, who occupied a front row seat in the gallery, swooned and almost fell over the railing, but was saved by the usually sedate and dignified Mrs. Randolph, who was cheering so loudly in a high soprano that her face was crimson.

Speaker Randolph pounded his gavel in vain, and ten minutes passed before order was restored.

Patrick rose to his feet again. "Mr. Speaker, I request the floor for the purpose of submitting a motion to the Burgesses."

"The chair recognizes the right honorable member from Hanover."

"Resolved," Patrick declared, "that a committee prepare a plan for embodying, arming, and disciplining the militia of Virginia, and that a committee be appointed forthwith for this purpose."

Again there was a cheer, and the Speaker dispensed with formality. "Unless there is objection, the chair rules the motion passed by unanimous consent, and appoints Mr. Henry as chairman of the special committee, empowered to name thereto such members of the House he himself selects."

For all practical purposes, Patrick had been given charge of Virginia's war preparations. It had not crossed his mind that he might be asked to shoulder such great responsibility, but his stirring address had made his selection inevitable, and he accepted the consequences. Bowing in response to another storm of applause, he looked around the chamber and quickly appointed eleven of his colleagues to serve with him.

Any hope that war might be averted had been dispelled by his speech, and speed was essential now in all things. Regiments had to be mustered, supplies would be needed to support the men in the field and plans had to be drawn for the defense of the colony. It was urgently necessary, too, that the Continental Congress reconvene at the earliest possible date to coordinate the efforts of all thirteen colonies. Patrick's speech had destroyed the flimsy and unrealistic belief still cherished by many that some sort of accommodation with England might yet be reached.

In effect, one man, standing alone, had declared war on Great Britain. The reaction of the Burgesses indicated that all Virginia was ready to march with him, and elsewhere men who shared the faith of the Virginians in their common destiny would prepare for battle, too. Patrick's oratory had made further delay impossible, and everyone in the House chamber knew that very soon the roar of cannon and rattle of musket fire would drown out the sounds of mere rhetoric. For as far ahead as anyone could see, the sword would be mightier than the pen.

4

A company of volunteer militiamen, their only "uniforms" white armbands and red, white and blue cockades on their hats, surrounded the Raleigh Tavern and admitted only those patrons the officers in charge trusted. No one was allowed to disturb the War Committee, as Patrick's group was now known, which was holding sessions beginning at breakfast and lasting far into the night. It was common knowledge that the militiamen would fight if British troops came near the Raleigh or made any other move that might result in the capture of Virginia's leaders. Lord Dunmore nearly solved his dilemma by pretending to be unaware of what was taking place in the Apollo room, and closed his eyes to the streams of messengers hurrying in and out of the tavern at all hours.

Washington was in charge of the military sub-committee, Pendleton became chairman of the group handling legal matters and Harrison was saddled with the task of trying to encourage the establishment of new manufacturing plants needed in time of war. Lee, who was Patrick's co-chairman, was kept busy writing to the Congressional delegations from other colonies, and Patrick himself, with the aid of Jefferson, began the arduous labor of trying to raise funds for a war chest by requesting voluntary contributions from all citizens of the colony.

Two rows of long tables had been placed along one wall, and there clerks sat, busily copying letters and reports written by the Committee members. Elsewhere in the cramped room several meetings were held simultaneously, orders were prepared and dispatched, and matters of policy were debated. There was so much to be done that men continued to work when their meals were brought to them, and everyone snatched only a few hours of sleep every night. The House ended its session after meeting for just four days, and virtually all of the Assemblymen volunteered their services to the War Committee, relieving the strain somewhat.

The Apollo room became so crowded that workers soon spilled into the main dining room, and the Raleigh literally became the headquarters of an organization that was usurping the powers of government from the royal administration. Lord Dunmore continued to do nothing, however, realizing that if he ordered his two companies of Redcoats to disperse the Assemblymen, shots would be fired and open warfare would begin. The governor had proved himself courageous as a civil administrator, but shrank from taking responsibility for the start of armed conflict.

Patrick and his sub-committee chairmen ignored their health as they tried to complete their preparations in the shortest possible time. Randolph, acting in his capacity as president of the Continental Congress, summoned the delegations from the other colonies to a meeting at Carpenters' Hall, Philadelphia, in May, so the Virginia leaders redoubled their efforts. Lack of sleep made them haggard, but Patrick drove himself unmercifully, and the others willingly followed his example.

Colonel Washington left Williamsburg for a tour of the colony to inspect militia units, and was accompanied by Colonel William Woodford, who had served with him in the campaign against the French and Indians. Pendleton's sub-committee carefully prepared writs of seizure that would enable Virginia to take possession of Crown property at a propitious time. Harrison, encouraged by the wealthy Byrd family, concentrated most of his attention on the expansion of Richmond as a manufacturing center. The citizens of that town, anticipating rapid economic growth, started work on the erection of two new inns and a large meeting hall.

Patrick and Jefferson were unable to leave Williamsburg, as men came to them every day from all parts of the colony with pledges of contributions to the war chest. In spite of the citizens' generosity, however, it was evident that Virginia would not be able to support herself on voluntary gifts of money alone once actual warfare broke out, and Patrick spent long hours with Jefferson devising a new system of taxation for use when the colony became truly independent.

Neither man enjoyed dealing with questions of finance, and their days were so busy that they had to spend their late evening hours working out possible schedules of taxation. They developed several elaborate plans, one based on the ownership of property, a second imposing levies on consumer goods and a third using farm produce and articles of manufacture as the yardstick.

"All of them," Jefferson said one night as they sat together in the Apollo room, "are going to be unpopular."

Patrick removed his glasses, polished them and rested them on the pile of documents containing full details of all three plans. "No one has ever devised a system of taxation that people like. But at least we'll have the satisfaction of knowing that the Burgesses have adopted one of these schemes, and that we'll be taxing ourselves."

Jefferson rubbed his eyes. "This period of waiting for something to happen is very strange. We've made our plans for self-government right under Dunmore's nose, and I'm certain that he's aware of everything we're doing. But he's as reluctant as we are to be the first to send troops into battle."

"Frankly, I dread meeting him face to face when I'm riding between our headquarters here and my room at the Williamsburg Inn," Patrick replied. "It would be embarrassing for both of us. Fortunately, he isn't up and about as early as I am, nor does he ride through the streets as late at night."

"Yes, we're living in a strange vacuum. Early this morning I was finding it difficult to sleep, and I was reading some of Dr. Franklin's work on the subject of the effects of creating an air vacuum." Jefferson smiled faintly. "We Americans are becoming experts in the science of making political vacuums."

"I know what you mean. No matter how late we work, I wake up at dawn every morning expecting to hear musket fire. And I find it disconcerting when I hear nothing but the usual babble of crowing cocks and barking dogs." Patrick put on his spectacles again. "Let's see how much more of the property tax list we can finish tonight."

"I think I can stay awake long enough for another county or two." Jefferson spread out a surveyor's map on the table before them.

A militiaman made his way past tables where others were working and halted in front of them. "Excuse me, Mr. Henry," he said, "but there's someone here to see you."

Patrick groaned. "As much as I enjoy receiving pledges, I wish people would find ways to confine their enthusiasm to reasonable daytime hours instead of seeking us out the moment they arrive in town." He laughed as he accepted a folded slip of paper the sentry handed him, but it died in his throat when he saw a familiar handwriting.

The message had been scribbled hastily: "*Papa—I must see you. Martha.*"

Murmuring something to Jefferson, Patrick dropped the note onto the table and followed the militiaman through the main room to the entrance. He couldn't imagine what had brought Martha back to Williamsburg and, glancing at the gold watch Sarah had given him as a twentieth wedding anniversary gift, he realized something out of the ordinary had happened, for it was almost one o'clock in the morning.

Martha was waiting in the shadows beyond the lighted windows, flanked by her husband and her teen-aged brother, Edward. Neddy burst into tears the instant he saw his father.

Martha tried to speak, but was unable to make a sound.

John Fontaine was forced to tell his father-in-law the news. "It's —Mrs. Henry, sir."

Scarcely realizing what he was doing, Patrick swept an arm around Neddy's thin shoulders and drew the sobbing boy closer.

Martha forced herself to speak. "It happened very suddenly, Papa, right after supper. Neddy took her a bowl of soup—and suddenly he called me." Her voice broke, but she stood erect, fists clenched. "She smiled, but I don't think she recognized me. She —she said, 'Tell P.H. I love him.' And then she closed her eyes."

Neddy's sobs became louder, more racking.

"She suffered no pain, Papa." Martha's voice was high and thin. "I'm sure of it." She was unable to continue.

"We thought her much improved these past few days, sir," John Fontaine said. "When Martha and I arrived at the house a little before supper time tonight, she was in very high spirits. She had been reading the accounts of your great speech in the newspapers from New York and Philadelphia that you'd sent to her, and she seemed very pleased. I know she was proud and excited." He searched in vain for something else to say.

Patrick leaned down to kiss the brow of his weeping son, then embraced his daughter for a moment, and almost buckled when she clung to him.

A militia sergeant stood nearby, making no attempt to hide his curiosity.

"Have my horse saddled, will you?" Patrick called to him, his voice so strained and rasping that it didn't sound like his own.

"Sure, Mr. Henry." The man hurried off to the stables behind the Raleigh.

"John, take Martha and Neddy to my room at the inn. They can rest there for the night. Pack my saddlebags, if you will, and I'll come for them shortly." Patrick was too stunned to feel anything other than a dull, aching sense of emptiness, but knew he had to maintain rigid self-control. If he allowed himself even a faint sense of sorrow, he would break down completely.

"We're going to ride with you, Papa," Martha said, and sounded remarkably like her mother.

Patrick turned away quickly, nodded and made his way back through the main room of the Raleigh. The glare of the oil lamps blinded him, tobacco fumes and the smoke rising from Virginia-made candles burned his eyes and gagged him. He raised his hand to loosen his neckcloth, but fumbled with the folds.

Jefferson looked up as he came into the Apollo room, and saw at once that he was deathly pale, but was too sensitive to ask any questions.

"I must go home for a few days—on personal business." Patrick realized he sounded stupidly wooden, but was afraid he would be rendered inarticulate if he tried to explain that his wife had died.

139

5

A heavy April rain fell on the mourners from six counties who had gathered to pay their last respects to Sarah Shelton Henry, but no one sought refuge indoors. The garden she had loved and tended had been selected by her husband and children as her last resting place, and they stood together, apart from all the others, at the foot of the open grave. Patrick's uncle, the Reverend Mr. Henry, had come out of retirement to conduct the Anglican funeral service, and his voice, still deep and powerful, rose above the patter of the rain and the weeping of the women.

"I am the resurrection and the life: he that believeth in me, though he were dead, yet shall he live. And whosoever liveth and believeth in me shall never die . . ."

Sarah's father and Patrick's parents sat together on plain chairs of pine at one side of the grave, and old Mrs. Henry, her face heavily veiled, pressed a handkerchief to her mouth. Behind them stood the Dandridge family, keeping a close watch over Patrick, who had insisted on making all of the arrangements himself. Not once had he broken down, but his friends were afraid that in this moment of intense sorrow he might collapse.

Yet, in spite of their fears, he stood erect, unmindful of the rain. His face was waxen, his eyes hooded, and not even those closest to him could guess the depth of his agony. His self-control had been remarkable from the outset of the ordeal, and did not waver now.

At his request, no sermon was preached. Instead, Richard Henry Lee read excerpts from the Books of Psalms and Isaiah. *"Thus saith the Lord, Keep ye judgment, and do justice: for my salvation is near to come, and my righteousness to be revealed . . ."*

Martha Henry Fontaine leaned heavily on the arm of her husband, but followed her father's example and was dry-eyed. Her younger brothers and sisters did not weep, either, but stared bleakly at the coffin of hand-rubbed oak made by a carpenter on Colonel Washington's estate.

Only old Isobel, who had served the family for so many years, was unable to restrain her grief, and as Lee's reading came to an end she fainted. Several members of the household staff quietly carried her away.

The Reverend Mr. Henry intoned a final prayer, then threw a handful of dirt onto the coffin. Patrick stopped, picked up still more dirt with a cold, unfeeling hand, and followed his uncle's example. The ceremony was over, and a burial detail, directed by Peter, waited for the mourners to leave before filling in the grave.

Those who had been invited to the service moved toward the house, and others walked quietly to their waiting horses and carriages. Sarah's father and Patrick's parents were helped from their seats and strong hands supported them as they made their way to the mansion. Patrick signaled to his children, and after a moment they, too, drifted off.

The bereaved widower stood alone at the foot of the grave. Several of his colleagues on the War Committee halted and glanced at each other, questioning whether one or two should go to him. But Jefferson, always so conscious of the feelings of others, shook his head. Colonel Washington concurred, and the group continued toward the house.

Patrick looked steadily at the box containing the mortal remains of the only woman he had ever loved. "Almighty God," he murmured aloud, "be good to her, for she was kind and gentle in all her dealings. Love her, for she followed Your injunction and loved her neighbor more than herself. Cherish her, for she was true to Your trust, cherishing all whom she held dear."

He bowed his head, closed his eyes for an instant and then turned away, walking rapidly in order to join his children before they reached the house. His step was leaden and he felt crushed by the tragedy, but knew he had to find new strength for the trials ahead. Sarah would not have wanted him to neglect his duty, and the people of Virginia, of all America, needed leadership in the travail that awaited the living.

6

News that shots had been exchanged by British soldiers and Massachusetts militiamen in the villages of Lexington and Concord on the morning of April 19 swept through the colonies like a hurricane. The war had come at last, and only General Gage, the British commander in Boston, misjudged the gravity of the situation. He considered the incident so insignificant that the report he sent to his superiors in London was brief, almost casual. But Americans knew better, and armed volunteers from every colony, acting solely on their own initiative, set out for Massachusetts.

In Virginia, Lord Dunmore became panicky. A detachment of royal marines from the armed schooner *H.M.S. Magdalen* came ashore in the hours before dawn on a night late in April. Acting under the governor's specific instructions, they entered the Williamsburg Arsenal, for more than fifty years the storage place for the colony's arms and gunpowder. Three of Dunmore's personal carriages were waiting there, and the marines piled fifteen half-barrels of gunpowder into them, then carried the precious powder to the *Magdalen*.

Word of the incident spread quickly, and the militia companies of Fredericksburg, Prince William County, and Albemarle County mobilized and requested permission from Colonel Washington to march on the capital. Peyton Randolph, the only member of the War Committee in Williamsburg at the time, received assurances from the governor that the matter would be adjusted to the satisfaction of everyone concerned. The representatives of fourteen companies of light horse were gathered at Fredericksburg, and Randolph, who hated violence, sent the governor's message to them, together with his own observation that Dunmore intended to keep his word.

The following day young Henry Lee, a nineteen-year-old graduate of the College of New Jersey whose father was Richard Henry Lee's cousin, appeared in Hanover County. He went first to the home of John Syme, and after a brief conversation they rode together to Scotchtown, where Patrick was putting his wife's affairs in order before returning to his War Committee work. His half brother and the young visitor found him in the library, going through Sarah's letters and other papers.

There were deep smudges beneath Patrick's eyes, and his suit of unrelieved black made him look far older than his thirty-nine years.

But he greeted his guests with his usual cordiality and, waving them to seats, offered them a choice of porter or mead.

"I'll take neither, Mr. Henry," Harry Lee replied quickly. "Only urgent business would force me to intrude on you at a time like this."

"I realized when you walked in that this is no ordinary call of condolence," Patrick replied. "But the dust on your boots is thick, and I'm sure you're in need of refreshment." He summoned a servant with the ivory-handled bell that had been Sarah's favorite, then turned back to the young man and raised an eyebrow.

"I've been in Fredericksburg," young Lee said, and told him about Peyton Randolph's letter. "The representatives of the militia companies," he concluded bitterly, "decided to accept the governor's word and have dispersed to their homes."

Patrick was shocked. "That wasn't wise. A blow must be struck sooner or later, and in my opinion it should be struck at once, before an overwhelming British force enters Virginia. Far too many people—including the commanders of militia companies, it seems—still regard the governor with almost superstitious awe. That spell must be broken, or we'll never develop our military resources!"

John Syme smiled grimly. "You see, Harry? I told you my brother would cut to the heart of the problem immediately."

"Delay would be fatal to Virginia's self-confidence." Patrick was concentrating, and paid little heed to John's remark. "If we send word to Colonel Washington and wait for him to summon the county commanders to another meeting, at least a week will pass before we put men on the march. Dunmore must be challenged immediately, or we'll lose our initiative."

"That's my feeling, Mr. Henry," young Lee said eagerly. "That gunpowder belongs to the people, not Lord Dunmore, and if he's allowed to escape punishment for this crime, Virginia will continue to let him exercise authority over us."

"Oh, he must make restitution, or our pride will be shattered. This is an impossible situation." Again Patrick rang for the servant. "Bring me the brace of pistols at the bottom of my chest of drawers," he told the man, "and the saber that the Whigs gave me as a birthday gift last year."

It hadn't occurred to John Syme that the grieving widower might want to go into the field himself, and he became alarmed. "What do you have in mind, P.H.?" It was difficult to break himself of the habit of calling Patrick by his initials, as Sarah had always done.

"We'll ride into Hanover, and I'll call up our own militia company. We can be on the road to Williamsburg within two hours."

Young Lee's eyes gleamed.

But John remained sober. "There are others who are capable of leading this expedition," he said. "Will Christian has been drilling recruits—"

"I'll expect Will to ride with me as my second-in-command." Patrick was unyielding. "The officers and men of the Hanover County company elected me their Captain, and their faith in me would be destroyed if I gave command of this little venture to someone else."

John could be stubborn, too. "Parliament's order for your arrest has never been rescinded. You'll be playing into Dunmore's hands —and giving him the excuse he needs to have you taken on board a warship as a traitor."

"He'll have to catch me first." Patrick smiled for the first time since Sarah's death. "My mind is made up. It's far better that I do something constructive than sit here brooding. I'll ask Martha to take charge here for a few days while I'm away, and maybe you'll be good enough to look in on the children now and again."

John was insulted. "Hellfire, P.H.," he said indignantly, "I'm coming with you! I'm as tired as anybody else of bending my knee to Lord Dunmore!"

7

The Hanover County company of light horse, two hundred and five strong, set out for Williamsburg at two o'clock in the afternoon on May 2. At the beginning of the ride Harry Lee was the only non-Hanoverian in the group, but word of the enterprise spread quickly, and fifty volunteers from Louisa County, who had ridden hard, joined the company shortly before nightfall. Patrick called a halt at a small inn about sixteen miles from the capital, and the delighted owner offered free accommodations to all the officers, but they preferred to sleep in the fields with their men.

Cooking fires were lighted, and in the next two hours men began to arrive from other counties. A party of forty militiamen from Henrico, most of them Richmond residents, were the first to appear on the scene, and were soon followed by mounted squads from New Kent, Chesterfield, and King George Counties.

When Patrick took a roll call at dawn, he was surprised and pleased to discover that he now commanded a small army of more than four hundred and fifty, each with his own horse, firearms, and emergency food supplies. The late arrivals all told the same story: news of the venture was spreading swiftly through the colony, and thousands of men, some of them organized in militia companies, others acting on their personal initiative, were hurrying to join the expedition.

Three horsemen from Williamsburg who appeared at sunrise, as the men were finishing their breakfast, told Patrick that an atmosphere of panic pervaded the capital. Marines had been sent from the frigate *Fowey* to help protect the Governor's person, and Lady Dunmore had left with their daughters during the night for an undisclosed destination. The two companies of Redcoats in the town were throwing up an earthwork barricade around the Governor's Palace, and the Loyalists of Williamsburg, expecting the worst, had sought refuge with Lord Dunmore.

Patrick promptly revised his tactics. Young Lee, who displayed the intelligence typical of his family, was sent to Lord Dunmore with a verbal message. "Tell him," Patrick said, "that I want no bloodshed and that I'm sure he shares my desire for an amicable settlement. But make it clear to him that I cannot restrain honest patriots who believe—with good cause—that the people have been robbed of property needed for their own defense. Tell him it must be returned at once, and I give him my word this army will disperse the moment we receive the gunpowder."

Harry Lee blinked incredulously. "You don't think he'll actually give it back, Mr. Henry?"

"Of course not. Dunmore may not be the brightest of men, but he's no imbecile. So I'll offer him an alternative. If he'll send me the sum of three hundred and thirty pounds in gold, today, we can buy an equivalent amount of gunpowder from the arsenal in Delaware."

"Three hundred and thirty pounds will buy a whale of a lot more than fifteen half-barrels, sir!"

"I'm well aware of it, Harry. That amount should net us at least twenty full barrels. We're going to need every ounce of it, too."

An escort of eight volunteers, one from each of the counties now represented in the force, accompanied Lee on his journey. Patrick settled down in the little village of Doncastle's Ordinary, in New Kent County, to await his emissary's return, and through the day his army kept growing. At noon he found himself in command of three thousand men, and by mid-afternoon there were more than four thousand in the camp.

Some wanted to push on to Williamsburg, but Patrick rode through the camp, calling the men to him several hundred at a time, and explaining the situation in detail. His logic was unassailable, and the radicals simmered down.

Some of the higher ranking officers who had joined the expedition disapproved of Patrick's familiarity with the militiamen, and Colonel Woodford acted as their spokesman when he said, "Soldiers obey orders, Patrick. They aren't members of an assembly who need to be persuaded and cajoled."

"They're free Americans, like you and me," Patrick retorted. "If there's to be a battle, I believe they'll fight all the harder now that they understand our situation."

Harry Lee and his party returned to Doncastle's Ordinary at sundown, and with them rode Richard Corbin, a member of the governor's personal staff who was accompanied by his own escort of eight Redcoats. Corbin had the money with him, and the Virginians cheered when he handed it to Patrick, who signed a lengthy receipt for it. The British cavalrymen sat rigidly in their saddles, staring out into space over the heads of the colonials.

Patrick's jubilation was tempered by his sympathy for the British professional soldiers. No man enjoyed being humiliated, and it was difficult for troops who had always enjoyed the respect of Virginians to bow to the superior force of a semi-organized rabble. Young farmers in homespun linsey-woolsey and artisans from the towns in cowhide breeches shouted insults at the Redcoats, and Patrick, somewhat ashamed of their manners, had to raise his voice above their jeers so Corbin could hear him.

"Now that our business is concluded, Mr. Corbin," he said, "I hope you'll join me in a toast to the future friendship of Great Britain and Virginia."

Corbin bowed coldly, and demonstrated greater courage than wisdom by replying, "Our business is concluded, sir. I don't drink with traitors." He mounted his horse, the cavalrymen moved into formation around him, and they rode off in the direction of the capital.

"Let's hang the bastards!" an angry militiaman called.

Others took up the cry, and Patrick hoisted himself onto the back of the nearest horse before his followers could translate words into action. He raised both hands, and gradually they became quiet, although some were still peering down the road after the Redcoats.

"You're under arms in the service of Virginia, lads," Patrick told them. "You're not a mob of unruly ruffians. Now is the time to learn a few basic rules of warfare. An envoy from the enemy enjoys our full protection. Any man who attacks Mr. Corbin or his escort will be responsible to me."

The men remained surly, and scores of them muttered to each other.

Patrick held aloft the bag of gold. "We've won the day, boys, don't you see? This money will buy us more than twice the powder taken from the arsenal. Go back to your homes until you're needed —and save your shot!" He knew, as the majority present apparently did not, that the governor would be forced to retaliate. "Take my word for it, you'll have all the fighting you want—and more— in the months ahead."

8

BE IT PROCLAIMED
To All Who Dwell in Virginia

Whereas I have been informed from undoubted authority that a certain Patrick Henry, of the county of Hanover, and a number of deluded followers, have taken up arms, chosen their officers, and styling themselves an independent company, have marched out of their county, encamped, and put themselves in a posture of war, and have written and dispatched letters to divers parts of the country, exciting the people to join in these rebellious and outrageous practices, to the great terror of all His Majesty's faithful subjects, and in open defiance of law and government; and

Whereas the said Patrick Henry and his followers have committed other acts of violence, particularly in extorting from His Majesty's receiver-general for the Colony of Virginia the sum of three hundred and thirty pounds, under pretense of replacing the powder I thought proper to order from the magazine;

Whence it undeniably appears that there is no longer the least security for the life or property of any man:

Wherefore, I have thought proper, with the advice of His Majesty's council, and in His Majesty's name, to issue this my proclamation, strictly charging all persons, upon their allegiance, not to aid, abet or give countenance to the said Patrick Henry, or any others concerned in such unwarrantable conduct, but on the contrary to oppose them and their designs by every means;

Which designs must, otherwise, inevitably involve the whole country in the most direful calamity, as they will call for the vengeance of offended Majesty and the insulted laws to be exerted here, to vindicate the constitutional authority of government.

Given under my hand and seal of the Colony, at Williamsburg, this 6th day of May, 1775, and in the fifteenth year of His Majesty's reign.

Dunmore

God save the King.

9

Annoyed and upset, Patrick paced up and down the portico of his house, his spurs jangling. "I willingly admit your arguments," he told his daughter and son-in-law. "General Gage tried to capture Sam Adams and John Hancock, and they were lucky to escape. I'm sure Dunmore would like to make me his prisoner and send me off to London as a prize catch—a genuine rebel in chains. But I don't need an escort on the road to Philadelphia! I intend to ride through friendly territory, and I'm embarrassed." He pointed accusingly at a body of more than a hundred horsemen assembled on the lawn.

John Fontaine started to speak, but Martha silenced him with a glance, indicating that she considered herself better able to deal with her glowering father. "All the arrangements have been made, Papa. John will go all the way to Philadelphia with you, and will stay with you while you're there. I take the rumors of Loyalist kidnaping plots seriously, even if you don't. Really, it will be a convenience to everyone if you'll behave sensibly. I'll move back here to look after the family, and all of us will be able to breathe more easily."

"I refuse to give Dunmore and the Loyalists a chance to call me a coward!" Patrick jabbed a finger at his son-in-law. "Tell your friends to disperse, or I'll be forced to treat them inhospitably."

John Fontaine coughed apologetically.

"Tell them to leave, Papa, but they won't," Martha said. "They're under orders to take you all the way to the Maryland boundary, where another escort will be waiting. And there will be still another in Pennsylvania." His astonished rage was so great that she couldn't help giggling.

"Who gave these orders?" Patrick demanded.

"Colonel Washington made the arrangements. Your friends know how touchy you are, and Mr. Lee asked me not to say anything unless you became impossible, which is what you've now done." Martha was totally unafraid of her father.

He peered at her suspiciously. "I suppose Colonel Washington acted at your instigation."

"In the first place, he didn't. Everyone has been worried about you since Lord Dunmore issued his proclamation. In the second place I'm not a witness being questioned on the stand by the eminent counselor, Mr. Henry. And above all, I beg you to use some of the common sense you've preached since I was a baby. Your speech to the Burgesses and your march on Williamsburg have made you the most renowned man in all America. I'm sure the Loyalists would call you the most infamous. They'll take any risk to capture you, and if you should be killed in the process, your murderer would be granted a royal pardon. He might even be knighted."

Patrick realized his reputation had grown enormously since the gunpowder incident, but believed both his fame and his danger were being grossly exaggerated. "For the last time, I don't want all the fuss!"

Martha played her trump card. "If Mama were here," she said quietly, "it's what she would have wanted for you. That's why I'm insisting, in her stead and in her name."

Patrick's intransigence wilted, and he turned wearily to his son-in-law. "Have my horse brought from the stables, John. I'm in your hands."

10

Crowds gathered at every town on the road to Philadelphia for a glimpse of the man who had defied Lord Dunmore, and the citizens of the largest city in America gave Patrick such a riotous welcome that he flushed scarlet as he and John Fontaine were escorted in triumph to their lodgings. The Continental Congress was already in session when he reached Carpenters' Hall, and the sedate John Hancock, who had just been elected president, led the members in a standing ovation of greeting.

For the first time in his life, Patrick was speechless.

He soon recovered his voice, however, as the delegates worked feverishly to prepare for the war that everyone had hoped to avoid. He and Richard Henry Lee were joint sponsors of a resolution appointing Washington as commander-in-chief of an embryo Continental Army, with the rank of major general. John Adams confided to his friend from Virginia that he had unwittingly made a personal enemy of Hancock, who had fancied that he would be offered the post. And Edmund Pendleton, who had long been jealous of what he considered a Lee-Henry-Washington clique, made no attempt to hide his irritation.

But there were far more important matters to consider than the ruffled feathers of irritated peacocks. While the Congress sat, debated, and organized, American irregulars led by Colonel Benedict Arnold of Connecticut and Colonel Ethan Allen of the Vermont District captured Fort Ticonderoga in New York, the gateway to Canada. A few weeks later, in mid-June, the Battle of Bunker Hill was fought in Boston, and Washington, who was working twenty hours out of every twenty-four in an attempt to muster and train, arm and supply his forces, create an efficient corps of officers and obtain enough cannon for two or three brigades of artillery, decided to lay formal siege to General Gage's army, which was already penned up in Boston by volunteer militiamen.

Jefferson, serving his first term in the Congress, had just won great applause for a pamphlet he had written, *A Summary View of the Rights of America.* Patrick nominated him for the chairmanship of a committee ordered to draw up a Declaration of the Causes and Necessity of Taking Up Arms, and the resolution was passed by unanimous vote, the members of several smaller delegations privately grumbling that all the best plums of office were going to Virginia and Massachusetts.

The Congress authorized itself to print money, and Dr. Franklin's offer of his printing presses for the purpose was gratefully accepted. Committees were set up to establish a Continental Navy, deal with the Indian nations of the frontier and supervise intercolonial commerce. And a special group, headed by Franklin himself, was assigned the delicate task of seeking financial aid and arms from Britain's traditional enemies in Europe, France and Spain.

The hope that Canada might join her neighbors to the south was fading rapidly. Quebec was the only town of consequence in the sparsely settled province, and the presence there of three fully equipped Redcoat divisions made it unlikely that the Canadians would dare to rebel. Nevertheless a new Congressional committee to encourage the northern colonists was appointed.

Hancock, who was the wealthiest of New England's merchants, made himself chairman of a committee to foster foreign trade and increase the American merchant fleet. John Adams was given the difficult task of grappling with unfamiliar problems of administration, and asked Patrick, already burdened with assignments to five other committees, to become his co-chairman. The offer was accepted, and at late evening suppers in a New Tavern booth the pair hammered out ways to transport and deliver mail between the colonies, establish permanent liaison between the thirteen legislatures and deal with such relatively minor but thorny questions as the extradition of criminals from one colony to another. For a time they wanted to codify the thirteen different law codes, too, but eventually abandoned the idea, being sufficiently realistic to realize that no colony would willingly give up any of its legal statutes for those of another.

Patrick also served with Adams and Richard Henry Lee as members of a steering or executive committee headed by Hancock, and in order to crowd their conferences into their schedules, all four developed the habit of rising before dawn in order to discuss developments at breakfast. Everyone was overburdened with work and carrying too many responsibilities, so it was inevitable that the quartet should be suffering from fatigue and bad tempers. Adams was sometimes waspish, Lee became sarcastic and Hancock, long accustomed to having orders obeyed instantly in his mercantile empire, raised his voice and pounded the breakfast table. Patrick was the calmest member of the committee, but when his temper exploded, the others learned to remove tankards and platters of food from his reach.

"There are times," Adams told him one day, "when you display all the bad traits of your Scots and French ancestors."

Patrick had just recovered his poise after delivering a tirade against some Congressional delegates from the smaller colonies who held up debate with claims that their interests were being neglected. Good humored and in command of himself again, he smiled and waved a hand. "You New Englanders," he retorted, "aren't just of pure English stock. You're all direct descendants of Oliver Cromwell and his Roundheads. Puritans never lose their tempers. That would be sinful. You simmer like that tasteless salt codfish you eat, and you never realize that losing one's temper can be as satisfying to a man of our age as kissing a pretty girl is to a boy of twenty."

The mutual exchange of insults became almost a ritual, and out of the greater mutual understanding, combined with the knowledge that all delegates were working toward common goals, grew tight bonds of personal friendship. "We who worked together that hot summer in Philadelphia," Hancock said many years later, "were members of the 1775 Club. We learned that the differences in our accents and regional attitudes weren't important, but that the freedoms we cherished in common were paramount. We were, I think, the first true Americans."

One morning in late July, when the Declaration of the Causes and Necessity of Taking Up Arms had been rewritten for the third time, Jefferson was invited to take breakfast with the steering committee. Platters of scrapple fried with bananas, beefsteak, and scrambled egg pies, and clams broiled with bear bacon were placed on the table, and Hancock turned to the newcomer as soon as the barmaids departed and closed the doors of the City Tavern's private dining room.

"We're anxious to the hear the reading of your declaration, sir," the president said.

Jefferson was still painfully shy. "You're an accomplished orator, Mr. Hancock, and Mr. Adams' speeches are always very clear." He glanced across the table at his fellow Virginians. "And I know better than to compete with Richie or P.H." He thrust several sheets of parchment at them. "Read it for me, would you? I'm afraid I'd stumble." He lowered his head and speared a clam on his two-pronged fork.

Patrick took the document, and his rich voice filled the room as he read Jefferson's arguments. "We are reduced to the alternative of choosing an unconditional submission to the tyranny of irritated ministers, or resistance by force. The latter is our choice. We have counted the cost of this contest, and find nothing so dreadful as voluntary slavery."

The Declaration presented a summary of the familiar grievances that were impelling the colonies to take drastic action, but left the door open if England wanted a peaceful solution of the dispute. The Whigs in Parliament were thanked for the "nobility" of their support and for recognizing "the justice of our cause." In three different passages, Jefferson had extended an olive branch, and in

153

the most emphatic of them had written, "We mean not to dissolve that union which has so long and so happily subsisted between us."

The Declaration ended on a conciliatory note, too, and Patrick meant every word as he read the final prayer, "May the Ruler of the Universe dispose our adversaries to reconcile on reasonable terms."

Everyone congratulated Jefferson on his accomplishment, and there were no suggestions of further changes in the document. Gradually the mood of exuberance changed, and the tired men lapsed into silence. Only Hancock enjoyed his usual hearty appetite, eating large portions of every dish and washing down his food with glasses of the watered Spanish Madeira he had brought with him from his private stores.

Patrick scarcely bothered to toy with his meal. He had lost a great deal of weight since Sarah's death, and knew he should eat, but the mere sight of food made him slightly queasy, so he carefully wiped his knife on his napkin, put it into its leather sheath and dropped it into his inner coat pocket. It was the last blade of English steel he would be able to buy for a long time to come, so he treated it with care.

"Tom," he said mournfully, "I'm sorry you had to spend so much effort and time on a paper that will do no good."

The others were jolted, and looked at him.

"Maybe it won't be wasted, though," he continued. "Maybe it will help our friends in England to bring about an accommodation in a year or two."

"You've been listening to Sam again," John Adams declared.

"No, to my own mind and heart. I'm as responsible as any man—in Congress or out of it—for our present situation, and I won't try to deny it. I keep thinking of a line from Seneca. 'Bonitas non est pessimis esse meliorem.'"

There was no need for him to translate. All of his colleagues held college degrees, so all were thoroughly familiar with Latin and knew the words meant "To be better than the worst is not goodness."

"You blame yourself too much, P.H.," Lee told him. "No one man on either side could have prevented this war, any more than one alone could have started it."

"That doesn't make life easier to live." To the astonishment of his friends, Patrick poured himself some rum from a jug that sat in the center of the table.

Lee and Jefferson, who knew him better than the New Englanders, exchanged quick glances. He had not wavered since his tragic personal loss, but the strain appeared to be telling now. It was as unusual for him to drink strong spirits as it was to hear him sound downhearted over the war.

"I have three sons," he said, "and last night I received a joint letter from them. All three, even the youngest, are enlisting in a Virginia battalion of Continentals. It's wrong of me to burden you with my doubts, gentlemen, and I beg your forgiveness. All I know is that if we've been wrong to push our dispute with England beyond a point of peaceful negotiation, the Almighty will punish me for my errors."

Adams tried to tease him. "You've told me I have a New England conscience, but I think Virginia breeds the same kind."

Patrick was unable to return his smile. "I'm not losing faith in our cause, John. Don't misunderstand me. Eventually justice must triumph. But right now, here in Philadelphia, we're unleashing all the furies of hell. The legions of Lucifer are on the march, and no one, not even Satan, knows where they'll lead us before we'll find the sunlight of freedom at the end of the road."

11

The Continental Congress adjourned on August 1, and the delegates from Virginia left Philadelphia that same day. The Burgesses were scheduled to meet in Richmond nine days later in a rump session, under the name of a convention, in order to avoid a brand of illegality. Lord Dunmore, still entrenched in Williamsburg, was continuing to demonstrate great personal courage by remaining at his post, and everyone in the colony was afraid that troops from Halifax or London might be landed to reinforce his authority.

The Congressional representatives spent only a day or two at home, and then went to Richmond, where they began anew their task of governmental organization, duplicating their Philadelphia efforts on a smaller scale. Party lines had disappeared, and the labels of Whig and Tory were discarded. All men faithful to Virginia had become Patriots, and the Loyalists who refused to forswear allegiance to the Crown were no longer taking an active part in the colony's public business. Some of the more prominent, like elderly John Randolph, were hastily putting their affairs in order prior to leaving America permanently.

But old alliances and animosities were not forgotten, no matter what the Assemblymen now called themselves. Edmund Pendleton, Peyton Randolph, and Richard Bland were still the spokesmen for the wealthy minority who lived in the old tidewater counties. Richard Henry Lee and Patrick Henry were still the leaders of what had been the dominating Whig element, but their council had been enlarged to include Jefferson, for whom a new place was made, and George Mason, who occupied General Washington's former seat.

Tentative committee assignments were drawn on the day before the convention opened, and it was agreed that, for the sake of harmony with the conservatives, the gavel of the presidency should be given to Peyton Randolph. The leaders, in spite of their exhaustion, kept a firm grip on the reins of power, or so they believed.

Routine business occupied the convention during its first hours, and the members didn't get down to serious problems until midafternoon. Only a few minutes of discussion were required before legislation was passed authorizing the raising of two militia regiments immediately and a third within a period of six months.

The next item on the agenda prepared in advance of the session by the leadership was the appointment of a colonel-in-chief, who would also become the commanding officer of the First Regiment. It was taken for granted that, when the third unit was formed, he would be promoted to the rank of brigadier general. A number of French and Indian War veterans were eligible for the top post, among them Harrison and Colonel Woodford, both of whom had served in the field with General Washington and had earned his respect. Woodford was favored, in part because Harrison was reluctant to give up his seat in the Burgesses, and had won the support of Pendleton as well as that of Tyler, Jefferson, and some of the other prominent younger men.

No more than three nominations would be accepted, Randolph told the members, and opened the floor for the purpose.

Assemblyman Clement Davis, a newcomer, leaped to his feet. "Mr. President!"

Randolph had to consult the clerk before saying, "The chair recognizes the right honorable gentleman from New Kent."

"Mr. President, fellow Burgesses, I reckon we won't need a long fandangle of an election. There's one man who ought to be our colonel-in-chief, and he has all the qualifications. The boys respect him, he's proved himself fearless and he's rightly earned his spurs. I had the honor of serving under him when he pulled the chin whiskers of old Dunmore, and I tell you plain and true, he's a great soldier." The enthusiastic Davis paused for breath. "I nominate the man who deserves to sit his horse next to our own General Washington, Captain Patrick Henry of Hanover!"

The House roared its approval, some members standing.

Patrick looked dazed by the unexpected move.

Lee, sitting beside him, chuckled and waited for the cheers to die down before his friend declined. Any man would appreciate the honor, but Patrick was a statesman whose administrative and oratorical talents would be wasted in uniform. Jefferson, who now occupied a seat in the front row, grinned broadly, and George Mason, sitting directly behind him, shook his head.

Patrick recovered his composure and, to the astonishment of his friends, turned in his seat and bowed from the waist to Davis.

Lee had to lean close and shout in his ear to make himself heard above the hubbub. "Decline quickly, P.H., or they'll call for your unanimous election!"

The pleasure faded from Patrick's eyes. "I'll serve in whatever capacity the representatives of the people want me," he replied sharply.

Lee was shocked, and Jefferson's silent shrug indicated that he, too, thought Patrick had taken leave of his senses.

The new members, sitting in the rear, stamped their feet in unison. "Henry!" they shouted. "Hen-ry!"

"Close the nominations, Mr. President," someone called. "We've got our man! Three cheers for Colonel Henry, boys!"

The unpainted pine walls of the new building shook as a mighty roar went up.

Randolph was unable to stem the tide. Benjamin Harrison leaned over to Lee and they consulted frantically, but it soon became evident that unless Patrick himself refused the nomination, he would be elected by immediate acclamation.

It was equally obvious that he had no intention of declining. For the first time since Sarah's death he looked genuinely happy, and he made only token efforts to resist when Davis and several others raced down the center aisle, hoisted him to their shoulders and began an impromptu parade.

President Randolph struck the table with his gavel repeatedly but in vain.

Edmund Pendleton, his face pale, came across the aisle to the dumfounded former Whigs. "If this is one of your political tricks," he said, his voice quivering with rage, "I don't appreciate it! I respect Mr. Henry, but he's no more a military man than I am. How dare we place our sons under his command? This is an outrage, gentlemen!"

Lee caught his breath. "I swear to you, Edmund, that we've had no hand in this idiocy."

The new members were singing the new marching song, "Yankee Doodle," that was sweeping through the colonies, and Jefferson's voice was inaudible when he cried, "Look at him!" He pointed, and the others turned to the paraders.

Patrick's smile was almost beatific, his eyes shone and spots of color burned in his cheeks. No matter what the opinion of his friends, he was already glorying in his new role.

12

General Washington's open letter to the Burgesses was a model of subtlety and tact. "Colonel Henry will be sorely missed by those who make and administer the laws," he said. "His skills as a counselor are unique, as are his executive talents. No other man has won such loyalty from all the people of Virginia, who wisely placed their trust in him. Now his voice will be heard in the field, rather than in the chambers of the civilians who must and ever shall be the true rulers of America."

Every literate man in the colony save one was aware of the general's hint. But Patrick, attired in a splendid new uniform of blue-and-buff, was too busy riding from county to county with the members of his staff to heed the delicate words of an old friend who had now become his military superior.

Woodford, who had been given the Second Regiment, summed up his own impressions in a confidential letter to the Assembly leaders. "Colonel Henry visited my headquarters yesterday," he wrote, "and left it a shambles. He delivered three orations to my troops, all of them inspiring, as only he can inspire men. But the orders he issued me, both written and verbal, are confusing and contradictory; violating, as they do, every rule of warfare in their insistence that the soldiers of each company be given a voice in its management, I find them disruptive.

"I can make neither cock's head nor mallard's tail of them, and must ignore them if the Second Regiment is to be made ready for combat with the foe."

The Convention's Committee of Safety, which was headed by Edmund Pendleton, with George Mason as vice-chairman, wanted to give the First Regiment to Hugh Mercer of Fredericksburg and promote Woodford to the top command. Mason visited Patrick in the field, hoping it might be possible to persuade him to resign, but even the broadest hints fell on deaf ears. Patrick was finding relief by absenting himself from Scotchtown, with its ever-present reminders of Sarah.

"The jealousy of petty men," he told Mason, "can neither hinder nor halt the performance of my duty."

Late in the autumn the situation became serious. The British garrison was reinforced by the arrival of two full battalions of regulars. Lord Dunmore slipped out of Williamsburg with them, and his numbers were soon augmented by a band of Loyalist volunteers. Too weak to meet the Patriots in open battle, yet strong enough to inflict damage on American property, this force began to conduct raids on towns and prosperous individual plantations, burning grain warehouses and meat storage sheds, slaughtering cattle and, wherever possible, otherwise weakening the Americans.

Woodford promptly marched against Dunmore, determined to scatter the governor's troops or drive them out of the colony. Patrick was annoyed because his subordinate had not waited for orders, and was further distressed because his own regiment was not yet ready for action.

Benjamin Harrison felt compelled to write him a strong letter, bluntly asking him to resign his commission and return to the civilian leadership for the good of Virginia. Patrick's reply was indirect. He sent no answer to Harrison, and instead wrote a letter giving up his seat in the Continental Congress.

When the news reached Williamsburg, where the Burgesses had reconvened after Lord Dunmore's evacuation of the capital, Patrick's friends decided something definitive had to be done. Richard Henry Lee rode at once to Hanover County, where Martha had become the mistress of Scotchtown.

She received the visitor in the drawing room, and he sipped a tankard of Patrick's mead, but was too embarrassed to open the subject that had brought him there. "What news do you have of Captain Fontaine?"

"I've had a letter written from Cambridge just last week. He's been made a member of General Washington's personal staff, and he's very pleased." The young woman hesitated for only a moment. "You're here to talk about my father."

"Well, yes." He found her frankness disconcerting.

"He's behaving like a madman. I—I think Mama's death has unhinged his mind."

"I wouldn't go quite that far, Martha. He's a proud man who lost sight of his goals when he was offered a high military command, and now he's reluctant to admit he made a mistake." Lee placed his tankard on a table of inlaid hardwood and, still uncomfortable, fingered his snuffbox. "The problem appears almost insoluble. He's the most popular man in Virginia, you see, and the people regard him as the primary symbol of resistance to the Crown. The Assembly has the power to retract his commission, but that would destroy the confidence of the whole colony in the Patriot cause."

"Then what can be done?"

"The first step has already been taken, and that's why I'm here. Two of his three battalions are as prepared for combat as they'll ever be, so they've been detached from his personal command and given to Colonel Woodford by the Committee of Safety. There's no question that it's an insult to your father. You understand him better than anyone—"

"I'm not so sure of that, Mr. Lee. I'm afraid Mama was the only one who really knew him."

"We must depend on your judgment, because there's none better. I'm leaving this week for a Congress meeting in Philadelphia, and there are good reasons for trying to determine your father's attitude before I go. What I want to know is this: Do you think this Committee of Safety slap will cause him to resign from the militia?"

"Oh, no!" Martha was emphatic. "He'll feel that his honor has been damaged, and he'll do everything in his power to vindicate it. The removal of the two battalions from his jurisdiction will make him more determined than ever to keep his command and assert his authority."

Lee sighed heavily. "That's what I feared."

Martha's eyes widened. "What will you do?"

"Our plan is only tentative at the moment, so I'd rather not discuss it."

"I'd hate—to see Papa hurt."

"So would I. But we must do what's necessary for him—and for America."

She nodded, fighting back tears.

"Ben Harrison has taken his place in our Congressional delegation, and Ben is a competent man, but there's only one Patrick Henry. How we'll miss him in Philadelphia! I can only pray he'll return to the work he does so well. He's needed, desperately, to help win the war."

SIX

1776

1

Early in 1776 the Military Affairs Committee of the Continental Congress incorporated Virginia's First and Second Regiments of militia into the Continental Army, and the officers of the two units were offered Continental commissions. No one was appointed commander of either the entire brigade or of the First Regiment, and Patrick Henry was sent a warrant offering him the rank of colonel, and the command of the First Regiment's First Battalion, which was still in training.

"It is enough," Patrick said, "that Edmund Pendleton tried to humiliate me through the Virginia Committee of Safety. He and my other enemies have now influenced Congress against me, and this insult is too great to bear."

He refused the offer, resigned from the militia and rode home to Hanover County.

There were patches of snow on the ground along the roads, a biting northwest wind blew steadily, and Patrick's fingers felt numb under the smart military gloves he was wearing for the last time. But he felt too miserable to be conscious of minor inconveniences, and spurred forward, not even bothering to halt at an inn for a noon meal. He had refused an escort, not wanting junior officers or troops to share the sense of disgrace that overwhelmed him. And when he finally reached Scotchtown late in the afternoon, he was relieved that his daughters were not at home.

He cut short the servants' warm welcome, and put off Peter, who was eager to talk about the business of the estate. He had neglected his own affairs for so long that another day or two wouldn't matter.

Every muscle aching, he climbed the stairs to his own bedchamber on the second floor, relieved that there, as elsewhere in the house, Martha had tactfully removed nearly all reminders of her mother. But a pier glass he had imported for Sarah was still installed in the space between the two windows that looked down across the front lawn, and in spite of his weariness he became angry when he caught a glimpse of his reflection. The dying rays of the sun picked up the gleam of the silver epaulets on his shoulders and the bright buttons on his tunic.

Patrick winced. "Henry," he said aloud, "you're an imbecile. You'll be forty years old in a few weeks, and you've been playing at soldier while the Redcoats burned Norfolk to the ground. You're lucky they let you resign. If I were Pendleton, I'd have insisted the Committee of Safety court-martial the—the impertinent minstrel play-acting at being a colonel."

He started to rip off his uniform, and to his dismay discovered that tears were rolling down his cheeks. He regained his dignity only because two servants were in his adjoining dressing room, pouring hot water into a gum-sealed cedarwood tub for his bath.

He soaked for a long time, enjoying his first real bath in months, and tried to take stock of his situation. At almost forty his life of service to his country and his family had come to an abrupt end. He was neither a military officer nor a member of the Continental Congress, and his empty seat in the Burgesses had been filled. It was useless to contemplate a return to his law practice; Will Christian was an officer in the Continentals, and all the junior members of the firm had accepted military commissions, too. Besides, as he well realized, the people of Virginia were thinking only of the war, and with their lives and property at stake, were not bothering to bring or defend civilian lawsuits.

His sons had left home, John and William having become Continental officers, while Neddy was an ensign-cadet in the militia.

For an instant his face brightened when he thought of Neddy; time passed so quickly it was difficult to picture the boy in uniform. And his daughters were even more adult. He wouldn't blame Martha if she secretly resented looking after his house instead of devoting her time and efforts to her own home. During his absence Anne had become engaged to marry Spencer Roane, one of his law clerks now serving in the Second Regiment, and Elizabeth was besieged by suitors. He had fulfilled all his functions as a father, and there was very little more he could do for any of his children.

Soldiers and civilians alike would need food, so he supposed he could devote himself to the plantation, but he had to admit to himself, candidly but painfully, that he had never been a successful farmer. Peter, who had demonstrated his efficiency for years, would continue to do well if the owner of Scotchtown allowed him to operate the plantation as he saw fit.

Patrick put on his small-clothes and slippers, then wrapped himself in a faded flannel dressing robe. Again he saw himself in the pier glass, and this time his gaze was steady. His face was haggard and wrinkled, the top of his head was almost totally bald and the fringe at the sides and back were gray. He couldn't read a word now without using his spectacles, and he guessed that enforced idleness would soon cause him to develop a paunch.

Aimlessly making his way downstairs, he knew he could blame no one but himself for his sorry state. Others, in Philadelphia and Williamsburg, were working to forge a new nation. But he, who had done as much as any man to bring about the revolution now developing, had caused himself to be banished from the ranks of the productive and useful.

Out of habit Patrick started toward his library, but paused when he saw someone in a pink silk dress standing before the drawing-room fire, warming herself. He started toward her, thinking she was one of his daughters, and by the time he saw masses of blue-black hair cascading down her back, it was too late. Dorothea Dandridge turned, her violet eyes making no secret of her pleasure.

"You've come home, Mr. Henry. Forgive me, I mean, Colonel."

"I'm just plain Patrick Henry again," he replied dryly. "I've resigned my commission. And you must pardon me. I didn't know anyone was here, or I wouldn't have come downstairs in my robe."

It was absurd to apologize to Dorothea, whom he had known so well since infancy, but she was an adult now—and exceptionally attractive.

She smiled, and a dimple appeared in her left cheek. "I'm not company, Mr. Henry. Besides, Martha asked me to spend the night with her. And you're sure to catch the ague if you stand in that draft. Please come over to the fire."

He obeyed, and warmed his hands. "Why aren't you entertaining one of your young men this evening, Dolly? I recall hearing something about you and some lad, but I can't remember who he was."

"His name is Jones, Mr. Henry, and the reason I'm not seeing him this evening is because he's gone to sea again." As always, she displayed great spirit.

The fire of hickory logs gave off considerable heat, but he still felt chilly, and shivered. "I don't know any eligible bachelors named Jones hereabouts."

"He's a Scotsman, and his name is John Paul Jones. He hates the English, and he's promised me he'll shoot one of their ships out of the water every month." Dorothea arranged a dark curl, twisting it and pulling it forward across her shoulder.

"That's quite a boast." Still shivering, Patrick frowned thoughtfully. "I know him. He's the brother of a fellow named William Paul who is a tailor in Fredericksburg. Why has he changed his name to Jones?"

She shrugged prettily. "He hasn't told me, so I haven't asked."

"If I remember rightly, he was an officer in the Royal Navy and had trouble of some sort. I met him once or twice—and he struck me as a braggart. I don't like him."

"I do." Her tone was flippant, but her eyes hardened.

"Don't be impertinent, Dorothea, or I'll be forced to speak to your father about this Jones person."

Dorothea lost her temper, and stamped a slippered foot on the polished hardwood floor. "I see anyone I fancy, sir, and I'll thank you to let me attend to my own business." Her anger drained away as swiftly as it had erupted. "Are you ill, Mr. Henry? You're shaking, and your face is as white as the lace on my petticoat." Slim fingers reached out to feel his forehead.

Patrick was still irritated. "There's nothing wrong with my health."

"It's as I thought. You have a fever. Sit down here, sir, at once." Paying no attention to his protests, she pushed him into a cushioned chair, then went to the bell-rope. "You need something to drink."

"I never touch strong spirits."

"So I've known, Mr. Henry, for about twenty of my twenty-one years." Dorothea hurried to the door and began giving orders to the servant who answered her summons.

Soon the whole house was astir. A chambermaid brought a blanket and pillow, another added logs and kindling to the fire, and Dorothea, after wrapping the blanket around Patrick, insisted he place the pillow behind his head and herself raised his feet onto a stool.

"I'm not an invalid!" he said in a loud, hoarse voice.

"You have a very unpleasant spleen, sir, and you should try to temper it. Your charm isn't enhanced by it, Mr. Henry."

"And I'm not charming!"

"Here, drink this turkey giblet soup." She handed him a pewter tankard.

"It's so hot it burns my fingers."

"Then I'll hold it for you. Gracious, Mr. Henry, you're behaving like a crochety baby, if there is such a person, instead of the most important man in Virginia." Dorothea started to laugh, but broke off sharply when she saw his expression.

Patrick had been become limp.

She held the tankard to his lips until he began to sip the steaming broth. "The Assembly will send you back to Philadelphia as soon as word of your resignation from the militia reaches Williamsburg."

"Impossible. Delegates sit in the Continental Congress for two-year terms now."

She allowed him to take the tankard from her, and flipped her curl back over her shoulder. "Surely the people of Hanover County will send you back to the Burgesses!"

"Why should they?" he asked dully. "I failed them. I let my vanity get the better of me, and I failed all of Virginia."

"That's nonsense, Mr. Henry," Dorothea said tartly. "The militia have been plagued with troubles in every colony, according to the speeches of the Congress I've been reading in the Philadelphia newspapers. You were honorably elected to a post you didn't seek, and although you may have been a trifle overly cautious, you were given no chance to prove whether you'd have been a good colonel-in-chief!"

Patrick briefly aroused himself from his lethargy. "You're the only female I've ever known who reads the political news. Why do you do it?"

"Because I want to know what's happening in America, of course."

He nodded, and his temples throbbed.

She drew up another footstool beside his chair, sat and wiped a film of perspiration from his forehead with a handkerchief she took from her sleeve.

"Don't hover over me, Dolly. I despise having people breathing down my neck."

"I wonder why it is," she murmured, "that a man always behaves like a horrid small boy when he's ill."

"I'm not ill!" Patrick's lids felt unaccountably heavy, but he opened his eyes wider to peer at her. "Besides, what do you know of men?"

"Only what I've observed. Finish your soup before it grows cold and does you no good."

"Miss Dandridge," he said, amused in spite of his misery, "you're an even more high-handed tyrant than Martha. I'm glad you're Nate's daughter, not mine."

"And I, Mr. Henry, am delighted that I'm not a blood relative of a man who feels so sorry for himself."

"Here, you young tyrant. I've taken every drop of this broth. Does that satisfy you?" Patrick's chill was gone, and he felt uncomfortably warm. Perhaps he really was running a slight fever, but he hated to admit that Dorothea might be right, and he wished that Martha would come home. Then she and her friend would disappear, and he'd be left in peace.

She looked at the porcelain and gold clock that stood on the top shelf of a corner bric-a-brac stand. "I'll wait a quarter of an hour, and if the soup hasn't cooled your blood by then, I'll send for a physician."

"I forbid it!"

"Why must you abuse yourself, sir?" Dorothea asked gently. "You've lost so much weight since dear Mrs. Henry left us that you look like one of Peter's scarebird dummies."

Everyone else avoided the subject of Sarah's death, but Dorothea spoke of her with such deep affection that he neither flinched nor took offense.

"I'm pleased that you're home, sir. You must have care and attention, so you'll be strong when Virginia calls on you again for help."

2

Patrick's illness was diagnosed as swamp fever, which he had apparently contracted when he had slept on the ground during training maneuvers.

"A man of his years," Dorothea Dandridge said in his bedchamber one day, "should know better than to act like a young boy. Lawyers and politicians develop their minds, and their bodies become prey to the elements."

"Papa takes little care of himself," Martha replied. "He needs us to look after him."

Patrick ordered them to leave the room, but they pretended not to hear him.

He had good reason to be grateful for their concern, however. His physicians bled him twice each week for a month, and he became so weak that Martha and her friend finally insisted that his treatment be changed. John Paul Jones, who paid Dorothea a brief visit after sailing north from the West Indian Islands, gave her a quantity of bark from the tropical cinchona tree that he himself found helpful for the same ailment.

The two young women tried for several days to persuade Patrick to chew the bark, and Dorothea was forced to lose her temper before he complied. His fever began to subside that same day, and thereafter he meekly chewed the bitter-tasting bark whenever ordered. Ten days later he left his bed. Isobel prepared all his favorite foods, Dorothea brought him delicacies from the Dandridge kitchen that she and her mother had cooked for him, and he was forced to eat several hearty meals every day.

"He listens to you," Martha told her friend. "It's because you treat him so much more firmly than I dare. I'm never able to forget he's my father."

Less than two weeks later Patrick began to take daily rides around his property, and soon was able to visit Nathaniel Dandridge, who brought him up to date on the war, which had been developing rapidly on many fronts. Benedict Arnold and Richard Montgomery had made a valiant effort to capture Quebec, but it failed, and the Americans were unable to hold the smaller town of Montreal, which they had taken previously. Perhaps the most spectacular military news was that the British had evacuated Boston. General Sir William Howe, who had replaced General Gage, had left discreetly, but his army was intact, and far more decisive battles were expected in the duel between him and Washington.

There had been American victories in the southern colonies, too. Lord Dunmore had withdrawn from Virginia rather than try to pit his small corps against superior forces. The biggest battle in the area had taken place in the Carolinas, where militiamen had defeated a combined Redcoat and Loyalist expedition.

Developments on the political front were less encouraging. King George had issued a proclamation formally branding the Americans as rebels and forbidding all nations to trade with them. Parliament had passed an act blockading the ports of all provinces, and a powerful Royal Navy fleet under the command of Admiral Lord Richard Howe, the general's brother, was being equipped for the purpose. The Continental Congress retaliated by openly appealing to France for help and declaring all American ports open to the merchant fleets of every nation.

Royal governors and their staffs had left every colony, and the Americans were organizing their own governments. The Whig party in England tried in vain to heal the growing rift, and the King, in a speech from the Throne, hinted broadly that he was hiring mercenary troops from the German principalities to augment the expeditionary force he intended to send across the Atlantic to subdue the rebels.

Patrick was deeply impressed by a pamphlet sent to him by Richard Henry Lee from Philadelphia, where Dr. Franklin's presses were printing copies by the tens of thousands to meet the demand. Called *Common Sense*, it was written by Thomas Paine, a recent immigrant from England, who already considered himself an American. "Reconciliation," Paine declared, "is a fallacious dream. Everything that is right or natural pleads for separation."

"Paine writes as you speak," Dandridge told Patrick one afternoon as they sat together before a fire in the planter's pipe-smoking room. "Aside from you, I've never heard a man plead so eloquently for freedom."

"It's good that someone else has picked up the torch of liberty," Patrick said, trying to conceal his gloom. "My voice has been silenced forever."

Nate grinned, but made no reply.

A few days later Dorothea appeared at Scotchtown, and went straight to the library, where Patrick was writing brief notes thanking the friends who had sent him letters during his illness. He stood when she came into the room, and realized he thought of her now as a woman, not a child.

"Martha has gone into Hanover for some panes of glass," he said, "but she should be home soon."

"I've come to see you, Mr. Henry, not Martha." Dorothea removed her silk-lined cape of violet-dyed wool that matched her eyes.

He couldn't resist teasing her. "Then your Captain Jones has gone to sea again."

"Well, yes. He has, but that's irrelevant. Did you know that county representatives are being elected to the Assembly next week?"

"Of course. But it's still being called a convention."

"You didn't register as a candidate."

It was difficult for Patrick to smile or speak calmly. "I wouldn't ask the voters for their confidence after disappointing them."

Dorothea was angry, and tugged at the black curl looped over her shoulder. "Mr. Lee and Mr. Jefferson have sent you letters begging you to reconsider. Mr. Mason stopped here for dinner day before yesterday and told you that you're desperately needed if Virginia hopes to organize her own government. You've had a message from General Washington, too, a note enclosed in a personal letter John Fontaine wrote Martha. He said we're going to be at war for a long time, and that we can't hope to win unless the civilian population is ably led, with its liberties protected. He hoped you'd reconsider, too."

"You keep yourself well informed on my private correspondence and meetings."

"Martha and I have no secrets from each other."

"Martha should be spanked, and so should you."

Dorothea's laugh was a challenge. "I'm too old for that."

"Unfortunately." A quill pen snapped between his fingers. "I'm grateful to my friends, and I'm trying hard not to resent the interference of young women who know nothing whatever of public affairs."

"I don't pretend to understand them." She rested her hands on her hips. "But there are two things I know. You feel you've disgraced yourself, which is untrue. And you believe the people have lost faith in you, which is equally false. In a speech you made to the Continental Congress last year, you said that under the democratic process of government, citizens with the right to vote have an instinct for survival. The people of Hanover County—of all Virginia, for that matter—trust you and recognize your talents."

She was as loyal to him as his own daughters, having spent half her childhood under his roof, and Patrick was flattered by her concern. "Thank you, Dolly, but that's a hypothetical assumption."

"Oh, it can be proved, Mr. Henry." She moved closer to his desk, her taffeta underskirts rustling pleasantly. For an instant she looked apprehensive, but her sense of mischief was greater than her fear. "It's going to be proved."

He was reminded of a time, many years earlier, when she and Martha had picked all the fruit, not yet ripe, from two pear trees in the yard. "What have you done?"

"I think it's only fair to tell you," she replied, her eyes enormous, "that your name was entered as a candidate for the Assembly an hour before the lists were closed."

He spluttered incoherently.

"There's no need to repay me the registration fee of five shillings," she said with mock innocence. "That was the very least I could do for you."

3

Nate Dandridge and his wife were visiting relatives in Goochland County before he went off to join the militia as a lieutenant colonel, so Dorothea was alone when Patrick came to call at the largest and most aristocratic mansion in the area. Simply dressed in a silk gown of pale green, she led him into the drawing room, looking very much at ease.

"Your conscience," he told her, "doesn't appear to have deprived you of any sleep since you played that trick on me."

Dorothea pretended she hadn't heard him. "I'm sorry that Papa and Mama are away."

"I've come to see you."

"Really, Mr. Henry? How wonderful! Let me give you some tea. It's green, imported from the East Indies by way of Holland."

"Hoard it, Dolly. The British blockade of our ports is becoming more effective every day, and it will be a long time before any more tea comes into the country."

She laughed. "Captain Jones doesn't agree. He says it's no problem to slip past British warships."

"Then your Captain Jones is a man of infinite resources, and you're lucky to be his friend."

"Why don't you like him, Mr. Henry?"

Patrick hoped her interest in the Scotsman wasn't becoming serious, and worded his reply carefully. "He lacks modesty. Men of real merit have no need to talk about themselves. Their deeds speak for them."

Dorothea leaped to the defense of John Paul Jones. "That isn't true of men who've made careers in armies and navies. Please sit

173

down, Mr. Henry. You look so distraught, walking around the room."

Patrick continued to pace. "Your father had a distinguished career in the Royal Navy, but there's no more modest man in Virginia."

"Papa's generation had fewer problems."

It was natural for the daughter of a sailor to become romantically interested in a sailor, but Patrick decided to speak privately to Nate about Captain Jones before Dorothea was carried away by her infatuation. The Scotsman had already performed valuable services for the American cause, it was true, but he was unscrupulous and a braggart who would not be a good match for a young lady reared as a gentlewoman.

Dorothea relaxed on a settee and regarded him calmly. "Did you come here to warn me against him, Mr. Henry?"

"No, I had another purpose. A far more personal one." Patrick halted in front of her, and bowed. "I've always made it my policy to apologize to one of my children when they've been proved right and I've been wrong in a dispute. I must treat you in the same way."

She smiled up at him, relieved that he did not intend to scold her.

"Less than an hour ago the Hanover County Election Board paid a call on me. Your interpretation of the voters' spirits was more accurate than mine."

She clapped her hands together, and the ruby ring on the little finger of her left hand picked up a gleam of sunlight. "You've been re-elected to the Assembly!"

"I have, thanks to you."

"Thanks to your own record, sir." She leaned forward, as excited as a child. "How did you stand in the final count?"

Patrick became embarrassed. "I was first."

"Out of five candidates. How many votes did you receive?"

He was still more uncomfortable. "It's difficult to believe, but the Board tells me that I was returned to the Burgesses almost unanimously. There were only three votes in the whole county cast against me. Of course," he added hastily, "that doesn't mean everyone voted for me."

"I had a wager with Martha of a half crown against a sixpence that more people would vote for you than for all the other candidates combined. Was I right?"

"You've won," he admitted, and tried to hide his feelings beneath a mantle of severity. "But I disapprove of gaming by young girls."

"I knew you'd do it! You have no idea how highly people regard you!" Ignoring his paternal glare, she stood, threw her arms around his neck and kissed him.

Patrick was pleased, but his confusion became worse. After all, she really wasn't his daughter.

"This is a great day for Virginia, Mr. Henry, and an even greater one for you. Now, I hope, you'll never again lose faith in yourself!" The radiant Dorothea was too happy to be aware of his discomfort.

4

Williamsburg was the same, yet everything was different. The Governor's Palace was empty, and a crudely stitched pennant displaying the Stars and Bars of the United Colonies flew from the flagpole on its front lawn instead of the Union Jack. There were no Redcoats in the town, militiamen occupied the barracks that British troops had evacuated, and young men with armbands and old-fashioned flintlocks had replaced the trim soldiers who had stood sentry duty for so many years outside the Capitol and other public buildings.

The impressive carriages of royal officials and wealthy Loyalists had disappeared, only a few light phaetons rumbled up and down Duke of Gloucester Street and no more than a dozen or two well-dressed ladies wandered in and out of the expensive shops. The young men had vanished from behind the counters of these establishments, as well as from the stables, and a recruiting sergeant for the Continentals had set up a small tent in front of the barracks, next door to the Governor's Palace.

However, with the members of the Burgesses gathered for the meeting they continued to call a convention, the hostelries and eating places were frantically busy, and thus looked normal. Every room in the stately Williamsburg Inn was occupied, some members sleeping four and five to a chamber. The dining hall was crowded at breakfast and evening supper, and those who had business of state to transact with the Assemblymen, militia officers, planters selling foodstuffs to the Continental and militia quartermasters, and the owners of privateers that slipped in and out of Virginia's waters in defiance of the British blockade, appeared at mealtimes, too.

There was the usual bedlam in the main room of the Raleigh, but only a select number of Assembly leaders were admitted to the inner sanctum, the Apollo room. "I suppose we could take over some of the offices that Dunmore's staff vacated," George Mason said soon after his arrival in the capital, "but we feel more at home here. Later, after we become more accustomed to governing ourselves, I reckon we'll spread out."

An informal caucus of members for various convention posts was made on the day prior to the start of the session, and so many familiar faces were missing that the legislators displayed some uncertainty. Peyton Randolph had died, while Lee, Jefferson, and Harrison held three of Virginia's seven seats at the Continental Congress. But John Tyler was there, as was Edmund Pendleton, and several younger men were admitted to the inner council. One of them was James Madison, whose almost encyclopedic knowledge of the law more than made up for his diminutive stature, and whose pugnacious record as director of safety for Orange County compensated for the fussiness of his personal attire.

Patrick left home late that afternoon, still a little shy of sitting down again with former colleagues, and arrived at Williamsburg well after sundown. He had intended to slip off somewhere for a quiet, solitary supper, but word of his presence in town spread rapidly, and several of his friends called on him and insisted that he accompany them to the Apollo room.

He was cheered as he followed Tyler through the main dining hall, and men stood on chairs to call their enthusiastic greetings to him. An even warmer reception awaited him in the Apollo room, and the younger members, who had not met him, clamored for the privilege of being presented. There was a brief moment of silence when Edmund Pendleton, who had been more responsible than any other individual for Patrick's troubles as a military man, rose from his own table.

Everyone fell silent, but the two principals carried themselves with the aplomb of professional politicians. Patrick's smile was as broad as Pendleton's, and his handshake was firm and cordial. Only when he accompanied Tyler, Mason, and young Madison to a table in the far corner did he sigh, very softly.

Tyler heard him. "We're taking care of Pendleton," he said grimly as Mason ordered sack. "There was a movement in the caucus to elect him president of the convention when we meet tomorrow, but we'll block him."

The others were in obvious agreement, Madison tugging at his lace-edged cuffs when Patrick studied him.

"We have enough votes," Mason added, "to give you the post by a comfortable margin, P.H."

Patrick's smile was pained. "I've learned to think carefully before accepting places offered to me by the Assembly. In this instance, I'm afraid I'll have to decline the honor."

His friends were shocked. "Think of the harm Pendleton did your reputation!" Tyler exclaimed.

Patrick shook his head. "I did myself more injury, and if Pendleton and I had exchanged places, I'd have been upset, too. I say it's wrong to punish a man for expressing an honest opinion, and although I appreciate the support of good men, I'll make my own situation clear by placing his name in nomination myself."

Tyler raised his hands in a gesture of despair. "I might have known," he said to the others, "that P.H. would be erratic and unpredictable—as always."

"I'm no saint, John, and I don't pretend I like Pendleton." Patrick spoke softly but earnestly. "All the same, we've got to look beyond the ends of our vengeance-seeking noses. I was ashamed to come back to Williamsburg, but here I am, no thanks to my own efforts. I was wrong to feel so reluctant, and I admit it. We've enlisted together in a struggle against the Crown, and any man who has a valid contribution to make is needed. If my friends and Pendleton's start squabbling, Lord Dunmore will soon be in his palace again, while we quarrel on our way to the gibbet."

Madison, still young enough to be an idealist, agreed emphatically.

"I hope every member of the Burgesses can be persuaded to feel as you do," Patrick told him. "Ever since I was nominated for my old seat without my knowledge, and returned to it without lifting a finger, I've been analyzing our situation, Virginia's and all America's, and there's a great deal of work ahead of us."

"I told you," Tyler said to Mason with an unhappy laugh, "that we should have waited until P.H. arrived before drawing up a tentative agenda."

"I failed the people once," Patrick said. "I don't intend to do it again. For one thing, we need a constitution for Virginia."

"Surely we can use the English common law," Tyler protested.

"To be sure, but there are hundreds of questions to be settled, and I think they should be put into writing and formally adopted."

Madison nearly spilled his glass of sack. "That's precisely what I've been saying for weeks, sir."

"It's a tremendous task, P.H.," Mason declared soberly.

"So it is, George, but in my opinion it's necessary. The people of England can rely on an unwritten constitution because they can fall back on seven hundred years of tradition. But even that heritage has done us no good. We must have specific, written safeguards against tyranny, including guarantees of personal liberty."

"What do you have in mind?" Tyler asked. "I don't think the Burgesses will accept radical reforms."

"Personal freedoms are never radical," Patrick retorted. "People must have the right to assemble where they please, and to express any honest conviction without fear of arrest. Newspaper editors and pamphleteers must have the right to publish what they wish. Every man must be allowed to worship the Almighty in his own way—"

"Not so fast, P.H.," Mason interrupted, emptying his glass of sack and pouring another from the decanter the barmaid had left on the table. "I hold the same opinion you do, but I can't see the convention adopting it as a principle. You're a member in good standing of the Anglican Church, so you certainly know that Virginia will never allow alien religions to flourish here."

"Maybe it's my Huguenot ancestry, a streak of undigested Calvinism that makes me rebel," Patrick said. "But I'll talk day and night, until the convention grows weary of my voice, to force agreement on the principle of religious liberty here."

Madison smoothed his silk waistcoat. "You've established precedent yourself, Mr. Henry. I've read your trial defenses of Baptists and Quakers, and they're unassailable."

"The past is useful, but we must break with it if it stands in our path." Patrick was becoming aroused now, and the cup of West Indian chocolate the barmaid had brought him instead of sack cooled at his elbow. "Papist troops from Maryland march beside Virginia Anglicans. Shall one discriminate against the other? If you saw last week's Philadelphia newspapers, you read that the entire membership of the synagogue up in Newport joined the Rhode Island militia. Shall we refuse to accept them as comrades in arms? We supported the Puritans of Boston, even though we disagree with their interpretations of the Bible. I believe our love of liberty is our greatest strength, and that freedom of worship is the most precious of all our rights!"

Mason held up a hand. "No speeches tonight, P.H."

Everyone laughed, but Patrick's amusement was fleeting. "I'd like to free the slaves, too, if we can find some equitable form of compensation for their masters."

"Now," Tyler said flatly, "you go too far."

"Do I, John? How can their servitude be just if ours is dishonorable?"

"There are wealthy planters from Georgia to Maryland who have been straddling the fence," Mason said. "Hundreds of them haven't decided whether to become Patriots or support the Crown. No matter how just the cause, we'll force them to take stands as Loyalists if we incorporate the freeing of slaves in our constitution."

"We need their help," Madison added, parting company with Patrick for the first time.

"Oh, I intend to be practical, but that won't stop me from bringing up the subject on the floor of the convention. I know that, unfortunately but realistically, I'll be voted down on the issue. All the same, at the appropriate time, when there aren't too many other matters occupying people's attention, I'm going to set my own slaves free as an example."

Madison took a pinch of snuff to hide his astonishment, but fooled no one.

"You have much to learn in your association with the right honorable gentleman from Hanover," Tyler said dryly. "After you've had time for rest and reflection, P.H., the earth itself trembles. Do you plan to explode any other sacks of gunpowder?"

"I do, as it happens," Patrick conceded. "Mind you, I'm not criticizing the delegates to the Continental Congress, and if it weren't for my own folly, I'd be in Philadelphia right now. I've done the next best thing since my reelection to the Assembly, and have been corresponding with Richie Lee and John Adams. Their letters confirm my belief that the members have so much to do they scarcely know where to begin. Everyone in Philadelphia speaks of freedom, but no one does anything specific to implement it."

"Until now," Mason said, "I hadn't realized how badly we've missed you here, P.H."

"The last bridge across the Atlantic has been swept away by the tides of liberty, and no man can claim otherwise. Our troops must have valid cause for risking their lives, and our civilians must have good reason for making sacrifices." There was a depth of passionate conviction in Patrick's voice that had been missing for many months. "Tomorrow, as our first order of business after the election of Pendleton as president, I'm going to offer a resolution. I'll request that Virginia's delegates to the Continental Congress be instructed to propose that the United Colonies declare themselves free and independent states."

5

The resolution of independence ordered by the Virginia convention was submitted to the Continental Congress by Richard Henry Lee on June 7, 1776. The moderates in the thirteen delegations were reluctant to take a vote on such a drastic issue, but the proponents of independence rejoiced because the question had been brought into the open at last. John Adams, a member of the committee appointed to draft a declaration, made one of his infrequent addresses to the Congress, and said, "Patrick Henry has accomplished more, even though absent from this body, than we who are here have been able to do in all these months."

Jefferson was the principal author of the declaration, although Dr. Franklin was chairman of the committee, and the others, including Roger Sherman and Robert R. Livingston, all contributed their opinions. In the meantime the Virginians, working closely with the Massachusetts delegation, worked to round up support for Lee's resolution. On July 1 nine colonies voted in favor of it, the number needed under the rules of the Continental Congress to pass legislation, and the United Colonies officially became the United States of America.

On the following day the other four delegations accepted the resolution, making the vote unanimous, and on July 4 the formal Declaration of Independence prepared by the committee was adopted unanimously.

Messengers rode off to all of the thirteen new states, and everywhere the news was celebrated with torchlight parades. No cannon were fired, as gunpowder was too scarce, but France had already hinted that she was willing to help alleviate the shortage. Although reluctant to form an open alliance that would plunge their nation into war with the British, the ministers of Louis XVI agreed to furnish both powder and armaments to an American company formed for the purpose. Terms of payment were deliberately vague, as everyone knew the new nation lacked funds to pay her benefactor.

Thousands of Virginians flocked to Williamsburg when word of the action taken by Congress spread, and were treated to the spectacle of a militia review held by Brigadier General Andrew Lewis. An impromptu picnic was held in Duke of Gloucester Street, and sides of beef, oxen, and venison were roasted in pits behind the Williamsburg Inn. Vast quantities of cider were consumed, and the taverns ran out of beer and ale.

Late in the evening a crowd gathered outside the Raleigh, demanding that Patrick Henry appear to make a speech, but he ignored the hubbub and remained closeted with a convention committee, headed by Mason, that was preparing a written constitution for the state. There was no precedent for the creation of such a document in a democratic society, and the group worked, as Patrick later described their efforts, "with feverish caution."

The Virginia constitution established three branches of government, executive, legislative, and judicial, and every article was debated at length by the committee members before being committed to paper by Mason and Madison. Speed was essential, as the state had no legal government until the constitution was adopted by the convention. No one had authority to levy taxes, raise new militia units or police the frontier, where Indian uprisings were reported.

Edmund Pendleton, as president of the convention, was the chief executive of Virginia for the time being, but he refused to give orders to the militia units already in existence, claiming that he had no right to command anyone. The homes of Loyalists were looted and burned in several towns, and when conditions threatened to become chaotic, Patrick finally took matters into his own hands. His only title was that of floor leader of the convention, but he did not hesitate to sign orders directing General Lewis to dispatch companies of militia to every community in which Loyalist families lived.

"Pending the establishment of duly constituted, permanent authority," he wrote, "it is the joint duty of the convention and the militia, the only arms of government now in existence, to keep domestic peace and wage war against the enemy."

His efforts won the undeviating support of the Congressional delegation, which returned home during a short recess, and their prestige helped to quiet Pendleton's complaints that Patrick was trying to make himself "a tyrant no less powerful than that of the Majesty whose yoke we have broken." Patrick was particularly grateful for the generous efforts made by Thomas Nelson, a member of the Pendleton faction. Nelson came straight to Williamsburg from Philadelphia, and after ascertaining facts for himself, let it be known that although members of the committee drafting the constitution had favored electing a governor for life, Patrick had insisted that no man hold the state's highest office for more than three terms, each of a single year's duration.

By late July the proposed constitution was ready for presentation to the convention, and so urgent was the need for a stable, permanent government that the members agreed when Patrick suggested that debate on each article be limited. Clerks copied the document from the original written in Mason's hand, and candles burned all night in most legislators' sleeping chambers. "The committee has worked a minimum of eighteen hours every day for weeks to prepare this extraordinary and history-making constitution," Patrick announced on the floor of the convention. "It is unique in all the world, and the brows of Mr. Mason and Mr. Madison will forever be wreathed in laurel. Sirs, most of you are already familiar with the contents of this great state paper. Be prepared to begin discussing it at seven o'clock tomorrow morning."

There were shouts of protest at the early hour from all parts of the floor.

"Virginia is in peril," Patrick said acidly. "Would you sleep, sirs, while she perishes?"

The debate began on schedule.

Mason read each article, explaining the drafting committee's thinking, and then Madison joined him in defending the section. Occasionally, when the opposition showed strength and the arguments became heated, Patrick stepped in and used his talents as an orator to win acceptance of the disputed passage. His greatest contribution, however, was that of marshaling votes for each article, and he ranged the floor of the convention constantly. Reason was his principal weapon, but he did not hesitate to appeal to the patriotism of the Assemblymen when necessary, and he insisted that sessions last from seven each morning until ten or later every night. The weary representatives grumbled, but were powerless to oppose him, and at the end of ten days the constitution was adopted with only a few minor changes.

Patrick presented the Bill of Rights to the convention himself, making an impassioned speech that brought the delegates to their feet repeatedly. Pendleton, who had seen no need for written guarantees of personal liberties, realized that the convention strongly favored the Bill of Rights and, changing his position, openly supported it. Debate was only desultory, and it was adopted a few hours after being submitted for consideration.

The convention then adjourned for twenty-four hours so the

representatives could sleep and rest. Patrick, who was exhausted, declined several invitations to join friends at dinner and retired to his room at the inn. He had no interest in food, his body ached and he felt his forty years. His canopied feather bed looked inviting, but before he could crawl into it, there was a tap at his door.

He pulled on his old dressing gown, sighed and admitted George Mason and John Tyler to the chamber. Both appeared disturbed.

"Don't you lads ever go to bed?" he asked.

"It will be a long time before we get there tonight, and you'd better put on your clothes again, P.H." Tyler was tense. "We have a long evening's work ahead of us."

"The Pendleton people are going to put up Tom Nelson for governor tomorrow. Most representatives like him, and I'm afraid they'll vote for him." Mason, haggard after the long ordeal he had suffered, spoke in a cracked voice.

Patrick accepted the news calmly. "Nelson is a good choice. He's conscientious, and from all I hear, he's done well in Philadelphia."

"He doesn't have your reputation!" Tyler said excitedly. "What's more, Pendleton and his friends have been working quietly for days, getting vote pledges, so you're the only man who can beat Nelson now."

"I'm not a candidate." Patrick yawned and wished they'd leave.

"We're going to nominate you," Mason said. "Please, get dressed and come with us. It'll help if you talk to representatives yourself in the dining hall here and at the Raleigh."

Patrick sat down on the side of his bed. "What do you have against Nelson?"

"We must have a governor who'll really unify the people. Tom is a fine fellow, but the public doesn't know him." Mason had prepared his arguments, and presented them forcefully. "Our own first governor must be respected by everyone in the state if the office itself is to have stature. He'll have to set his own precedents, so he must be capable of making decisions, even unpopular ones."

"You sound to me as though you're describing Richie Lee," Patrick said with a tired grin.

Tyler gestured impatiently. "In the first place, Richie is a legislator, not an executive. In the second, the people don't look up to him. You're a symbol of our resistance to the Crown, and in the public mind he's simply someone who has helped you. What's more, he's in Philadelphia, and we're physically incapable of getting his consent to run before the convention meets tomorrow afternoon. Don't sit there arguing, P.H. Get dressed and come with us!"

There was a long silence, and Patrick ran the sash of his robe through his fingers. "I'm flattered that you think enough of me to place my name before the convention, gentlemen, and your confidence in me is pleasing to my vanity. But it wouldn't be right for me to go vote hunting like a newcomer to politics canvassing his county. No, that wouldn't do."

"Why in blazes wouldn't it?" the exasperated Mason demanded.

"Only a moment ago you yourself said that the office of governor must have stature if this new system of government is to be effective." Patrick shook off his fatigue, and his manner became crisp. "The public must look up to the governorship. If we can succeed in creating the right impression, the man who holds the office will almost automatically gain prestige. That would be impossible if he behaved like a candidate for the Burgesses."

Tyler was interested in practical politics, not theories. "You intend to let Tom Nelson win by default."

"Not necessarily. An election of this kind must be decided on the Assembly's judgment of the men who are nominated. If their opinions are formed on the basis of anything other than the qualifications of the candidates for the office, the very type of government we're setting up will collapse of its own weight." Patrick started to pace the floor, his hands plunged deep in the pockets of his flapping robe. "You've spoken of the precedents a Governor of Virginia must set. You were quite right, and I intend to set one right now. I consider it unseemly for any man to seek the office."

Mason let his hands drop to his sides in despair.

"George, you've spent weeks writing and polishing a constitution, so it's plain that you have faith in the principles of democratic government. Will you abandon them when we must meet the first test? Tell the Burgesses my feelings, if you wish. I'm sure Tom Nelson will agree with me, and perhaps we can set a standard that will be followed in later years."

"Persuasion is a waste of breath when you've made up your mind. Come along, George." Tyler started toward the door. "We'll pass along your message, P.H., but don't set your hopes too high. Under these circumstances, I don't believe you have a chance to win tomorrow."

"If Virginia is to survive, if the United States itself is to become more than an ideal," Patrick said, "our philosophy of governing and being governed is more important than the hopes of any one man. Naturally, I'd like to be elected, and I believe I could fill the office. Whether the convention agrees with my somewhat biased view is something we'll learn tomorrow. Thank you, gentlemen."

The visitors glumly shook his hand and took their leave.

For a moment or two Patrick stared at the closed door. Then he shrugged, blew out the oil lamp and climbed into bed. His abortive experience as colonel-in-chief of the militia had taught him that the satisfaction of personal ambition didn't necessarily determine a man's ability to assume the responsibility of high office. He couldn't trust his own judgment in this election, so he had to place his faith in the delegates to the convention.

He dismissed the matter from his mind, stretched and pulled up the quilt. Drowsiness overcame him, and a few moments later he fell asleep.

6

Thomas Nelson, Jr., was not a member of the Virginia convention, and therefore was not allowed to present himself on the floor of the Assembly chamber. Therefore Patrick, to the despair of his friends, deliberately absented himself from the Capitol. "I don't want it said that I tried to use personal influence to sway the electors," he declared, and invited Nelson to dine with him at the Apollo room.

They sat together over bowls of tripe chowder, platters of liver dumplings made with cornmeal and the Raleigh's specialty, beef and oyster pies, while their peers decided their future. For a time, neither man mentioned the election. They discussed the affairs of the Continental Congress at length, Patrick inquired about friends there and Nelson, who had been planning to return to Philadelphia before his friends had nominated him for governor, candidly revealed his impressions of the strengths and weaknesses of Congress.

"Hancock is an able president," he said, "but it's difficult for him to limit debate. Let someone from Virginia or Massachusetts deliver a speech, and delegates from the smaller states clamor for the floor. They're so afraid we'll put our interests first that they flinch before they're attacked."

"That's the great weakness of a confederated government," Patrick replied. "Pennsylvania, with several times the population and size of Delaware or Rhode Island, should have a larger voice in voting rights. But I believe we'll learn from our errors and rectify them. The beauty of George Mason's constitution is that it's flexible. If you should return to Philadelphia, I wish you'd take a copy to John Adams, Tom. He's anxious to study it." With only a trace of self-consciousness he added, "Of course, I can always send him one in the post."

Nelson laughed and adjusted his wig. "When I told Edmund Pendleton we were going to dine together, he wanted to know what we'd talk about. I said I hadn't the least notion, but I knew I could rely on you to keep up a flow of conversation."

"It strikes me," Patrick said carefully, "that you and I must set an example."

His opponent raised a bushy eyebrow.

"We're the first men ever to run against each other for high office—anywhere in the United States. So it seems to me we have a responsibility in this matter that goes beyond the boundaries of Virginia. Luckily, neither of us initiated the activities of our friends. That's as it should be. No governor can maintain his dignity if he buys rum and hams for the electorate. But there's more to it than that. We're both Americans, we both believe in the same basic ideals, and we must impress people with the fact that—no matter which of us may win in the convention today—we're friends. The weakness of a democratic system is that it could provide two or three groups permanently opposed to each other."

"In this instance, there are no theories of government that separate us," Nelson said. "But I can imagine a situation in which men honestly favor different principles. What then?"

"The question has been worrying me," Patrick admitted. "It can be the great weakness of a democratic system. Whether we'll develop political parties, as the English have done, is something that only time will determine. And we have a lesson to learn from them, Tom. Their differences are in manner and approach, not in fundamentals. The Whigs favor more liberal attitudes than the Tories, but both are devoted to the monarchy."

"Then our problem is that of creating as great a love for democracy."

"Don't treat the thought lightly. The monarchy is a living entity —as Americans discovered to their sorrow. The Crown isn't just a vague dream. There's a man who sits on a throne in accordance with hereditary traditions that all Englishmen automatically accept, regardless of whether they label themselves Whigs or Tories —or whatever." Patrick lost interest in his meal, as he always did when he found conversation stimulating. "But democracy is an abstract principle that no one has ever tried to apply to the realm of practical politics."

"The ancient Greeks—"

"They had a form of democracy, to be sure, but it wouldn't be acceptable to us. Pericles may have been a great man, but he was a ruler who accepted or rejected the advice of his elected counselors, as he saw fit. It was the Greeks, remember, who conceived the idea of giving power in times of crisis to an absolute ruler whom they called a tyrant. The Romans took the same scheme and abused it. The Roman Senate was an ornament to emperors who ruled as they pleased. If we let that system develop here, we're defeating our own purposes, and the whole world will laugh at our folly."

"It isn't easy to feel a fierce loyalty to an abstraction that was created in the mind of John Locke and existed for decades only in his writings."

"That's our dilemma," Patrick said. "If we fail to prove that we love freedom for its own sake, we'll lose our liberty for all time."

A young man approached the table somewhat hesitantly, and

Nelson frowned when he recognized his law clerk. "What do you want?"

Philip Aylett ran his hand through his thick blond hair. "I—I want to make an appointment with Mr. Henry, if he has time to spare a few minutes later in the day."

Patrick and Nelson glanced at each other. "Your election must be assured, P.H.," the delegate to Congress said. "Philip has applied for a commission in the Continentals, and now he's looking for a place when he comes out of service."

The youth didn't join in the forced laughter. "It's more personal than that. I want to talk about Elizabeth."

For an instant Patrick remained blank, but suddenly the pieces of the puzzle fell into place. "I've seen you at Scotchtown. You were there with a group of young people just before I left for the convention."

Aylett swallowed hard. "Yes, sir. I've been there quite often. Mrs. Fontaine has allowed me to call on Elizabeth."

Patrick realized that Martha had been trying to spare him, but knew he was about to lose the youngest of his daughters and would be completely alone in the world. "I'll be very pleased to meet you this evening, Mr. Aylett," he said, trying to conceal the sense of emptiness that swept over him.

The youth bowed and retreated.

"We seem destined to become more closely associated than either of us anticipated, P.H.," Nelson said. "He's related to me through my wife's family. He's a gentleman, an able lawyer, and a good lad."

"He needs no credentials other than your recommendation, Tom." Patrick still thought of Elizabeth as a child, but could not deny her the right to become betrothed when the young man she wanted to marry was about to leave for military duty. Sarah would have known whether he was right, but he had to depend on his own judgment, and he wished he felt as sure of himself in dealing with family matters as he did in handling affairs of state.

Nelson tactfully returned to the subject they had been discussing. "I'll tell you something that worries me. Locke says no man's knowledge exceeds his experience."

"Quite so." Anne would be married soon, but it might be possible to persuade Elizabeth to wait a year or two. Perhaps Martha would help, and Dorothea's aid might be enlisted, too. Elizabeth had always looked up to her. On the other hand, Patrick didn't want his own feeling of loneliness to be the determining factor. In all fairness to Elizabeth—and to Philip Aylett—he thought it might be wise to make no final decision until the shock wore off and he had a chance to study the question more objectively.

"If that's the case," Nelson said, "democratic government can't succeed. "All of us are inexperienced, but that doesn't dampen our enthusiasm."

Patrick found it impossible to concentrate on democracy and Locke.

Nelson pretended to be unaware of his silence, and gave him still more time to recover. "I'm told that in your address on the Bill of Rights you claimed men have an instinct for democracy. If that's true, then we don't really need the experience Locke believes necessary."

"I was misquoted. Every man instinctively loves liberty," Patrick replied, making a great effort. "The meanest savage proves it by his demeanor when he's carried here from Africa on a slave ship. But I see democracy as a higher form of freedom than untutored liberty. To be a democrat, one must feel responsible for the freedom of others as well as himself."

"Would you curb a man's right to preach anarchy? Wouldn't that be an abuse of freedom of speech?"

"You raise a delicate point, Tom. Under my concept of freedom, I'd let him make his speech, because I assume that Americans have already learned to distinguish the bad from the good. The impairment of their own liberties by the Crown has taught them what they could have learned in no other way. So they'd laugh at the anarchist. Try to silence him, and he becomes a martyr. Then people will start listening to his nonsense."

"You'd let him speak to a gathering of slaves?"

"Certainly! Their love of liberty is so great and their appreciation of it so keen that they'd stone the anarchist. What I don't know is whether I'd let him speak before a gathering of semi-literate English immigrants. Their understanding of freedom is limited, so I might want them to spend six months or a year here before subjecting them to influences that might confuse or corrupt them. That brings up a problem, Tom, that one of us will have to face as governor. Shall Virginia, an independent partner in a voluntary alliance of states, continue to grant citizenship to immigrants the moment they land on our shores? Or shall we change our policies and require them to wait long enough to absorb our way of thinking?"

"Have you been corresponding with Dr. Franklin? He raised the same questions on the floor of Congress."

"I regret that he's never included me on his list of correspondents. The problem occurred to me independent of anyone else's thinking, and it's one we may have to face sooner than we realize. If we move toward a closer alliance with France, it's inevitable that at least some of the French troops who come here to fight will want to settle here. Should we grant citizenship to men who've been trained to obey the dictates of a near-absolute monarch? It's a point worth considering."

Nelson glanced toward the door at the far end of the room. "One of us will have to consider it very shortly, it appears."

A half-dozen men were coming toward them, with Pendleton and Mason in the lead. All were smiling, and it was impossible to guess from their demeanor who had won the election.

The newcomers halted and bowed formally.

Patrick returned Nelson's lead in rising and returning the salutation, feeling a trifle foolish.

"As president of the convention, it is my duty to inform you of the results of our deliberations," Pendleton said, unaware of his pomposity.

Two barmaids chatting in a corner inched closer, and the cook stopped turning a half-side of beef on a spit.

"Milord," Pendleton continued, bowing again to Patrick, "you have been elected Governor of the Dominion by a vote of sixty to forty-five."

"I'm no man's lord!" Patrick spoke quickly, without thinking, and had no idea his words would be repeated from one end of the United States to the other.

Everyone crowded around him, offering congratulations, and Nelson was the first to shake his hand.

Pendleton, still stiffly formal, searched for another title and finally found one. "Your Excellency, the convention remains in session. Will you come with us to the Capitol to take the oath of office, or do you prefer another place?"

"I'll be very pleased to take the oath in the company of my colleagues," Patrick said quietly, and thought it strange that he felt no sense of excitement. "If you don't mind a brief delay, I'd like to get Mrs. Henry's Bible from my quarters at the inn." He paused for an instant, realizing he had an immediate opportunity to put into practice the concept of friendship between candidates for office in a democracy that he believed so important. "What's more, I'd very much like Mr. Nelson, acting in his capacity as a delegate to the Continental Congress, to administer the oath."

7

"I hate using someone else's furniture, but Lady Dunmore's taste was exquisite." Martha walked into the master bedroom on the second floor of the Governor's Palace, still fresh after a long morning of inspecting the place from wine cellars to attics.

Dorothea went to the windows that looked down on a small, well-trimmed grove of fruit trees. "These drapes are lovely." She fingered the heavy maroon velvet. "They would have made a handsome ball gown and cloak."

"I'm afraid they'll just gather dust here. Papa won't sleep in all this splendor."

"He must! It's expected of him."

"If I try to persuade him, he'll never leave his room at the inn. Perhaps you can convince him, Dolly. You have more influence with him these days than I have." Martha linked her arm through her friend's, and they moved together into the corridor. "Do you know," she asked with a giggle, "that the stables are actually bigger than the whole house John and I expect to occupy for the rest of our days? I'll be incurably spoiled by the time Papa's term of office ends."

"You can't possibly manage this place with the Scotchtown staff. You'll need more servants."

"I know, but Papa says there's no provision in the state budget for them."

"Then he'll have to pay for them himself. Poor old Isobel was in tears, and I can't blame her. Mr. Henry shouldn't have announced on such short notice that there will be eighteen at evening dinner tonight." Dorothea hastened to reverse herself. "Of course, it really isn't his fault. He had no idea that three liaison officers from General Washington's staff would arrive unexpectedly, or that he'd have to entertain Mr. Jefferson, too."

"I'll lose my wits trying to act as housekeeper here, Dolly. I'm efficient only on a small scale, and I don't have your training for managing scores of guests simultaneously. I honestly wish you'd stay here with me through the winter, until I know what I'm doing."

"Well, I may, now that my father has left for militia duty and my mother is going to stay in Culpeper until March or April." They walked into another bedchamber, and Dorothea paused before a long pier glass to smooth her curls and adjust the lace modesty-frill at the neckline of her gown. "There's just one problem. When John Paul comes home on his next shore leave, I'll have to find some place for him to stay."

Martha giggled again. "Really, dear! We counted fifteen bedrooms here—or was it sixteen? I'm a little dizzy."

"Mr. Henry doesn't like John Paul."

"But that's impossible. Papa doesn't really know him."

"They've met several times, and Mr. Henry becomes very cold and stiff whenever his name comes up. I've learned not to mention John Paul in front of him."

"Papa has very few prejudices—"

"—but he's stubborn."

"Very." Martha looked at her friend. "Have you made up your mind about John Paul?"

"Not yet. It isn't easy when a man is off at sea so much. He appears for a few days unexpectedly—literally out of the blue—and I'm in such a whirl when I see him that I really can't think coherently."

"I'm sure you'll know what to do. Would you like this room, Dolly?"

"Oh, no. It's far too grand for me. I'd feel dwarfed here."

"Now you sound like Papa."

Their laughter was interrupted by a servant. "Miss Martha, Isobel says she's broiling some trout and venison chops for Mr. Patrick's dinner. She says to tell you they'll be spoiled if he don't come to the table in ten minutes."

"Then we'll have to interrupt him. Help me, Dolly."

The two young women walked together down the broad, spiral staircase that led to the ground floor, and made their way to the wing where Lord Dunmore's suite of offices had been located. Patrick had found the arrangement suitable, and had made no changes in it. Four clerks were hard at work in a small chamber, beyond which was an anteroom in which seven or eight men were sitting patiently, chatting in low voices as they waited for an opportunity to snatch a brief word with Patrick whenever he came through.

Behind a door still bearing the legend, lettered in gold, "*Secretary to His Lordship*," Philip Aylett was ensconced. Competent assistants were becoming hard to find, and Philip had reluctantly agreed to postpone his acceptance of a Continental commission for a year in order to take the post of secretary. The compromise had been made easier to bear by Patrick's promise that at the end of that time Elizabeth would be old enough to marry before Philip, himself only eighteen, went into military service.

"His Excellency doesn't want to be disturbed," the young man said, rising as Martha and Dorothea came into his office.

"That's too bad for His Excellency," Martha replied. "These are handsome quarters, Philip."

"Too handsome by far for me. Please don't go in there, Martha. He'll skin my hide."

"We'll take full responsibility." Martha comforted him with a smile and opened the inner door.

Lord Dunmore's former office was thirty feet long, with leaded windows on three sides. Thick Turkish rugs were scattered on the polished hardwood floors, and a bare spot on the wall above a fire crackling in the hearth marked the place that had long been graced by an oil portrait of King George III. A cushioned settee and several large, comfortable chairs looked insignificant in a chamber dominated by a huge, leather-topped desk of mahogany, on which papers were piled in orderly stacks.

The man who sat behind the desk looked anything but neat. His coat and wig had landed on the floor near the chair at which he had aimed them, the sleeves of his worn shirt were rolled above his elbows and his fingers were ink-smudged. He was writing feverishly in a small, cramped hand, and didn't look up when he heard the door latch fall into place.

"Get out," he said. "I'm busy."

Martha braced herself. "Papa," she said tentatively.

"Oh, it's you. Go away."

She froze, unable to continue.

Dorothea came to her rescue. "I never knew that election to great office could make a gentleman an ill-mannered, crotchety tyrant," she said.

At the sound of her voice, Patrick stood and tugged absently at his unbuttoned waistcoat of homespun wool. "I've just appointed a privy council," he told her, sounding vaguely apologetic, "and I'm sending the Burgesses a message explaining its functions."

Martha seized her opportunity. "Your noon dinner is waiting, and Isobel says the meat will be burned if you don't come at once."

"I must approve plans for a string of forts on the lower James River," her father replied, tapping a pile of documents, "and it's essential that I prepare for a meeting this afternoon on various schemes to promote and encourage the growth of our merchant marine." He sat down again.

Martha's glance at her friend was a plea for help.

"Is food so plentiful," Dorothea demanded, addressing her question to no one in particular, "that the Governor of Virginia can afford to set a bad example? Only yesterday he signed a proclamation urging people to conserve food so he can send more supplies to the Continental and militia quartermasters."

Patrick shoved his spectacles on his forehead and grinned; then, without another word of protest, he retrieved his coat from the floor.

Dorothea pressed her offensive. "Martha says your clothes are a disgrace, sir, and she's right."

His annoyance was tempered by amusement.

"At the very least, Mr. Henry, you should be seen in a suit of black broadcloth, a yellow silk waistcoat and a scarlet cloak. And only apprentice stonemasons wear stockings of black cotton."

"May I remind you, Miss Dandridge, that I'm Governor of Virginia, not a popinjay taking the waters at Bath while hoping someone will present me to the King?"

Dorothea's temper flared. "I'm far more aware of your exalted position than you appear to be, Mr. Henry!"

Martha made a frantic but vain attempt to silence her friend.

"You preach a doctrine of dignity, sir, but you don't practice it in your person. Your demeanor can't compensate for an appearance that makes you resemble a Hanover County lawyer starving for want of clients! You've replaced the royal viceroy, but people won't respect you if you look like an ignorant hay-foot, straw-foot militia recruit." Dorothea picked up his wig from the floor, then flung it into the fire. "Disgusting."

Martha tensed as she awaited her father's explosion, but to her amazement he chuckled.

"You may be right, Dolly," he said mildly. "One of the penalties of being a busy widower is that a man becomes careless in his dress. Perhaps you girls will be good enough to buy the materials I'll need for some new clothes. The shops on Duke of Gloucester Street are bursting with goods brought in by the brig from France that slid past Lord Howe's blockade two days ago."

Martha needed no second invitation. "We'll do it this very afternoon."

Her father frowned. "I'd prefer that you wait until tomorrow, and concentrate instead on a grand dish for Mr. Jefferson this evening. He's developed a keen palate, and it's my hope he can be persuaded to leave the Continental Congress and become floor leader of the Burgesses. He's badly needed here."

Dorothea improvised swiftly. "Tonight's menu is already planned, Mr. Henry. We're having wild fowl baked according to a French receipt of my mother's. The birds will be stuffed with West Indian olives and basted in Malaga wine." She took his arm in order to urge him toward the door. "Will that suit your purposes?"

"I know so little of elegant dining that I'll gladly take your word for it. Jefferson," he said gallantly, "is as good as Assembly leader now."

Martha wished she knew her friend's secret. Not even Sarah had managed Patrick with such seemingly effortless, discreet ease.

8

The last of the French tapers had been used, and the candles made in Fredericksburg emitted thick, pungent smoke that filled the governor's huge office. But neither Patrick nor his guest suffered any discomfort; both he and Jefferson had grown to manhood in homes that had rarely been free of the rancid odors in late autumn and winter months. Observing the twice-weekly ritual they had established since Jefferson had become leader of the Burgesses, they sipped tea brewed from leaves grown in Georgia. The lingering, bitter taste puckered their mouths, but they were too patriotic to complain, believing it was their duty to help make the United States less dependent on goods imported from abroad.

Jefferson absently pushed his cup to the far side of the table beside him, and crossed his legs, which were too long for the chair in which he was sitting. "These recruiting goals aren't realistic, P.H.," he said. "I don't see how we can maintain a quota of six thousand Virginians in the Continentals and at the same time build a militia army of five thousand more."

Patrick sipped his tea and wished he hadn't. "I see no choice, Tom. I've shown you General Washington's confidential letter, so you know his situation has become desperate. His losses in the Battle of Long Island were staggering, and after he was forced to give up New York Town to Sir William Howe, his militia began to desert by the thousands. Only the Almighty knows how many left him on his retreat through New Jersey."

"I'll grant you that Virginia and Massachusetts are the best potential sources of manpower for the Continentals, but the most energetic recruiting sergeants on earth can't fill a quota of six thousand in a year."

"Six months," Patrick replied grimly. "I'll issue a proclamation to be read in every county seat, and I'll depend on you to squeeze unanimous support through the Assembly."

"They'll be willing enough—until they learn that we want a militia of five thousand. Then I'll have a real insurrection on my hands."

"The man who persuaded them to pass the bill freeing non-Anglicans from paying the Church tax can perform any miracle."

"Thank you, P.H., but you haven't been sitting in the Capitol lately. You don't understand their mood."

"I understand only that this is a time for action, not rhetoric. Independence must be won through sacrifice because there's no other way."

Jefferson sighed patiently. "You got my message this morning. They became panicky when they heard that Washington has retreated into Pennsylvania and that nothing stands between us and Sir William's Redcoats except open land."

"I hope you read them my letter saying I intend to stay right here—with my family."

"Oh, I did, and there was a little applause when I read them your line that you'd fire on the vanguard from the windows of the Palace, if need be. But that won't stop them from taking to their heels if Howe really decides to march south."

Patrick shoved his spectacles onto his forehead and grinned. "Neither will my marksmanship, if you want the truth. I didn't touch firearms during that nightmare period when I was chief of the militia, and I haven't gone hunting in years. Between us, I'll have to flee with the rest if Howe actually marches on Williamsburg."

"Frankly, I'm relieved to hear it. Heroics may be inspiring, but the capture of Virginia's governor would destroy public spirit." Jefferson smiled, too. "It would also destroy the governor. I honestly believe the King and Lord North would attend your hanging in person."

"I hope to deprive them of the spectacle. I'm putting my faith in Washington's belief that Howe will stay in his snug Jersey quarters until spring. We're luckier than many people realize, Tom. Sir William may be winning battles, but he's demonstrating again and again that he has strong Whig tendencies and doesn't want to press too hard against us."

"Well, it may be true, as Washington wrote to you, that now is the time to recruit and train a dependable army, before Howe is replaced by someone anxious to win himself an earldom by smashing us. All the same, I don't see how Virginia can put eleven thousand men into uniform. The effort will bankrupt us, but we have no real alternative. We'll either be free paupers or slaves in rags."

"Precisely."

"I'll find some way to win Assembly support. Several members have hinted that they'll vote in favor of increasing the militia if you'll give them—or their sons—commissions as captains or majors. I took it on my own initiative to say I felt certain you'd be amenable to no such arrangements."

"Thank you, Tom. Aside from my own miserable experience in the militia, our defeats make it more obvious than ever that we must have a trained officer corps. Washington is being very strict in maintaining the principle that he'll only promote within the ranks to higher grades—"

"—even though the Continental Congress grants commissions as generals without consulting him."

"In spite of political handicaps imposed on him in Philadelphia. We must do the same. I've been thinking of establishing a promotion board consisting of our two militia brigadier generals and the senior Continental liaison officer. They'll be free of all civilian influence, and it's within my prerogative as commander-in-chief of the state's army and navy to set up the board without consulting the Assembly or seeking its approval. However, if I do it, I realize it will be more difficult for you to handle the members."

Jefferson couldn't make himself comfortable, and stood to stretch his legs. "They'll be unhappy, but I have a few more surprises of my own in store for them. I want to abolish the old law of primogeniture."

"Good! It's absurd, in a democratic state, for the eldest son to inherit his father's estate while the younger sons go begging."

"When I hear of similar things being done in every state, I begin to realize that this war is going to be far more sweeping in its results than any of us realized a few years ago when we were agitating for self-government. We're doing more than fight for our independence, P.H. We're creating a nation unlike any other on earth."

"This is just the beginning, and sometimes it frightens me. But we can only move forward. It's strange, you know. In the Declaration of Independence, you wrote of life, liberty and the pursuit of happiness." Patrick looked reproachfully at his cup of cold, medicinal-tasting tea. "We may lose our lives, our liberty is in jeopardy, and it will be years, if ever, before we can allow ourselves the luxury of seeking happiness. Yet all our goals are within our grasp if we're willing to work hard enough."

"At the risk of sounding like a New England Puritan," Jefferson replied, "self-discipline will solve our problems. In the kind of world we're trying to make, every man must be his own master."

"To be sure, but we lose sight of our ideals, and it's easier to speak in glowing terms of our high principles than to live up to them day by day." Patrick stood, too, and began to wander around the still unfamiliar room. "We seek safe, high-ranking staff posts for our sons. We go out of our way to curry favor with our friends from the western counties, where game is still plentiful. A man who wants to hang a side of venison in his meat shed is always willing to compromise. Everyone likes to cheer when there's a parade, but so few want to march in it because they'll go off to battle when it ends. We must put eleven thousand men into uniform and keep them there, no matter how heavy the burden."

"You and I," Jefferson said wryly, "may be forced to do the recruiting ourselves."

"I'm ready, and I'm sure you are, too. But a few men can't carry the whole weight of our enterprise. Last year's patriotic fervor has burned away, and people are reluctant to make sacrifices." Patrick took a worn leather purse from his pocket and emptied its contents onto the desk. A few coins clattered, and he scooped them up again in a theatrical gesture. "In a few more months, I won't have a ha'penny to my name. I've refused, on principle, to accept my wages as governor, but there aren't more than a half-dozen members of the Burgesses who have followed my example."

"Perhaps we expect too much. By creating a new type of society through acknowledging the equality of all, we must be patient and give our people a chance to grasp the concept. Then they'll change."

"No, Tom. We expect too much of them. Man's nature doesn't change."

"But it will! When the poor man realizes he can become wealthy, when the indentured servant discovers he can be a social leader and the illiterate learn that through education they can earn the provostship of William and Mary, or of Princeton, they'll have to change. They'll have no choice, really, because the very world in which they'll live will be changed. It was Simonides of Ceos, I believe, who said that not even the gods can resist necessity."

"Simonides was an optimist, and so are you. The parents of Lobsterbacks pray in their churches for victory, as we pray in ours. We appeal to the same God, and I sometimes wonder whether He listens to those whose voices are the loudest. I'm afraid I must agree with Pindar, who said that war is sweet only to those who have never tasted battle."

"He also said that the slave appreciates liberty more than the freeman, and we've been a nation of slaves." Jefferson paused, and his voice became gentle. "You've already changed, P.H., and not for the better, I fear. The man who cried for liberty or death wouldn't have allowed the greed and self-interest of others to discourage him."

Patrick's mood changed abruptly. "You must forgive me," he said. "A man who lives alone becomes overly sensitive to the faults of others while forgetting his own." He laughed humorlessly. "I sound as though I'd been reading the homilies Dr. Franklin sometimes writes when he's in need of funds."

Jefferson thought he sounded like a very lonely man, but smiled politely.

"I don't think my faith in humanity is less than yours, Tom, or I couldn't have prodded and jabbed at the public conscience as I did for so many years. But I don't have your patience. Our crisis grows worse, and I grow angry when I see men losing heart. It doesn't require much courage to join a mob sacking the house of some unfortunate Loyalist—"

"That won't happen again, I'm sure. There hasn't been a single such disgraceful incident since you threatened to hang the leaders of that herd in Warrenton last month."

"That didn't take courage, either. Three thousand militiamen have sworn oaths to obey the orders of their governor. The real heroes are the people of New York Town who are living under Redcoat rule, and if other Americans keep blinding themselves to our peril, we'll all become that same, unfortunate brand of hero. Then your Declaration of Independence will become a curious little footnote in history that students at Oxford and Cambridge may read some day for their private amusement. Something needs to be done to rekindle the torch of liberty before it's too late, but I don't know what. We need a miracle, or freedom will perish."

SEVEN

$1777-1778$

1

"Play the British game, and you'll be whipped every time!" There was a trace of a burr in John Paul Jones' voice, which penetrated to the far corners of the drawing room in the Governor's Palace. Smiling and self-confident in a self-designed blue uniform and the silver epaulets of a captain in the Continental Navy, he enjoyed being the center of attention. Assemblymen and members of the Privy Council, militia officers and their ladies crowded around the ruddy-faced, stocky man who seemed to take his good health and physical strength for granted. "They make their own bloody rules of warfare, and then they expect you to obey them. They know the infernal rules better than you, so they'll send you to the bottom, gentlemen."

Patrick, standing with several guests near the rum and Madeira punchbowl, found it difficult to carry on a conversation when Jones' quarterdeck roar cut through the sounds of more genteel voices. In all fairness to the man, however, he had to admit that the captain was making the governor's first annual reception a success, and although he had consumed uncounted cups of punch, he appeared to be sober.

"I know their rules because I've played their game," Jones continued. "I can guess their moves in advance, and when they expect me to counter in one way, I do it in another."

His audience inched closer, men nodding in awed agreement. A sailor who had sunk at least ten British warships, captured more than a dozen enemy merchantmen and conducted a spectacularly successful raid on the Royal Navy's storage base at Canso in Nova Scotia obviously knew his business. The winner of one or two victories might have been lucky, but the one American commander who had not yet been defeated on either sea or land had good reason to boast that he understood his foes.

"Expose yourself to a frigate's broadsides, and you'll be ripped to kindling. Sail past a ship-of-the-line, and you'd best strike your colors. But if you tack, gentlemen, if you weave in and out as my sister-in-law does when she's sewing a new sampler to grace the wall of her Fredericksburg parlor—the devil who is waiting for you to present yourself as a clear target won't know what to do."

A representative from Reedville, on Chesapeake Bay, who owned a small fleet of privateers, nervously cleared his throat. "Then you advocate slipping away from them, Captain?"

"In the name of hell and damnation, sir, I do not!" Jones' voice became still more penetrating. "Train your gun crews, gentlemen. Send them to battle stations late at night, in rough seas and when it's so cold the coating of ice on your decks is as thick as pastry crust of a meat pie in a Boston tavern. Ah, your men will curse you and mutter of mutiny when they crawl back into their hammocks. But by the living God, gentlemen, they'll be gunners who can split a mainmast on their third volley—even on the second if your bo's'n has an eye for range and the tossing of a ship in the sea."

Such talk was not suitable for ladies, Patrick thought, but the women were as absorbed as the men. It was particularly annoying to see Dorothea standing beside Jones, her violet eyes shining as she took in every word.

A lieutenant colonel of militia frowned slightly, and there was a hint of asperity in his voice as he said, "Your tactics may be successful at sea, Captain, but we face a far different problem on land."

"Damn me if it isn't the same, Colonel!"

Patrick wished Jones would be more careful of his language in mixed company.

"General Washington broke their rules when he made his night attack on the Germans at Trenton." The captain's booming laugh filled the room. "Ah, that was rich. He knows how to fry those devils. And look at him now. He maneuvers. He slips and slides and weaves so Willie Howe can't bash at him, and meantime his lads are learning the art of soldiering. Yes, Colonel, it's the same, right enough. Thumb your nose at British rules, and you can't lose!"

Patrick had heard enough. Handing his cup of West Indian chocolate to a servant, he made his way through the crowd. "Captain Jones," he said, still resenting Dorothea's infatuation with the brute, "these good people have taken advantage of your good nature long enough. I'd like a word or two in private with you."

The guests moved aside to let them pass, and Dorothea, after a moment's hesitation, remained behind.

The chamber that Lady Dunmore and her daughters had used as a cloakroom was empty. Pier glasses still stood on three walls, but there was no furniture in the room and the striped satin wallpaper was beginning to peel. But there weren't enough funds in the state treasury to make unnecessary repairs.

Patrick came to the point at once. "I've been told the Continental Congress gave you a low place on its list of Captains," he said.

Jones' eyes darkened. "Aye, Governor, that the bastards did. I've sent them a complaint that would blister the tar off a hull, but they've sent me nary a word in reply. It's that Hancock, I think. He shows a preference for his Massachusetts captains."

"Don't blame President Hancock." Patrick weighed his reply. "I'll grant you he's kept the chairmanship of the Committee on Naval Affairs, but he has no easy task. Every state has its favorites, and if he wants legislation passed, he must accommodate the interests of others in order to win their support."

"Politicians are the curse of mankind, begging your pardon, Governor. When a nation is at war, it must win!"

"True, Captain, but our states are just learning to work together. You see war from one point of view, and the delegates in Philadelphia view it from another."

"To hell with what they think."

Richard Henry Lee had written to Patrick that Jones' lack of tact had been as much responsible as any other factor for the refusal of Congress to grant him higher seniority on its list of captains. The blunt, almost savage contempt that enabled him to win victories at sea proved to be a handicap in the advancement of his own career.

Patrick could understand another Scotsman's cold rage, but was afraid of its consequences. "There are rumors, Captain, that you may resign your commission."

"That would be cowardice, Governor, and I'll challenge any man who dares make the accusation to my face. As long as there are British ships on the seas, I'll sink them."

"I'm delighted to hear it, Captain, and I'm pleased you haven't lost heart. Virginia is loyal to her sons, and I've been trying to right the wrongs done you in Philadelphia. Our delegation there is as powerful as any, and I'm not completely lacking in influence myself."

"You're too damned modest, Governor." Jones grinned and hooked his thumbs in his broad leather belt. "People talk of you as though you were the first cousin of the Almighty."

The man's blasphemy was shocking, but Patrick concealed his feelings, wondering at the same time who had been talking about him. Surely he wasn't a topic of conversation when Dorothea and Jones were alone.

"Are you using your twelve-pounders to win me higher seniority, Governor?"

Patrick sympathized with his sensitivity over rank. "I'm doing what I can, Captain. I've sent an official letter to President Hancock, and private communications to John Adams and Richard Henry Lee, the most influential member of the Virginia delegation."

Jones extended his hand, and caught Patrick's in a bone-crushing grip. "Sail or sink, you're my friend, sir!"

Patrick winced, but resisted the urge to rub his aching hand. "Don't set your hopes too high. The smaller states are jealous because a Virginian commands the Continental Army, and they oppose rewards to others here."

The captain cursed fluently, displaying imagination and an excellent command of the language.

"Even if I can't win you higher rank, there's one thing I definitely can promise you. I've nagged so hard that Philadelphia has promised to give you the finest new ship in the Navy."

Jones forgot his grievances, and became as excited as a schoolboy. "The *Ranger*, Governor?"

"She'll be yours the day she's commissioned. Hancock has sent me official notification, and I'll glady show you his letter tomorrow morning. The official announcement will be made shortly."

"How soon will she be ready for sea trials?"

"There's a shortage of experienced carpenters in New Hampshire, but some workmen have been sent up to the Portsmouth yards from Boston. President Hancock believes she'll be launched in May."

"That means June," Jones declared sourly, but brightened again immediately. "Ah, with a real frigate under my feet at last, I'll gladly meet Lord Howe's flagship—and sink her. How many guns are they giving me?"

Naval armaments meant little to Patrick, and he carefully searched his memory for the details of John Hancock's letter before replying. "Eighteen six-pounders, I believe."

"Nothing bigger? Ah, well. With nine to a side, I can still bleed the bastards."

Patrick had to admire the man's ferocious determination, and wished that other commanders shared it. "I also insisted that you be given the right to select your own officers, and President Hancock assures me you'll be granted the courtesy."

"I'll leave this very week to find the right crew!"

"So soon, Captain? You arrived only last Thursday."

"I'll be honest with you, Governor. Here's a secret I'd tell no woman. I feel a restlessness so bad that my skin itches when I'm not at sea. God help my wife when I marry, sir, for I'll beat her hide with a captain's cat-o'-nine if I'm away from salt air too long. I need it as bad as a drunkard craves spirits, and that's no lie."

Patrick hoped Dorothea would have more sense than to marry a man who apparently loved ships and fighting at sea more than he could ever love a woman.

Relaxing now that his future seemed assured, Jones laughed slyly. "They say that men who go out to sea are a fickle lot, but don't you believe it, Governor Henry. We want snug homes, the same as other men, but when we're in far places we can dally a bit, with no one at home ever the wiser." He nudged Patrick in the side.

"I'm sure you'll want a little more rum-and-Madeira before it grows too warm, Captain," Patrick said hastily.

Jones threw an arm around his shoulder, unconsciously compromising the dignity of Virginia's first citizen. But he seemed unaware of the guests' surprised stares when they walked back into the drawing room.

Again the two shook hands, and again Patrick's joints ached. The United States was in great need of men like John Paul Jones and could use fifty others of his extraordinary caliber, but Dorothea would be miserable if she married him. Perhaps it might be wise to drop a discreet word to Martha in the morning.

The handsome clock that Governor Spotswood, Dorothea's grandfather, had installed in the palace fifty years earlier, chimed midnight, and the guests began to leave. Patrick stood in the spacious entrance hall, Martha beside him, and formally bade each of them farewell. He had thought of relaxing for a time before the fire, but had forgotten that Captain Jones was a house guest, and when he saw from the drawing room entrance that a half-dozen young people, including another Navy officer and a major in the Continentals were still chatting there, he drew back. Dorothea and Jones stood apart from the others, and were conversing earnestly near the handsome French doors that led into the garden.

Patrick felt very old and unaccountably lonely. Realizing that his daughters' friends would be unable to relax informally in the presence of the governor, he wandered off through the deserted corridors, feeling at loose ends and more than a little sorry for himself. The social evening, in itself unusual, had jarred him awake, and he didn't feel like going to bed.

Footsteps echoed behind him, and he turned to see Philip Aylett.

"Is there something you want, Your Excellency?"

"A great deal," Patrick said. "Freedom and peace for my country, happiness for my children and a sense of accomplishment for myself."

Either Philip was too young to appreciate irony, or the hour was too late. "I saw you going toward the office, sir, so I thought—"

"No, thank you." Patrick patted him on the shoulder. "Go back to Elizabeth. I'll be fine."

Embers were still glowing in the hearth, and dry kindling caught fire almost at once. Patrick eased two logs into the flames, then lighted an oil lamp with a spill of plaited tobacco stems and glanced at his desk. As usual, papers were piled high there. John Page, the head of his Privy Council, had submitted two financial reports he hadn't yet read, and if he spent an hour or two preparing a message to the Assembly asking for legislation to prevent the persecution of Loyalists, he might be subjected to less pressure in the morning. He hung his new coat of black broadcloth on a wall peg, carefully removed the splendid wig just made for him in Philadelphia and unbuttoned his yellow silk waistcoat.

It would be a shame to soil the lace cuffs of his extravagant lawn shirt, he decided, and rolled up his sleeves, although the growing fire hadn't yet removed the chill from the air. Polishing his spectacles with a limp square of buckskin, he wondered what Dorothea and Jones were talking about. Probably the captain was boasting of his exploits, and the girl was listening in adoring wonder. Patrick sighed and reached for Page's report on revenue and taxation.

Years of self-discipline enabled him to shut everything else from his mind, and he concentrated on the document, occasionally scribbling questions in the margin. Friction was already developing between the Burgesses and the Privy Council, which was unfortunate but probably unavoidable. Both the legislative and executive branches of the government were so jealous of their authority that neither willingly yielded to the other. A sharp reminder of their need to cooperate might help clear the air temporarily.

It gradually dawned on Patrick that someone had come into the office, and he looked up to see Dorothea standing part way between the entrance and his desk, the firelight intensifying the sheen of her oyster-colored satin gown. Her long hair was piled high on her head and held in place by a diamond and pearl studded coronet she had inherited from her grandmother, and at first glance she looked regal. But, Patrick thought as he rose, her eyes were deeply troubled.

"Your door was open, Mr. Henry," she said apologetically. "May I disturb you?"

"You're always welcome here." He waved her to a chair.

She ignored the invitation and, twisting a tiny handkerchief, continued to stand.

"Why aren't you with—the other young people?"

"I had to see you." Dorothea shivered and rubbed her bare arms.

Patrick went to the peg for his coat.

"Please don't, Mr. Henry. My shoulders are dusted with rice powder that will stain your handsome new coat."

He paid no attention to her protest, wrapped the coat around her and guided her toward the hearth.

"This feels better, thank you. But I'm being a nuisance."

"That's absurd." Patrick guessed she had quarreled with Captain Jones. Anne had displayed similar signs of tension before accepting Spencer Roane's proposal. But it was wise, in dealing with young women, not to ask too many questions, so Patrick waited for Dorothea to tell him what was disturbing her.

She seemed in no hurry, however, and stared into the fire.

Eventually her silence made him ill at ease. "Would you like me to send for a cup of punch? No? A platter of barley cakes from the buffet table, then."

"They'd make me fat and old and ugly," Dorothea said with a sudden display of bad temper. "Not that it matters. Here, sir," she went on, removing his coat and holding it out to him. "I refuse to be guilty of staining the lining of the first new suit of clothes the governor has bought in years."

It was the last he would buy for a long time, Patrick thought; his pounds were draining away at an alarming rate, and the specie issued by the Continental Congress was virtually worthless.

In a sudden, impatient gesture, Dorothea snatched off her

coronet, and her black hair tumbled in thick waves down her shoulders and back. "I'm the most stupid human being on earth."

He rescued the coronet before she could throw it into the fire. "Speaking strictly from the viewpoint of an *amicus curiae*, the evidence of the past twenty-two years indicates that the testimony submitted by the witness is inaccurate."

She forgot her misery long enough to look at him. "What's an *amicus curiae?*"

"Literally, a friend of the court. Someone called in for advice by a magistrate, usually a counselor of standing who is familiar with the legalities of a case."

"Am I on trial, Mr. Henry?"

"You appear to be trying yourself, Dolly." He was finding it difficult to maintain a surface calm.

"And are you sufficiently familiar with my problems to qualify as an expert on me, sir?"

"An interesting challenge. I submit to the court that I've known the witness from the time of her birth. I also submit that although no man ever understands the mind of a woman, I have three daughters who are approximately the same age as the witness. Their inconsistent behavior and temper tantrums have helped to make me old and bald before my time." When he saw that her expression remained unchanged, he tried new tactics. "If you were my daughter, I believe I'd spank you."

Dorothea's gaze was haughty.

"In fact, standing *in loco parentis—*"

"You'll drive me mad with your lawyer's phrases. What's this one?"

"In place of a parent. A substitute parent, armed with full parental authority. We were speaking of spanking. I'm sorely tempted, Dolly." He took a single step toward her.

"You wouldn't dare!" she cried, and began to weep.

Patrick was horrified, and didn't know how to explain that he had been half-joking.

"Not that I'd blame you! I deserve it—and worse!"

Her sobs unnerved him, and he hastily closed the door. Gossips would whisper for months if it became known that a handsome young woman in a low-cut gown had become hysterical in the governor's office. "I cannot abide tears," he said sharply. "I presume you came here for a purpose, but I can't help you unless you tell me what's wrong! Stop it at once, Dorothea, and be quiet!"

She was stunned into silence, gained partial control and suddenly giggled. "How can I possibly be quiet and at the same time tell you my troubles?"

"I bow before superior logic," Patrick replied acidly. "Well?"

Dorothea's full lower lip began to tremble again. "Captain Jones," she said in a scarcely audible voice, "has asked me to marry him."

Patrick felt as though the breath had been knocked from his lungs, although he certainly was not surprised. "Everyone except the bride-to-be, it seems, has been expecting him to propose for many months. I wish you great joy." Her behavior certainly wasn't that of someone who had just become betrothed, and he was bewildered.

"You don't understand at all!" She stamped angrily. "I haven't accepted."

He gaped at her. "You refused him?"

"Not in so many words. I—I behaved dreadfully, Mr. Henry. He assumed I'd fall at his feet, and that made me angry. Captain Jones has a high opinion of himself."

"Luckily for us, and unfortunately for the Royal Navy." Patrick tried hard to be fair.

"There must have been twenty girls at tonight's reception ready to swoon if he as much as held their hands. Any one of them is welcome to Captain Jones, with my blessings." Dorothea stood very straight. "I don't love him."

Patrick became still more confused. "My observations have led me to believe otherwise."

"I just realized it tonight—less than a half hour ago!"

He put his hands on her bare shoulders and forced her to sit in a chair before the fire. "Never trust a sudden decision. Apparently something in Captain Jones' attitude irritated you, but you'll probably change your mind again by morning. Rash judgments are always dangerous."

"My decision was sudden, I'll admit," Dorothea said coldly, looking up at him as he loomed before her, "but it wasn't rash.

I hadn't been able to make up my mind about him for months, but the moment he proposed to me, I knew. I realized many things, and I'm certain I could never love him, just as he doesn't really love me."

"What makes you so sure of his feelings?" Patrick felt as though he was examining a witness on the stand.

"He's a hero, Mr. Henry, and he needs nothing but his victories to sustain him. He can be happy only if he's fighting in a war, and he's sustained by his belief in himself."

Her wisdom surprised him. "How have you learned so much?"

Color rose slowly into Dorothea's face. "I've watched you, so I've seen the difference. You're sustained by your faith in freedom. No, it's more than that. You have a genuine concern for people, and you can't rest until you've won them the rights that you're convinced are their birthright."

Patrick smiled wearily. "You make me sound very noble, but I suppose many young people draw idealized portraits of old family friends."

Dorothea drew a deep breath. "I do not think of you as a family friend, Mr. Henry," she said, speaking slowly and distinctly.

He looked at her, helped her to her feet and could not resist the overpowering urge to take her into his arms. Their lips met, and Patrick was staggered by the emotions that swept through him. Never had he known such intense desire nor felt such infinite tenderness.

At last they moved apart, both of them struggling for breath, and Dorothea was radiant.

"I need time to think," Patrick muttered. "I won't insult you by apologizing, Dolly, but I'm aghast to discover that I love you."

She laughed at him, her eyes shining. "You're the last person in all Virginia to realize it, Mr. Henry."

"That couldn't be true."

"But it is, sir. Even Captain Jones saw it—and knew I loved you, too."

The room seemed to spin, and Patrick put his spectacles on the table beside him before he twisted their metal arms out of shape. "It will be necessary," he said, trying to recover his dignity, "to write at once to your father and ask him for your hand."

"Papa has been expecting a letter all winter, and so has Mama. They knew how we felt—almost as soon as I knew it myself."

"They don't object?" he asked faintly.

"Really, Mr. Henry! Too much modesty in a great man is unbecoming."

"Posterity must judge whether I'm able or only a dreamer. I believe I know myself—and my worth. But this," he continued, his throat dry and his voice rasping, "is an extraordinary situation. Nate Dandridge has been one of my closest friends for almost a quarter of a century. You and Martha have been like sisters. The world will laugh at an ancient fool, and at a girl who marries a man old enough to be her father."

"The people who matter to us won't laugh, and the others will learn in time that they were mistaken."

He blinked, still unable to accept the reality of the miracle. "Martha?"

"I know she's been praying for this, and so has Anne. Elizabeth has wanted it, too, although she's been too shy to say so. And Martha has hinted that her brothers will be very pleased."

She looked so lovely that Patrick reached for her again.

"Wait, please. There are some things I want to say, Mr. Henry."

He let his arms fall to his sides.

"When I first discussed my feelings—and yours—with my parents, I found it hard to believe, too. I was sure of my love for you, but not of your affections for me. There were many times when you seemed to be—well, Martha's father, being kind and loving and sweet to your daughter's good friend."

"I'm almost twenty-two years older than you," he murmured.

"As if a few years mattered," she replied scornfully. "And I'll thank you not to interrupt, sir."

Patrick tried to keep a straight face, but chuckled.

"The reason I didn't discourage Captain Jones in all these months is because I felt my love for you was hopeless. I tried to become interested in him. I even tried to persuade myself that I was learning to care for him. But tonight, when he asked me to marry him, I gagged, Mr. Henry. I couldn't pretend to him or to myself, and I couldn't have lived a lie for the rest of my days. It would have been better to become a spinster."

For the first time he looked at her boldly, relishing the perfection that would be his. "I have a lively imagination, but I cannot picture you as a spinster."

"For the last time, sir, let me say what I must!"

She needed taming, and the prospect excited him.

"When I came into this room tonight, I didn't know what to say or do. I've been tortured for so long, believing one moment that you care for me, but feeling sure the very next that you've thought of me as a child. That's one reason I wept, Mr. Henry. But I'm not just a romantic little girl. My tears of despair were caused by something far deeper than my frustration." Dorothea clenched her fists, and her voice trembled. "May we talk about Aunt Sarah?"

The unexpected request caught Patrick completely off guard, and he could only nod.

"I think I know how you felt about her. I—I knew her almost as well as I've known my own mother, and felt nearly as close to her. The thought of—of presuming to take her place has filled me with terror." Suddenly she lowered her head and fell silent.

Patrick understood now why she had begged him not to interrupt. She had needed great courage to reveal her innermost feelings, and deserved equal candor in reply. "You won't take Sarah's place," he said, his manner grave but his voice very gentle. "I've never been able to speak of her to anyone else, but you must know the truth, Dorothea. I loved her with all my heart and mind, might and soul. She was the light that illuminated my life from boyhood, and she bore me six children I cherish. She will always occupy a place, a special place, within me."

Dorothea forced herself to look at him, and a tear crept slowly down her face.

He made no attempt to touch or comfort her, and his voice became harsh. "Memories aren't enough to nourish a man, no matter how precious they may be, as I've learned to my sorrow. Now I'm finding that one can love the living without losing one's love for the dead."

She flicked away the damp streaks, and her smile was tremulous.

Patrick could wait no longer, and again kissed her, surprising himself with the shattering intensity of his passion. Sarah had been the only woman he had ever known intimately, and their relations had been as natural and easy as breathing itself. But his yearning for Dorothea was so explosive that he realized he didn't know himself as well as he had always believed.

She, too, was shaken when they reluctantly moved apart.

"You'll want a family," he said gruffly.

Dorothea's last vestiges of aplomb vanished. "I'd always hoped —I mean—"

"But you thought I'd be too old to rear another brood, is that it?"

Her face turned scarlet.

"One of my daughters is married, the second may beat you and me to the altar, and the third will be gone in a year. My sons are men, fighting for the freedom of their country. Marriage lacks meaning without children."

"I'm glad you feel that way," Dorothea whispered.

He realized that behind her surface sophistication she was very vulnerable. But now was the time to tell her the problems they would face. It was far better to give her the chance to back out of an agreement before she suffered too much heartache. "You should know," he said, "that I have no real right to ask Nate for your hand. Living is dear these days, and children are a great expense."

Her laugh indicated that she had no real understanding of what he was saying.

"By late spring my strongbox will be empty."

"But you're the governor!"

"Indeed I am, and the cost of maintaining the position is staggering."

"It's true you won't accept your wages?"

"They'd cover only a small part of the cost, and my conscience would give me no peace if I took money needed to buy arms and gunpowder and food that troops in the field need so badly."

"I'm sure Papa will lend you money."

"A marriage based on a father-in-law's fortune would be precarious. If I were a young lad starting out in the world, I'd be willing to accept a dowry payment. But I earned a good living as a trial lawyer for too many years. Besides, the office of governor would be subjected to ridicule if I accepted funds from Nate. No, that would be a bad mistake.

"Then what will we do?"

"I'll have to borrow from the bankers in Philadelphia, putting up some of my property as security. I've come to know Robert Morris fairly well, so I believe he'll charge me fairly low interest rates. But you should think twice before you consent to marry a debtor, Dolly."

She recovered her high spirits instantly. "If you ever say such wicked things again, I shall become very angry. I intend to marry you, Mr. Henry, not your strongbox, and it wouldn't bother me in the least if we were forced to beg in the streets—provided we did it together."

2

John Henry was too feeble to leave his home, so Patrick and Dorothea were married there, although work continued to pile up at the Governor's Palace in Williamsburg. The Reverend Patrick Henry came out of retirement for a second time to perform the ceremony, and Martha Fontaine acted as her friend's matron of honor. Lieutenant Colonel Nathaniel Dandridge, who gave away his daughter, and Colonel John Syme, who stood up with his half brother, rode down to Hanover County together from Pennsylvania on brief leaves of absence.

No one wanted a large wedding, and Dorothea had hoped that only members of both families would be present. But it was impossible to turn away the Virginia Congressional delegation, an official committee representing Congress itself and an even larger group from the Virginia House of Burgesses. Members of the Privy Council were miffed until they and their ladies received invitations, and it proved impossible to leave out the commanders of the militia regiments stationed in the state, two Continental Navy captains and a trade commission from Maryland that happened to be traveling north after a conference in Williamsburg.

Major Henry Lee and Captain Alexander Hamilton represented General Washington, who was unable to leave his troops, but Mrs.

Washington made the journey from Fairfax County. Old friends and neighbors in both Hanover and Louisa Counties announced that they planned to attend, regardless of whether they received invitations.

The principals bowed to the inevitable. The old Henry house wasn't large enough to accommodate so many guests, which made it necessary to resort to desperate measures. The ceremony was held on the open portico in spite of raw, windy weather, but Dorothea, attired in a white lace gown made for an ancestress who had worn it at a ball celebrating the restoration of Charles II to the throne of England in 1660, seemed impervious to the elements. Only the bride's mother and the bridegroom's youngest daughter wept.

The excitement proved to be too much for old Mr. Henry, who was put to bed and given a dose of sassafrass tea flavored with ginger root and essence of mulberry, which put him to sleep. Everyone then adjourned to the Dandridge mansion, for an informal reception. Patrick had insisted that there be no extravagance at a time when troops in the field badly needed additional supplies, so the only foods served were cold roasted turkeys, baked hams, glazed ox-tongues and several huge vats of lobster which were an unexpected gift from a party of Princess Anne County fishermen who made the journey to Hanover, unbidden, to pay their respects to the governor.

Nate Dandridge opened his wine cellars, and countless toasts to the bridal couple were offered in French, Spanish, and Portuguese wines, West Indian rum, Amsterdam gin, and pre-war whiskey from Scotland. The speeches rambled and became increasingly incoherent, but Patrick responded courteously to each with a few words of his own.

It was imperative that he return to Williamsburg in time for a meeting at noon the following day with the Assembly committee chairmen, so in mid-afternoon Dorothea quietly changed into a dress of pale green satin and matching plumed hat, which were more suitable for travel. The guests went onto the lawn to wish the bride and groom Godspeed, and Patrick's elderly mother gave them a final word of advice. "When there are two tinder boxes on one mantel," she said, "remember that either of them can light the hearth, and both of them can burn down the house."

An honor troop of fifty horsemen from the Fourth Cavalry, which thereafter called itself the Governor's Own, formed around the carriage. Philip Aylett and several other members of the staff rode with the vanguard, which started off at a rapid clip in the hope that the party would reach Williamsburg at a reasonable hour.

"I don't care for this coach," Patrick said, smiling and nodding to the guests clustered on the Dandridge lawn.

"It seems very comfortable." Dorothea waved, too.

"Oh, I doubt if there's finer in all America, but I can't help thinking of it as stolen property. You may have noticed that the royal seal has been scraped from the doors."

"You could argue that the Palace was Crown property, too. But I'm not in the least bothered by the idea of living there."

"Of course not. Your grandfather built most of it." He grinned at her.

They were on the open dirt road now, and Dorothea glanced quickly out of the windows to make certain the troopers weren't looking, then leaned toward her husband.

Patrick kissed her lightly on the side of the face.

"That wasn't very satisfactory."

"You're a public figure now, Mrs. Henry." He was conscious of her youth, and didn't like the feeling. Her impetuous desire to be kissed was natural enough, but she would have to learn that the governor's wife could relax only in strict privacy.

Dorothea giggled. "I won't disgrace you, Mr. Henry."

Her ability to read his mind startled him, and he flushed.

"Never fear, sir. I'll try to do you credit."

"I'm sure you will." He leaned back against the cushions stuffed with goats' hair, and took her hand.

The long ride was uneventful. Thanks to the careful precautions Patrick had taken, residents of the towns along the route had no advance warning that he would be passing through with his bride, so there were no ceremonies, celebrations, or exchanges of speeches. By the time that casual bystanders recognized the governor and his escort, the entourage was gone.

Brief halts were made at two country inns for light refreshments, and at both Patrick insisted on buying tankards of ale for the cavalrymen, whose frank admiration pleased and embarrassed Dorothea. At the second stop, a courier from Williamsburg appeared with several documents that needed urgent consideration, so Patrick spent a few minutes with Philip, telling him what he wanted done. The young secretary then rode ahead to the capital.

"I'm afraid you'll become accustomed to these constant interruptions," Patrick told his bride as they resumed their journey.

Her eyes became serious. "I have my own thoughts on that subject. I can't count the number of times I've seen you forced to leave the dinner table—and then complain later that the crisis could have waited until you had finished your meal. I've already made up my mind that no one is going to disturb you when you're eating."

He shook his head. "I'm sorry, Mrs. Henry, but I've left standing orders that anything of importance is to be brought to me at once. I'm the only one in a position to know whether the interruption was justified. We can't take needless chances or risk negligence in a time of war."

"You eat and sleep too little because selfish people take unfair advantage of you. And not even you can win the war single-handed, Mr. Henry! Have you taken as much as one complete day of rest since you were elected governor?"

Patrick thought hard. "No, but—"

"I won't tolerate such abuse, sir. It's my duty to take care of you, and I shall!"

Her ferocity was so intense that he smiled weakly and said nothing.

Dorothea fell silent, too. She knew he would protest if she persisted, so she would speak privately to the members of his staff and request that they disturb him at table only when real emergencies threatened. She was conscious of the difference in their ages, too, and had no intention of letting him kill himself with too much work.

Williamsburg was quiet when the party arrived, and Duke of Gloucester Street was virtually deserted. A small crowd was waiting patiently in front of the Palace, however, and began to cheer as the carriage pulled to a halt at the main entrance. Patrick acknowledged the salutes as he climbed out and handed Dorothea to the ground, but his pleasure was marred by the realization that lamps were burning in every room of the office wing.

Philip was waiting in the entrance hall, as was Lieutenant Colonel Robert Carter, the governor's military aide, and both looked grim.

Patrick wasted no words. "What's wrong?"

Carter remembered to bow hastily to Dorothea. "A column of Indians and Loyalist irregulars has filtered through the mountains into the western counties, Your Excellency. I've presumed to call a meeting of the militia commanders who are in town, sir, and they're waiting for you in your office." Acutely conscious of the fact that this was the governor's wedding night, he went off rapidly down the corridor.

Philip hesitated for a moment, but could think of nothing constructive to say, and followed the colonel.

"This is unfortunate, Dolly, but it can't be helped," Patrick said apologetically.

"People are being scalped, sir, and their homes are being burned! I require no explanations." She smiled gallantly. "This will give me an opportunity to unpack some of my belongings."

He realized that Martha had helped her put away her clothes in the cupboards and closets of the master suite at least a week earlier, but gratefully accepted the white lie intended to ease his situation.

The meeting lasted a long time, in part because the regimental commanders had not yet returned to their posts from the wedding, and their subordinates were afraid to act on their own authority. Patrick listened to several plans for crushing the infiltrators, who seemed to be operating at approximately battalion strength. At last he made the final decision, giving orders to dispatch a regiment of infantry and two cavalry squadrons to the west immediately.

By the time he finished writing letters to the militia brigadier general and colonels, telling them what he had done and giving them the opportunity to make last-minute changes in his retaliatory strategy if they deemed it wise, the Palace had grown very quiet. Philip hastened to the barracks with the letters, carrying instructions that couriers were to be sent with them at once, and Patrick rose wearily from his desk.

He blew out the candles, turned up the wick of the silver oil lamp that was burning on his desk and, gripping it by its mahogany handle, started down the corridor. The clock in the entrance hall chimed, and a fleeting, tired smile crossed his face. It was two o'clock in the morning, the day had been long and he had been subjected to strains he had never before faced. It was small wonder he felt exhausted.

He made his way up the central staircase, slowly went toward the master suite and peered into the bedchamber from his dressing room entrance. A gutted candle stood on a nightstand, and Dorothea's quiet, even breathing told him she was asleep in the canopied bed.

Patrick undressed, put on a new dressing robe over his nightclothes and crept into the bedchamber. He carefully turned down the wick so its light wouldn't disturb his sleeping bride, and placed it on the table at his side of the bed.

Dorothea opened her eyes, smiled, and extended her arms to him.

He extinguished the lamp and, as he joined her, forgot his weariness. In her arms he found the joy and solace, tenderness and love he had been denied for so long, and when at last they fell asleep, together, he was at peace within himself.

3

The fruit trees in the palace gardens were in bloom, honeysuckle blossoms were pleasantly fragrant and the April sun directly overhead was as warm as it was brilliant. Patrick inhaled deeply as he strolled with Jefferson on gravel paths laid out by Lord Dunmore's gardeners. "These flower beds will soon be choked with weeds," he said, "but it can't be helped. When we've won the war, there will be time to grow pretty ornaments again. Meantime, I've had another request from General Washington for food."

"What does he want?"

"Anything we can send him, except grain. The Pennsylvania farmers are giving him all the wheat and oats he needs at present, but he's afraid some of the newer units will desert before summer if they don't get enough meat."

"Men yearn for liberty, no matter what their condition, but they'll fight for it only if their hunger has been satisfied." Jefferson paused to admire the blossoms on a peach tree. "It's strange, isn't it, how little we know of human nature until we're forced to endure hardships worse than any we've ever imagined?"

"I have few regrets," Patrick replied, "but on a day like this I wish I could go hunting in the forests or sit for hours beside a river with a fishing line."

"You make the purpose of my call more difficult, P.H."

Patrick smiled and waited.

Jefferson wondered whether to mention the news, which the governor had apparently confided in others, that Mrs. Henry was expecting a child. Under the circumstances, he decided, it was better to approach the subject obliquely. "A family man," he said, "must always think of his wife's welfare."

"Not these days, Tom. If we think first of our country's independence, our wives and children will be safe." Patrick took it for granted that the Assembly leader had heard of his personal situation. "It's better by far not to bring children into the world than shackle them with chains. My responsibility to my wife is to make certain her sons and daughters are free."

Jefferson smiled wryly. "You've either heard or guessed why I'm here today, P.H."

"A little of both. I knew there was to be a meeting of the leadership at the Apollo room last night, and this morning's closed session of the Burgesses was unusual."

"Only one name was considered at both sessions, and the choice was unanimous."

Patrick was surprised. "Surely Pendleton's friends intend to put up a candidate."

"Edmund doesn't claim to be your friend. In fact, he makes no more pretense of liking you than you do him. But he admitted last night at the Apollo that he can find no fault with your stewardship—"

"Very generous of him," Patrick muttered.

"—other than a possible failure to persuade or force the Continental Congress to prosecute the war more vigorously."

"Impossible! The government of the Confederation would need greater authority—which the states won't relinquish."

"There's no need to flare up at me. I'm well aware of Congress' unfortunate situation, but I certainly don't favor the transfer of power from the states to a stronger central authority. The state is the natural unit of government, just as the individual's little farm is his own natural source of livelihood."

"I'm not sure I agree with you, Tom. I can see advantages as well as drawbacks to a stronger Confederation government."

"Centralized authority will lead to the establishment of a monarchy here, just as it has done elsewhere, throughout history."

"Don't cite the Greek city-states or Rome, if you please. Their electorate was a small minority of the wealthy and privileged. We're the first nation in all the world to give every freeman the vote, the first to grant the people the exclusive right to choose their own leaders. The Confederation is weak because we've made it that way, and I haven't decided yet whether I think that's for the good or bad. Whatever the faults in our system, we'll find them out by the time the war ends, I should think, and can correct them. I only hope they won't prove too severe a handicap and delay victory. But you haven't come here to discuss the philosophy of democratic government. I know you're expected on the floor of the House in an hour."

"And you have the usual crowd in your anteroom." Jefferson spoke more briskly. "No matter what the weaknesses of our system, we've learned that the states must have strong governors. You've already contributed so many years of service, P.H., that I'm reluctant to ask a further sacrifice of you. But—will you accept another term?"

"Frankly, I was looking forward to a term in Congress, which would have given me at least part of the year for my private law practice." Patrick made no attempt to hide his glumness from an old friend. "You say the caucus produced no other candidates?"

"None. But everyone will understand if you decline." Jefferson looked at his watch, an old-fashioned silver timepiece which he carried, incongruously, in a pocket of his breeches. "Shall I come back tomorrow for your answer, after you've had a chance to discuss the offer with Mrs. Henry?"

"There's no need for delay." Dorothea would be bitterly disappointed, and would protest when he told her he'd have to borrow still more money from Robert Morris, but there was no choice. Officers in the Continental Army would not retire from service until the war ended, and a civilian—particularly one who had been instrumental in creating the conflict—could not retire to private life when he was still needed. "I'll accept, Tom, but let's use this situation to our advantage."

"How?"

"Tell them I'm dubious and must be persuaded. Push through the new tax bill on property that the Pendleton people have been fighting. And tell them I won't consider another term unless they increase the term of militia duty to six months. I think we'll pick up extra votes for both bills if we use my acceptance as a weapon."

The idealistic Jefferson was shocked. "That isn't ethical!"

Patrick pointed to an oriole's nest high in the branches of a pear tree. "The mother bird yonder uses a great many techniques to teach her young to fly. Sometimes she shows them by example, sometimes she feeds them and sometimes she threatens. Her one concern is that they actually learn to fly. I trust my analogy is clear."

"You've become Jesuitical, P.H."

"Had anyone else made that accusation, I'd take offense. You and I know self-government is an exercise in self-discipline, Tom, but others are just learning it. Right now the Burgesses need prodding. We've got to have more money, and the militia can't function on a basis of three-month enlistments. Maybe I have become Jesuitical. We need funds and manpower to win the war, and I'll use any means to get them."

"You govern in the same way that you rule a family," Jefferson said, wryly amused. "I thank the Universal Creator for your love of liberty. Without it, you'd be a tyrant. Very well, Governor, I accept your conditions. You shall have your legislation, and Virginia will have you for another term."

4

Patrick tried in vain to curb his anger as he paced the second-floor sitting room that Dorothea had fashioned for herself. The new baby was howling in a chamber directly overhead, which gave him an excuse to raise his voice. "If Martha had told me she intended to join John, I'd have forbidden it! Pennsylvania has been dangerous for travel ever since Philadelphia fell to Sir William, and she's old enough to realize it!"

"She's also old enough to be responsible only to her husband, Mr. Henry." Dorothea had taken pains to wear her most attractive gown and arrange her hair in a high pile on her head, knowing he would be furious this evening, but he appeared totally indifferent to her appearance. "Be glad, sir, that your son-in-law has been promoted to colonel and commands the garrison guarding the Continental Congress."

"They're deep in the interior of Pennsylvania somewhere, and it's ridiculous for Martha to go there!"

"The reason she didn't tell you is because she knew you'd behave like a mean bear awakened from his winter nap at the wrong time. Please sit down." She tried to speak gently, realizing he'd had a difficult day: the son of an old Louisa County neighbor had deserted a militia battalion during battle, and Patrick had refused to pardon the youth, who would be executed the following morning.

"Can't you do something about that infant's infernal noise?"

"I've already offered to soothe her."

He changed his mind abruptly. "No, let her exercise. It's better for her health, and I've heard the sound often enough in years past to shut it out of my mind." Suddenly he stopped roaming and pointed an accusing finger at her. "What does disturb me is the discovery that my wife is engaging in conspiracies with two of my older daughters!"

Dorothea was prepared for a fresh outburst. "I suggested that Elizabeth wait another day or two before speaking to you, but she was too anxious."

"You've actually encouraged her to marry Philip Aylett immediately!"

"Why shouldn't they marry?" she countered. "You promised them you'd give your approval this year."

"I can't afford to release Philip for military service. He knows the routines of my office so well that he's become indispensable. He'll have to stay with me as long as I'm governor. I realize I've broken my word to him, and I can sympathize with his desire to join the Continentals. But I must have him at my side until spring."

"All the more reason to let Elizabeth marry him now," Dorothea said calmly. "Why should he be doubly penalized? And why should Elizabeth be made unhappy? I told her I'd do everything in my power to help persuade you to be fair and reasonable to them. I understand your reluctance. You don't want the world to accuse you of playing favorites, but everyone knows Philip will become your son-in-law some day, so I don't see what you lose. Surely you aren't so thin-skinned that you'll be hurt if a few malcontents criticize you. They'll find fault, you know, no matter what you do."

Patrick's anger subsided, and he sank into a chair, burying his face in his hands. "I reckon you're right," he said in a muffled voice.

She wanted to cradle his head in her arms, but had learned he hated to be touched when showing signs of weakness. "When will you listen to me—and the physicians, Mr. Henry? Your need for a rest grows more desperate every day."

"So does our military situation. Troops have deserted General Washington by the hundreds since we lost Philadelphia, and his supplies are running low. If Lord Burgoyne beats the corps we've mustered in upper New York, the United States will be cut in two. I have little faith in General Gates, and I wish Congress had been sensible enough to give the corps to Benedict Arnold instead of posting him as second-in-command. Dr. Franklin and Silas Deane haven't been able to persuade France to increase their aid to us, and men everywhere are becoming discouraged. Spend an afternoon in the gallery at the Burgesses, Mrs. Henry."

"I went often before little Dolly was born."

"The atmosphere has changed, I assure you. Misguided imbeciles make speeches daily, urging that we find an honorable accommodation with England. They won't listen when I tell them the Crown will demand total surrender, and I'm afraid that if I spend as long as a single day away from my desk, they'll do our cause damage that can't be repaired. Apparently you didn't read the new pamphlet by Tom Paine that I gave you."

"I've studied it many times, Mr. Henry." It wasn't easy for Dorothea to curb her own annoyance. "I can't disagree when he says these times try men's souls, but they tax the strength of my husband to the breaking point."

Patrick stared at her. "I haven't broken yet."

"Must you become ill before you'll stay in bed later than dawn?"

"I beg you, don't nag at me." He rose, walked to the windows and stared out at the outlines of the bare tree branches in the garden, barely visible in the dark.

Her penitence was swift and genuine. "I'm sorry. You're upset because of the boy who'll be shot tomorrow."

"I had no choice, although in my own heart I can't blame a lad of eighteen for showing cowardice when he faced professional soldiers for the first time. If he goes unpunished, a score will desert under fire next time, and then whole companies will run from the field."

His willingness to talk about the cruel decision he had been forced to make was encouraging, and Dorothea wanted to lighten his burden. "Did the parents come to see you?"

"No, they sent me a letter. They begged me in the name of God—and our friendship—to pardon him." Patrick continued to gaze blindly out of the window. "I'll have to answer them before I go to bed tonight."

"What will you tell them?" she asked softly.

His weary shrug was eloquent. "Will they understand if I say that for the sake of all America their son must die? I think not." Patrick turned toward her, his voice and manner savage. "If I dared to mention the Almighty, I'd be guilty of blasphemy! All I can do is send them a stiff note citing military regulations. I'm committing legal murder, Dolly, and it makes me feel no better to know that by doing it I'm saving other lives."

His anguish was so great that Dorothea lost her sense of caution. "How I wish you'd stayed in Hanover all these years, practicing law and minding your own affairs!" she cried.

"That would have been impossible. We must be free, no matter how many young men die, or how many old ones—like me—suffer the torments of living hell."

5

The Burgesses guarded their traditions zealously, and expected the elected Governor of Virginia to observe the unwritten rule, followed so long by the Crown viceroys who had preceded him, that he should not appear in person before the legislature. Even Patrick's closest friends in the Assembly were shocked, therefore, when he sent a formal message to the Speaker requesting the privilege of making an immediate address before a joint session of both the upper and lower chamber.

The bid was so unexpected that many members argued in favor of granting the request, and a full-scale debate erupted in both Senate and House. Patrick swiftly took advantage of the confusion, and sent Philip Aylett to the Burgesses with the announcement that he would present himself in less than an hour.

Bludgeoned into granting the unusual prerogative, the representatives were surly and suspicious as they crowded together in the House chamber to await him. And when he moved slowly down the center aisle, preceded by an escort of sergeants-at-arms, the splendor of his appearance did nothing to allay the members' misgivings. For the first time in the memory of his oldest associates he was wearing a powdered wig, and trailing on the floor behind him was a rustling cloak of scarlet taffeta. No one knew that Dorothea had made it for him herself, and insisted that he wear it in order to give his office greater dignity.

The voice of the senior sergeant-at-arms echoed through the chamber. "His Excellency, the Governor of the Old Dominion."

Applause was perfunctory as Patrick mounted the dais.

He was aware of the antagonism and made an immediate effort to dispel it by grinning disarmingly. "I've changed," he said, throwing his cloak from his shoulders, "but you haven't. It's good to come home."

A few old friends appreciated his mild humor, but no one laughed aloud.

"I am grateful for the rare privilege of appearing before you, gentlemen, and have come here only because of a development in our struggle for freedom so monumental that I felt it necessary to bring you the tidings myself."

The members became even more tense.

"I have received a brief communication from General Washington, gentlemen, informing me that the Army of the North, commanded by General Horatio Gates and led in the field by General Benedict Arnold, has won our greatest victory of the war. Burgoyne's invaders have suffered a staggering defeat, and Lord Johnny has been taken prisoner, together with nearly two thousand of his men."

The representatives leaped to their feet, cheering wildly.

Patrick raised a hand, and they sat down again. "General Washington feels confident, as do I, that France will now enter into a formal treaty of alliance with us and give us the help in men, ships, and armaments we so badly need."

Again his words were cheered.

"We have reached a turning point in the war. Until now, the liberty we have sought has been a dream, and the more diligently we have pursued it, the farther it has slipped from our grasp. Now, at long last, we have the promise of fulfillment. Now, at long last, we can say to ourselves with confidence, 'The United States shall be free.'"

He was interrupted by a fresh storm of applause.

Waiting for it to subside, his manner changed. "As the troops who have defeated Burgoyne know full well, as the corps that has gone into winter quarters at Valley Forge in Pennsylvania with General Washington knows full well, the price of freedom is high. Governments move slowly, even the governments of states, as you and I have sometimes learned to our sorrow.

"Many months may pass, gentlemen, before a treaty with France is signed and the mighty fleet of King Louis brings guns and powder and cloth for uniforms to our shores. Until then, we must rely upon our own efforts.

"General Washington's corps is badly in need of all the necessities of life, food and shelter and clothing, as well as arms and lead for bullets. If that corps perishes, the British cannot be driven from Philadelphia, no matter how much help we receive from France. If hunger and cold destroy Washington's brigades, the victory in the north will have been won in vain, and liberty will once again become a dream, remote and unattainable."

Patrick looked searchingly at his audience, stopping to gaze into the eyes of one friend after another. "It is the supreme irony of our struggle that in this hour of triumph, our need is greater than ever before. Therefore, under the powers vested in me as governor, I shall send several messages to the Burgesses in the next few days.

"Once again, gentlemen, taxes must be raised. General Washington's need for blankets, cloth that can be made into uniforms and nails to build barracks is urgent. He must have elixirs for the sick. He must have meat and grain to feed eleven thousand starving men. In one message, I shall suggest that each of you return to your homes, and there appeal for voluntary contributions of beef, vension, and fish, wheat and dried corn and oats. It is my devout hope that the people of Virginia will respond to that appeal with generous speed, so that a militia convoy will be able to leave for Valley Forge within a fortnight.

"I have no desire to curb or hamper the deliberative processes of this great body. But I must remind you, gentlemen, that each day of delay hurts our cause, and that too much talk can destroy liberty. You have placed your trust in me by twice electing me your governor. Rest assured, gentlemen, that I shall utilize the full powers of my office, as defined in our Constitution, to insure that there is no needless delay in the procurement and dispatch of the supplies that must be sent to General Washington if the torch of freedom is to burn brightly in our land."

Patrick gathered his cloak around his shoulders, left the dais and walked quickly up the aisle. To the surprise of the representatives he did not wait outside the chamber to chat, but mounted the horse that Philip was holding for him and, unattended, cantered back to the Palace.

231

His mask of grim self-confidence vanished as he joined Dorothea in her sitting room, and he looked old and haggard.

She poured him a cup of steaming herb tea and wished she could do something to dispel the pain in his eyes. "Was your address successful?"

"I believe so. I've given them something to think about." Patrick sipped the brew, which was potable when it was very hot.

"The news of General Arnold's victory must have delighted them."

He nodded.

"Do they agree to the new tax increases and contributions to the Continentals?"

"They were given no choice."

Dorothea steeled herself. "Did you—read them the other letter?"

"I couldn't." Patrick reached into the pocket of his waistcoat, removed a single sheet of folded paper, and opened it. His fingers trembled as he placed the sheet on his knee, smoothing it, and although he wasn't wearing his spectacles, he remembered every word:

> *Headquarters at*
> *Valley Forge, Penna.*
>
> *My dear Governor Henry:—*
>
> *Our long, close association makes it Mandatory that I write this Communication to you in person, rather than entrust its sad contents to the Adjutant General or some other member of the staff.*
>
> *Duty compels me to transmit to you the tragic news, my dear Governor Henry, that your beloved son, Lieutenant Edward Henry, was killed while taking part in a Skirmish with the Enemy. Captain Harry Lee, his immediate superior, who was in command of the patrol, and who will write to you of the action in greater detail when he has had an opportunity to compose his Thoughts, begs me to inform you that Lieutenant Henry died gallantly and, as befitted the son of so noble a father, comported himself with his usual Courage. He died instantly when struck in the head by a ball fired at close*

*range from a Pistol, and I am assured by Major Lee that he
suffered no pain.*

*Please accept, sir, for yourself and Family, my most sincere
expressions of Condolence, in which Sentiment I know I am
joined by Mrs. Washington.*

I am, sir, now as always,
Your Obdt. Svt.,
G. Washington.

6

The bronzed young man in faded, soiled buckskins pounded his
hard fist on Philip Aylett's desk, and, to the astonishment of the
visitors waiting in the anteroom and the clerks beyond it, shouted
in a voice that echoed through the corridors. "I'll be damned if
I'll write the governor a letter, and maybe wait until my powder
gets moldy for an appointment. I aim to see him now, here, today."

Philip eyed the bone-handled hunting knife, gleaming naked in
the man's belt, but held his ground. "Governor Henry's schedule is
very crowded, and everyone except Congressmen and Burgesses
must make appointments in advance."

The visitor pushed back a shock of his long, blond hair. "I was
elected, fair and even, by folks out in Kentucky to be their
spokesman, and by God, I'll speak to the governor if it means
scalping you and feeding your heart to the crows."

One of the clerks became alarmed and ran to the office of the
military aide-de-camp for help.

Meantime Philip refused to be intimidated. "The last man who
threatened to serve my head on a platter was Governor Rutledge
of South Carolina, but I'm still here."

"Damn me, you've got grit, I'll say that for you. I bear you no
personal grudge, mind, but I'm going in there if it means walking
over your body!"

The door leading to the inner office opened, and Patrick stood
in the frame, his spectacles precariously balanced on his forehead.

"You've lost weight in the last three or four years, George," he said calmly. "Come in."

"You don't look any younger yourself, Governor." George Rogers Clark grinned at Philip to show he harbored no hard feelings, picked up his long rifle and, tucking it comfortably under his arm, sauntered into the inner sanctum.

"That's my new son-in-law you were threatening out there," Patrick said as he shook hands.

"If I'd known, I'd have treated him with more respect."

"I doubt it." Patrick poured his visitor a drink of whiskey. "Life in Transylvania hasn't made you any gentler, lad."

"There has been no Transylvania since Dan Boone's venture failed. It's all lumped together as the Kentucky District now, Governor." Young Clark slumped on his spine as he eased himself into a chair, and he raised his glass in a salute. "Here's to you and your pretty wife. I'd have courted her myself if the Ohio Company hadn't hired me as a surveyor."

Patrick took the observation as a compliment, certain that was how it was intended, and inclined his head. "You'll have dinner with us this evening, George."

"I haven't sat at a table for years, but I reckon I haven't lost the knack."

"I've heard you've become a property owner of consequence."

"Oh, I've picked up my fair share of land, Governor. And, my God, what land it is. You've never seen soil so rich and creamy and black. There are forests all the way from the mountains to the Mississippi River, and they're filled with game."

"I envy you, lad." Old, half-forgotten desires stirred in Patrick.

"Don't envy anybody who lives out there these days, Governor. It's a hard lot, what with the Erie and the Illinois and Miami on the warpath, and all the nations of the Iroquois coming south on raids."

Patrick sighed. "I've had reports every few months on conditions in the District, but I've had no militia to spare."

"Kentucky needs no men, Governor. We'll look after ourselves if you'll give us other help." Clark sat upright. "I'm here as the representative of the settlers. We've hatched a scheme, and if you'll give us what we need, I can pretty damned well guarantee that the whole of Kentucky—all the way to the Mississippi—will be safe."

Patrick removed his spectacles and leaned forward in his chair.

"The British have stirred up the tribes for the past year. Fort Detroit is the main headquarters, and the Redcoats hand out money and rum there to any Indians who'll promise to drive us out of the Kentucky District."

"It sounds logical."

"The savages don't think as we do, Governor. Promises mean nothing to them, and they'd as soon spend their days hunting after they've bought knives and blankets with British silver and filled their bellies with British rum. That's known to the generals in Quebec and the colonels at Fort Detroit, of course, so they've devised a system that's been right effective. There's more silver and more rum waiting for the warriors at every British wilderness fort on all the rivers in the Kentucky District and the rest of the Ohio country.

"Very clever, but not clever enough. The forts are undermanned, and the troops stationed there are lazy and gluttonous. They have all the meat and fish they can eat, and you can be sure they don't give all their rum to the Indians." Clark slapped the desk sharply. "Governor, I can take every damned one of those forts with a small expedition of no more than two to three hundred men, and I have all the volunteers I need in Kentucky. Once we control the outposts, the savages will scatter and the whole wilderness will drop into our hands like a ripe peach that falls when you shake the tree."

"What do you need from me, George?" Patrick asked bluntly.

"Gunpowder and lead for bullets. Enough dependable rifles and pistols and blankets to supply a battalion. Boats built to my specifications that can navigate the rivers. And boots of strong cowhide or buffalo leather. These damned moccasins wear out on long marches." Clark held up a large foot.

"If I accomplished nothing else as governor, I'd like to be known as a man who helped make the west secure for the United States. But there's a problem, George. The Burgesses have been bleeding Virginia white, and there's sure to be a scream of protest in the Assembly because the Kentucky District pays no taxes."

"That's what I was afraid you'd say."

Patrick pushed back his chair and began to pace. "You tell me the settlers elected you as their emissary. Do you have any documents to prove it?"

"Hell, no!" Clark said resentfully. "You'll have to take my word for it."

"Easy, lad." Patrick was amused, but became lost in thought again. "Were you given any specific instructions?"

"I'm here to get help, and nobody cares how."

"Mmm. Is there much political consciousness in the District, George?"

"I don't rightly know I understand you, Governor."

"Do men there still think of themselves as Virginians?"

"Certainly! That's why I'm in Williamsburg."

Patrick walked up and down more rapidly. "Where are you staying in town?"

"I just got here. I aim to look up some friends later, and I hope I'll find someone who'll give me a bed."

"You have one. You're the official guest of the governor."

Clark thanked him, but realized that more than hospitality was on his mind and waited expectantly.

"You say you've been granted extraordinary powers to deal with the situation here."

"Yes, sir. The boys will accept any conditions, provided we get help we need to take those forts."

"I'm assuming that you can capture them, George." Patrick smiled fleetingly. "Now, then. The reason your visit is official is because you're here as a petitioner. Kentucky is asking that it no longer be regarded as a District, and that it be incorporated into the state as a county."

"That would be great, Governor! Everybody out yonder would be as happy as a deer that just found a new salt lick."

"Good. I'll send a message to the Burgesses telling them you're here for that purpose, and we'll arrange a series of meetings between you and the Assembly leaders. We'll take Jefferson, Mason, and perhaps one or two others into our confidence, but I want you to discuss your military plans with no one else."

"I don't—"

"You will, George, if you listen carefully. If I ask the Assembly for funds to buy the supplies and equipment you need, there will be weeks of debate, perhaps months. Your whole strategy will be exposed in public, and it'll be a miracle if the British don't learn it. There are still Loyalist sympathizers in the state, even in Williamsburg."

"Hang the bastards, Governor."

"We assume a man's innocence until he's proved guilty. That's a British legal tradition, George, and I thank the Almighty we've kept it, because democracy couldn't function without it. You aren't to discuss your strategy with anyone, understand?"

"Yes, sir. But—"

"Wait until I've finished, George. You'll be asked to testify before a committee of the Burgesses set up for the exclusive purpose of deciding whether Kentucky should be admitted to the state as a county. Talk as much as you please about your rich land and timber. The members of the committee will be thinking of property taxes."

"Folks out yonder don't have much hard cash, Governor."

"Few people do these days, anywhere. Those paper Continental dollars are a national curse. Personally, I'm not worried about the question of whether Kentucky does or doesn't pay its taxes. It will carry its share of the burden after the war ends and more settlers make their homes out there." Patrick went back to his desk, shaking his head approvingly. "Yes, this is the best way."

Young Clark was still bewildered.

"I'll send a special message to the Assembly, asking for the admission of Kentucky. I can imagine no reason why there should be opposition from anyone. Not even the tidewater conservatives will protest. The bill can be passed before Christmas without difficulty, and I'll sign it at once. The rest will be easy."

"Hell, Governor, I need gunpowder and boats and—"

"Yes, George, I know." Patrick ignored a sudden feeling of fatigue. "Under the terms of the Constitution, the Governor may appropriate and assign state funds for use within the state as he sees fit. Once Kentucky is a county, I'll deem it proper to give you every last rifle, pair of boots, and blanket you request. Make out your list now, to save time, and I'll put Philip to work finding out where we can put our hands on the supplies you want and need."

Clark understood at last, and bellowed so loudly that Philip opened the door and peered into the office to make certain the governor was suffering no harm. "By God, sir," the Kentuckian declared, "you're sharp enough to be a wilderness man!"

"That," Patrick replied a trifle wistfully, "is the greatest compliment I've ever been paid."

7

George Rogers Clark's boats, lightweight but sturdy, were loaded with precious supplies, and forty Virginia volunteers who had joined his expedition planned to sail the little flotilla up the James River to its headwaters. Several long portages lay ahead before the company reached Kentucky County and the commander, accompanied by the newcomers, joined the wilderness men who awaited him there. But spirits were high, and Clark himself felt certain his daring scheme to drive the British out of the western lands would succeed.

Patrick shared his optimism. The maneuver to make Kentucky an integral part of Virginia had succeeded, Clark had all the munitions, gunpowder, and other items he had requested, and strenuous efforts had been made to maintain the utmost secrecy. Even the volunteers had been kept in the dark and knew only that they would cross the mountains to take part in a vaguely defined campaign on the frontier. The only political leaders who had been told the details of the ambitious project were Jefferson and Mason.

Both of them, accompanied by their wives, attended a small farewell dinner for Clark at the Governor's Palace. In a surprise ceremony, Patrick tendered the young wilderness fighter a commission as a Colonel of Virginia Militia, accompanied by orders granting him the right to recruit men, buy supplies as needed and conduct operations as he saw fit. Jefferson administered the oath to the new officer, using Dorothea Henry's Bible, and toasts were offered in Madeira, porter, and West Indian chocolate. Clark himself drank whiskey for the last time, strong spirits being scarce in the wilderness.

The following morning Dorothea joined her husband and their guest for an unusually early breakfast, as Clark intended to leave before sunrise for a rendezvous with his volunteers on the James. He ate heartily, as always, and praised Dorothea's sausage meat so extravagantly that she had a package of it made up for him to take on his journey. The atmosphere was relaxed and convivial, but Patrick realized that Dorothea was tense beneath her façade of gaiety. Clark appeared somewhat nervous, too, although he was full of his usual blunt good humor.

The dreadful suspicion struck Patrick that his wife and the rugged young wilderness man, who were members of the same generation, had learned to care for each other. The very idea shocked him, and he tried to dismiss it from his mind, but could not. In a sense, he wouldn't be able to blame either of them. Dorothea was lovelier than ever, and he felt sure that marriage to a man almost twice her age was a strain. And he didn't see how any woman could resist the forthright, masculine charms of Clark, who radiated so much strength and robust health as well as intelligence.

Suddenly, however, he knew his fears had been misplaced. Shortly before the meal ended, Elizabeth Henry Aylett arrived with her husband, and everything fell into place when Patrick saw that Philip was dressed in buckskins similar to Clark's, and carried a brace of pistols in his belt, a long rifle over his shoulder and a knife in his boot top.

Everyone looked at the governor as he half-rose from his chair, clutching his linen napkin, then sank into it again. "I dislike conspiracies," he muttered. "Someone should have told me."

Dorothea started to answer.

But Philip silenced her. It was his place to speak, and he faced his father-in-law courageously. "If I had told you my plans, sir, you'd have forbidden me to go."

Patrick knew he was right, but was reluctant to admit it.

"Please don't be angry, Papa," Elizabeth begged. "It's Phil's right to fight for America—and Virginia."

He reached up and wearily patted her arm.

239

"I reckon I'm at fault, if anyone is, Governor," Clark boomed. "He's a damn—a very good shot, and there aren't many who stand up to me as he did the day I came here. He'd make a good officer in any commander's corps, and I'm glad I got him."

"You've accepted a commission, Philip?"

"Yes, sir. Colonel Clark swore me in late last night as a lieutenant."

"Very tidy, indeed. I granted George the right to issue commissions as he pleases, and I can't revoke the privilege without damaging his whole cause."

Clark reddened beneath his tan, and Philip shifted his weight from one foot to the other as he stared down at Lord Dunmore's Turkish rug.

Elizabeth stepped into the breach. "Spencer Roane will be here in a week or two, now that he's being discharged because of his wounds. Anne wrote that she's bringing him home from Valley Forge. He's really a much more experienced lawyer than Philip—"

"I see." Patrick wiped the corners of his mouth, hoping to hide his wry amusement, and then dropped his napkin onto the table. "I'm expected to exchange one son-in-law for another as my secretary."

"You've always admired Spencer," Dorothea interjected, entering the conversation for the first time. "You know he'll be far more competent than Philip."

Patrick raised an eyebrow. "I suspect, Mrs. Henry, that your delicate hand guided this whole operation."

She smiled impudently, to the dismay of the others, who were very much ill at ease. "The defendant pleads guilty, Your Worship, and realizes she can't appeal her case—because there's no higher court."

There was a long silence, which grew more uncomfortable with each passing moment.

"Philip," Patrick said at last, "you'll need a good meal before you start out on a long march. Mrs. Henry, send for another platter of sausages and grits, if you please. And Elizabeth, stop hovering! It's a childhood habit you haven't conquered, and if you're moving back in here with us while your husband is away, you'll have to remember not to irritate more than you can help.

George, you're making me suffer a great inconvenience, so don't waste his talents. If a British garrison is too strong to be stormed, it's plain he can take it by intrigue. Will someone pass me the pitcher of mead?"

8

Spencer Roane, neatly attired in a dark suit, raised himself to his feet with the aid of his walking stick as Dorothea came into the governor's office.

"I've told you a thousand times not to stand on formality with me," she said.

"It's different in the family quarters." He insisted on holding her chair for her.

Patrick waited for them to subside. Youth, he had discovered, loved protocol, and a young wife had taught him new patience. "Tell Dolly the news from the Capitol," he said as soon as they were settled.

"Mr. Mason and Mr. Tyler are preparing a petition asking the governor to serve a third term," his son-in-law said, "and Mr. Jefferson is urging that no one else be nominated."

"I knew it!" Dorothea was on her feet again.

She was so distraught that Spencer decided to remove himself as quickly and discretely as possible. "Jamie Madison is coming in to see me," he murmured, "so please excuse me." He limped out, realizing that neither Patrick nor his wife was aware of his departure.

"It's an imposition, Mr. Henry. You'll simply have to tell them I'm expecting another baby and that you can't afford a third term." Dorothea's voice was shrill.

Patrick hated to upset her still more, but felt he couldn't compromise. "If I'm needed again, I must serve."

"Surely there are other men capable of acting as governor!"

"I dare say there are many. But the principles of democracy are inviolable, Mrs. Henry. If the electors want me for the office, I'd be guilty of criminal negligence if I refused."

"You take yourself too seriously."

"Maybe I do. But I can't let myself forget, ever, that I'm setting a precedent with every move I make. If the first citizen of Virginia tends his own garden instead of the public's, who can blame a young farmer for refusing to serve in the militia?"

"You'll set a magnificent precedent, I'm sure," Dorothea flared, "if you're the first high official of the state to be sent to debtors' prison."

He tried to mollify her. "There's a bill pending in the Assembly right now that will abolish imprisonment for debt."

"How convenient. I hope a special section will provide that idealistic public officials who should know better than to accept office can't be punished for bankruptcy."

"That's no way for a lady to talk." Her sarcasm grated, and Patrick felt his patience wearing thin.

"I'm not a lady, Governor Henry. I'm the wife of a man who puts his country ahead of his family. I have one baby to feed, and will soon have another, but my starry-eyed husband doesn't care if we starve." There was a faint note of hysteria evident in Dorothea's voice, and she brushed angrily at a curl that had become unpinned and fell from the crown of her head across the front of a shoulder.

Patrick decided to call a halt before she worked herself into a rage. "The feeding of my family is my responsibility," he said coldly. "You'll have no legitimate complaint until there is actually a lack of food in our larder. Now, if you'll excuse me, Mrs. Henry, matters of state require my full attention. We can continue this— ah—little chat—later in the day."

Dorothea sat down in the chair opposite his desk. "You can't get rid of me as you would a delegation of citizens who've come to see you about some trifling complaint. I'm your wife, sir!"

"You give me no opportunity to forget it, ma'am." He bowed deeply, polished his spectacles and picked up a sheaf of papers from the desk. "If it pleases you to stay here, I won't ask the honor guard to remove you by force. Much as I'm tempted. I'll simply take myself to Spencer's office, where I can work without interruption."

She leaped to her feet and, hurrying to the door, blockaded it. "I beg you to be sensible, Patrick. You're piling up so many debts that you'll never be able to repay them, not if you live to be a hundred years old."

"The aggravations to which I'm subjected every day and every night make that possibility remote." Patrick checked himself when he saw the pain in her eyes. It was unfair of him to engage in a debate with someone who wasn't his equal. "Dolly, my dear, I give you my solemn word that I'll find a way to relieve our debts. I can't tell you how I'll go about it because I honestly don't know. Nor can I afford the luxury of planning until we win the war and Parliament ratifies a treaty granting our independence."

Tears of frustration came to her eyes.

He gave her a handkerchief. "Three thousand of Virginia's sons are facing real starvation at General Washington's winter camp. Do you think I could live with my conscience if I didn't do everything in my power to find meat and grain for the men at Valley Forge? I'd be disloyal to my trust if I put my own convenience and comfort ahead of their need."

"I beg you to be sensible, that's all. Papa will gladly let you have as much money as you want—and won't charge you a ha'penny in interest rates."

Patrick's expression froze. "Under no circumstances could I accept funds from Nate."

"If Spencer Roane or Phil Aylett came to you for money, you'd give it to them."

"My relationship with my sons-in-law is not the same as my lifelong friendship with my father-in-law. I'm sure that a great many people have criticized me for marrying a young girl. If I accepted a loan from Nate, the whole state would know about it— and would laugh. I'd be accused of marrying for an ulterior purpose."

"You and I know it wasn't your motive, and so does Papa! What does it matter if others believe you had secret reasons?"

Patrick's voice became soft, almost caressing, and in his accent was a hint of the Scottish burr that appeared only when he was in great emotional difficulty. "Do you not yet know a Henry's pride?"

Dorothea was exasperated. "It's false pride!"

He stood, unmoving, and stared at her.

She flinched, afraid he intended to strike her.

Patrick reached past her, raised the latch and opened the door, then walked stiff-legged into Spencer Roane's office. Perhaps he had been wrong to marry someone so young—and so wealthy, although it was too late now to berate himself, and he could only hope she would grow more mature in the years ahead. Adversity would temper her or break her spirit, and for her sake he felt the deep, anxious pangs of personal fear he had never known for himself. America's greatest trials were still ahead, and Dorothea would know real suffering before ultimate victory was won.

EIGHT

1779–1781

1

The bell in the corner of Spencer Roane's office tinkled discreetly, and he quietly left the meeting over which he had been presiding. The governor, who took no holidays and worked late every evening, was always in a foul mood these days, and was inclined to become caustic if he was kept waiting.

Patrick sat back in his padded chair, spectacles pushed high on his forehead, and surprised his son-in-law by grinning amiably. "Here is a draft of a very short letter," he said, waving a single sheet of paper. "Have enough copies made to send one to each member of our Congressional delegation and all leaders of the Burgesses. You might alert the commander of the cavalry detachment at the barracks, too. I'll want special couriers to deliver the copies. I'm writing another in my own hand to General Washington, and I'd like a squad commanded by an officer to carry it to him."

Spencer took the sheet of paper and, unable to curb his curiosity, read it swiftly.

Patrick chuckled. "I've had a full report from George Clark within the hour. He's done it, the rascal. Kaskaskia and Vincennes are ours, along with a half-dozen smaller posts. The whole of the Northwest Territory is in our hands, and I'm sending him reinforcements so he can take Fort Detroit. After all, there's a limit. A force of fewer than two hundred men can't perform miracles."

Spencer blinked and read the letter again. "I'm blamed if I know what you call a miracle, sir! Not one of his boys has been killed, only seven have suffered injuries and he's sending Colonel Henry Hamilton, the British commander in the territory, to Williamsburg as a prisoner. Are you sure these figures are accurate, Governor?"

"I'll take George Clark's word for it, but I'm a mite puzzled about housing a distinguished prisoner, and I hope to pass him along to Washington. But I mustn't sound ungrateful. The western lands are doubly ours now—by rights of charter and of conquest. I reckon you won't regret your partnership with me in buying that parcel of Kentucky land. It will be worth three times what we paid for it when this news becomes known—even though we won't be able to collect more than promises if we sell now. I suggest we accept no offers before the war ends."

"Whatever you say, sir." Spencer stared at the calm man behind the desk. "You don't seem in the least surprised by this victory, Governor. To me it's incredible."

"Oh, I could pretend I expected it all along, but I'd be a liar. I didn't know what to hope, Spencer. I suspected Clark might be a madman, but I couldn't be certain. When men have lived out in the wilderness for years, they don't think or act like ordinary mortals any more. Clark saw great visions—and made them come true. I envy him, and I'm proud of him." Patrick's mood changed abruptly, and he pulled his glasses down to the bridge of his nose. "Here's Colonel Clark's report. Consider it confidential military information, and show it to no one until I notify you otherwise."

Spencer glanced through the document written in Clark's angular hand. "Phil Aylett is in command of the detachment guarding Colonel Hamilton!"

"Keep that news to yourself. Elizabeth is visiting my mother in Hanover, so I'll have to find some excuse to bring her here."

"Surely you're going to tell Liz her husband will soon be home!"

"I'll tell no one, and neither will you. If word leaks out, the Loyalists will notify the British, and a relief column will be sent out into the mountains to rescue Hamilton."

The precaution was wise, and Spencer admired his father-in-law's foresight. Nevertheless he hesitated.

Patrick knew what was going through his mind. "I'll take full responsibility in the family as well as outside it. Elizabeth will understand the need for secrecy when I'm finally able to tell her the full story."

He wasn't thinking of Elizabeth, and both of them knew it. Dorothea would be furious when she learned that Patrick had not taken her into his confidence, and probably would make a scene. He sighed, his joy over George Rogers Clark's magnificent achievements vanishing. Perhaps he was wrong to anticipate Dorothea's reaction, but she found fault with everything he did these days, so it would be just as well to brace himself for still more domestic trouble.

2

War came to the Southern states with a vengeance in 1779. Companies of Loyalist troops, armed and supplied by the British, made swift, unexpected raids on scores of small towns and settlements, burning, looting, and killing. The militia of Virginia and North Carolina, Georgia and South Carolina struck back with equal brutality, and men everywhere suspected the patriotism of their neighbors.

The French alliance, now ratified by a formal treaty, had given General Washington new arms and uniforms for his battle-hardened Continental regulars, but he still lacked the strength to come to grips with General Sir Henry Clinton, Sir William Howe's successor. A great French fleet had been sent to help him, but British seamanship was still superior, and the blockade of American ports remained effective.

Pennsylvanians rejoiced when Clinton evacuated Philadelphia, but the news offered small comfort to the South, where it was rumored that a major Redcoat force would soon be landed to isolate and occupy the whole area. Tension mounted steadily as spring approached and the armies left their winter camps.

"I have it on no less an authority than General Washington

himself," Patrick told George Mason and John Tyler, whom he was entertaining at mid-day dinner in the Governor's Palace at Williamsburg, "that Horatio Gates will be sent from Pennsylvania and New Jersey to protect us." He made a wry face.

"You don't hold a high opinion of Gates, P.H.?" Mason asked.

"I wish I could share Washington's faith in him. I would have preferred Benedict Arnold, but he's still recuperating from the injuries he suffered at Saratoga, so he'll stay on as Military Governor of Philadelphia."

"I reckon his marriage to a girl half his age has robbed him of his energy as a warrior." Tyler chuckled, then broke off abruptly. "Sorry, P.H. No personal offense meant."

Patrick needed all his self-control to remain calm. "None taken, John. Help yourselves to more tripe and turnip greens, gentlemen. I must apologize for the fare, but the governor's table is no richer than any other these days."

Mason made an effort, too, giving Tyler a chance to recover from his embarrassment. "I hear rumors every week that French supplies are being landed, but I've yet to see a barrel of wheat or beef."

The thin, high-pitched wail of an infant drifted down into the dining room, and there was an uncomfortable silence. Patrick wondered whether to make a light, passing comment, but realized anything he might say would sound defensive. So he smiled, as graciously as he could, and passed the decanter of Canary wine. "You said in your message of this morning that you had urgent business to discuss with me, gentlemen?"

Tyler was poised again, sure of himself. "It's the unanimous opinion of the Assembly's steering committee that Virginia's worst days are ahead, P.H."

"I'm afraid you may be right."

"For that reason, we've been named a sub-committee of two to wait on you with a request. Will you accept another term of office as governor?"

"My personal feelings in the matter are irrelevant," Patrick said. "George, you wrote the Constitutional provision stipulating that no governor may serve more than three consecutive terms. As I understand it, I'd be eligible again in another year. But I'm barred from succeeding myself this spring."

Mason pushed his plate away. "The Assembly is willing to amend the Constitution."

"No," Patrick declared firmly. "I'd veto any such amendment."

His visitors looked at him in surprise, and both wondered whether Dorothea's well-known attitude was responsible.

"If we change the Constitution at will, it'll soon become a meaningless document. We limited a governor's tenure to prevent any man from becoming a tyrant—"

Mason interrupted with a laugh. "Everyone in Virginia knows you're no tyrant, P.H."

"Does any human being know another that well? I favor the abolition of slavery when the war ends, in spite of the personal inconvenience my family and I would suffer. I'm well aware of the harm that would be done to the state's economy at a crucial time, when we'll need to reorganize our agricultural production. But the principle of freedom for all men—not just some—is more important. Do you suppose there are some who'd call me a tyrant if I announced my position on the subject today?"

Tyler shuffled his feet and tugged at his lace cuffs. "You aren't serious."

"Indeed I am. As it happens, I don't want to cause unnecessary dissension, so I'll keep my views on slavery to myself until the war ends. But that doesn't change my basic views on the question." Patrick sipped his cup of mead. "I'm flattered by your offer, but I can't consider it."

"Virginia needs you at the helm again, P.H.," Mason protested.

"Nonsense. No man is indispensable. And if the citizens of a democracy believe otherwise, they're denying that a government such as ours can succeed. I'd be derelict in my duty if I permitted the Constitution to be changed so that I—or any man—could benefit."

His guests looked at each other, and Tyler smiled wanly. "I told you this is what he'd say, George."

Mason nodded, then turned back to the governor. "The members of the steering committee share your faith in representative government, P.H., but the majority view is that the Constitution should be altered in time of great danger."

"Then we don't hold the same views. We can end the danger tomorrow—today, if you will—by abandoning our experiment and swearing allegiance to the Crown. If we intend to survive as a separate governmental entity, we must demonstrate our loyalty to the system we've created. I'll grant you it isn't easy, but there's no alternative." Patrick's manner was that of a severe schoolmaster, but suddenly he relented. "Have you thought of Richie Lee for the post?"

"He's been away from home for too long, and he's more valuable in the Continental Congress," Tyler said.

"Jefferson, then?"

"If you won't change your mind, he's probably the best available," Mason said, and laughed wryly.

"May I know what you find so amusing?" Patrick asked.

"I'm just remembering a remark Jamie Madison made at the steering committee meeting. 'If Governor Henry turns us down,' he said, 'we'll have to take Jefferson. One way or another, we must have an idealist. Only a man with his head in the clouds would be foolish enough to govern Virginia in such perilous times.'"

3

"It's so good to be back in Virginia." Martha Fontaine sighed happily as she looked around the sewing room on the second floor of the Governor's Palace. "It even feels good to be here. You've made so many changes that I scarcely know this place."

"Mrs. Jefferson is welcome to the Palace, believe me," Dorothea replied ardently.

Martha laughed and, reaching out, patted her friend's hand. "You've had your problems living in a mansion too large for any family, and I've been miserable living in one room and sharing a kitchen with three other families. It was worth any inconvenience to be with John, even after little Patrick was born, but I shall always think of waiting in line to boil water whenever I think of

York. Not that I have anything against the town, mind you. But with the Congress there, it was the most crowded place in Pennsylvania. Even so, I was more contented there than I've been in Philadelphia these past months."

"Tell me about Peggy Arnold."

"I don't like her. She's very young—"

"Younger than we are?"

"Oh, yes. By several years. She's pretty enough, in a bold way, and she leads the general around like a trained bear with a ring in his nose."

"In that event," Dorothea said caustically, "we aren't in the least alike."

"Oh, dear. I was afraid you'd hear talk."

"How could I help it, Martha? A principal topic of conversation in Williamsburg has been gossip about middle-aged men who marry young wives. I'm sick of it!"

"I'm glad you're going home, too," Martha said sympathetically. "I'm opening our house again. John and I decided it would be best for me to stay in one place now that he's been given a regiment in the Marquis de Lafayette's new division. And you'll be only a ten-minute ride away. Why, it'll be like the old days again —except for the babies."

"You haven't heard," Dorothea said dully. "No one knows yet. You're the first, and you needn't pretend ignorance to your father. I've got to tell someone—or burst. We aren't going back to Hanover."

Martha was too shocked to speak, and could only gape at her.

"Scotchtown has been sold."

"Oh, no!"

"I'm going there this week to pack the last of our belongings still in the place. And on the very day that His Excellency's term ends," Dorothea continued, bitterness and another, unidentifiable quality in her voice, "we leave at once for our new home. We have quite a journey ahead of us."

Martha steeled herself, and waited.

"The settlers in the Blue Ridge foothills, down in the southwestern part of the state—near the North Carolina border—have named a county for him. That's where we're going to live."

"Henry County?"

"It's about two hundred miles from here. My lord and master has bought a house and more than sixteen thousand acres of land with a small fraction of what he's being paid for Scotchtown."

"But why, Dolly? It sounds mad to me!"

Dorothea smoothed her skirt, tucked in a stray lock of hair and spoke slowly, with great care. "In the first place, he's always wanted to live on the frontier—as you know."

"But this is no time to give in to a whim!"

"He doesn't consider it a whim because—and this is his second reason—he believes land values in the west will rise very sharply after the war. We're almost hopelessly in debt, so he's using the rest of the Scotchtown sale money to buy still more land, some of it in Henry County, some in Kentucky. If the land really should be worth more in peacetime, we might be lucky enough to pay off some of what we owe. He hasn't earned a farthing in five years or more, you know, and he goes wild at the mere suggestion of accepting any help from my family."

"But surely his wages as governor—"

"He won't accept them." Dorothea laughed savagely. "He says Virginia is in such great financial difficulty that it would be wrong to add to the taxpayers' burdens."

Martha looked at her friend's delicate, soft hands and skin that had always been carefully protected from the sun. "I—I'm overwhelmed. I don't know what to say."

"In a strange way, I'm rather looking forward to it."

"But you've always lived in luxury, Dolly. You aren't the type to make your home in the wilderness."

"I'll manage. Besides, we're taking the household staff with us."

"Even so, there's so much you'll have to do yourself."

"I'm not completely helpless." Dorothea became aggressive.

Martha shrugged. "I'm only thinking of your happiness."

"So am I. My own—and his. You had a taste of public life when you were his hostess. But it isn't the same when one is his wife. We've had no privacy since the day we were married. I've never known how many guests to expect for noon dinner, and the evenings have been nightmares. I've thought myself lucky when we've had breakfast alone once or twice in a week."

"I had no idea the strain was so great."

"It's been much worse for him than for me. Mr. Henry is no boy, Martha, and he's been subjected to a frightful strain that's making him an old man before his time. I sometimes curse his sense of duty, but we'll be free in Henry County. It's time that others take up the task of guiding Virginia."

4

Official Williamsburg crowded into the palace gardens, and Patrick's last order as governor was a request to the militia commander on duty at the gate, asking him to admit more than two thousand ordinary citizens who had come to watch the unprecedented transfer of power from one elected chief executive to another. To most onlookers the event was a disappointment. Patrick and his successor shared an intense dislike of pomp, and although a militia fife and drum corps offered to play for the occasion, both refused.

The brief ceremony of swearing in the new governor was scheduled to take place promptly at noon, and Patrick had planned to retire quietly to private life. But James Madison, now acting chairman of the Assembly steering committee, urged him to speak a few words to the throng, and others added their pleas. Although reluctant to dim another man's glory, Patrick finally consented, and climbed onto a bench near the tables where a light fruit and wine punch would be served to the invited guests.

Governor-elect Thomas Jefferson led the applause, and the young militiamen on duty in the garden cheered.

Patrick raised a hand for silence. "This is too sunny and pleasant a day for me to make an address," he said, and although he seemed to declaim effortlessly, his voice carried to the farthest reaches of the crowd. "The record of my three-year stewardship speaks for itself, ladies and gentlemen. Where I have erred, a defense of my actions would be a waste of breath. Whether I have succeeded will be determined in the years to come.

"There is only one criterion of success or failure. Has Virginia done her share in our fight for liberty?"

"Yes!" The response was spontaneous.

253

He shook his head. "No, good friends. You and I cannot yet make that claim. When our independence is won, it will be time enough. Until then, all of us must work with Governor Jefferson, accepting his direction in our struggle for freedom. I pledge him my own constructive support in all things. May the Almighty grant to the United States of America freedom from bondage."

The crowd roared its approval, and a half-dozen hands helped him to the ground. Dorothea, in a gown of pale yellow velvet, and by far the most attractive woman present, took his arm and he shook hands with the governor-elect who stood a few feet away with the shy, delicate Mrs. Jefferson.

"Listen to them, P.H.," Jefferson said. "I swear, you could read to them from the *Iliad* in the original Greek, and they'd love you for it."

Dorothea, in a gayer mood than she had enjoyed for many months, laughed brightly.

"We hope, ma'am," the governor-elect told her, "that you won't bury yourself in the forests of Henry County."

His wife nodded her assent.

"In fact, we'll be honored if you'll stay at the palace with us whenever you come to Williamsburg with P.H."

The laugh died in Dorothea's throat, and she looked apprehensively at her husband.

"Tom has offered me a place in our Congressional delegation," he said quickly, "but I've felt it needful to refuse. Others are more familiar with the situation in Philadelphia, and can perform a more valuable service there."

"Nevertheless," Jefferson interrupted, good-humored but firm, "I agree with General Washington. Your talents must not be wasted in our hour of peril." He turned blandly to Dorothea. "You've seen the general's letter, I trust?"

"We've been so busy I've had no chance to show it to her," Patrick said, unable to meet his wife's eye.

A committee headed by George Wythe appeared to escort Jefferson to the sundial beside the fishpond, where he would take the oath of office, and the conversation was terminated abruptly.

Dorothea continued to stand motionless beside Patrick, and only the tightening of her fingers on his arm indicated her tension.

"Scarcely a day has passed in the last five years without one politician or another speaking of our hour of peril. The phrase is a tired cliché, and I'm heartily sick of it," she murmured.

"So am I, but it happens to be true," Patrick replied. "We've been spared the worst of the war so far, but if the British really invaded the South, I dread to think of what our people will be forced to endure."

The brief ceremony began, and he was grateful that Dorothea was forced to fall silent. This moment, when he was leaving high office, was not the time to tell her his conscience would not permit him to retire completely from public life. He didn't know specifically what he would do, but it was enough that Virginia still needed him.

5

"Leatherwood" was no crude frontier dwelling, but a surprisingly gracious house of weathered pine clapboard, three stories high and located at the crest of a hill dominating its domain, which stretched out toward the horizon on all sides. Adjacent to the main building was a kitchen made of Blue Ridge rocks, fitted together with infinite patience, and behind the house stood the barns, stables, servants' quarters and cedarwood storage sheds. Off to one side stood a partly completed sawmill, powered by the waters of a deep, swift-running brook.

The rugged mountains of the Blue Ridge chain towered on the horizon to the west, and everywhere—on the crests and slopes of hills, in little valleys and gorges—were countless thousands of trees. Most were pines, some rising thirty feet and higher, yet dwarfed by magnificent poplars. There were elm and oak and maple, yellow ash and cedar, hickory and chestnut and blue spruce, all blending together and forming a solid blanket of green that, in late spring, stretched out toward the horizon.

Patrick stood alone some distance from the house, gazing out toward the mountains and inhaling the crisp air. His eyes glistened, and when his wife joined him he slipped an arm around her and kissed her.

"Dorothea is eating porridge," she said, "and Sarah is asleep."

"You've explored the house, Mrs. Henry?"

"I have, sir, and I can find no fault with it."

"Nor I with this countryside. I've seen trout in the brook yonder, and these forests must be teeming with game. If I haven't lost my eye, I'll put meat on our table seven days a week. Our crops of wheat and corn are hardy, and the tobacco out here is smaller than the crop grown farther east in the lowlands, but it's a strong plant." He handed her a small bouquet of yellow and violet flowers. "I picked these for you beside the brook."

"They're so pretty you should have let them grow." Dorothea reached up to kiss him, then twined the flowers in her hair.

"You look like a girl in her teens, Mrs. Henry. No one would suspect you're the mother of two children—and soon to have a third."

"I've watched the years roll away from you, sir, on our journey out here. I was afraid you'd lost your wits when you first told me you'd bought this place. But you were right, and I salute your wisdom."

"You're happy, Dolly?"

"Happier than I would have imagined possible. The world seems so far away. Mr. and Mrs. Henry of Henry County live in a world of their own!"

6

Less than twenty-four hours after Patrick and Dorothea moved into "Leatherwood," neighbors called on them in such numbers that the parlor overflowed and everyone had to go outdoors into the yard. The women brought gifts of deermeat sausage, wild boar bacon they had cured themselves, fruit pies, and the most precious of all offerings in a community far from produce markets, carefully nurtured young vegetable plants for Dorothea's kitchen garden.

The men, all armed with loaded rifles and carrying powder-horns, brought jugs of hard apple cider and of a potent, virtually colorless corn whiskey. Patrick took a token sip of each, and his guests settled down to serious drinking. A pit was dug near the kitchen, and an elderly man took charge of roasting two sides of venison. The women produced loaves of fresh bread, some of wheat flour, some of barley and some of corn, and there were huge bowls of cold sliced beets spiced with onions, roasted Cherokee squash and melons with pink meat from vines that flourished in some of the more protected valleys.

Small children were constantly underfoot, laughing, shouting, running and, occasionally, weeping. The women took Dorothea's measure, and warmed to her when they discovered she was completely lacking in ostentation. "You don't look like a governor's wife or a rich man's daughter," one of them said, and meant the observation as the greatest of compliments.

The men, most of them farmers and planters, with a sprinkling of artisans in the crowd, were mature and quiet, and weighed their words carefully when Patrick asked about crop prices and weather. Only the absence of young males and, indeed, of men in their thirties and even their early forties, was a reminder that Virginia was engaged in a grim struggle for her existence.

Everyone departed in mid-afternoon, intending to reach home before sundown. The power of the Cherokee had been so thoroughly diminished earlier in the war, the men said, that the savages no longer dared to attack in daylight, but travelers who ventured into the forests after dark still ran the risk of being assaulted by small war parties of raiders.

Dorothea, flushed with the excitement of having achieved success and won acceptance in her own right, put her babies to bed and then went in search of Patrick. She had expected to find him either in the parlor or in his new library, where stacks of books tied in bundles with vines still awaited their owner's attention. But he appeared to have vanished, and she hunted for a quarter of an hour before seeing him in a small clearing near the brook.

She went down the hill from the house to join him, found him staring down with unseeing eyes at the water swirling over smooth stones, and her smile became less confident. However, she saw no point in borrowing trouble, and spoke with self-assurance. "That was one of the best parties we've ever given, Mr. Henry. And I didn't lift a finger."

Patrick raised his head, glanced at her vaguely and frowned.

Dorothea slipped her arm through his. "I hope you didn't eat too many venison ribs. They always give you indigestion."

"I have indigestion of another sort, the kind caused by fear."

She saw he was serious, and was amazed. From earliest childhood she had thought of him as fearless.

"I'm afraid I'm going to make my wife unhappy."

Dorothea laughed.

Patrick remained solemn. "I was told today that the voters of Henry County held a special election when they heard we were moving out here. They've elected me—unanimously—to represent them in the Burgesses."

She caught her breath. "I see."

"Do you? I couldn't have lived with my conscience if I'd refused to serve. I can be of help to these good people. Maybe I fancy myself, but I believe I can do more for them than anyone else they might send. I've accepted—because I have no choice, even though I don't know what harm it will do to our relationship."

Dorothea stared at him, her face wooden.

"I shouldn't have married you. I can see it clearly now."

"You're sorry, Mr. Henry?"

"For your sake, Dolly. You should have had a husband nearer your own age, rather than an old man who offers you no real companionship and is burdening you with a large family."

"You're suggesting," she said softly, "that I should have married John Paul, perhaps."

"You're more nearly the same generation. You think alike."

Dorothea made a swift, vehement gesture. "I married my husband because I love him, Mr. Henry."

He stooped, picked up a round stone from the bank and hurled it downstream into the brook. "My sense of guilt is all the greater, then, because I haven't earned such loyalty."

"I knew before we left Williamsburg that this—this honeymoon would be temporary. Governor Jefferson told me how badly you're needed in the government. So did Mr. Madison and Mr. Tyler. And George Mason—how little he knows you—begged me to use my influence and persuade you to accept a new post."

Patrick looked at her uncertainly.

"I've been spoiled all my life, sir, but my selfishness has limits. Suppose I were married to John Paul—whom I don't love. He's off at sea, I have no idea where—"

"He's been given command of a powerful squadron embarked on a secret mission."

"No matter. Such things mean nothing to a woman. All I know is that I wouldn't see him from one month to the next. Martha and John are separated, possibly until the war's end—assuming he survives—and so are thousands of other couples. I should be grateful for any time you can spare me."

Patrick was bewildered. "What causes this change in your attitude, Dolly?"

"It isn't in the least changed. I resent the drain on your strength made by public office. I was hoping—in vain, I know—that you could resume your law practice and reduce our debts. I feel lost and confused when we aren't together, and it will be even worse, now that you'll have to travel to Williamsburg for Assembly sessions."

"Richmond. We're moving the state government. Williamsburg has become too crowded."

"The difference in distance is slight."

"You could come with me, Dolly, and we could rent quarters there."

"No, Mr. Henry. I've been a child long enough. This is our home. I intend to live here and rear our family. I'll rejoice whenever you can spend a little time with me."

Patrick reached for her, and to his horror she burst into tears, wrenching free.

"Don't touch me!" she cried. "I must fight this battle alone if I'm to be worthy of your name."

He forced himself to remain at the bank of the creek as Dorothea gathered her skirts and ran, sobbing, up the hill to the house. He supposed he should feel relieved, but instead was filled with an overwhelming sadness. The war had robbed her of her youth, and she would never again be carefree and joyous. The unending struggle claimed victims in many places other than the fields of battle.

7

Richard Henry Lee seldom found time to visit Richmond when he came home from Philadelphia, but an unpublicized mission on behalf of the Continental Congress brought him to the new state capital in the autumn of 1780. He spent a day and a night as the governor's guest, then attended a meeting of the Burgesses, where he was accorded the privileges of the floor, heard flattering addresses by former colleagues and greeted old friends. Then, duty done, he retired to the Richmond Inn and dined privately in the suite of Assembly Leader Patrick Henry.

"It was like old times," he said, "sitting there in the front row with you, P.H."

Patrick smiled wearily and absently cut the food for which he had no appetite. "You don't know how often I wish I had you beside me again, Richie."

"Tom leaves a great deal to be desired as a governor, doesn't he?"

Patrick shrugged diplomatically.

"He deserved a second term, of course, but he lacks your executive talents. He's too busy converting the College of William and Mary into a university and establishing his new system of universal education."

"Comparisons are a waste of time. I did my best when I held the post, and Tom does all he can now."

Lee was disturbed by his old friend's dull, almost indifferent tone. "Had I known of your father's passing, I'd have left Philadelphia a week earlier for the funeral."

"Thank you, Richie. But he wouldn't have wanted any man to waste effort on the dead. In his quiet way he was a patriot."

"Your mother is well?"

"Well enough, everything considered. Johnny Syme is still on convalescent leave after his brush with that imp of Satan, Tarleton, so he's escorting her out to Henry County. She and Dorothea will be good for each other. Dorothea's mother is out there, too, and I wish I could persuade Martha to make a journey west. Between you and me, I don't think any of the seaboard counties are safe, what with Tarleton's Redcoat cavalry burning and looting. He appears to be a real fiend."

"I tried to explain to Tom last night that Tarleton's method of waging war represents British desperation. Lord Cornwallis is encouraging units like Tarleton's to commit outrages in the hope that we'll become panicky and surrender."

"We won't," Patrick said, awakening from his lethargy. "Clinton and Cornwallis don't understand Americans if they think anyone of standing will follow Benedict Arnold into their camp."

"I hope you're right." Lee dropped a chunk of bread onto his plate and appeared to be concentrating on mopping up gravy with it.

Patrick looked at him sharply. "Are you free to explain?"

"Only to you—and Jefferson. General Washington is badly shaken by Arnold's defection. He's afraid the infection may spread, and he knows the British high command is deliberately sowing terror in the Southern states. Clinton and Cornwallis have several goals in mind. They're trying to frighten us into submission, force American leaders to renounce our cause—"

"If we must, we'll fight them with our bare hands!"

"I wish Tom had your fury. Washington can spare no more men for the area. He doesn't know which way Clinton will jump, and he needs the bulk of his troops in New York and Pennsylvania. That means Virginia, Georgia, and the Carolinas will have to continue the fight without more than token support from the Continentals. I urged Tom to call up two more regiments of militia, but he's afraid the economy can't stand the strain."

"The governor is the only man in a position to know all the facts, Richie. I need hardly remind you that he'd resent interference from me."

Lee sighed deeply. "Thomas Jefferson remains calm in the face of catastrophe, and Patrick Henry takes refuge in diplomatic delicacy." He stood, went to the door of the parlor and, opening it, peered out into the corridor to make certain they weren't being overheard. Satisfied, he returned to the supper table. "You and Jefferson are in greater danger than ever before, P.H. Your danger is personal—and immediate."

261

Patrick remained unflustered.

"I've come to Richmond on General Washington's behalf to deliver a message to each of you from him. He's gained possession of captured enemy documents—I don't know how he got them, and I'm not really concerned with such details—that indicate you're major figures in the Redcoat plans. Colonel Banastre Tarleton is under orders to capture you and Jefferson. You're to be handed over to the commander of a Royal Navy squadron that's standing somewhere off the Virginia coast for the express purpose of delivering you to Sir Henry Clinton in New York."

Patrick leaned back in his chair, and laughed until tears filled his eyes.

"Tom thought it was amusing, too," Lee said angrily. "What neither of you seems to realize is that the British scheme is exceedingly clever. You're the two most popular leaders in the Southern states. Clinton hopes that—by hanging you—he can frighten and persuade others to reaffirm allegiance to the Crown."

"Oh, I understand Clinton's strategy, Richie, and I'm sure Tom sees it, too."

"Then maybe you'll share the joke with me." Lee drained his glass of Madeira so hurriedly that he coughed.

"I'm unfailingly astonished by the British inability to understand the people of this country. How long has Clinton been here now? At least since '77, as Howe's deputy, and maybe longer. His trouble is that he takes Great Britain with him wherever he goes." Patrick's smile faded. "He's incapable of conquering us because he doesn't know our minds and hearts. If Jefferson and I were hanged, the resolution of every other patriot in the United States would be stiffened. There's only one Benedict Arnold, and I thank God there are dozens like George Washington—and Richard Henry Lee!"

Lee inclined his head. "I'm grateful for the compliment, P.H. But," he added after a slight pause, "rhetoric won't save your neck or Jefferson's!"

Again Patrick laughed. "No, it won't. But before Clinton can swing us from a scaffold, his Colonel Tarleton will have to catch us."

8

The full fury of the war descended on Virginia in late 1780 and early 1781. Captured Charleston in South Carolina was the principal British base in the South, and Lord Cornwallis struck at will throughout the area, his cavalry under Tarleton creating so much havoc that the bumbling Horatio Gates, the choice of the Continental Congress for the American command in the South, was finally replaced by Washington's personal choice, Major General Nathanael Greene, a one-time Quaker and a blacksmith by trade who, it was said, never smiled.

New militia units were hastily called up, and every man capable of bearing arms was urged to join the colors. The Burgesses sat in continuous session, working day and night with Governor Jefferson in an effort to raise enough money to continue the struggle. Only Patrick Henry was absent from his post. The need for new volunteers was so desperate that he conceived and executed a plan of his own, and traveled incessantly from county to county, making recruiting speeches. He spoke so frequently that his voice became too hoarse for ordinary conversation, but he managed to summon reserves of energy and will to make himself heard whenever he mounted the stump.

In spite of Richard Henry Lee's warning the previous year, he was careless of his own safety. Washington, alarmed, wrote him a letter urging him to be more cautious, and Patrick replied in a short note. *"I am always in the company of fellow Virginians, my friends,"* he wrote, *"so I am always safe."*

His optimism proved to be unfounded, however. In neighboring North Carolina, hundreds of men banded together in Loyalist companies, and were joined by many Virginians. Sir Henry Clinton's grand strategy seemed to be working, and Cornwallis sent recruiting teams into the western hills.

Militia from the Carolinas, Virginia, and the Tennessee district of North Carolina learned that a large force of British regulars and Loyalists was traveling north, just east of the mountains, and moved with unaccustomed speed to meet this new threat. One of the most vicious fights of the war took place in what was to become known as the Battle of Kings Mountain, in North Carolina, and the Americans, the majority carrying their own weapons and wearing no uniforms other than armbands, won a smashing victory. In their fury they broke the supposedly inviolable rules of warfare by executing a number of prisoners.

By the time Patrick learned of the event, the battle had ended, and there was no reason for him to feel concerned for the welfare of his family at "Leatherwood," just a short distance above the North Carolina border. He soon learned that no part of Virginia was now safe: while he was recruiting in Louisa County, in January 1781, a British expedition was landed by sea and marched on Richmond.

Governor Jefferson, state officials, and the Assembly were forced to flee to Charlottesville, in Albemarle County. Patrick joined them, and from the governor heard the incredible news that the enemy force, which burned fifty buildings to the ground before being forced to withdraw, was commanded by none other than Benedict Arnold, now a brigadier general in Clinton's corps.

A half-regiment of untried militia commanded by Colonel Will Christian, Patrick's brother-in-law and former law partner, was given the task of protecting the legislators. But Christian himself doubted their effectiveness. "They're good lads," he confided to Patrick, "who should be conjugating Latin verbs, not carrying muskets they've never fired at a living enemy. I'll grant you our real troops are needed elsewhere, but I'd hate to depend on these boys in an emergency."

That emergency arose swiftly but not unexpectedly. Patrick and Christian, sharing a room in the overcrowded Piedmont Inn, formerly the Queen Charlotte, were having breakfast in the taproom with Tyler and Benjamin Harrison, who had recently returned from Philadelphia. A young militia lieutenant dashed in to find Christian, and was so agitated he forgot to salute.

"Colonel," he cried, "Tarleton and his devils are riding this way. They'll be here within the hour!"

The men at the table jumped to their feet.

"Have the troops been alerted?" Christian hurriedly buckled on his sword.

The junior officer looked abashed. "Well, they've heard the news right enough. But they've scattered, sir. Not more than a dozen or two are still at the barracks."

The story had been the same for more than six years: American veterans, Continentals and militia alike, fought courageously, but youthful recruits who had received no training often bolted at the first indication of trouble.

There was no time to regret what had happened. Christian sent his remaining men through the town to warn members of the Burgesses and other officials that the dreaded Tarleton was approaching, and sent two others to the governor's home at Monticello, three miles from Charlottesville, to make certain that he, too, had an opportunity to disappear into the wooded hills.

Patrick calmly remained at the breakfast table with Harrison and Tyler, and when the harassed Christian returned, he was explaining to his friends how a study of Plato's theories could be profitable in the establishment of a post-war American government. No one else was in the taproom.

"Come along!" Christian shouted. "I've ordered horses saddled for us."

Patrick stood slowly, smiling and shaking his head. "We'll walk," he declared. "Take my spare coat and clock, Will. They're in our room. You don't want the enemy to see you in uniform."

Christian hesitated.

"Do as I tell you," Patrick commanded. "I've been giving this situation serious thought, and I'm convinced that three middle-aged civilians and one colonel of infantry can't possibly escape from a full regiment of healthy young fellows who are professional horsemen."

Will Christian saw his point, and raced off for the civilian attire.

Five minutes later the quartet headed toward the west on foot, walking briskly but without undue haste through the suddenly deserted streets of the town. Most citizens of Charlottesville had already gone off to the surrounding countryside, taking with them their family silver, precious mementos, and other possessions of value. Tarleton's reputation had preceded him.

"P.H.," Harrison said mildly, "I reckon the Redcoats have a general description of you."

"Maybe so." Patrick removed his wig, jammed it into a pocket and carried his hat in his hand. "I'm glad it's a cloudy day," he remarked to no one in particular. "My head would blister in the sun."

"Take off your spectacles, too," Tyler urged him. "London newspapers always show you wearing them in their cartoon-portraits."

"What I dislike most about a situation like this is one's loss of human dignity." Patrick placed his spectacles in a small deerskin bag. "Death isn't the worst of war, you know. The degradation of the living is far more humiliating. It was Cicero who first made the observation, I believe. Or was it Horace?"

"Walk a little faster," Christian told him, "and save your erudition for another day."

"I know it was Cicero who said that statesmen are reduced to the level of slaves by generals. How odd, when there's an even greater need for statesmen than for soldiers in time of war." Patrick expected no reply, and was not surprised when his companions remained silent.

The day was warm and humid, and within a short time all four were perspiring. But they kept up a steady pace, and Patrick continued to chat as they followed the road used by frontier settlers headed for Kentucky. Occasionally they caught glimpses of Charlottesville residents on the heights ahead, but they themselves appeared to be something of a rear guard. Others were fleeing in earnest, and their own walk was relatively leisurely.

About two and a half hours after they had left the town, they paused for a moment's rest at the crest of a wooded hill, and Colonel Christian pointed in the direction of Charlottesville. "Tarleton," he said harshly, "is leaving his calling card."

A plume of thick, black smoke was rising high into the air.

"We'd better leave the trail," Tyler said. "Patrols are sure to head this way."

"We'll do no such thing," Patrick replied cheerfully. "Any Redcoats who might follow us into the forest would know we're running away. I have a far more logical plan."

"Trust P.H.," Harrison muttered, "to think in logical terms at a moment like this."

They resumed their walk, and about a half hour later Patrick

266

beamed when they passed a sharp bend in the road and suddenly came upon a large building, made of logs, with clay filling in the open spaces between them. "This must be the place," he said. "The Kentucky Road Tavern."

He moved ahead of the others and tapped at the locked door.

There was a long wait. Then a male voice called, "What do you want?"

"Drink and food, if you please!"

A bolt slid back, and the door opened a few inches to reveal a gray-haired, unshaven man who was clutching an ancient, cocked pistol. He eyed the quartet for a moment, then asked sourly, "Ain't you heard the Lobsters are in Charlottesville?"

"There's been a rumor to that effect," Patrick replied, slipping past him and beckoning to the others. "If I were you, my friend, I'd keep the door open, and be prepared to entertain company. Make sure your more expensive spirits have been removed, of course." He led the way to a table. "A locked door might be regarded as a challenge by the British, you know. They display the manner of boors when traveling abroad, and they'd need no provocation to burn this place to the ground. Bring us four cups of your whiskey, if you please, and some bread and meat."

The proprietor of the tavern obviously thought him mad. "All the bread is hidden in the barns," he declared, "except for a few stale loaves I was aiming to use as bait in 'coon traps. The same with the other things. There's nothing at hand except some pickled beef that wasn't worth moving."

"We aren't particular. But please hurry." Patrick turned to his companions. "Take off your neckcloths," he directed. "Only gentlemen wear them. John, you and I have lace on our cuffs. I suggest we roll up our sleeves." He stripped off his coat and, rolling it into a ball, threw it onto a pile of kindling beside a corner hearth. "Ben, get rid of that gold watch fob on your waistcoat. Will, your civilian disguise is perfect, except for your silver spurs. And your boots are too clean." He went quickly to the fireplace and smeared ashes on his own boots.

After a brief wait the proprietor returned with a platter of the stale bread, chunks of gray, pickled beef and four cups of evil-smelling, colorless corn whiskey. He grinned when he saw his guests' transformation.

Patrick sniffed the whiskey and shuddered. "Do you suppose we might have a little water to cut the strength of this questionable nectar?"

"Folks hereabouts drink it straight," the man told him.

"Then we'd better do the same. As for you, I advise you to put away your pistol. I've been given to understand the British are rather sensitive to the sight of firearms."

The suggestion made sense, and the man hurried away, talking to himself.

"Ben, I'll be obliged for the loan of a pipe and some tobacco," Patrick said.

"But you don't smoke, P.H.!" Harrison was bewildered. "You've always said it makes you ill."

"Precisely. The fact is well known. Even to Tarleton, I presume." Patrick held his breath, swallowed some of the whiskey and shuddered. "There. I trust my breath is now as atrociously strong as the Greek fire of the Dark Ages. It's also known that I don't drink distilled spirits."

Christian studied him. "I thought I knew you, but my wife—bless her—is right. She's said a thousand times that Patrick would still be a dirt farmer if he hadn't discovered the pleasures of hearing an audience applaud him. By God, P.H., you're a play-actor. And you're actually enjoying all this."

Patrick laughed, then coughed as he had difficulty lighting the borrowed pipe. "I won't deny," he said, "that I find a certain titillation at the prospect of matching wits with the enemy. I refuse to cower in the brush like a rabbit run to ground by hunting dogs. I prefer to make a virtue of necessity."

"The stakes," Harrison reminded him, "are rather high, especially for you."

"They are for the rabbit, too. But he defeats himself because he's incapable of using intellect." Patrick squinted at the pipe bowl, uncertain whether he had lighted it. "I'm relying on the British inability to deal with an unexpected situation in a land they haven't bothered to understand. Tarleton is searching for a man wearing a label, 'Patrick Henry,' who fits a neat description.

Any departure from the anticipated will confuse him. Just remember that had London shown malleability in '74—even in '75—there would have been no war."

"I hope," Tyler said fervently, "that your analysis of the British cavalryman's mind is correct!"

For a quarter of an hour or more they made desultory conversation, but became tense when they heard the steady drumming of approaching hoofbeats. Patrick deliberately ate some of the bread, spilling crumbs down the front of his waistcoat, and took another swallow of the corn whiskey. He reached for a piece of the beef, too, but changed his mind; there was no need to go that far.

The proprietor came into the taproom, nervously rubbing his hands together.

"Stay out in back where you can't be seen," Patrick told him. "And before I forget it, what's your name?"

"David Johnson. I—"

"Later, my friend. They'll be here at any moment."

The man disappeared just as the thunder of hoofbeats ceased outside the tavern. Suddenly the door burst open, and a major of Royal Cavalry, impeccable in a scarlet tunic and plumed, brass helmet, stalked into the room, an unsheathed saber in his hand. Behind him was a junior officer and a half-dozen soldiers, all armed with sabers and pistols.

Patrick blew a cloud of tobacco smoke toward the ceiling. "Well, now," he said amiably. "We heard tell you boys was in the neighborhood."

The major was not interested in four bumpkins. "Has anyone passed this way?" he demanded.

Patrick laughed raucously, and his companions joined in, somewhat more hesitantly. "Gawd A'mighty!" he exclaimed, spitting on the floor. "Half the folks o' Charlottesville has been on this here road all day, hurryin' so fast they couldn't stop t' pass the time o' day. Here, boy." He thrust his cup under the major's nose. "Set yourself and be sociable."

The major drew back from the whiskey as though he had been handed a cup of hemlock.

"Dave!" Patrick bawled. "Bring out that there jug. Ye got comp'ny." He grinned blandly at the major. "It's the last jug o' whiskey he's got, so ye be in luck, boy. Folks has been sufferin' a mighty ferocious thirst all day."

Johnson, who had been eavesdropping from behind a partition, appeared with an earthenware jug.

"Give this boy and his friends a taste o' your wares, Dave," Patrick said, drinking from his own cup and almost gagging on the contents.

Several of the Redcoats were trying unsuccessfully to hide their broad smiles, the junior officer looked embarrassed, and the major, the discipline of his unit at stake, became even more defensive. "Impossible, sir. We're on duty."

"Oh, it's my treat, boy," Patrick assured him, blinking innocently.

The commander of the search unit was laboring under a distinct disadvantage. He could not betray the code of gentlemen by ordering the establishment's supplies confiscated after the amiable rustic had displayed such generous hospitality. And at the same time his own fastidiousness made it impossible for him to accept the offer.

He made a desperate attempt to concentrate on the business that had brought him so far into the American interior. "By order of Colonel Tarleton, I have been directed to find and apprehend two notorious traitors to the Crown, Thomas Jefferson and Patrick Henry. In the King's name, have either of them been seen in this vicinity?"

Patrick's harsh, wheezing cackle surprised his own companions. "The likes o' them don't come t' places like this, boy," he said, stuffing a piece of pickled beef into one side of his mouth, then chewing on it and dribbling down his chin as he spoke. "Ye can bet them there fancy boots they skedaddled out o' Charlottesville ahead o' everybody else. Sure as shootin' a buck at a salt lick, they're a-settin' snug as ye please at some cozy cabin fifty miles from here, drinkin' French brandywine and eatin' food fit for the table o' the King hisself."

The major nodded. Under similar circumstances, were he in the position of Jefferson or Henry, he would undoubtedly hide out somewhere with the best wine and beef available in this barbaric land. "Colonel Tarleton," he said, "will make his headquarters in Charlottesville until tomorrow. If you—or anyone you know—

learns the whereabouts of these fugitives, please notify him immediately. There's a price of two hundred fifty sovereigns—in gold —on the head of each of them, provided they're captured alive."

Patrick's astonishment was genuine. He hadn't known that a real fortune, a sum large enough to enable a Virginia family to live in comfort for years, was being offered for him. Sir Henry Clinton was far more anxious to stage a hanging than he had imagined.

Harrison came to Patrick's rescue. "That's a right bold sum, lad," he said, puffing hard on a pipe. "Five hundred sovereigns, say ye? A prince's ransom."

"Pass the word to your friends," the major told him. "Colonel Tarleton is carrying the money, and there'll be no delay. Deliver the traitors, and the gold is yours." He nodded slightly, the gesture of an aristocrat condescending to bid farewell to his inferiors, and went off to his horse.

The junior officer was close behind him, and the soldiers followed, wanting but not daring to stay behind long enough for a drink.

Johnson stood in the entrance, watching them, and finally turned to the four silent men at the rough-hewn table. "They're gone," he said. "They've headed back in the direction of Charlottesville."

"Then we must be leaving, too." Patrick rose. "Let me pay your fee for these—ah—refreshments, and we'll be on our way, too. I shall also be obliged to you for a cup of water to rinse away certain tastes that are alien to me."

"I'll bring you a pitcher from the spring," the proprietor declared. "But you'll not pay me a penny, Mr. Henry."

"You know me?"

"I've never set eyes on you until this day, sir. But when I heard you talking like a woodsman to flummox the Redcoat, I knew you couldn't be anybody else. There's not another like you in all of the United States, Mr. Henry. You and these gentlemen are welcome to stay here until Tarleton leaves the area, longer, if it pleases you. And I'll feel honored if you'll be my guests. If it wasn't for the way you offered him this whiskey I made last month, with your manner so sly-like and all, he'd have raided and robbed me until I was beggared."

"We'll be very pleased to accept your hospitality, Mr. Johnson." Patrick realized it was far safer to remain here than to continue wandering through the hills of the Piedmont. "Now, if you will, satisfy my curiosity. You knew me, yet you didn't give me away to the major. Two hundred and fifty sovereigns would buy you the finest tavern in Virginia, with enough left in your strongbox for a farm, a team of horses and a half-dozen head of cattle."

"I'm no Judas, Mr. Henry!" the man declared indignantly. "I'd rather have my tongue cut out than harm the best friend me and my kind have ever had."

Tears came to Patrick's eyes, and he bowed his head. Never in his forty-five years had anyone paid him a greater or more sincere tribute.

9

The burning of Charlottesville and scattering of the Burgesses disrupted the government of Virginia, and the military events that followed in the summer of 1781 further hampered civilian rule. Lafayette moved into the state with his division of Continentals, and Lord Cornwallis followed him. Nathanael Greene and his deputy, Dan Morgan, remained in North Carolina and bided their time.

Clinton sent reinforcements to Cornwallis, who was finding it impossible to catch the elusive Lafayette. Thus the British in New York were weakened, and General Washington saw an unprecedented opportunity to smash the enemy. Lafayette's troops and crack cavalry commanded by Colonel Harry Lee made life so miserable for the British in Virginia that Cornwallis, trying to protect his flanks, withdrew his entire force to Yorktown, a thin strip of land between the York and James Rivers.

Greene received orders from the commander-in-chief to keep him penned there at all costs, and Washington made his major moves in a chess game involving thousands of men as pawns. The French fleet sailed north to Chesapeake Bay from the West Indies, cutting off Cornwallis by sea, and Washington, supported by a French corps, moved south from New York and Pennsylvania.

The Royal Navy grasped the situation, and made a desperate attempt to relieve Cornwallis, but the French ships-of-the-line and frigates drove off the vessels of their ancient enemies.

Early in September the armies of Washington and his allies closed their pincers. Cornwallis fought violently, gallantly, but there was no escape from the trap into which he had blundered. The end was drawing near.

Patrick, scarcely able to believe the miracle that was taking place, went to Richmond with Richard Henry Lee and Benjamin Harrison. On two occasions early in October they paid brief visits to Washington's headquarters in the field to see the situation for themselves. But, aware of the commander-in-chief's preoccupation, they did not linger, and returned to the newly rebuilt Richmond Inn, which Arnold had destroyed.

There, as anxious spectators rather than participants, they awaited the outcome of the military operation. Cornwallis' frenzy increased, but the Americans knew that ultimate victory was at last in sight, and redoubled their efforts. Morgan's celebrated riflemen, long the backbone of the Continentals, led one attack, and Lafayette, commanding other Virginians and Pennsylvanians, was in charge of another.

The pressure became unbearable, and at last, on October 19, the Battle of Yorktown came to an end when the British hoisted a white flag. That same day General Lord Cornwallis surrendered his entire army to General George Washington, and for all practical purposes the war was at an end, even though Sir Henry Clinton still held New York.

A jubilant courier brought the news to Richmond, and that night the town went wild. Huge bonfires were lighted, taverns and inns served free food and drink to everyone, and private citizens opened their doors to total strangers. Impromptu parades were held, and when a battalion of Continentals arrived with captured British supplies and ammunition, virtually the entire unit had to stand guard duty to prevent the enthusiastic civilians from making off with the provisions.

Patrick and Lee took no active part in the celebration. Finding the atmosphere in the taproom of the inn too noisy, they retired to their own quarters, and finally went up to the roof of the four-story building so they could watch the crowds in the streets below without participating in the frenzied activities. Neither felt like making the speeches they would be asked to deliver if they mingled with the citizens, and both were unusually silent.

"It will be strange," Lee said at last, "to live at peace after six and a half years of fighting."

Patrick nodded. "My sons will come home soon. And my sons-in-law." He had seen Colonel John Fontaine at Continental head-quarters, and had been shocked by the younger man's gaunt appearance. "It won't be easy for young men to adjust to peacetime living. Nor will it be easy for the community. We've been without young males for so long."

"You've been thinking of the problems we face, too, I gather."

"Yes. There will be a clamor to reduce taxes, but we can't for several years. Idle farms and plantations must be made active again, there are industries to build and shipyards to convert to the making of cargo ships."

"The difficulties of establishing a stable government worry me even more," Lee declared. "People have accepted wartime regulations, but they'll expect greater freedom now."

"They'll have to learn that a democracy will fail if its citizens don't exercise self-discipline." Patrick sighed heavily.

His old friend looked at him, raising an eyebrow.

A crowd of shouting men and boys passed the inn in the street below, and Patrick waited until they moved off before speaking again. "For two and a half years, ever since I gave up the governor-ship, I've comforted myself with the thought that when the fighting ended I could devote myself to my new farm and my law practice. Dorothea has been so patient that I've marveled. How she'll react now, I don't know. I've spent no more than a few weeks at Leatherwood every year, and I have growing children who scarcely know me."

"You'll keep your seat in the Burgesses?"

"I must. In this transition period we'll have a greater need than ever for experienced leaders. I hope you'll consider coming back to the Assembly, Richie."

274

"I will."

"Sometimes I wonder whether we fool ourselves." Patrick clasped his hands behind his back and moved away from the edge of the roof. "Are we so enamored of power—for its own sake—that we make excuses not to retire? Does public office actually mean more to us than the chance to earn a good living for our wives and children?"

"Eventually we'll have to hand over the reins to others."

"I know. I've been training young John Marshall to take my place as Assembly Leader. But I find I'm reluctant to step down in his favor, or Jamie Madison's, either. They're bright lads, you know. Their knowledge of the law is greater than yours or mine."

"But they're incapable of getting things done—the things that need to be done." Richard Henry Lee smiled wryly. "We're not unique, and I don't claim that we have greater intelligence than the younger men. But we do have the experience they lack. Circumstances forced us to take up politics as a vocation, and we shouldn't feel badly because we're still needed. We'll lay down the burdens when our successors have learned to take our places."

Patrick pointed down the street at a company of Continental infantry, armed with muskets and bayonets, that was marching off to protect a complex of storage warehouses before the crowds became transformed into an unruly mob. "I envy those boys. Yes, and I envy Washington and Greene and Henry Knox and all the rest who wear the epaulets of generals. They've become professional soldiers, but there will be no more need for them now. Washington can retire to his plantation, and Knox can open a new bookstore in Boston. But there can be no rest for the professional statesman."

"I wonder," Lee said quietly, "whether we'd have accepted our responsibilities had we known there would be no end to them."

Patrick straightened, squaring his shoulders. "Of course, because there was no choice then, just as there's none now. We depend on the electorate. But, may the Almighty help us all, they depend on us even more."

NINE

1783–1786

1

Dorothea Henry, now the mother of four small children, brought them to her parents' home in Hanover County early in 1783 for a visit of several months' duration. It was the first time she had gone there since moving to Henry County and, as she explained to them, she despaired of seeing her husband if she remained at home. Patrick, still active as Assembly Leader, continued to spend most of his time in Richmond.

He rode up to Hanover County on familiar roads during a brief recess of the Burgesses, and on the evening of his arrival, still deeply immersed in the affairs of his nation and state, he remained at the dinner table with his father-in-law after the ladies had gone. Nathaniel Dandridge, who had retired from the Continentals with the rank of colonel, looked remarkably youthful and robust now that he had resumed an active life as a planter.

"P.H.," he said, "you're too thin and pale. You ought to spend more time outdoors."

"I wish I had time." Patrick dismissed the subject with an impatient wave and returned to his favorite theme. "We couldn't have asked for better peace treaty terms, Nate. Our independence is recognized, our rights to the territory west to the Mississippi are granted and even our fishing rights off the Canadian coast have been included. We can thank John Adams for refusing to give up when the British offered less."

Nate had already heard the treaty terms, and nodded as he sipped his port, which came from the first consignment sent to the United States from England since the war's end. "Would you like to go hunting with me tomorrow?"

"I wish I could, but I'm expected in Richmond for a meeting tomorrow night."

"Your wife will be less than pleased."

"I hope I can persuade her to leave the children here and come with me for a few days." Patrick's mind was still on non-domestic matters. "In a sense, you know, there's been a miracle. The King swore he'd abdicate before he admitted our independence, but Jefferson wrote to me that he actually received our commissioners. And the biggest miracle of all is the change in the British government. Lord North is so badly discredited he'll never come out of retirement—"

"When will you think of following General Washington into retirement, P.H.?"

Patrick frowned. "As soon as we settle some of our more pressing problems. I've changed my position on taxation, you know."

"I've heard rumors."

"Cash money is scarce, and men returning from military duty need a moratorium to get on their feet. I'm proposing they be granted complete freedom from state taxation for twelve months."

"I'm not sure I like that. It'll place a heavier burden on me— and men like me."

"Precisely, Nate, because you can afford the luxury of paying taxes." Patrick's smile took the sting from his words. "I'm sorry to say that Richie Lee opposes me, but I have the votes to beat him. I swung John Tyler over to my side this week, and there are always a dozen men who'll follow the Speaker. Then there are some other problems I want to settle. We need more colleges, and must have funds to establish them. I'm in favor of state support for the clergy—"

"Not so fast. How do you reconcile that view with your stand in favor of freedom of religion?"

"I don't propose to limit support to Church of England ministers. I favor helping clergymen of every denomination, and I'm proposing a bill to that effect before the Burgesses adjourn later in the summer. I'm specifically including Catholic priests and Jewish rabbis. A democratic society can't flourish without sound morals. Without the churches there will be decay and, eventually, complete ruin. The clergy have been having a far too difficult time establishing themselves again since the end of the war, and they need help as much as Washington's veterans."

"You'll have a fight on your hands."

"I'm accustomed to fights. Then there's the very pressing question of what to do about the Loyalists."

"That one is easy to handle. I'm in favor of hanging the bastards if they try to come back to Virginia!"

"No, Nate, you're wrong! We—"

"Mr. Henry!" Dorothea stood in the dining-room entrance, trying to curb her temper. "Mama has just gone off to bed, and I'm going to do the same if you and Papa intend to spend the night solving the world's affairs."

The men rose, and Nate coughed behind his hand, well aware that Dorothea and Patrick had spent no time together in three months. "I'll join your mother," he said, "and I accept full blame for keeping P.H. overly long at the table."

Patrick followed his wife into the handsomely appointed parlor, bracing himself for an unpleasant scene. "I was bringing your father up to date on our legislative calendar."

Dorothea seated herself on a divan. "How fascinating," she said, and poured him a cup of tea, which was now being imported again in large quantities.

Patrick gratefully inhaled the fragrant aroma.

"I wonder if you realize, sir, that little Patrick doesn't know his father."

"That, Mrs. Henry, is a situation I hope to remedy in the immediate future." He paused, but she made no response. "You'll be pleased to hear that Governor Harrison has just appointed Spencer Roane a judge."

"Will he ride a circuit?"

"Of course."

"Then my heart goes out to Anne. She'll be a political widow —as I am."

Patrick spent a moment or two adjusting his wig. "I believe our temporary inconveniences are coming to an end. Will you ride to Richmond with me tomorrow? The Harrisons have asked us to spend a few days as their guests, and I'm sure your mother will be delighted to look after the children."

Dorothea's gaze was coldly speculative. "I scarcely know Mrs. Harrison, and I've met the governor only a few times."

"Ben hopes to have a little chat with you."

She folded her hands in her lap and waited.

He stirred sugar in his cup, nervously clattering his spoon. "The truth of the matter is that the leadership wants me to become governor again."

She wasn't surprised. "By the 'leadership,' you mean you've given in to your own vanity. Others are usurping your fame, and you're hungry for more glory."

There might have been an element of truth in the charge before the war's end, but the accusation was no longer valid. "The responsibility of high office outweighs its pleasures," he replied soberly. "For the sake of my children and grandchildren, I want to finish the work I began so many years ago. For your sake—and my own—I want us to be together again." He placed his cup on a table and reached for her hand.

Dorothea tried to withdraw.

Patrick caught her wrist, and his fingers closed over hers. "Hear me out, Dolly. If I take the governorship, we'll buy a house near Richmond. We'll live under the same roof again, and I'll see the children every day."

Her laugh was shrill. "Are you asking me to make still another move?"

"Indeed. I fulfilled a lifelong dream when we moved to Henry County, and I've had no chance to enjoy either our home or the countryside. In a little more than two years I'll be fifty years old, so my chances of doing what I please in this world are limited. I doubt if I have that much longer to spend on this earth."

Dorothea heard the gravity of his tone, and her pique gave way to concern. "Are you hiding an illness from me?"

Patrick regretted his slip. He had been suffering from dizzy spells whenever he was tired, but didn't want the question of his health to interfere with far more important issues. "I was speaking rhetorically, but there are realistic problems at stake. Our debts are crushing, but I've found a way to reduce the immediate pressures."

"As governor?"

"Yes. No one has cash, of course, but I've been able to make a barter deal that will show us a good profit in a few years, when gold and silver are plentiful again. A company of land speculators has agreed to take 'Leatherwood,' and to give me, in exchange, thirty thousand acres in Kentucky, located in a region that Phil Aylett knows and approves. They'll throw in a handsome estate near Richmond that we can sell for a profit when I retire from office, and a property in Prince Edward County, about eighty miles southwest of the city, where we can move as soon as I leave office."

"How will that relieve our debts?"

"The Kentucky tract is enormous! Eventually I'll get two to three dollars an acre for it."

"I still think in pounds and shillings."

"We'll be out of debt by the time our children are grown."

Dorothea began to weaken.

Patrick seized his advantage. "What's more, I swear to you that I won't serve for more than two years. That will give me enough time to accomplish my goals." His grip became firmer. "And I give you my solemn promise that I'll never again accept public office of any kind, under any conditions, without your voluntary consent."

"I—I wouldn't want to hold you to a pledge like that, Mr. Henry."

"I give it to you of my own free will, ma'am. Once I've discharged this last obligation, I'll devote the rest of my life to the welfare of my family. I beg your indulgence only because we live in extraordinary times."

She sighed, then smiled. "And as I knew long before I married you, you're an extraordinary man. I can't deny the people your guidance, so I accept your terms, Mr. Henry."

He drew her to her feet. "We've been separated far too long. I won't permit it to happen again."

They looked at each other, then with one accord started toward the staircase.

2

John Fontaine looked as uncomfortable as he felt in the sparsely furnished office of Virginia's Chief Executive. "If I take the post, it'll be said that you gave it to me because I'm the only one of your sons-in-law who hasn't worked for you."

"People are entitled to their own opinions." Patrick pounded the new oak desk that the carpenters' guild of Norfolk had made and given him as an inauguration gift. "I want you as my personal assistant because I need your help. I've given myself a limit of two years to complete what needs to be done, but I can't do it without you young fellows. My generation can't lead forever. John Marshall has promised to become assistant Leader in the Burgesses, and young Monroe, our new delegate to the Congress, will do everything in his power to strengthen the abominably weak Confederation government. I'd have gone to Phil Aylett or Spencer Roane—even though he'd have to give up his seat on the bench— because they've worked for me previously and know my methods.

"But neither of them is strong enough. I want someone who grasps the principles I believe in, who shares my convictions, and who is able to work independently, on his own initiative. Above all, I need someone whose common sense I can trust. A process of elimination leaves you as the only candidate."

John Fontaine chuckled. "When Uncle John Syme heard you say you wanted a private word with me after the inauguration, he told me to hide my purse and load my pistols."

"So that's why Martha was so annoyed with him."

"She won't let any man say a word against you in her hearing." Still grinning, the younger man removed his spectacles in a gesture remarkably similar to his father-in-law's, and cleaned them with a square of soft leather.

"Because of her—and your children—I've hesitated to ask this sacrifice of you. I realize you haven't completely recovered yet from the wound you sustained at Yorktown, and I know you've had no chance to put your plantation on a paying, sound basis. But it will take much longer if men like you and Monroe and Marshall and Jamie Madison don't pitch in now to work for Virginia and the country. There's a little nine-room house at the far end of the property outside of town where we're going to live, and I gladly offer it to you and Martha, rent-free. It's the least I can do for you."

"I'm sure Martha would like it," John Fontaine said. "She and Dorothea are still very close."

"Yes," Patrick replied dryly, "they can commiserate with each other and curse all husbands who believe more in public service than in earning a good living for their families. Talk it over with her, if you wish, and let me know tomorrow."

"I'd rather not. I think a man must make his own decisions in these matters."

Patrick beamed at him. "When can you start?"

"I'm at your disposal now, sir."

"Good! I'll take you at your word. We'll go back to the reception, and I'd like you to seek out General Washington. He's always partial to his former colonels, and he'll unburden his mind to you more freely than he does when he's talking with politicians. He doesn't trust us, you know. Find out if he has any ideas on how we can shore up the Confederation government without taking authority from the states. Then have a private word with Harry Lee, and see if you can persuade him to take a seat in either the Burgesses or the Confederation Congress. Try to see young Edmund Randolph, too. He's competent, and I've had to keep him in my Privy Council as Attorney General, but I don't pretend to understand him, much less like him. I'll hold you responsible for getting a detailed opinion from him—within a week, if possible, two at the most—on the legality of the Kentucky movement in favor of creating a separate state there. Then—"

John Fontaine held up his hand. "The reception won't last more than another hour, sir!"

Patrick blinked behind his spectacles. "Quite true. Well. These little assignments will keep you busy for that time, I dare say, but see me again before we go to the Richmond Inn for the inauguration banquet. We can put the time to good use."

His son-in-law wondered, as they rejoined the guests in the rotunda of the new Capitol, whether he would regret his acceptance of a position. Never had he seen anyone so determined to accomplish so much so quickly.

3

"His Excellency, the Governor!" The principal sergeant-at-arms started down the center aisle of the new Assembly chamber.

Patrick followed close behind his escort, smiling and nodding at old friends, then paused when he reached the front row to shake the hand of Richard Henry Lee, who had given up his post as Assembly Leader to become President of the Confederation Congress in Philadelphia, and was present as a guest.

"I suspect," Lee murmured, "that you're up to your old tricks, P.H."

Patrick smiled blandly.

"Whenever you address the Burgesses in person rather than send over a written message, I know you're planning to force legislation on them that they don't like."

Patrick's eyelid fluttered in a suggestion of a wink before he mounted the rostrum and accepted the official greetings of Speaker John Tyler. This was the first personal appearance of his term before the Assembly, and the members applauded him warmly, but it was obvious that many were apprehensive. The governor had taken care to conceal his purpose, and Richmond had been filled with rumors for three days.

"Mr. Speaker, gentlemen, and our honored guest, President Lee." Patrick spoke quietly, completely at ease on the podium. "I asked for the privilege of appearing before you because of a desire to discuss with you, face to face, a problem of great urgency."

Suddenly his voice rang out sharply. "When Americans are intolerant, they become traitors. When Virginians are intolerant, they deny their identity and their heritage. In peace as in war, it is the duty of Virginia to lead the United States on the broad but often tortuous path of freedom and enlightenment."

There was a brief stir in the chamber, and men glanced at each other uncertainly. Governor Henry was beginning a speech at the peak of his unrivaled oratorical form, which meant that he intended to use all his powers, official and personal, to have his way in a matter he had not yet chosen to disclose.

"Gentlemen, this free and independent land of ours is rich in many resources. The Almighty had dealt kindly with us, and has given us minerals and timber, salubrious climate and rich soil, water power and other blessings too numerous to mention. Yet we remain poor because we are an extensive country without population.

"People constitute the real strength and form the real wealth of a nation, any nation.

"I am impatient to see the United States fulfill her natural destiny. If this be a fault, I willingly admit it. I admit that I want to see our vast forests filled by a process more rapid than the ordinary course of nature. I want to see these, our United States, rapidly ascending to the rank which their natural advantages authorize them to hold among the nations of the earth."

The audience remained mystified and tense.

Patrick took his time, his voice resonant and rich. "Cast your own eyes over this extensive country, gentlemen. Observe for yourselves the salubrity of your climate, the variety and fertility of your soil, and see that soil intersected in every quarter by bold, navigable streams, flowing to the east and to the west, to the north and to the south, as if the finger of heaven were marking out the course of your settlements, inviting you to enterprise, and pointing the way to wealth.

"Gentlemen, you are destined, sooner or later, to become a great agricultural and commercial people. This is no idle dream. It is fact. The only question is whether you choose to achieve greatness by slow gradations, and at some distant period, lingering on through a long and sickly minority, and subjected meanwhile to machinations, insults and oppressions of enemies, foreign and domestic, without sufficient strength to resist and chastise them—or whether you choose to rush at once, as it were, to the full enjoyment of those high destinies and be able to cope, single-handed, with the proudest oppressors of the Old World.

"If you prefer the latter course, as I do, and as I trust you do, encourage the husbandmen, the mechanics, the merchants of the Old World to come and settle in this land of promise—to make it the home of the skillful and the skilled, the industrious, the fortunate and the happy, as well as the asylum of the distressed.

"Ah, America—blessed haven of refuge for the oppressed minorities of the Old World! You and I, gentlemen, like every other citizen fortunate enough to call himself a native of this land, is descended from a victim of tyranny. We are the great-grandsons, the grandsons and sons of the weak and helpless, the minorities who were persecuted for their beliefs in God and in liberty, in government and in their unalienable right to seek happiness in their own way.

"The United States, gentlemen, is the only nation in the history of the world founded on a principle, the principle that the convictions of the individual are inviolable!" His voice soared, sending chills up the spines of his listeners. "If we deny that right to any man, we deserve to perish. Let our forests return to their pristine state, let our rich land lie fallow, let no boats travel down the waters of our rivers and seas and lakes, let our cities crumble and become dust.

"I have spoken, gentlemen, of tolerance, of opportunity and of principle. They are separate topics, say you, each fit for a discourse of its own, yet unrelated to the others? Not so! They are intertwined, like the roots of the mighty oaks that grow in our forests.

"This nation needs men, we say. Where shall we find them? Open your doors, gentlemen, and they will come in. They are already standing on tiptoe at the edge of these, their own native shores, looking to your coasts with wistful and longing eye.

"I refer to those whom we called Loyalists, those men who refused to take up arms against their King when we declared ourselves a free and independent people. Some fled from the terror imposed on them by their neighbors. Some, broken of heart and spirit, left of their own free will, afraid it would no longer be possible for them to live where they and their fathers and grandfathers had made their homes. Still others, a courageous and militant minority, took up arms for the cause in which they believed.

"Today these former Loyalists see a land in which liberty has taken up her abode. They desire, with all their hearts, to return to their homes. Some have repented of their former views. Others proudly cling to them. But changed or unchanged, they think of themselves still as Americans. Dare we deny their heritage? I say we cannot. We lack the right."

Patrick paused, searched the faces of his audience and then spoke very slowly and distinctly. "We cannot claim to be champions of freedom if we deny freedom to these, our countrymen. We cannot call ourselves defenders of liberty if we close our gates to our brothers. Is it just or fair, is it in the traditions first established in Jamestown almost one hundred and eighty years ago to strike down the hands of our own flesh and blood?

"Justice, gentlemen, must be tempered with mercy. Think you of the parable of the prodigal son, and then search your own hearts and minds. Follow the dictates of your own consciences!"

Patrick's voice was a musical instrument, and its trumpet call became pure, almost sweet. "Prepare legislation at once permitting the former Loyalists to return in safety and honor to their homes. Prove to them and to the whole world that this nation, dedicated to the cause of freedom, honors herself by honoring those of her sons who erred.

"Let us have the magnanimity, gentlemen, to lay aside our antipathies. Let us have the compassion to cast off our prejudices. Let us have the courage to overcome our fears!

"Our fears! I, for one, have no fear of any mischief these misguided and humbled refugees can do us! They beg forgiveness. Let us forgive!

"Afraid of them? Shall we, who have laid the proud British lion at our feet, be afraid of his whelps?"

Before the stunned Assemblymen realized he had finished, he descended from the rostrum and walked quickly up the center aisle. Not until he approached the door at the rear did the applause start. Then, rising to a tumultuous crescendo, it followed him into the lobby beyond the chamber.

4

"This is my last term." Patrick, looking worn and haggard, paced his office. "Twenty-four months of service as governor is enough. In all, I'll have served in the post five years. It's time others take over."

Congressman James Monroe, a tall, ungainly young man with unruly hair, tried to interrupt, but John Fontaine warned him with a glance to remain silent.

"I've had more than my fair share of victories. It's to Virginia's eternal credit that we're readmitting the Loyalist refugees without prejudice. New York and Massachusetts have followed our example, and other states will do the same. Madison and his friends beat me on the bill to subsidize the clergy, and I bow to the will of the majority. I feel my work is done."

Monroe could remain quiet no longer. "The work of the United States is just beginning, Governor. Edmund Randolph's proposal at the meeting of the states in Annapolis to revise the Confederation government is gaining strength. If you've read Madison's pamphlets, the papers he calls *The Federalist*—"

"I'm familiar with them."

"Then you know he's advocating a new Constitution to strengthen the national government at the expense of the states. We need your help to defeat his proposals."

Patrick stopped abruptly, hands clasped behind his back. "I'm of two minds on the idea, and so are some of my friends in other states. Governor Hancock of Massachusetts isn't certain whether a stronger national government would be a boon or a curse, and neither am I. Sam Adams is afraid that individual liberties would be neglected, and I stand with him. The rights of our citizens must be protected at all costs."

John Fontaine took a folder from the desk. "The governor has been corresponding with General Washington on the subject. We understand he'll be made president of the Constitutional Convention in Philadelphia." A sudden fit of coughing made it impossible for him to say more, and he lay back in his chair, gasping for breath until Patrick handed him a bottle containing an elixir. He drank a small quantity, and it gave him partial relief.

Monroe was sympathetic, but the question he had raised was too important to permit him to change the subject. "Surely you'll serve as a delegate to the convention, Governor."

"I will not, sir." Patrick shook his head. "General Washington has enjoyed several years of retirement, and has been able to put his personal affairs sufficiently in order to give his full attention to the affairs of the convention. No one can doubt his patriotism, and I'm willing to leave matters in his hands."

"If all delegates are as high-minded as the general," Monroe said gloomily, "we'll have nothing to fear."

Patrick smiled. "You're as pessimistic as Richie Lee. He's afraid the convention will draw up a Constitution that will destroy the United States."

Monroe wondered how hard he dared prod this complex man who seemed so determined to retire from public life. "With all due respect, Governor, Mr. Lee and I have been in Philadelphia, and we know the mood of men from other parts of the country. The smaller states are jealous of Virginia and Massachusetts. They resent the power and wealth of Pennsylvania and New York. They want to clip our wings."

Patrick looked covertly at John Fontaine, who had recovered, and hiding his concern over his son-in-law, returned to his desk. "I can't blame them, you know. I'd feel as they do if I came from Delaware or Rhode Island, I'm sure. What puny power is vested in the Confederation rests with the stronger states. I think there's little doubt that we need a more centralized national government, although I'm reluctant to see us establish the system that Madison and Hamilton of New York favor. Certainly the national government should give equal representation to the states. I'll go that far.

"But a state isn't helpless. I think we've performed something of a minor miracle here in Virginia by retiring the paper money printed during the war years—"

"You're the miracle worker," John Fontaine said, his voice still husky and indistinct. "Your campaign to find new sources of revenue and cut expenses worked wonders."

"It certainly did, Governor," Monroe added. "New York and Massachusetts have been following your example—as usual."

Patrick was pleased, but waved aside the compliments. "It shouldn't be necessary for the states to take this sort of action. The national government should have the power to levy taxes—and to control the currency through a contract of some sort with a chartered bank. There's much to be said for the Madison and Hamilton scheme, although I'd feel happier if they showed as much concern for freedom of speech, assemblage and religion as they do for establishing equal, balancing branches of government. It seems to me they're too intent on the mechanics of their scheme, and too inclined to forget that the purpose of government is the service and protection it renders its people."

Monroe thought he saw an opening. "You've devoted your life to that kind of service, Governor! That's why we hope to persuade you—"

"I'm not needed. So many men who hold freedom dear will sit at the convention that I'm convinced the future of the United States is secure. As for me, I can't afford to wait until my Kentucky lands increase in value." Patrick spoke calmly, but was far more disturbed than anyone knew. His debts had soared again during his two new terms as governor, and he now owed his creditors the fantastic sum of fifty thousand dollars. Unless he took immediate steps to regain his financial health, he would soon be forced to declare bankruptcy, and in that case all his possessions, even the land that might some day be worth a fortune for his wife and children, would be lost. "I haven't earned a ha'penny in more than twelve years. It's time I think of feeding my family."

5

The house on the Appomattox River in Prince Edward County was only two stories high, and the rooms were small. But Dorothea insisted on giving her mother-in-law a suite consisting of a parlor, dressing room, and bedchamber. Patrick needed a library he could also use as an office, so the mistress of the house did without a sewing room, the first time since her marriage she had been without one, and the children shared two tiny cubicles at the rear of the second floor, overlooking the small kitchen and barn.

There was no town of consequence in the immediate vicinity; Farmville, the county seat, a village with a population of about six hundred, was fifteen miles away, riding cross country. The dirt roads were so narrow and rutted that Patrick ordered both of the carriages dismantled, as he was afraid their axles would break if Dorothea or his mother dared to venture out in them.

The property had not been farmed since pre-war years, and although the soil was rich, at least two years of hard work would be needed before a profitable tobacco crop could be produced. But even that modest goal had to be postponed, as free farm labor was too expensive to hire, and Patrick stubbornly refused to buy slaves to work as field hands. "I've claimed for years that I disapprove of slavery in both principle and practice," he told his wife, "and the time has come for me to prove it. We'll keep our household servants for the present as there's nothing to be gained by getting rid of them. But I refuse to buy men to work the place, even though the land will lie fallow. I'm a lawyer, not a farmer."

A neatly lettered shingle was suspended from chains outside the library office, informing the world that this was the legal headquarters of *P. Henry, Counselor.* But only a few neighbors who came to pay welcoming calls saw it.

"You'd think," Patrick said to Dorothea one morning in November 1786, as they strolled around the house, "that I died the day I left office. We've been here five weeks, and not one client has come to me."

She tried to hide her own concern. "I agree with your mother. She says it'll take time for people to realize that you're available."

"That's something else that bothers me. Ma isn't happy here. Folks aren't as friendly as they were in Henry County, and she's getting too old to traipse around the countryside on horseback. She doesn't have a blame thing to do except help you look after the children. There won't even be any fruit until late in the spring, so she can't even put up those preserves she loves. People of her age wither if they aren't made to feel useful." He sighed, but didn't know it. "I've been wondering whether she ought to go back to Hanover County and spend the winter with Johnnie Syme."

"No," Dorothea replied firmly. "If she's made to feel her sons are passing her from one to another, she'll be sure she's useless and has no place in the world. I'll give her more responsibility in the house. I know she'd enjoy supervising our meals."

"You're very kind. And thoughtful." It occurred to him that he had been taking Dorothea for granted, that he hadn't realized how much she had matured in recent years.

"Nonsense." She smiled as they paused beside a grove of black locust trees and looked across a smooth expanse of lawn toward the river. "What was in the letter you received from Richmond this morning?"

"An unacceptable offer of employment, unfortunately. Governor Randolph wrote that the Burgesses unanimously voted me a place in our delegation to the Constitutional Convention. I'll send him my regrets this afternoon, and I'll drop it off in the post at Hampden when I ride over there tomorrow—or is it the next day? —to deliver that lecture at the college."

He seemed so much at a loss that Dorothea ached for him. After a lifetime of furious activity, he had literally nothing to occupy him except deliver an occasional address at Hampden-Sidney College, which he had helped establish. "Perhaps," she said hesitantly, "you might want to reconsider Governor Randolph's offer. I know you'd enjoy Philadelphia, and there's no doubt you'd make an important contribution to the convention."

"There are others who think as I do, and are capable of expressing themselves." His voice rose, as it did when he made a speech. "I've postponed my return to private life long enough. Too long, if we're to judge by the lack of interest that people are showing in a lawyer who has no practice. My creditors have been patient, but I can't wait forever before starting to repay them. I'm here, and here I'll stay."

She supposed she should be grateful, as he was doing what he had always wanted. But with each passing day he looked older, and her uneasiness persisted. "I can't help wondering if it was a mistake to move out here. Perhaps we should have kept the house near Richmond."

"We needed hard cash, Dolly. The sale of that house will feed and clothe us for a few more months."

"Then it might have been wiser to move back to Hanover County, where you're known. Or even to Henry County."

"Land prices in Hanover are too high for my purse these days. And there isn't enough legal work to keep a man busy in the frontier settlements." He laughed without humor. "From the looks of it, there isn't enough here, either. I'm either well enough known everywhere in Virginia by now, or I'll have to accept the fact that people don't want to hire a counselor who has never appeared in an American courtroom before an American judge and an American jury." He was reluctant to tell her that, if he failed to build up a new practice, they would be compelled to move out to the real frontier in Kentucky. The prospect of starting life anew in his fifty-first year, clearing a plot of land with his own hands and growing his own crops was too dismal to contemplate, and he doubted that he had the physical strength or stamina to succeed in such a questionable venture.

"Here," he said gruffly. "Don't plant your kitchen garden on this side of the house."

Dorothea was surprised by the seeming irrelevance, and couldn't understand his sudden leap from important matters to the subject of kitchen gardens. But she asked no questions, and said meekly, "I thought it would be perfect. There's plenty of sun here, and the drainage is good."

Patrick shook his head, realizing that, ironically, he could still sound like a farmer, even though afraid to live as one. "The roots of those walnut trees yonder extend this far. They're poisonous, and will kill your vegetables."

One of the children started to cry, loudly, and Dorothea hurried off to the house, calling an apology over her shoulder for her abrupt departure.

Patrick continued to stand, staring at the handsome walnut trees. It was a weakness to feel sorry for himself, but he couldn't help thinking he and the trees were alike in many ways. Like them, he had performed useful functions, but he contaminated those who were close to him. He had been wrong to marry a lovely young woman and burden her with children. It had been a grave error to bring a new family into the world, to crush his young daughters and sons with the load of debts that, it appeared, he would never be able to repay.

The citizens of Virginia thought of him as a public servant, but it had not crossed their minds that even a man who had served five terms as Governor and another ten years as Assembly Leader needed money. He couldn't blame people, of course. They had their own problems, and his financial worries weren't the concern of anyone else.

He started toward the house, then paused and looked back at the walnut trees. If Dorothea really wanted to plant her kitchen garden in the adjoining field, he would cut them down.

6

Patrick had been closeted in his library for more than an hour with Colonel John Holcombe, the wealthiest planter in Prince Edward County, and Dorothea couldn't rid herself of a restless, nervous feeling. They were talking politics, she felt sure, and the very thought made her queasy. It was one thing for her to urge Patrick to attend the Constitutional Convention in Philadelphia, knowing that the meeting would not last for more than a few weeks. It was something far different for him to hold a lengthy conference with Holcombe, who had been one of his trusted militia commanders during the war.

She was certain the colonel was trying to persuade Patrick to represent the county in the Assembly. She knew all the arguments, and she could see her husband rising slowly to the bait. Not that he needed much urging. An appeal to his sense of duty would suffice. He'd peer at her over the top of his spectacles, stammering slightly, and would shamefacedly admit he'd agreed to one term.

Then, before he realized it, he'd be caught up once more in the press of state business. His delighted colleagues would elect him Assembly Leader again, and in another few years they'd make him governor. The thought of their debts mounting still higher made her panicky, and she fled from the kitchen, where her mother-in-law and Isobel's daughter, now the chief cook, were discussing the menu for evening dinner.

Dorothea had to exercise all her self-control to refrain from raising her skirts, running off into the black locust grove and weeping hysterically. Her fists clenched, she forced herself to walk sedately around to the French doors that opened onto the dining room.

To her surprise, she saw that Colonel Holcombe was just leaving, and she halted, sure that her worst fears were confirmed. If this were an ordinary neighborly visit, the colonel would have stayed for refreshments. So she felt positive he had persuaded Patrick to run for office and, afraid of facing her, was taking a discreet departure. She continued to stand, unmoving, as her husband saw his guest off.

Patrick turned, caught sight of Dorothea and walked toward her across the side lawn.

She steeled herself, hoping she wouldn't lose her temper. "Colonel Holcombe didn't stay for a cup of tea or sack," she said, hoping the flat statement didn't sound belligerent.

"No, this was strictly a business visit."

His expression as well as his guarded words told her that something unusual had just taken place.

Patrick removed his spectacles and cleaned them slowly, with great care, a sign that he was under emotional stress.

Dorothea waited. She supposed she should make the situation easier for him, but couldn't.

He reached into his inner coat pocket, brought out a worn deerskin bag and, opening it, thrust it at her.

She was astonished to see it filled with silver coins.

"This," Patrick said huskily, "is a retainer fee. John Holcombe has asked me to represent him in a complicated case that will go to the Supreme Court in Richmond before we're finished. He's paid me one hundred dollars as a retainer, and I reckon I'll earn ten times as much by the time the last appeal is heard."

Dorothea caught her breath.

"His cousin, Ed, down in Lunenburg, has need of a lawyer, too. John said that Ed has wanted me to handle his suit, but he was shy of a famous man." Patrick laughed hoarsely. "When I made it plain to him that famous men have to pay seven cents per pound for beefsteak, the same as anybody else, he told me there must be at least fifty planters and merchants in the area who have wanted to come to me. But they were too bashful to seek legal help from the former governor."

She burst into tears, threw her arms around him and clung to him.

"I have an idea," Patrick said, awkwardly comforting her, "that the dry spell may be ended."

TEN

1787–1788

1

A heavy rain turned the dirt roads of Prince Edward County into rivers of mud. The roof leaked, and Dorothea had to send to Colonel Holcombe for help to patch it. The newest member of the family, Fayette, named for the French marquis who had done so much for the cause of American freedom, became ill and ran such a high fever that Dorothea became alarmed. No physician was available, so Patrick's mother fed the infant tiny quantities of an old-fashioned herb tea for two days and two nights, and at last the fever broke.

A colt broke through a fence and disappeared, and while Dorothea was scouring the area for the animal, getting thoroughly soaked in the process, the older girls dared Patrick III to climb a black locust tree. He did, then promptly fell to the ground, spraining his left wrist. Raccoons stole a ham from the smokehouse, and the rain ruined several bales of hay at the rear of the barn, seeping in under a wall. John Syme, Jr., who was attending Hampden-Sidney College, came to pay his respects to his grandmother and aunt, and shot a small, deadly snake, a water moccasin, only fifty feet from the house. Dorothea was forced to order her children to stay away from the Appomattox, a request so seemingly unreasonable that little Sarah became hysterical and had to be sent to bed without supper.

After five days of rain the weather became a trifle better, and a light drizzle fell for the next twenty-four hours. Old Mrs. Henry went to bed with the ague, and Dorothea, who didn't feel like dining alone, made a fire in the master bedchamber hearth, brewed herself some tea and drank it with a few cold water-biscuits. Thunder rumbled in the distance as she undressed, and for no good reason she felt like weeping. Instead she spread a lotion made of cedar oil on her face, first fastening her hair at the crown of her head with a frayed string, the remains of a toy that one of the children had left in the room. Clad in her oldest flannel dressing robe, she huddled in a chair near the fire, damp and miserable, and wanted to scream as she heard the crashes of thunder moving closer.

The bedroom door opened, and Patrick stood in the frame, water dripping from his bicorn hat and cloak onto the new hooked rug.

Dorothea had no chance to wipe the oil from her face or otherwise make herself more presentable. "Don't kiss me!" she exclaimed. "You'll smear cedar lotion on your face and clothes!"

He ignored the command. "I hoped to be home day before yesterday, but the circuit court extended its sittings in Charlotte for forty-eight hours." He began to shed garments as he moved across the room, soaking portions of the rug that were still dry. "Have you eaten supper yet? I'm starved."

"I'll get you something, Mr. Henry." She hurried to her dressing room for quick repairs as he went to his. If she weren't a lady, she thought, she would curse the thunder that had prevented her from hearing his approach.

A quarter of an hour later they sat together in the dining room, a platter of cold meat, cheeses, and bread piled high before them. Patrick ate ravenously, and seemed in high spirits. "I argued thirty-nine cases in eleven days," he said. "I think that's a record of some sort. And I won all but two of them."

She smiled appreciatively and decided to postpone her tale of unrelieved woe.

"I'll have to get someone to go into partnership with me. It's too much to hope that Will Christian would be interested in moving out this far from Hanover County, but I'd be delighted to take John Fontaine in with me as soon as he recovers his health. You might sound out Martha the next time you write to her. I'm getting far more work than I can handle."

Dorothea knew she should feel elated, but was too tired to react.

"In fact, I've already hired two young law clerks. They'll move out here in the next week or so."

"Where will we find room for them, Mr. Henry?"

"I'll leave all that to you, ma'am," he answered cheerfully, cutting himself another slice of cold beef and refilling his mead cup. "Eventually we'll have to add a new wing to the house, I reckon."

She knew she couldn't complain, and tried to figure out some new sleeping arrangement for the children.

"This past week has been incredible, Dolly!"

She assumed he was talking about the rain, and opened her mouth to start telling him of the misfortunes that had accompanied the weather.

"They're talking about the new Constitution everywhere. And everyone is saying the same thing. I can't for the life of me understand how the delegates to the convention could have left out safeguards that guarantee personal liberties. There isn't one word in the Constitution on them."

Nothing was farther from Dorothea's mind than politics.

"I'm told Richie Lee has sworn he'll fight adoption of the Constitution at the Virginia Convention. I wouldn't be surprised if he's written me about it. You've left the mail in my library."

"Yes, I—"

"Stay where you are. I'll get it." Patrick hurried to his office, returning after a few moments with a bundle of letters. "It's as I thought. There's a letter from Richie." He broke the wax seal, and smiled across the table as he opened the letter. "Did anything much happen while I was gone?"

Dorothea wondered which tragedy to relate first.

"Well! It's more serious than I'd realized. George Mason is opposed to the Constitution, too, and has had words with General Washington. It looks like a real fight is brewing!"

"It was very quiet here," Dorothea said.

He scarcely heard her as, his excitement mounting, he broke the seal on another communication. "This is from Sam Adams. Let's see his reaction." He scanned the closely penned lines. "There's organized opposition in Massachusetts, too. Sam is actually suggesting a revival of the old Committees of Correspondence, and blamed if he isn't serious." Patrick chuckled, shaking his head.

The provisions of the proposed Constitution meant far less to Dorothea than her mother-in-law's illness and her infant son's recent bout of fever. But she knew from long experience that Patrick would pay no attention to anything she might say when political affairs had captured his imagination and attention.

"By the way," he said, "I've had the third request this month to act as a delegate to the state convention."

"Are you going to attend?" She surprised herself by asking the question in a calm voice.

"I haven't time. I'll send Richie a letter expressing my conviction that the Constitution is worthless without a Bill of Rights guaranteeing the individual freedoms for which we fought the war." Opening still another letter, he smiled at her reassuringly. "I gave you my pledge, and I mean to keep it. I'm through with public life."

2

The rain drummed steadily against the leaded panes of the library windows, and the fire crackled in the hearth. For what seemed like a long time there was no other sound as Patrick, hands clasped behind his back, stood and stared at his guest. "I find your story difficult to believe, sir!"

James Monroe ran long fingers through his hair. "It's true, sir. The New Yorkers and New Englanders favor the treaty with Spain—at our expense."

"I can't believe General Washington would be a party to such an outrage!"

"I can't speak for him, Governor, but I feel certain he and Jamie Madison are willing to take the risk that the Federal government proposed in the Constitution would find some way to reject the treaty."

Patrick started to pace the room, but was too shaken. "I suggest you give me the full details of this infamous affair, sir. And as one attorney to another, I demand proof, not hearsay evidence. This matter is far too important for innuendo. Give me the pure facts, nothing else."

"Very well, Governor." Monroe began to enumerate on his fingers. "Don Diego Gardoqui arrived in the United States with documents certifying him as minister plenipotentiary to this country from the court of the Spanish king. He presented his papers to Mr. John Jay of New York, acting as the Confederation Congress' secretary for foreign affairs. I believe they had met when Jay was sent to Madrid to negotiate a treaty with Spain during the war."

"You believe, sir?" Patrick's voice rose above the sound of the rain. "Not good enough, Mr. Monroe."

"Whether they met in Madrid is irrelevant, in a sense. As you know, Governor, his attempt to negotiate a treaty failed because of Spain's refusal to grant the United States navigation rights on the Mississippi, and Jay came home empty-handed before becoming a member of the commission that negotiated with Great Britain."

"Let's return to the present. At the time that Don Diego arrived in this country, Mr. Jay was already working with Jamie Madison, Hamilton of New York and others in behalf of the new Constitution. Is that correct?"

"Yes, Governor." Monroe, obviously agitated, drank a small quantity of sack. "I have here a copy of the letter that Jay sent to the foreign affairs committee of Congress. As it's only a copy, it isn't substantive evidence admissable in court, but I copied it with my own hand, and I swear to you that I haven't changed a comma." He reached into his pocket and handed the older man a folded document.

Patrick opened it with trembling fingers. "First, the Jay-Gardoqui treaty proposes that Spanish ports be opened to American shipping without payment of landing taxes by brigs' masters or of customs duties on any American products, raw or manufactured, exported by us to Spain. Very generous."

"Incredibly generous, Governor. You'll find the second provision equally intriguing."

"Well. Spain also agreed to purchase masts and timber for her royal navy from New England merchants. Do I gather correctly that she would also agree to have warships built in New England and New York yards?"

Monroe shrugged. "The wording is open to that interpretation, sir. I asked Mr. Jay the selfsame question myself, and he couldn't give me a direct answer. The Spaniards hinted—very cleverly, in my opinion—that they would give business to shipyards in the states of the North. But as that's only an opinion, I can't allow it to influence you."

"It's plain enough that the wording is anything but plain." Patrick laughed at his own wry humor.

"The next article is the key to the entire treaty, Governor."

There was a long silence as Patrick, white-faced, read the paragraph several times. "There can be no doubt of this. The United States would have to agree to give up all shipping rights on the Mississippi."

Monroe said nothing.

"This is impossible, sir!" The most renowned orator's voice in the United States rose to a roar. "Our settlements in the Ohio Valley would be cut off from their natural commercial outlet. The settlers in Kentucky and Tennessee would starve! They'd have to send their produce east across the mountains—at exorbitant cost."

"Obviously, Governor, it couldn't be done."

"This is a crude attempt to break up our settlements in the western lands!" Patrick was still seething. "It's a conspiracy offered by the Spaniards to the states of the North—at our expense and North Carolina's." He forced himself to become more rational. "Of course, Connecticut owns vast tracts west of the mountains, too."

"Her statesmen are realists, Governor. They know a small state can't continue to administer a huge territory for all time. They're reconciled to a movement in their western lands favoring the establishment of new states there."

"So, for all practical purposes, Connecticut stands with the other states of the North." Patrick went to his desk, but was still too overwrought to sit for more than a moment. "What I can't understand is how patriots like John Adams and Governor Hancock can tolerate the prospect of a deal that's harmful to our natural rights."

"You forget, sir," Monroe said, almost apologetically, "that Mr. Adams is still in London as our minister and has had no part in the proceedings. As for Mr. Hancock, he hasn't yet declared himself on the issue of the Constitution."

Patrick nodded, and was lost in thought for a time. "Under the terms of the Confederation agreement between the states, nine would have to ratify the treaty before it would become effective. Jay knows he can't get the support of nine states. But—under the new Constitution—all treaties would be ratified by an upper legislative body, a Senate."

"That's correct, Governor. I think Madison and John Marshall are being shortsighted and naïve. So is General Washington, if you'll forgive me for criticizing him. They argue that each state would have equal representation in the Senate, and that we'd be able to block the Jay-Gardoqui treaty—or some modification of it. For instance, I've heard some Northerners talk of closing the Mississippi to American navigation for twenty-five or thirty years."

"That's sophistry! After a quarter of a century, our settlers would have been driven eastward again, and the valleys would belong to Spain. George Clark's expedition would have accomplished great deeds in vain. The West is as much a part of the United States as Philadelphia or Boston. Or Richmond and Charleston, for that matter. Our rights to use the Mississippi aren't negotiable, now or ever!" Again Patrick was forced to curb his rage. "What I don't yet see, Mr. Monroe, is how the New Englanders and New Yorkers could accomplish their purpose under the new Constitution."

James Monroe smiled cynically. "The Vermont District is agitating for statehood. So is the Maine District. Spain isn't particularly interested in the Ohio and Indiana territories north of the Ohio River, and Virginia's claims to that region are tenuous. The area is being settled rapidly by New Englanders, and within a few years several other new states can be formed there."

"I see," Patrick replied grimly. "In other words, we'd be outvoted in the Senate within a few years. And meantime Kentucky and Tennessee would die on the vine, and Georgia would lose her claim to the Alabama River country."

"That's the general idea, Governor."

Patrick walked to the rain-streaked windows and stared out at the grove of black locust trees. "Mr. Monroe, I would rather part with the Confederation itself and establish a republic composed only of the Southern states than relinquish the navigation of the Mississippi River."

"Then you'll join our fight to prevent the adoption of the Constitution, sir? I'm here to enlist your help."

"This foolish plan will fail, of course." Patrick didn't hear the question. "General Washington loves his country too much to be hoodwinked for more than a short time. John Marshall, Jamie Madison, and Edmund Randolph are patriots, too. For that matter, so are thousands of men in the Northern states. They're Americans, as we are. No, I'm not really afraid of losing the western settlements, and I suggest that the Virginia Assembly go on record by passing a resolution opposing the treaty."

Monroe started to reply, but fell silent when his host turned suddenly and pointed a finger at him.

"What I fear is the parochial self-interest of the generation that's been coming to adulthood since we won our independence. I'm afraid there are men in New York and Pennsylvania and the New England states who will put sectional interests ahead of national concerns. I find many faults with the Confederation. It's weak, and we need a strong government to administer the affairs of all our people. But we need safeguards to prevent exploitation by one region at the expense of another, just as we need safeguards to prevent the larger states from harming the smaller."

"You'll join us, Governor?" Monroe persisted.

"I distrust any new system of government prepared in haste. Why the hurry? We fought the British for six and a half years, and then waited two more for the peace treaty. We need time to study the Constitution. Parts of it seem admirable, but I have doubts about others. Let's not ruin in a year or two what we needed the better part of a decade to accomplish." Patrick's manner changed, and he became the genial host. "Let me show you to your room, Mr. Monroe. I'll have a basin of warm water and some towels sent up to you. And," he added softly, "I'll give you an answer before dinner."

3

"I don't ask you for a permanent release from my promise, Dolly." Patrick spoke calmly, as he did when presenting facts to a jury. "I wouldn't have come to you at all if I didn't believe this cause vital to our future and that of our children."

"I knew your private career was too lucrative and pleasant to last," Dorothea replied bitterly, jabbing a needle through the shirt she was mending. "In another two or three years you'd have actually been free of debt. Think of it. After all these years, we could have called our souls our own again."

"That day will be postponed for a short time, nothing worse. The Virginia Constitutional Convention won't sit forever."

"When it ends, you'll find something else. Politics—and debts —are in your blood, Mr. Henry!"

"I wouldn't ask this boon of you if I didn't think it right for me to become a delegate."

"Why must you go? Aren't there others capable of taking up the burden, as you've claimed for so long?"

"It appears," he replied quietly, "that I still have a standing in Virginia. Men listen to my views, and are influenced by them. I feel strongly in this matter, Dolly—so strongly that I'm willing to spend whatever prestige I've accumulated."

"I wish we had cash to spend, instead." Dorothea dropped her sewing into a basket on the floor beside her. "Do what you will. How can I stop you? No, Mr. Henry—don't touch me, please. I— I couldn't bear it just now."

Patrick stood motionless before her. "I appreciate this, ma'am. And once the new crisis is ended, I'll never need to ask the same favor of you again. The United States is suffering childbirth pains, but when her labor is finished, the infant will be strong enough and sturdy enough to stand alone in the world."

She made no reply.

Patrick waited, realized that she didn't intend to mention the subject again, and left the room to tell Monroe he would attend the state convention.

4

General Washington was spending twenty-four hours in Richmond on personal business, and Patrick, arriving in the capital on the same day, went at once to the general's suite. James Madison, who had been conferring with the general, departed quickly, obviously embarrassed, and the two old friends confronted each other in the impersonally furnished parlor.

Washington, always reserved, seemed even chillier than usual, and Patrick's sense of dignity restrained him, making it impossible for him to unbend. The general's elegant coat, handsomely cut breeches, and silver-buckled shoes made him conscious of his own suit of rusty black and worn boots, and the thought crossed his mind that Washington's powdered wig had cost more than he himself could earn in a busy week. It was pleasant, he supposed, to be independently wealthy.

"You're looking well," they said simultaneously, but neither smiled.

"May I offer you a glass of watered rum, Governor?" Washington asked politely.

"You're very kind, General, but I've never developed a liking for strong spirits, and I'm too old to change my ways." Patrick knew that someone as sensitive as his host would appreciate the subtlety.

"Some coffee, then? I lost my own taste for tea during the war years, and I'm afraid I have none on hand."

"Nothing, thank you." It was odd, Patrick thought, that he couldn't break through the barriers of reserve. Other old friends stood on the opposite side, but he and they would have pounded each other on the back and exchanged insults. But he had never established an intimate relationship with the distant Washington.

They inquired after each other's wives, Patrick thanked the general for the silver cup he and Mrs. Washington had sent to Fayette, and they spent several minutes discussing Jefferson's successes as United States Minister to France.

"A man of your experience," Washington said, "would be extremely valuable as head of a major foreign mission, or as Secretary of State under the new form of government."

"I have no intention of holding public office again," Patrick replied firmly. Afraid he sounded rude, he added, "I've been told you're the leading candidate for President in all parts of the country, should the Constitution be adopted. It's the one bright ray of hope in the dark. You're the one man I'd trust not to make himself a tyrant or a king under a system that would give an unscrupulous President unlimited power if he chose to exercise it."

"I haven't given serious thought to the Presidency," Washington replied with scrupulous honesty. "In my opinion we must move one step at a time, and the first task that faces us is winning the support of the states."

There was an uncomfortable pause, both men realizing that their battle was joined.

Washington was not to be outdone in generosity, however. "Any man elected as President would be wise to follow the example you set as governor. No man could have been more honorable or treated his foes more fairly. You were an inspiration to men in every state, Governor Henry."

They half-rose and exchanged bows.

"That's why I find it so surprising," Washington continued in his grating voice, "that you should oppose the Constitution now."

Patrick smiled coldly. "As an American citizen, General, I'm entitled to my views, and to express them as I see fit."

"To be sure, although I regret the harm you'll inflict on people who follow leaders blindly rather than decide issues on the basis of merit."

"It's my hope that I'll influence a great many delegates to the convention." Patrick paused, and when there was no reply, he added, "I'm sorry you won't be sitting as a member. I'd enjoy debating the Constitution with you in a public forum."

"As I was president of the Philadelphia Convention, I feel it would be unseemly for me to represent Fairfax County here." Washington's tone was glacial. "However, the cause of the Constitution will be presented by true patriots who love their country."

Patrick felt his cheeks burn. "Do you insinuate, sir, that such men as Richard Henry Lee and George Mason—whose records of public service are self-evident—are lacking in patriotism?"

"I do not, sir," Washington replied in a tone equally crisp. "No one can quarrel with their past services."

Two proud men faced each other, each of them accustomed to command, each unwilling to compromise when he considered his honor at stake. Patrick stood erect, his shabby clothes and old, undressed wig forgotten. "Do you also consider me misguided, General?"

"No, Governor." Washington drew himself to his full, imposing height. "Let it suffice that I expected more of you, Governor."

"Because I don't agree with you? I'm not one of your staff officers, General, who stands at attention and salutes when he's given an order."

Washington lost his temper, too. "And I, Governor, am not one of your errand boys."

They glared at each other, both struggling to hold back still more offensive insults.

Patrick bowed stiffly from the waist, his left hand resting formally on the hilt of his dress sword. "I see nothing to be gained by prolonging this conversation."

Washington returned the bow. "I bid you good day, Governor."

"Goodbye, General."

As Patrick walked stiff-legged out of the suite, Harry Lee, now permanent brigadier general of Virginia militia, a member of the Confederation Congress and of the state's Constitutional Convention, arrived with two of his colonels to pay a courtesy call on their former commander. They stared in dismay as Patrick, not seeing them, brushed past them in the corridor, and then they caught a glimpse of Washington, who stood as still as a marble statue, lips compressed, in the parlor.

"May the Almighty help Virginia and the United States," Harry Lee murmured to his companions, "when two such giants quarrel."

5

Eight of the thirteen states had adopted the new Constitution —some with reservations which included demands for guarantees of personal liberties—by the time the Virginia Convention met at Richmond on June 2, 1788. Massachusetts, where Sam Adams had gone down in noble defeat, had endorsed the new form of government, Governor Hancock taking the lead in requesting that a Bill of Rights be voted by the first new Congress. Pennsylvania had listened to the advice of her most distinguished elder statesman, Benjamin Franklin, and had also ratified the Constitution.

The favorable vote of one more state would bring the new, controversial Federal government into being, but more was at stake than a mere technicality. Stubborn little Rhode Island and recalcitrant North Carolina were using delaying tactics, but the opponents of the Constitution in both states privately admitted that the fate of the Federal system rested elsewhere. Realists everywhere knew that the new type of Union would have to be abandoned if either of the two key states that had not yet made up their minds, New York and Virginia, voted against the Constitution.

In New York the two factions were evenly divided, but it was generally believed that Alexander Hamilton and John Jay would win the battle for the government they had been so instrumental in creating. Therefore Virginia became the center of national attention. General Washington, working quietly from his home at Mount Vernon, directed the operations of the Constitution's proponents, and his field commander was Madison, in Richmond.

The principal opponent of the Constitution was Patrick Henry, who worked ceaselessly, and with such consummate skill and cunning that Madison was frequently in despair. For two months prior to the opening of the Convention, Patrick toured the state, visiting every county and delivering scores of speeches. Former governors Thomas Nelson and Benjamin Harrison announced that they, too, sought the defeat of the proposed system. In mid-May Patrick received a letter from former governor Thomas Jefferson, who wrote that he found many features of the new government unsatisfactory and even dangerous to individual liberty. Finally, Governor Edmund Randolph, who had attended the Philadelphia Convention and had been a leading figure in the deliberations there, announced that he was joining his predecessors. After due reflection, he declared, his conscience prompted him to take a stand against the Constitution. Thus all the men who had held Virginia's highest office were united.

Richard Henry Lee and George Mason, working closely with Patrick, obtained strong support from members of the bar, and a few days before the convention was scheduled to open, a startling proclamation was published. It was signed by an overwhelming majority of Virginia's attorneys, who announced themselves opposed to the Constitution.

Madison frantically sought more active support from General Washington, whose personal prestige was at stake. Governor Randolph was invited to visit Mount Vernon, and twenty-four hours later announced that he had once again changed sides in the controversy.

It had been planned to hold the convention in the Assembly chamber, but on the hot, humid morning of June 2 the visitors' galleries were filled soon after dawn, and hundreds of other citizens milled around outside the building, vainly seeking admission.

Patrick was calmly eating breakfast with John Tyler and James Monroe in the taproom of the Richmond Inn when he learned that a huge throng had assembled, and he wasted no time. Crossing the room to the table of John Marshall, one of Madison's principal lieutenants, he proposed that the meetings be moved to the auditorium of the New Academy, the largest building in town.

Marshall agreed, even though he knew that Patrick hoped to obtain vocal support from the galleries.

Promptly at nine o'clock former governors Henry, Nelson, and Harrison walked down the center aisle of the auditorium together, went to the front row and acknowledged the frenzied cheers of their supporters with grave bows. Other delegates presented their credentials to the clerk of the convention, and at the joint request of Edmund Pendleton, a champion of the Constitution, and John Tyler, one of its leading opponents, the windows of the hall were opened in the vain hope that the chamber would be less suffocating. It was the last time the two sides were in agreement for the twenty-three days that the convention was in session.

The spectators were continuing to applaud, and Patrick turned in his seat to whisper to George Mason, who was seated directly behind him. "What a pity," he said, "that our friends can't vote. As nearly as I can judge—in spite of all our efforts—Washington and Madison have won the support of a majority of delegates. They're using the general's prestige to help them, and all we have on our side is logic. We'll have to work twice as hard!"

The morning was devoted to the organization of the convention, and Madison won the first round by pushing through the election of Patrick's lifelong foe, Edmund Pendleton, as permanent chairman. During the noon recess the opposition camp sustained an even more severe blow when word was received that Richard Henry Lee was ill and could not attend. His alternate was assigned to his place, and the talents of one of the most able debaters in the state were lost.

Patrick sat quietly through noon dinner at the Richmond Inn, paying little attention to the talk swirling around him. Harrison and Mason thought him unusually gloomy and tried to cheer him, but Tyler urged them to leave him alone. Apparently he had something out of the ordinary on his mind, and his old associates respected his silence.

He made his tactics clear to the entire convention by requesting the floor when the convention reconvened that afternoon. Madison had expected to open the debate with an address explaining the strengths of the proposed Constitution, but he and his friends realized too late that the wiliest politician in Virginia had stolen a march on him.

"Gentlemen," Patrick said with a broad smile, "make yourselves comfortable. I expect to hold the floor for a spell." The galleries applauded, but he pretended to take no notice. "There's been a great deal of talk in Richmond these past few days about the position I'm taking in the matter that brings us together here. I want to set the record straight.

"My objections to the Constitution submitted here for our consideration do not spring from any hostility to the union of our thirteen states, or from any preference for a separate union of the Southern states. There was a time, to be sure, when I felt so provoked by the outrage planned by some so-called statesmen in the North over the navigation rights on the Mississippi River that I felt there was no security for Virginia in the Confederation, and that this lack would have spelled certain disaster under the Constitution.

"But I am convinced that, no matter now sinister the machinations of men opposed to our interests, the thirteen states must remain united. Separate confederacies would ruin us."

He paused, and his voice rang through the hall when he resumed. "The first thing I have at heart is American liberty. The second thing is American union. I do not, nor will I to my dying day, breathe the spirit nor utter the language of secession."

The applause was so loud and prolonged that he had to wait until it subsided before he could continue. "Mr. Chairman, gentlemen, I freely admit there are great defects in the Confederation. I believe they ought to be cured by giving greater strength to the Federal government. But does the proposed Constitution embody such improvements? On the contrary, it replaces our entire system of government with something radically different and radically dangerous.

"The convention at Philadelphia ought to have amended the old system. For this purpose they were solely delegated. The object of their mission extended to no other consideration.

"The distinction between a national government and a confederacy is not sufficiently discerned. In my opinion the delegates at Philadelphia had no power to propose a consolidated government. They have exceeded their prerogatives, and have submitted to us a resolution as radical as that which separated us from Great Britain. Our rights and privileges are endangered, and the sovereignty of the individual states will be relinquished."

Again he paused, and then spoke very slowly and distinctly. "The rights of conscience, trail by jury, liberty of the press, all your immunities and franchises, all pretensions to human rights and privileges, are rendered insecure, if not lost, by this change, so loudly talked of by some, so inconsiderately by others.

"A number of our citizens, of the greatest eminence in this

country—Mr. Sam Adams and Mr. Gerry of Massachusetts, the good friends who flank me on either side and scores of others whose patriotism is beyond reproach, object to a form of government that offers the individual no security for his freedoms. This is not imaginary. It is a formidable reality. If this consolidation destroys our liberties, if it proves to be as mischievous to this country as it has been to other nations, what will the poor inhabitants of this nation do?

"This government will operate like an ambuscade. It will destroy the liberties of the people without giving previous notice. If gentlemen are willing to run the hazard, let them run it! But I shall exculpate myself by my opposition and monitory warnings within these walls.

"What does the new Constitution provide for the protection of individuals? Almost nothing. It creates a new and tremendous power over us, but it fails to cover us with any shield, or to interpose any barrier by which, in case of need, we might save ourselves from the wanton and fatal exercise of power that could make the freedom for which we fought a mockery.

"A bill of rights, gentlemen, is indispensably necessary for the protection of our citizens. It is far more urgently needed than a whole new system of government.

"Gentlemen, I trust you will see that the great objects of religious freedom, liberty of the press, trial by jury, interdiction of cruel punishments and every other sacred right are secured. I beg you, in the name of the Almighty God in whom we place our trust, that you will insure this guarantee of our freedoms before you agree to consider the rights and wrongs of any other portion of that paper submitted here for your consideration."

Another wave of applause interrupted Patrick, but he gestured for silence, and his audience was so completely under his spell that delegates and spectators alike immediately fell silent.

"The necessity of a bill of rights," he went on, "appears to me to be greater in this government than it ever was in any government before. Let me observe that the sense of European nations, and particularly Great Britain, is against the construction of rights being retained which are not expressly relinquished.

"I repeat, gentlemen. All nations have adopted the principle that all rights not expressly and unequivocally reserved to the people are impliedly and incidentally relinquished to rulers, as necessarily inseparable from delegated powers.

"What are the sentiments entertained by the American people on this subject? At the Revolution it was their purpose to set down those great rights which ought, in all countries, to be held inviolable and sacred; Virginia did so, as we all remember. We are indebted for all time to our distinguished colleague, Mr. George Mason, for his work in drawing up a bill of rights for the citizens of Virginia, the first such expressly worded document in the history of the entire human race.

"Virginia made a compact to reserve, expressly, certain rights. She most cautiously and guardedly reserved and secured those invaluable, inestimable rights and privileges which no people, inspired with the least glow of patriotic liberty, ever did—or ever can—abandon. She is called upon now to abandon them, and dissolve that compact which secured them to her. Will she do it? This is the question you and I must decide, gentlemen, here, in this chamber.

"If you intend to reserve your unalienable rights, you must have the most express stipulation, for if implication be allowed, you are ousted of those rights. You default. You lose them."

James Madison looked glum, as did most of his supporters, and only John Marshall, taking notes furiously, seemed undismayed by the persuasive power of Patrick's oratory.

"If the people do not think it necessary to reserve their precious rights, they will be supposed to be given up. And a crime will have been committed against the citizens of the United States, the good people of Virginia. You act for them, gentlemen. The decision is yours alone to make.

"If you give up these powers, without a bill of rights, you will exhibit to all mankind the most absurd spectacle that ever the world saw—a government that has abandoned all its powers—the powers of direct taxation, the sword and the purse. You will dispose of them to a Federal Congress without a bill of rights, without check, limitation or control.

"Think of the paradox, fellow Virginians. At this very moment you have powers that prevent your state government from acting

314

against your best interests. No tyrant can destroy your freedoms here. You have a bill of rights to defend you against the state government. Yet you will have none against a Federal Congress if you meekly adopt the proposed Constitution.

"You arm yourselves against the weak and defenseless. Will you expose yourselves naked to the armed and powerful?"

There was a stir in the hall, and delegates muttered to each other, some nodding in obvious agreement.

Patrick bowed to Edmund Pendleton. "Mr. Chairman, I've concluded my introductory remarks. From time to time in the days to come I shall again ask for the privilege of making my views known to our colleagues."

He sat down, and Madison, who immediately obtained the floor, was brutally honest. "I can't hope to compete with Governor Henry's rhetoric or logic," he said, and appreciative laughter greeted his candor. "I can only wish, with all my heart, that he stood with me in this debate."

6

Patrick continued to fight with a vehemence that heartened his friends and dismayed his foes in the days that followed. The opponents of the Constitution, deprived of Richard Henry Lee's services, had only one great orator in their ranks, and Patrick carried the burden of the battle almost single-handed. He made as many as fifteen separate addresses in a single day's session, and as the debate neared a climax he spent seven uninterrupted hours on the floor, making a speech—without written notes—in which he discussed at length every phase of the proposed Constitution.

Madison's majority dwindled steadily, the final outcome was in doubt, and General Washington's aid was once again enlisted. The high-minded patrician refused to campaign directly on behalf of the Constitution in which he so fervently believed, but he was finally persuaded to meet Patrick privately at Governor Randolph's home.

Then Madison, justifiably fearful, approached Tyler, Monroe, and several other leading members of the opposition, asking if they might persuade Patrick to meet the general. All said they were unable to speak on his behalf, so Madison was forced to go directly to his principal foe. Patrick's immediate reply surprised him.

"Of course I'll see the general," he said. "Our personal relationship is totally irrelevant. This question is far more important than friendships or enmities."

At four o'clock on the afternoon of June 24, Patrick arrived at the governor's home and found Washington alone, awaiting him in the parlor. They exchanged stiff bows and, their previous encounter fresh in both their minds, did not bother to indulge in the usual civilities.

Washington opened the conversation with military bluntness. "I'm informed, Governor, that the vote will be a virtual draw. Either side can win, as things stand at present."

"Your count tallies with mine, General."

"I'm deeply distressed."

"So am I," Patrick said. "No matter who wins, Virginia—and the United States—will be the losers. I hope you'll accept my word when I assure you that I think it a tragic spectacle. No one will benefit when the first state in the Union reveals herself so badly split."

"My own melancholy over this unfortunate situation is what has brought me back to Richmond. The future of the nation is more important than any disagreements that may divide us."

"Agreed, sir," Patrick said crisply.

"I consider it essential that we present a consolidated front to the world. I've therefore asked Mr. Madison to make a conciliatory gesture, and he has volunteered to introduce a resolution to the convention tomorrow morning. It will express the convention's firm opinion that a bill of rights must accompany the Constitution's adoption, and will bind Senators and Representatives elected to office from this state—as well as members of the Executive elected by the nation as a whole—to press for such safeguards."

Patrick smiled appreciatively. Washington was alleged to be no politician, but in one simple, master stroke he was disarming the Constitution's opponents. "I'm overwhelmed by your generosity, sir," he said, "and for the sake of the country and state both of us love, I hope I can prove myself equally gracious."

The conversation was at an end, and far more significant than what had been said were the opinions and feelings that neither expressed.

7

Tumultuous applause greeted James Madison's resolution, which the delegates to the convention adopted by unanimous, standing vote. Virginia was now on record demanding, without equivocation, a bill of rights that would guarantee personal liberties.

When the cheers subsided, Patrick asked for the floor and was recognized. He walked to the rostrum, surprising Pendleton, but the chairman realized he had something extraordinary to say, and relinquished the podium to him as a sudden hush settled over the chamber.

"Virginia," he said, "has acted wisely and well to protect those freedoms which we hold sacred. Americans of generations yet unborn will be grateful to this body for so acting.

"Now, if I may be indulged, I would like to say a personal word, the last I shall deliver in public life." His voice became husky, and he removed his spectacles, cleaned them and placed them on the bridge of his nose again.

"I beg pardon of this House for having taken up more time than came to my share, and I thank them for the patience and polite attention with which I have been heard.

"If I shall be in the minority in the vote we are about to cast, I shall suffer those painful sensations which arise from a conviction of being overpowered in a good cause.

"Yet I will be a peaceable and good citizen. I will abide by the will of the majority. I will work to the best of my ability as an American and a Virginian to support the will of that majority.

"My head, my hand, and my heart shall be ever vigilant to retrieve a loss of liberty inflicted upon us by a new and untried system of government, and remove the defects of that system in a Constitutional way.

"I will not, now or ever, resort to violence. I shall wait, with high hopes that the spirit which predominated in our Revolution is not yet gone, nor the cause of those who are attached to the Revolution lost. I shall therefore patiently wait in expectation of seeing our new form of government changed, so as to be compatible with the safety, liberty and happiness of the people.

"To the day I die, I shall be thankful to the Divine Creator for having granted me the privilege of living as an American and a Virginian."

The delegates saw tears trickling down his face as he descended from the podium and resumed his seat. No one applauded.

Chairman Pendleton asked the clerks to poll the delegates on the question that had been the primary concern of the convention, and an hour later the results were counted again and checked. Virginia adopted the Constitution by a majority of ten votes. As she was the ninth state to ratify the document, it became the law of the land.

James Madison immediately made his way across the center aisle to shake Patrick's hand. "Governor," he said, "you stand above us all as a patriot. I hope you'll accept my support for a seat in the new Senate, where you can work for the adoption of a bill of rights."

"Give your support to Richie Lee instead," Patrick told him. "He'll carry out the will of this convention as diligently as I might have done." Sighing inaudibly, he looked around the chamber, where delegates were standing in small groups, chatting animatedly. Here was the verve and excitement, the sense of high purpose and the drama of public service that had been his life for so long, and it was difficult for him to speak. The inside of his mouth felt dry, and his heart hammered in his ears as he said, "I am retiring from public life for all time."

ELEVEN

1794–1799

1

The First Congress of the United States under the new Federal system was true to its trust, and so was General Washington, chosen by his fellow citizens as President. A Bill of Rights was incorporated in the new Constitution in the form of ten amendments, which the states ratified. "These amendments," Senator Richard Henry Lee of Virginia told his colleagues, "are a lasting monument to two men who love liberty more than life itself, Patrick Henry and Sam Adams."

The nation expanded rapidly in the years of Washington's first administration, and by the time he was re-elected in 1792, the country's total population stood between four and five million. Vermont had been admitted to the Union as a state in 1791, and was followed by Kentucky in the next year. Tennessee, to which North Carolina was gradually relinquishing its claims, was preparing for statehood, and the Ohio Valley was burgeoning.

Only a few of the Revolutionary War leaders were still active in public life, chief among them being President Washington and Vice-President John Adams. Benjamin Franklin was dead, mourned by the entire nation, and in 1794 Secretary of State Thomas Jefferson let it be known that he intended to retire, at least temporarily.

Prince Edward County in Virginia was far from the seat of the Federal government, which was located in New York, and Patrick Henry had kept his word to take no part in public affairs. He remained interested in the government's activities and maintained a steady correspondence with friends in both Federal and state service, but refused to give advice to others.

"I would not presume," he wrote Jefferson, "to tell any office-holder how, in my poor opinion, he should discharge his responsibility. Only in the unlikely event that I—and no one else—should discover my country in mortal danger because of acts committed or left undone, would I venture to offer advice or criticism to those who carry the burdens of state."

No one, not even Dorothea, knew whether Patrick was satisfied with his new, non-political existence. Only once did he raise the question. On the eve of President Washington's second inaugural he dropped a brief, unusual comment to a few neighbors, saying, "I shall always regret the coolness that has marked my relations with the President since the Constitutional Convention."

Embarrassed by his own outburst, he changed the subject and did not refer to the matter again.

Dorothea would have pursued it, but life at the estate in Prince Edward County was so hectic that she had no immediate chance. There were seven children in the family now, and the oldest, Dorothea and Sarah, were sixteen and fifteen years old, respectively. Patrick's mother had died, and was mourned by the whole family.

A separate building located a stone's throw from the house now served as Patrick's office, and five assistants worked there in what Assembly Leader John Marshall jokingly called "the busiest law factory in the United States." There was no question that Patrick was almost frantically overworked, and by 1794 was handling in excess of one thousand cases per year. The load was all the more remarkable because he carried it alone. Will Christian had been reluctant to move west, and persisting ill health had prevented John Fontaine from joining his father-in-law.

The physical strain on Patrick was enormous and unceasing. His services as an attorney were in constant demand throughout Virginia, which made it necessary for him to travel constantly from one county to another in order to appear before the local courts everywhere. He accepted only those cases that interested him, refusing to represent potential clients of whom he disapproved, and he was the envy of fellow members of the bar because he consistently charged higher fees than any other lawyer in the United States.

But he remained unswervingly devoted to the common people, and insisted on giving one-third of his time free of charge to the poor, who could not afford to hire legal representatives. When Dorothea protested that he was working too hard, complaining that he came home only on weekends and urging him to drop his charity clients, he disposed of the subject succinctly.

"I would prefer," he said, "to abandon my entire practice."

In the spring of 1794 he paid off the last of his debts and became the master of his own financial house.

Dorothea persuaded him to celebrate by taking his first vacation in more than a decade, and his sons and daughters by his first wife were invited to Prince Edward County with their husbands, wives, and children for a grand family reunion. Dorothea, her eldest daughters, and two cooks worked for ten days in the kitchen preparing for the family party, and the stone hearth, two charcoal stoves and the roasting pit were in constant use. Neighbors contributed feather mattresses, the youngsters agreed to give up their rooms and it was arranged that adults would sleep in the bedrooms, with the children using the parlor and even the dining room as a dormitory. Only the separate law office building was considered inviolable.

Patrick came home on the first day of May, forty-eight hours before anyone was expected, and was surprised to find Martha Fontaine sitting on a bench with Dorothea near the grove of black locust trees. Unmindful of the dust that coated his clothes, he went to her at once and enveloped her in an embrace.

"This is the best surprise I've had in a long time," he said heartily, and kissed her.

Dorothea, standing behind Martha, gestured frantically.

Patrick stared at her over his daughter's shoulder.

Suddenly, to his horror, Martha began to weep.

Dorothea knew she had to intervene. "Martha was widowed seven days ago," she said.

Only then did Patrick notice that his daughter was dressed in unrelieved black. For a moment he was too stunned to speak, and when he recovered his voice he couldn't help shouting. "Why wasn't I told?"

Martha recovered a semblance of her poise. "John wanted it this way, Papa. He knew for a month that he was dying. He begged me not to let you interrupt your work, and he insisted that he be buried with only the children and me there."

Dorothea, Patrick saw at a glance, had known from the outset that John's illness had taken a grave turn. "I scarcely know what to say," he murmured, and kissed Martha again.

"I didn't know whether to come here," she said. "But it's been so long since all of us have been together that I didn't want to deprive the the children of this visit."

"She's been talking of leaving the children here and going back to Hanover to close the house," Dorothea told him.

Patrick settled the matter. "You'll stay," he said.

Martha nodded, then buried her face in his coat. "I—I don't want to spoil the celebration."

"Families draw together when there's trouble or sorrow. It's important that we try to help you. Besides, I've never yet known a Henry who enjoys roistering." Patrick made a heavy-handed attempt to sound casual; then his stiff smile faded as a sudden thought occurred to him. "Why are you closing the house?"

"I've got to move out our belongings. John and I sold it only a few weeks ago." Martha seemed reluctant to discuss the subject.

Her father stepped back and held her at arm's length. "I don't understand."

"John's illness was so expensive, Papa. We needed cash." Martha's shoulders drooped. "The final payment will bring in just about enough to pay off our creditors. John can rest quietly, knowing he left no debts."

"You still have property in Hanover County and out in Kentucky."

"No, we had to sell it last year."

Patrick made no attempt to hide his concern. "How do you intend to support yourself and four children?"

Martha shrugged helplessly. "I haven't thought about it yet. All this is so—so new to me."

"I've already told her," Dorothea said, "that she and the children must make their home with us."

Never had she displayed greater generosity, and never had Patrick loved her more. "Of course. It's the only possible solution."

"I refuse to be a burden on you," Martha cried.

"It will be our great joy to have you with us," Dorothea replied. "Our children are as close as brothers and sisters, as close as you and I have always been. So they'll create no problems. Mr. Henry and I insist!"

"But you haven't even discussed it privately!"

"There's nothing to discuss," Patrick said gently.

Martha's pride forced her to make a last, desperate effort. "You don't have enough room for me and my brood."

"That's the very least of our concerns," her father declared. "We'll find another house somewhere. The subject is closed."

2

Red Hill was an estate of more than twenty thousand acres, southwest of Prince Edward County, and the Staunton River ran through the property, part of which was located in Campbell County—named for one of Patrick's brothers-in-law—and part in Charlotte County. There were trout in the Staunton and its tributary, the Otter, and the thick pine forests were teeming with game. "It's almost like living in the wilderness," Dorothea said, "but we're only a two-hour ride from Lynchberg and even closer to Appomattox."

One of the most attractive features of the property was the complex of dwellings that made up a family village. Open tobacco fields spread out in the Staunton Valley, and above them, surrounded by chestnut and ash, poplar and oak and hickory, stood the buildings. The "main house" was two stories high, made of clapboard and painted white, and attached to it was a single-story

323

annex, which contained the parlor and dining room, master bed-room and library-office. Patrick installed a tin roof over his work-room because, he confided to Dorothea and Martha, he loved the sound of rain overhead when studying his law books.

A stone's throw to the north was a smaller home, where Martha and her children were installed, and another house was built on the opposite side for Anne and Spencer Roane. Judge Roane, wor-ried about the financial security of his family, retired from the bench because his pay was so small, and entered into a partnership with his father-in-law. The idea originated with Patrick, who had no hesitation in adding another daughter, her husband and their children to his list of dependents until Spencer began to earn his way.

"I'm fifty-eight years old, and I find that constant travel tires me," Patrick said frankly at a family council. "I'll find it a blessing for Spencer to follow the circuit courts while I stay at home and prepare my briefs. If all goes as it should, I can cut my own court appearances by fifty percent or more."

The relationship was a success from the start, and to Dorothea's relief her husband found time to go fishing and hunting occasion-ally on his own property, usually with at least three or four of his young sons and grandsons accompanying him. "We talk and laugh so much that we frighten off the deer and the trout vanish," he said, "but I can't remember when I've enjoyed myself as much."

Unavoidably, he was in debt again. The estate had cost him almost twenty-five thousand dollars, and he had spent seven thou-sand more adding the new buildings. Above all, he was responsible for the support of a wife and seven children, a grown daughter and her four youngsters and, at least for the moment, another daughter, her husband and their brood of three. But he remained cheerful, and so did Dorothea. Neither doubted his ability to earn a substantial income, and with Spencer as his new partner, there was every reason to believe he could bring in enough money to provide for his rapidly approaching old age.

Autumn came late to southern Virginia in 1794. One morning in early October the sun blazed in a cloudless sky, and not a ripple of a breeze stirred the leaves of the trees. Patrick found it difficult to concentrate on his work. He remained at his desk, however, until his sons and grandsons came home from school early in the afternoon, and then, suddenly, decided to spend the rest of the day as he pleased.

"We're going trout fishing," he announced. "Get some meat and bread from the kitchen, and we'll have a picnic."

Thirty minutes later he and seven small, giggling boys were lined up on the bank of the Staunton River, each armed with a fishing pole. The heat was even more intense, and Patrick, stretching out on the mossy bank, ignored the hum of childish conversation and dropped off to sleep.

He was awakened by fifteen-year-old Sarah, who stood above him, panting for breath.

"I've been searching everywhere for you, Papa," she said. "Governor Lee has come to see you."

Still sleepy, Patrick thought for a moment that she meant Richard Henry Lee, and it was a shock when he remembered that Richie had died four months earlier. He pulled himself to his feet, and stood for a moment or two, blinking, before he recalled that Sarah undoubtedly meant Harry Lee, who was completing his third year as governor and who owed his election at least in part to Patrick, who had written a number of open letters on his behalf to the newspapers.

Harry owned an estate in the neighborhood, but it was surprising that he should be here at this season, when the Burgesses were meeting in Richmond. "I'll be back, lads," he called, and carrying his fishing pole over his shoulder, walked through the woods with Sarah to the house.

General Harry Lee, chatting on the lawn with Dorothea, was wearing a handsome coat of green velvet with a yellow waistcoat, white silk breeches and a powdered wig. Patrick chuckled as he realized that his own appearance could not have been shabbier. His linsey-woolsey shirt was old, his buckskin trousers were stained and his bald head was bare. It was good, he thought, that such things no longer mattered to him.

The two men shook hands cordially. "How are the fish biting, P.H.?" Lee wanted to know.

"The boys were playing at being Chickahominy warriors the last

I heard, and it discouraged the fish. What brings you out here, Harry?"

"You."

Dorothea quickly absented herself and went off to the house for refreshments as Patrick led his guest to a latticed pavilion where they would be shielded from the sun. "I've heard that you're being called to Federal Army duty when you retire from the governorship."

"Yes. President Washington has a mission he wants me to perform." Lee glanced at his host. "For a man who buries himself in the wilds, you keep yourself informed of what goes on in the world."

"I was in court at Lynchburg for two days earlier in the week. Would you like to make a tour of the property?"

"Later, P.H." Lee, still more the soldier than the politician tried without success to speak casually. "You know, I couldn't help thinking as I was riding over here just now that it's a damned shame you and the President should be on bad terms. You were close for so many years, and you worked together so hard for our independence."

It was obvious that the governor hadn't come to make idle, small talk about an old feud, and Patrick decided on the spur of the moment to break his long silence on the subject. He couldn't divine Lee's motives, but saw no reason to be less than candid. "Every man does something stupid in his life that makes him ashamed of himself," he said. "And too often pride gets in the way. Maybe it's the other way around, I'm not sure. I've often thought of a line from the Book of Proverbs, 'When pride cometh, then cometh shame.' My only excuse—and it's a mighty feeble one —for behaving as I did in '88 is that I was carried away by the fight over the Constitution. Well, I was wrong in more ways than one. The new Federal system is working out far better than I imagined it could. So I don't blame Washington for holding a low opinion of me."

"He doesn't." Lee spoke slowly. "I was the President's house guest less than a week ago, and we spent the better part of an evening talking about you. He feels he was to blame for your difficulties, and he quoted a line, too. From Ovid, I think."

"I know it. 'The proud man closes his mind and locks out thoughts.' Very generous of him."

"It has long been President Washington's opinion," Lee said, phrasing his thoughts with care, "that the talents of the most able man in the United States are being wasted. I'm very pleased that you bear him no grudge, and I know he'll be delighted. You've been on his conscience for a long time, P.H."

Patrick's face felt stiff as he smiled. "I look forward to the day when I can shake his hand."

"That day is at hand, if you wish it. I'm here as an unofficial emissary on official United States business." Lee rose from the bench on which he had been sitting. "President Washington would like you to join his Cabinet, and wants to offer you the highest post he's authorized to give any man, that of Secretary of State. He asked me to tell you that if you feel you've been absent from government service for too long, he'll gladly send you to Madrid first, for a period of months, as our Minister to Spain."

Patrick was stunned. Clasping his hands behind his back, he paced up and down the pavilion.

Lee respected his silence.

"Tell the President I'll be grateful for the honor and this sign of his trust and friendship until the day I die. But I must refuse."

Lee had apparently been prepared for a rejection. "I'm sorry. But I agree with the President that you're being wasted in private life. On my own behalf I'd like to offer you Richie's seat in the United States Senate. I canvassed the Assembly before I left Richmond, and I've been assured of unanimous approval if I appoint you."

Patrick moistened his lips with the tip of his tongue. "I can't accept, Harry, but I thank you."

"Please don't be too hasty."

"Let me explain my situation. I have no private fortune, and I support a very large family. If I were to die tomorrow, my wife and children would be destitute." Patrick shoved his spectacles up onto his forehead. "I'd enjoy serving as Secretary of State. I flatter myself that I might be able to do even more for the people as a Senator from Virginia. But my hands are tied, Harry. I don't know how much longer the good Lord will permit me to walk this earth. A year or two, perhaps—"

"More than that, surely!"

"I hope so. But I don't know. My first obligation is to provide for my family. Once I've made them secure, there's nothing would give me greater joy than the right to serve my country and my state. But until I've provided for them, I can't even think of anything else." Patrick was horrified to discover that his eyes were misty. Not until now had he allowed himself to realize how badly he missed public life. But his duty to Dorothea and their children, to Martha and to Anne came first, and only after he discharged his duty to them could he allow himself the luxury of working once again for the American people—and living in the limelight he relished.

3

The continuing growth and expansion of the United States was spectacular. Thousands of brigs built in American yards joined the nation's merchant marine, and the New England fishing fleet doubled its size in years between 1794 and 1796. Hundreds of textile plants and other commercial enterprises were established in Massachusetts, Connecticut, and Rhode Island, scores of industries were founded in Pennsylvania and, much to the chagrin of Boston and Philadelphia, New York—now a city—was increasing in size so rapidly that it promised to become the country's largest community.

Renewed warfare between England and France brought thousands of immigrants to the shores of the New World, land was settled as far west as the Mississippi River, and Tennessee formally applied for admission to the Union as the sixteenth state. President Washington, nearing the end of his second term as Chief Executive, steered a careful course of neutrality and refused to become embroiled in the quarrel between France and England. There was some sentiment in the cities favoring the cause of France, America's ally in the Revolution, and in parts of New England, where merchants maintained strong ties with London, there was a great deal of talk about a common Anglo-Saxon heritage. But the President, supported by an almost united Congress, insisted that the young nation develop her own resources and avoid unnecessary risk of foreign entanglement.

Washington, anxious to retire, would not listen to the suggestions of friends that he consider acceptance of a third term. If a President was limited to two terms, he believed, the danger that any man who held the office might want to make himself a king would be vastly reduced. When word of the President's decision became known, various potential candidates for the Presidency appeared, but it seemed likely that only a token contest would develop. Washington, most members of his Cabinet and the more influential Senators and Congressmen felt that Vice-President John Adams was entitled to the post.

Virginia was enjoying unprecedented prosperity. Her tobacco was selling in the world's markets at the highest prices in history, her other agricultural products were in demand at home and abroad, and Norfolk's commercial shipping rivaled Philadelphia's. Small consumer goods factories were springing up all over the state, and Richmond, still growing rapidly, was now the largest city in the South.

Real estate values doubled in the two years between 1794 and 1796, and Patrick Henry, disposing of half his estate, suddenly found himself solvent. Never in his sixty years had he enjoyed such great financial security. The law firm of Henry and Roane was in demand everywhere, there were now eight clerks in the office and Patrick, leaving the management of daily affairs in the hands of his son-in-law, was at last free to accept only the cases that challenged him or that paid him the highest fees.

He tried in vain to confine his trips to the county seats closest to his home, and in mid-summer of 1796 complicated litigation forced him to travel to Fairfax, in the northern part of the state. He was the principal attorney representing the plaintiff, and conducted his case with his usual vigor and skill, virtually assuring his client a victory. On the last afternoon of the three-day trial he was sitting in the courtroom, listening to the final summation of the defense counsel, when he became aware of a stir at the rear of the chamber.

Turning, he saw a young captain in the blue-and-buff uniform of the Army. Most of the spectators were gaping at the officer, and Patrick smiled quietly. Moments such as this made him aware of his age; most of the people present had rarely seen the once-familiar uniform in all their adult lives.

The captain seated himself at the rear of the courtroom, and Patrick forgot him. Counsel for the defense completed the presentation of his case, and evidently expected an adjournment of an hour or two. But the magistrate felt no need for a delay to ponder the case, and handed down a verdict in favor of the plaintiff.

A dozen men surrounded Patrick, eager to congratulate him, and he accepted their praise with as much grace as he could muster. The truth of the matter was that he had grown accustomed to winning his cases, and he was weary, even a trifle bored.

The crowd parted to let the Army officer through. "Mr. Henry?" he asked.

"What can I do for you, young man?"

Lawyers, their clients and even the magistrate listened curiously, and the captain indicated he wanted a private word, so Patrick accompanied him to the courthouse portico.

"I'm Captain Henry Harrison, sir—"

"Ben's nephew? Well. I knew you as a boy."

"I didn't think you'd remember, sir." The officer was pleased. "I'm military aide-de-camp to President Washington, sir, and I'm here at his order. He and Mrs. Washington are spending a few days at their plantation, and would be honored if you'd join them for dinner and spend the night. It's only a short ride from here."

"I'll be delighted," Patrick replied unhesitatingly, then added dryly, "I know the distance from Fairfax to Mount Vernon, Captain Harrison. I made the journey many times, long before you were born."

Thirty minutes later, after paying his bill at the local inn and collecting his belongings, Patrick started out for the estate, the officer beside him. The unexpected invitation was even more gratifying than Patrick had realized, and his sense of anticipation grew as the horses moved at a steady gait down the dirt road. He and Washington had corresponded sporadically since their reconciliation, but had not met face to face since their unpleasantness eight years earlier.

The sun was still high when they arrived at the plantation, but a soft breeze was blowing, and it seemed a trifle cooler on the bluff overlooking the Potomac River. President Washington came out of the mansion house to greet his guest, and Captain Harrison took Patrick's mount.

The two old friends looked at each other for a moment, smiled simultaneously and extended their hands.

"You don't look a day older, Governor Henry," Washington said.

"If I told you the same, Mr. President, we'd both be liars."

Members of the household staff, who rarely heard Washington laugh, were surprised by the sound of his uncontrolled mirth.

The two men discussed affairs of state in general terms until Mrs. Washington joined them for dinner. The conversation turned to domestic matters during the meal, and then Washington took his guest on a stroll through the gardens.

Neither mentioned the unfortunate period when their relations had been strained. They paused to admire trees that had been planted by the Marquis de Lafayette and others, and Patrick agreed to plant one himself before departing in the morning.

"I envy you this place, Mr. President," he said.

"I'll admit I'm looking forward to retirement. And you, Governor?"

"The thought hadn't occurred to me. I try to spend a day fishing now and again, but my balance of humors wouldn't permit me to be idle, I'm afraid. I become restless when I have too little to do, more's the pity."

"Perhaps you're the one who should be envied." Washington hesitated for a moment, then said delicately, "I trust your personal affairs have improved since Harry Lee visited you as my intermediary."

"They're much improved, sir." Patrick could see that his reply did not surprise the President.

"I'm pleased to hear it, both for your sake and the country's." Washington offered no immediate explanation.

They returned to the house and made themselves comfortable in the main drawing room, where a servant brought them silver mugs, into which they poured small quantities of wine and liberal amounts of cold well water.

"This visit is opportune," Washington said. "You've been much on my mind of late, and a meeting in person is better than correspondence or dealing through an emissary."

Patrick felt himself growing tense.

"The United States has long needed your services, Governor, and that need has never been greater than it is at present. I'm no lawyer, but I'm told our judiciary needs to be strengthened. The Attorney General and several others believe there's no better lawyer in the country than you, and your record as an executive speaks for itself. I've wanted you in the government for years, and I'd like to offer you the post of Chief Justice of the Supreme Court."

Never had Patrick felt so honored. He flushed and, his composure momentarily deserting him, blurted the first words that came to his mind. "I'm too old."

"You're four years younger than I am."

Patrick slowly recovered his poise, and smiled. "I wonder if you know, sir, that I had a letter from John Adams less than two weeks ago. He'd like me as his Vice-President, and he said he felt positive that Jefferson's friends as well as Hamilton's would support me."

"The Vice-President discussed the situation with me, Governor. He deplores the split into factionalism, as I do, and he believes you'd exert a healing influence. I dare say you would, but in my opinion you'd perform a more valuable service to the country as Chief Justice."

"I usually know my own mind," Patrick said, "but I hope you'll forgive my confusion, Mr. President. I don't know what to tell you."

"Give me your decision when you can, Governor. It's wonderful to know that you're going to consider both places. From your own standpoint, you'll have to decide which will make you happier. To me it's heartening that the American people will benefit either way."

4

Dorothea, her hair still showing no trace of gray, sat in the four-poster bed, and after adjusting the pillows of pine needles behind her back, picked up her cup of early morning tea from the table beside her. "I must be truthful with you, Mr. Henry. I've been disturbed for the past two years, ever since you told me you'd been asked to be Secretary of State and rejected the offer. Surely you know I wouldn't have stood in your way."

"I had no choice. It was a luxury I couldn't afford." Patrick was already dressed, and sat in a chair near the windows overlooking the side yard as he drank his own tea.

"Well, our situation is improved now, and I'd be the most selfish woman alive if I discouraged you from accepting one of these new offers. When the government's demands are so insistent, it would be wicked to close the door."

"I must admit I've been giving them serious consideration. I believe Spencer can function alone for a few years, and I'll arrange to have him give me a portion of the partnership's income while I'm away, although I must warn you, Dolly, that it will be no more than a small fraction of what I'm earning now."

"We'll manage."

"It will be a sacrifice for us—and for Martha. Government wages are still very small."

"At least we own the property now, and you'll be able to resume your practice when you leave office."

"The Lord willing." Patrick was reluctant to tell her that his physical strength was ebbing, and was no longer a match for his mind. "That's one reason I'm a little afraid of taking the Vice-Presidency. If there's no further growth in factionalism—and I can only pray they'll reconcile their differences because the growth of political parties in this country might destroy democracy—the

Vice-President is the logical successor to the President. I'd be sixty-five if John Adams serves only one term, and sixty-nine, if I lived that long, after two. I don't want the responsibilities of the office at that age. I'm not sure I could discharge them."

"Of course you could!"

He shook his head. "Washington's appearance would shock you. I've never seen a man look older or more tired." He was silent for a moment, then brightened. "Besides, as an attorney I know of nothing I'd enjoy more than to serve as Chief Justice."

"Then you've made up your mind." Dorothea finished her tea and shook her head when he would have poured her another cup.

"Provided you approve, of your own volition. I haven't forgotten my promise to you, Mrs. Henry."

"I thought you understood that I'm releasing you from it."

"Thank you." He stood, walked to the bed and kissed her.

"You'll come with me, of course?"

"No, it would be too expensive to find a house large enough in New York. If the new town they're starting to build in President Washington's honor is finished in time, we might go there. At least it's in Virginia. Otherwise, I think the children and I should stay here. Martha and her family will stay in any case, of course."

His sense of well-being evaporated, but he knew she was being sensible. "You're right, I'm afraid. We don't have enough money to be reckless. I wonder if the sacrifice will be worth it. I'll be spending even less time at home than I did when I was following the magistrates around the circuit."

"I can't let you refuse, Mr. Henry!"

He chuckled. "We live in a strange and contrary world, Dolly. Had someone told me, even six months to a year ago, that I'd ever hear you urging me to accept a position with the Federal government, I wouldn't have believed it possible. And remembering my opposition to the Constitution in '88, who'd have dreamed I'd some day take the post of Chief Justice? I'm going to be particularly busy today, what with Spencer and Anne on holiday in Norfolk. But I'll draft a letter of acceptance this afternoon, and mail it to President Washington when I ride over to Lynchburg on Thursday afternoon."

5

The final draft of the letter was the best:

To the President of the United States,
Sir:

   I accept with great pleasure and in full consciousness of
my responsibility to Justice and the Public Weal in so doing,
the position as Chief Justice of the Supreme Court of the
United States, tendered me by you, and effective at your con-
venience.

   I am deeply appreciative of your confidence in me, and
beg you to accept my sincere and lasting protestations of the
high regard in which I hold you.

   I remain, sir,

                              Your Obdt. Svt.,
                              P. Henry.

Satisfied with his effort, Patrick sanded and folded the letter, then sealed it with a blob of wax he heated over a taper in a copper sealing spoon. In the eight years that had passed since the Virginia Constitutional Convention he hadn't allowed himself to dwell on the public service career he had given up, but now he could afford the luxury and admit that private law practice, no matter how successful, gave him no feeling of lasting gratification. Now, at last, he would be able to use his accumulated wisdom and experience for the benefit of the entire nation he had helped to form. It was good to know he would be useful, and it flattered his vanity to realize that another chapter would be added to his record.

It was difficult for him to concentrate on the case he intended to plead at Lynchburg, but he forced himself to put everything else from his mind and studied the material his clerks had prepared. He planned to leave right after noon dinner, which gave him just enough time to absorb the facts of the case. It would seem odd, in the next few weeks, to appear before lower state courts when he would soon become the presiding magistrate of the highest bench in the land.

Someone came into the room, and he looked up in surprise at Dorothea. She rarely disturbed him at work, and, not knowing when a client might be with him, made a point of knocking at the door before entering. Now, however, a quick glance at her pale face and stricken eyes told him that something out of the ordinary had happened, and he jumped to his feet.

Dorothea thrust a letter at him. "This just arrived by special messenger," she said in a strangled voice. "It's from Anne." Her voice trailed off, and she was unable to continue.

The communication was as brief as it was shocking. Spencer had gone off for a day of fishing, Anne wrote, and had been drowned when the boat in which he had been a passenger had overturned. His body had been recovered, and she was bringing it home for the funeral.

Dorothea threw herself into Patrick's arms, clung to him and sobbed.

He stared bleakly into space over her shoulder. The tragedy was heartbreaking for Anne, and he ached for her.

The news completely altered his own situation, too. With no partner to continue his practice and bring in an income for him, he could not afford to accept the Chief Justiceship. In fact, he would have to work harder than ever now, in order to support Anne and her family as well as his own wife and children.

Dorothea raised a tear-streaked face, and Patrick murmured a few words of consolation, promising to join her in a moment. He was expected in Lynchburg by clients who were depending on him, and would have to make the journey in spite of the terrible loss.

His wife raced from the room, attempting in vain to curb her hysteria, and Patrick stood silently, trying to adjust to the cruel facts of the unexpected situation. Reaching out with numb fingers he picked up the letter of acceptance he had written to President Washington, and tore it into narrow strips. A fate harsher than he could have imagined was depriving him of the high office—and the glory—for which he had hungered.

6

At sixty-two Patrick looked and felt his age. The fringe of hair at the sides and back of his bald head was white, his face was lined and he had lost at least ten pounds, which gave him a wizened appearance. Only his eyes, alert and calm, seemed unchanged, but he wore his spectacles most of the time now, hiding them in part. He traveled unceasingly from one Virginia county to another, and no other lawyer in the state appeared in court as often.

His energy was inexhaustible, and younger men, John Marshall among them, marveled at his memory. He rarely referred to the notes his clerks had prepared for him, carried no law books with him and seldom asked local attorneys for the privilege of studying their reference works. Yet he delivered long addresses to judges and juries without erring in his presentations.

He made few appearances in Richmond, finding memories of the capital and of the life he had been forced to abandon too painful, but in the autumn of 1798 was compelled to appear there in a case involving a snarled real estate transaction.

The cordiality of the proprietor and staff of the Richmond Inn surprised him when he reached the city late in the afternoon of a chilly October day, and he was flattered by their attentions. He was given a suite at the cost of a bedchamber, a tub of hot water was sent to him so he could take a bath before evening dinner, and a waiter brought a huge bowl of peaches to his quarters with the compliments of the owner. Private citizens were never accorded such treatment, which was reserved for high-ranking officials.

Patrick enjoyed his bath, but decided to wait until bedtime before indulging himself. His appetite had diminished so sharply in recent months that he knew he would lose all interest in his meal if he ate a peach now. He sat down at the desk in the parlor of the suite to write a brief letter to Dorothea, but had scribbled no more than a few lines when a tap at the door interrupted him.

James Monroe, who had returned to private law practice after serving as United States Minister to France, came into the room,

337

followed by John Marshall, who was regarded by many as second only to Patrick as a lawyer. "Welcome to Richmond, sir," Monroe said. "Your instincts are infallible—as always."

"Congratulations, Governor!" Marshall exclaimed, shaking hands.

Patrick waved his guests to chairs. "Has my case been settled out of court—to my client's benefit and without my knowledge?" He was mildly amused.

His visitors exchanged glances. "You mean you really don't know?" Monroe was incredulous.

Patrick shook his head as he slipped into his waistcoat and coat of black worsted.

"Just this afternoon," Marshall told him, "the Assembly elected you to a sixth term as Governor! The vote was virtually unanimous."

Patrick sat down abruptly.

"He actually hadn't heard," Monroe murmured.

"I was given no advance notice," Patrick told them, "and no one sought my consent. Is the Assembly sitting this evening?"

"No, there's an adjournment until ten tomorrow morning," Monroe said.

"The sergeant-at-arms will have a message from me for the Speaker no later than ten o'clock. I'm obliged to decline the honor." Patrick sounded old and brittle.

"You can't!" Marshall was indignant. "The people of Virginia need you!"

"My family has an even greater need for me. And I've agreed to represent a great many clients in the months ahead. I'm bound by my word to them."

"Surely you could transfer their cases to other lawyers," Monroe protested.

"Only in the event of a great national emergency," Patrick replied, "in which my services—and mine alone—could save the United States. I'll grant you that President Adams is having his troubles with France, but we aren't at war, and if both sides show enough common sense, the peace will be kept. No, gentlemen, I can't justify acceptance of another term as governor."

338

Marshall laughed helplessly. "There are men who'd give their souls for the positions you turn down."

"It's good to know that people have such a good opinion of me," Patrick said wistfully, "but I gave up all thought of public service after Judge Roane died. Your generation must assume the burdens now, you know. You belong in the governor's seat, Mr. Monroe, and I'll gladly give you my full support for the place. As for you, young man," he continued, pointing a bony finger at Marshall, "you're being wasted in private practice. If you'll run for Congress, which is where you belong, I'll write to every citizen in your district on your behalf. Now, if you have nothing better to do, come along to dinner with an old man who has had his day in court, so to speak, and is living out his days in the shadows. Don't look so disturbed, lads. It's too late for regrets."

7

Patrick continued to work at a furious pace through the autumn, winter, and early spring. Still believing that property offered the best investment potential, he purchased tracts of land in various parts of Virginia that were beginning to grow. "You'll be a wealthy widow," he told Dorothea with a half-smile, "and the children will never be in want. The land I've bought will treble in value in the next few years."

Late in the spring of 1799 his health began to deteriorate, in spite of constant treatment by his friend, Dr. George Cabell, who prescribed various elixirs to restore his appetite. He became increasingly emaciated, but refused to change his habits or lessen his work load. His mind had not weakened, his reasoning powers were still strong and only a faint hoarseness in his resonant voice indicated that his vitality was being sapped to the breaking point.

Irritated by the persistent rasp in his voice, he practiced public speaking on his estate, going alone to the head of the little valley and making addresses to an imaginary audience as he stood on a hill overlooking the tobacco fields. Occasionally he became melancholy, but took great pains to insure that no one realized he had become seriously concerned over his health.

339

Dorothea learned that he was reluctant to discuss his condition with her, and when Martha and Anne tried to persuade him to spend more time at home, resting, he pretended to be deaf. "There's nothing wrong with his hearing," Dorothea confided to Martha, "but he won't tolerate being coddled. It makes him furious."

In spite of his infirmities, Patrick kept up his interest in the nation's affairs. Relations between the United States and France continued to worsen, and many leaders were critical of the firm stand being taken by President Adams. Patrick wrote him a long letter, approving of all he was doing, and used some of his precious strength actively campaigning for John Marshall, who won a seat in the House of Representatives by a narrow margin and immediately became one of the President's most vocal supporters.

Patrick's support also guaranteed Monroe's election as Governor of Virginia, and no other candidates presented themselves for the office. "You still command more popularity and respect than any other man in the state," former President Washington wrote to Patrick from Mount Vernon. "Now that you have at last achieved the financial security you sought, I wish—for the sake of the entire nation—that you would turn your thoughts once more to the possibility of accepting Federal service."

Before Patrick could reply, he collapsed in the Lunenburg County courthouse at the end of a trial and had to be transported home in a carriage. Dr. Cabell put him on new medication and ordered him to remain in bed.

Twenty-four hours later a special courier arrived, bearing a private communication from President Adams and an official letter from Secretary of State Timothy Pickering. Patrick read them, with Dorothea standing beside his bed, and she was startled when he pushed his spectacles up to his forehead in a familiar gesture and made no attempt to stem the flow of tears down his cheeks.

"This," he said, "is the final irony. John Adams tells me I'm needed to restore relations with France—that I'm the only man in the United States with enough prestige to negotiate as an equal with the Foreign Minister in Paris, Talleyrand." He laughed hollowly. "Secretary of State Pickering writes that the President nominated me as Minister to France, and the Senate confirmed my appointment. I'll have to refuse. It's my destiny never to serve my country again."

Dorothea made a valiant attempt to smile. "Don't be too hasty, Mr. Henry. You're truly free to do what you please now, and you'll soon be strong again."

He wiped his face with the sleeve of his nightshirt. "Let's not fool each other, ma'am. I'm not well." He made the remark quietly, without a display of emotion. "My future is no longer in my own hands."

8

With each passing day in May, Patrick grew weaker, his condition complicated by the development of an intestinal inflammation that stubbornly resisted treatment. Dorothea, who remained day and night at his bedside, sent word to his brothers and sons by his first marriage, and they hurried to Charlotte County with their own wives and children.

Each tried to greet the invalid casually, but Patrick was not fooled. "I know why you're here," he said, "and I'm grateful for the chance to bid you farewell."

Two physicians from Richmond were summoned, but could do nothing for the distinguished patient, and agreed that it was necessary to resort to drastic means.

On the morning of June 6 Dr. Cabell sent Dorothea and several of Patrick's older sons and daughters from the sickroom, closed the door and turned to the man propped on pillows in the four-poster bed. "Governor," the physician said gravely, "I want to try a new remedy, but I can't administer it without your consent and full knowledge." He reached into his inner pocket and removed a small glass phial, which he handled with great care. "If you know anything of medicine, this is an essence of liquid mercury."

"Forgive my ignorance," Patrick said courteously, "but I assume from your tone that this is your last resort."

"I'm sorry to say it is, Governor. The inflammation of your

intestines must be removed. If not, mortification will set in, and you'll die a painful, lingering death."

"What is the effect of this medicine?" Patrick's self-control was superb.

"It works very quickly, either way. It will give you immediate relief or—" Cabell was unable to complete the thought.

"Or it will prove fatal immediately?"

The physician nodded. "You can only live a very short time without it. And there's a chance, remote perhaps, but nevertheless a chance, that it may relieve you."

There was a long silence. "Have you informed Mrs. Henry and my children?"

"I told them last night, Governor."

Again there was a silence. "Be good enough to help me to my chair," Patrick said at last. "I consider it undignified to die in bed." He struggled into his dressing gown, and the physician half-supported, half-carried him to a rocking chair beside the open window looking out on the trees and front lawn. "I'd like a moment or two alone to compose myself. Then, if you will, ask Mrs. Henry to join me."

The physician left the chamber, closing the door behind him.

Patrick looked out at the green, thick carpet of grass and the stands of pine and ash and oak. "Almighty God, Creator of all good," he said, his voice resonant and strong, "I am thankful for the blessings You have visited upon me through my many years, and for Your infinite mercy in permitting me to die without pain. I commend my wife and children to Your care. Watch over them, and over the nation I have loved with all my heart and soul." He bowed his head.

Dorothea came into the room, and her husband's tranquillity enabled her to refrain from weeping as they embraced.

"I've loved you for a very long time, Dolly," Patrick said. "I shall always love you."

She caught her breath. "How I wish—"

"That I could have accepted a place in the government? It's too late for wishes. It wasn't in God's scheme. Never waste breath on regrets. Concentrate instead on what can be done, now and in the future."

They kissed again, and then, at his request, Dorothea opened the door. His children and grandchildren filed in, and he kissed each of them in turn. Only when the younger members of the family had been sent from the bedchamber did Martha, Anne, and Elizabeth begin to weep. Young Dorothea turned away, and Sarah buried her face in a handkerchief.

"I'm ready," Patrick called, his voice surprisingly firm, and Dr. Cabell returned with the phial. "Observe, Doctor, that a man of faith can be at peace in a moment such as this."

Martha sobbed aloud, and her father patted her hand. "You—all of you—share that faith. Let it sustain you." There was one thing more he could do for them, he thought, and laughed aloud. "In years to come, you may tell my enemies that even at the last, Patrick Henry needed an admiring audience." He held out his hand.

The physician hesitated for an instant, then gave him the phial.

Patrick raised it to his lips and drained the contents. He smiled at Dorothea and the weeping Martha, then leaned back in the chair and, sighing very softly, closed his eyes.

His eldest grandson, Patrick Henry Fontaine, stood erect near the door. "The world," he said, "will never see his like again."

An Afterword

Patrick Henry would have enjoyed the paradox of his fame that has developed in the two hundred years since he achieved immortality.

Every American—and millions of men and women of other nationalities—can repeat his ringing challenge, "Give me liberty, or give me death." Almost as well known is the concluding line of his address opposing the Stamp Act, "If this be treason, make the most of it."

But only the student of American history is familiar with the life story of this extraordinary man, "the great Virginia rebel," as John Adams fondly called him. This book has been written in the hope that the circle of his present-day admirers will be enlarged.

His career was extraordinary, to put it mildly. Speculation may be a waste of time, as "P.H." himself would have been the first to insist, but I cannot help wondering whether he might have remained a small-town failure all his life had he not discovered the law. His transformation from lazy, shiftless lout to brilliant attorney was almost incredible, all the more amazing because of the short time he needed for the study of the law, a task that required others, including such a genius as Thomas Jefferson, years to complete.

I have found that most histories of his time fail to do justice to Henry, and only in the correspondence of his contemporaries

345

does he emerge as a giant among Americans until the time of his death. Surely no other man in the nation's public life has ever been offered—and compelled to reject—so many high offices. The personal tragedy that forced him to refuse the Chief Justiceship was, I believe, a blow from which he never fully recovered. Washington's earlier offer to make him Secretary of State meant relatively little to him, in my opinion. Certainly he dismisses the subject lightly in his letters, as he does his election—without his knowledge or consent—to his sixth term as Governor of Virginia, which he turned down so casually.

The influence of the "Virginia hierarchy" in the early days of the United States is evident through these pages. Patrick Henry was a close associate of Washington and Jefferson, Madison and Monroe, the first, third, fourth, and fifth Presidents of the United States. I find it fascinating that he was also on intimate terms with the second President, John Adams of Massachusetts, whose complicated personality made it difficult for him to become truly friendly with many men. It is remarkable, too, that three later Presidents, General William Henry Harrison of Ohio, John Tyler of Virginia, and Benjamin Harrison of Indiana, were directly descended from members of Henry's immediate political circle.

John Marshall, perhaps the greatest Chief Justice in history, often said that he owed his career to Patrick Henry. So did a score of other prominent Americans who helped to form the United States and shape her destiny. The list is too long to enumerate here.

In his own time, Patrick Henry's greatest fame rested on his skill as an orator. Everyone who heard him make an address was dazzled, and there are countless references to his great gift in the letters of his contemporaries. Even Benjamin Franklin, who was impressed by no man, was moved to declare after hearing the Virginian speak in the Continental Congress, "I thank God Henry is on our side, for he has the tongue of an angel. If he stood with the King, he would be Satan incarnate. The sound of his voice keeps me awake at night, ringing in the ears of my imagination like the chiming of a great church bell."

No novelist or biographer, unfortunately, can re-create the magical spell that Patrick Henry cast when he delivered an address, and I felt it unfair to give more than an intimation of his powers. His recorded words, still strong in themselves, must suffice, without the added punch he himself gave them.

The private life of this unique man is as interesting as his public career. Little is known of his loyal first wife, his childhood sweetheart who died before his career reached a climax. Her sons and daughters praised her unceasingly, and it appears that she was surprisingly literate in an age when relatively few women could read and write.

Patrick's marriage to the tempestuous and beautiful Dorothea Dandridge, half his age and his eldest daughter's closest friend, is in itself a "storybook romance." It is surprising for the modern reader to discover that John Paul Jones, the great American sea captain of the Revolution—who remained a bachelor—was an unsuccessful suitor for her hand, and that she chose instead to marry her parents' neighbor and close friend, the governor.

In spite of its storms, the marriage was a happy one, and Dorothea was a devoted wife. After Henry's death she married Judge Edmund Winston, his cousin, but prior to her own death many years later—in 1831—directed in her will that she be buried on the Charlotte County estate beside her first husband.

Only a few books have been written about Patrick Henry through the centuries. To those interested in a more detailed account than can be presented in the pages of a biographical novel, I recommend the following:

Everett, Alexander H., *Life of Patrick Henry*, (Sparks's Library of American Biography, 2nd Series, Vol. 1), Boston, 1844.

Henry, William W., *Patrick Henry: Life, Correspondence and Speeches*, 3 vols., New York, 1891.

Morgan, George, *The True Patrick Henry*, Philadelphia, 1907.

Tyler, Moses Coit, *Patrick Henry*, Boston, 1887 (reprinted in paperback by Great Seal Books, Cornell University Press, Ithaca, New York, 1962).

N.B.G.

Waterford, Conn.

G50